PRAISE FOR THE READER

"Most world-building shies away from tackling the question of literacy within fantasy cultures, but here it serves as the beating meta-heart."
—*NPR*, Best Book of the Year

"Masterfully written . . . This is a book you will not soon forget."
—Renée Ahdieh, #1 *New York Times* bestselling author of *The Wrath & the Dawn*

★ "A good read with genuine character growth, mystery, unique world-building, adventure, unyielding bonds of loyalty, and pirates . . . Highly recommended."
—*SLJ*, starred review

★ "Commanding storytelling and vivid details . . . the first of what promises to be an enchanting series."
—*Kirkus Reviews*, starred review

★ "An intricate, multilayered reading experience . . . Absorbing."
—*Publishers Weekly*, starred review

★ "This is a series fantasy lovers will want to sink their teeth into."
—*Booklist*, starred review

"Readers will find themselves lifted out of reality to become totally absorbed in the story."
—*Romantic Times*, Top Pick

★ "With evocative language, fascinating world building, multi-faceted characters, and a compelling plot, this is a series fantasy lovers will want to sink their teeth into."

—*Booklist*, starred review

"Those looking for complex fantasy will enjoy and look for the next installment." —*SLC*

★ "Chee's debut is an intricate, multilayered reading experience . . . An exploration of self-determination and the magic of the written word, Sefia's story is an absorbing introduction to the Sea of Ink and Gold series."

—*Publishers Weekly*, starred review

"Wide in scope, a rich mine of overlapping stories and time-lines." —*Shelf Awareness*

"'Look closer,' exhorts an inscription at the novel's opening, and readers will feel inspired to look for hidden clues in this intricately and unconventionally structured fantasy novel."

—*BookPage*

"Ripe for optioning!" —*Hollywood Reporter*

"Chee's impressive fictional world is developed so clearly that readers will find themselves lifted out of reality to become totally absorbed in the story." —*Romantic Times*, Top Pick

"[F]illed with adventure, friendship, and mystery set in a rich world that won't leave you anytime soon."   —BuzzFeed.com

"For a story about the almost magical power of books, Traci Chee certainly does the tale justice with her own book."

—Bustle.com

"Traci Chee has unleashed a new series that will suck readers in."   —Minnesota Public Radio

AN ALA TOP TEN BEST FICTION PICK

A *SCHOOL LIBRARY JOURNAL* BEST BOOK OF THE YEAR

A *KIRKUS REVIEWS* BEST BOOK OF THE YEAR

AN NPR BEST BOOK OF THE YEAR

A *BUZZFEED* BEST YA BOOK OF THE YEAR

A *BUSTLE* BEST YA BOOK OF THE YEAR

MINNESOTA PUBLIC RADIO BEST YA BOOK OF THE YEAR

A BARNES & NOBLE BEST BOOK OF THE YEAR

A NERDY BOOK CLUB AWARD WINNER

THE READER

Book One of Sea of Ink and Gold

TRACI CHEE

speak

SPEAK
An imprint of Penguin Random House LLC
375 Hudson Street
New York, New York 10014

First published in the United States of America by G. P. Putnam's Sons,
an imprint of Penguin Random House LLC, 2016
Published by Speak, an imprint of Penguin Random House LLC, 2017

THE LIBRARY OF CONGRESS HAS CATALOGED THE G. P. PUTNAM'S SONS EDITION AS FOLLOWS:
Names: Chee, Traci, author.
Title: The reader : sea of ink and gold / Traci Chee.
Description: First edition. | New York, NY : G.P. Putnam's Sons, [2016]
Summary: "Set in a world where reading is unheard-of, Sefia makes use of a mysterious object to track down who kidnapped her aunt Nin and what really happened the night her father was murdered"—Provided by publisher.
Identifiers: LCCN 2015039924 | ISBN 9780399176777 (hardcover)
Subjects: | CYAC: Books and reading—Fiction. | Robbers and outlaws—Fiction. | Adventure and adventurers—Fiction. | Kidnapping—Fiction. | Murder—Fiction. | Orphans—Fiction. | Fantasy. | BISAC: JUVENILE FICTION / Fantasy & Magic. | JUVENILE FICTION / Action & Adventure / General. | JUVENILE FICTION / General.
Classification: LCC PZ7.1.C497 Re 2016 | DDC [Fic]—dc23
LC record available at https://lccn.loc.gov/2015039924

Speak ISBN 9780147518057

Printed in the United States of America

1 3 5 7 9 10 8 6 4 2

Photographic elements courtesy of Shutterstock.

For Mom,

who always knew

HELLO.

IF yOu'RE READING THIS, THEN MAYBE YOU KNOW

YOU OUGHT TO READ EVERYTHING. AND MAYBE

YOU KNOW YOU OUGHT TO READ DEEPLY. BECAUSE THERE'S

WITCHERY IN THESE WORDS AND

SPELLWORK IN THE SPINE.

AND ONCE YOU KNOW TO LOOK FOR SIGNALS IN THE SMOKE,

FOR SECRETS IN THE SEA, THEN YOU UNDERSTAND WHAT IT IS

TO rEAD. THIS IS A BOOK. YOU ARE THE READER. *LOOK CLOSER.*

THERE'S MAGIC HERE.

The Book

Once there was, and one day there will be. This is the beginning of every story.

Once there was a world called Kelanna, a wonderful and terrible world of water and ships and magic. The people of Kelanna were like you in many ways—they spoke and worked and loved and died—but they were different in one very important respect: they couldn't read. They had never developed alphabets or rules for spelling, never set their histories down in stone. They remembered their histories with their voices and bodies, repeating them over and over until the stories became part of them, and the legends were as real as their own tongues and lungs and hearts.

Some stories were picked up and passed from mouth to mouth, crossing kingdoms and oceans, while others perished quickly, repeated a few times and never again. Not all the legends were popular, and many of them lived secret lives in a single family or a small community of believers, who whispered among themselves so the stories would not be forgotten.

One of these rare tales told of a mysterious object called a *book*, which held the key to the greatest magic Kelanna had ever known. Some people said it contained spells for turning salt into gold and men into rats. Others said with long hours and a little dedication, you could learn to control the weather . . . or even create an army. The accounts differed in the details, but on one thing they all agreed: only a few could access its power. Some people said there was a secret society trained precisely for that purpose, toiling away generation after generation, poring over the book and copying it down, harvesting knowledge like sheaves of wheat, as if they could survive on sentences and supple paragraphs alone. For years they hoarded the words and the magic, growing stronger on it every day.

But books are curious objects. They have the power to trap, transport, and even transform you if you are lucky. But in the end, books—even magic ones—are only objects pieced together from paper and glue and thread. That was the fundamental truth the readers forgot. How vulnerable the *book* really was.

To fire.

To the damp.

To the passage of time.

And to theft.

CHAPTER 1

The Consequences of Thievery

There were redcoats on the road. The gravel path that cut through the tangled jungle was teeming with people, and the mounted Oxscinian soldiers rode above the sea of foot traffic like lords in a parade: their fine red jackets unblemished, their black boots polished to a high shine. At their waists, their sword hilts and gun grips glinted in the gray morning light.

Any law-abiding citizen would have been happy to see them.

"No good." Nin grunted, shifting the pile of furs in her arms. "No good at all. Thought this town would be small enough for us to escape notice, but that doesn't seem likely now."

Crouched in the undergrowth beside her, Sefia surveyed the other shoppers, who carried baskets or towed rattling carts with burlap nests for their infants, the parents calling sharply after dirt-smudged children if they wandered too far. In their trail-worn gear, Sefia and Nin would have blended in well enough, if not for the redcoats.

"Are they here for us?" Sefia asked. "I didn't think the news would spread so fast."

"Word travels quick when you've got a face as pretty as mine, girl."

Sefia forced out a chuckle. Old enough to be her grandmother, Nin was a squat woman with matted hair and a face as tough as rawhide. Being pretty wasn't what made her memorable.

No, Nin was a master criminal with hands like magic. They were nothing special to look at, but she could slip a bracelet from a woman's wrist with a touch as soft as a breath. She could undo locks with a twitch of her fingers. You had to see Nin's hands at work to really see her at all. Otherwise, in her bear-skin traveling cloak, she looked something like a hill of dirt: dry, brown, ready to crumble in the humidity of the rain forest.

Ever since they'd fled their home in Deliene, the northernmost of Kelanna's five island kingdoms, they'd kept a low profile as they roamed from one land to the next, surviving on what they could find in the wilderness. But in the hardest winters, when the scavenging was poor and the hunting was worse, Nin had taught Sefia to pick locks, pick pockets, and even steal huge hocks of meat without anyone noticing.

And for six years, they hadn't been caught.

"Can't stay here." Nin sighed and hefted the pelts in her arms. "We'll unload these in the next town."

Sefia felt a twinge of guilt in her stomach. It was her fault, after all. If she hadn't been so cocky two weeks ago, no one would have noticed them. But she'd been stupid. Overconfident. She'd tried to steal a new bandanna for herself—all viridian with gold paisley, much finer than her faded red one—but the clothier had noticed. At the last second, Nin had slipped the bandanna into her own pocket, taking the blame so Sefia wouldn't have to, and they'd left town with redcoats on their heels.

It had been too close. Someone might have recognized Nin.

And now they had to leave Oxscini, the Forest Kingdom that had been their home for over a year.

"Why don't I do it?" Sefia asked, helping Nin to her feet.

Nin scowled up at her. "Too dangerous."

Sefia plucked at the topmost pelt in Nin's arms. Half of these were kills she'd brought down and skinned herself, enough to help them pay for passage out of Oxscini, if they ever got into town to trade them. Nin had kept them safe all these years. Now it was Sefia's turn.

"It might be more dangerous to wait," she said.

Nin's face clouded. Though the old woman had never explained exactly how she'd met Sefia's parents, Sefia knew it was because someone had been after them. They'd had something their enemies wanted.

And now Sefia had it.

For the past six years, she'd carried everything she owned on her back: all the tools she needed to hunt and cook and camp, and at the bottom, slowly wearing holes in the leather, the only thing she had left of her parents—a heavy reminder that they had existed, and now were gone. Her hands tightened on the straps of her pack.

Nin shifted her weight and glanced over her shoulder, into

3

the thick of the jungle. "I don't like it," she said. "You've never gone in alone."

"You *can't* go in."

"We can wait. There's a village a five-day journey from here. Smaller. Safer."

"Safer for you. No one knows who I am." Sefia lifted her chin. "I can go into town, sell off the goods, and get out of there by noon. We'll be twice as fast if we don't have these pelts to lug around."

Nin hesitated for a long moment, her shrewd gaze darting from the shadows in the undergrowth to the flashes of red on the road. Finally, she shook her head. "Be quick," she said. "Don't hold out for the best price. All we need is enough to hop a ship out of Oxscini. Doesn't matter where."

Sefia grinned. It wasn't every day she won an argument with Nin. She wrested the heavy stack of pelts from Nin's sturdy arms. "Don't worry," she said.

Frowning, Nin tugged on the red bandanna Sefia used to tie her hair back. "Worry's what keeps us safe, girl."

"I'll be fine."

"Oh, you'll be fine, will you? Sixty years of this life, and I'm fine. Why is that?"

Sefia rolled her eyes. "Because you're careful."

Nin nodded once and crossed her arms. She looked so perfectly like her grouchy old self that Sefia smiled again and gave her a quick peck on the cheek. "Thanks, Aunt Nin," she said. "I won't let you down this time."

The woman grimaced, wiping her face with the back of her hand. "I know you won't. Sell the furs and come straight back to camp. There's a storm brewing, and I want to get going before it breaks."

"Yes, ma'am. I won't let you down." Turning away, Sefia glanced up, noting the moisture in the air, the speed of the clouds as they crossed the sky. Nin always knew when the rains were coming, said it was the chill in her bones.

Sefia stumbled off, hefting the furs in her slender arms. She was almost at the edge of the trees when Nin's gruff voice reached her again, quick with warning: "And don't you forget, girl. There's worse than redcoats out there."

She didn't look back as she struck out from under cover to join the other people on the road, but Sefia couldn't stop herself from shuddering at Nin's words. They had to avoid the authorities because of Nin's reputation for thievery, but that wasn't the reason they lived like nomads.

She didn't know much, but over the years she'd gathered this: Her parents had been on the run. They'd done all they could to keep her isolated, safe from some nameless, faceless enemy.

It hadn't been enough.

And now the only thing that kept her safe was her mobility, her anonymity. If no one knew where she was or what she carried, no one would find her.

Sefia shrugged her pack higher on her shoulders, feeling the weight thump against the small of her back, and weaved seamlessly into the crowd.

By the time she reached the edge of town, Sefia's arms were aching with the weight of the furs. She tottered past the docks, where a few small fishing boats and merchant ships were moored to the tipsy piers. Beyond the cove, the crimson hulks of Oxscinian Royal Navy ships lay at anchor, decks spiked with cannons.

Five years ago, a handful of patrol boats would have sufficed, but now they were at war with Everica, the recently united Stone Kingdom, and they'd tightened the restrictions on trade and travel. Sefia and Nin could no longer get to the embattled shores of Everica, and even the stretch of Central Sea between the two kingdoms was rife with at-sea skirmishes and bloodthirsty privateers. To ordinary citizens, the sentinel ships might have been protectors, but to Sefia, who had never been ordinary, they were prison guards, barring her escape.

At the entrance to the town square, she paused to study the layout of the market, searching for alleys she might use if she needed a quick exit. Around the perimeter were rows of shops easily identified by the crests over their doors: a cleaver and a pig for the butcher, an anvil for the blacksmith, crossed wooden peels for the baker. But it was the cluster of covered stalls in the center of the square that drew the crowds. On market days, traveling merchants and local farmers came from miles around, selling everything from bolts of cloth to scented soaps and balls of twine.

Sefia wove among vendors hawking mangoes and passion fruit, sacks of coffee and catches of silver fish. Through the throngs of shoppers, she spied loose clasps on bracelets and jackets bulging with coin purses, but now was not the time for thievery.

She passed the newsstand, where a member of the newsmen's guild, a woman in a short-billed newsman's cap and brown armbands, greeted her with more news of the turmoil abroad: "Another merchant ship lost to Captain Serakeen off the Liccarine coast! Queen orders additional naval escort for ambassadors traveling to Liccaro!" At her feet, the collection tin rang with the *plink! plink!* of copper coins.

Sefia shuddered. While Everica and Oxscini warred in the south, the sweltering desert kingdom of Liccaro had problems of its own: Serakeen, the Scourge of the East, and his fleet of brutal pirates. He terrorized the seas around the poor island, pillaging coastal cities and extorting others, attacking traders and supply ships bringing aid to a kingdom that hadn't had a king in generations. She and Nin had barely escaped one of Serakeen's warships when they'd left Liccaro over a year ago. She still remembered the bursts of fire from distant cannons, the explosions of water on either side of the ship.

As she made for the furrier's stall, elbowing her way past people dressed in work shirts and old trousers, long cotton dresses and pointed coattails, a flash of gold caught her eye: a light no bigger than a puddle, rippling beneath the boot heels of the crowd. She smiled. If she looked too closely, it would disappear, so she contented herself with knowing it was there, on the edge of her vision.

Her mother had always told her there was some hidden energy to the world, some *light* simmering just beneath the surface. It was always there, swirling invisibly around her, and every so often it would bubble up, as water appears from a fissure in the earth, a golden glow visible only to those who were especially attuned to it.

Like her mother. Her beautiful mother, whose copper skin

would tan to bronze in the summer months, who had given her the same slender build, the same unusual grace, the same special sense that there was more to the world than its physical forms.

When Sefia had brought it up with Nin, her aunt had gone sullen and silent, refusing to answer any questions or even make casual conversation for a whole day.

She'd never mentioned it again, though that didn't stop her from seeing it.

As the little pool of light began to ebb away, a man crossed in front of her. Stiff black hair flecked with gray, a stoop accentuated by an oversize sweater. She looked again.

But it wasn't him. The shape of his skull was wrong. The height was wrong. He didn't share her straight brows or her teardrop eyes, dark as onyx. Everything was wrong. It was *never* him.

Her father had been dead for six years, her mother for ten, but that didn't stop her from seeing them in complete strangers. That didn't stop the ache in her heart when she remembered, again, that they were gone.

She shook her head and blinked rapidly as she approached the furrier's, where a harried-looking woman was pawing through chinchilla furs with one hand while gripping the arm of her young son with the other. The little boy was crying, her hold on him so tight her fingers puckered his pink skin.

"Don't you ever leave my sight again! The impressors will get you!" When she shook his arm, his entire body wobbled.

The furrier, a plain woman with spindly arms, leaned over the counter, digging her hands into a stack of fox pelts. "I heard another boy disappeared this week, just down the coast," she whispered, glancing sideways to see if anyone was eavesdropping. Half-hidden behind her armful of pelts, Sefia pretended to take a greater interest in the paper envelopes of goods in the next stall, each one painted with a picture of the spices inside: cumin, coriander, fennel, turmeric . . .

"See?" The mother's voice rose in pitch. "This is impressor country!"

Sefia's pulse quickened. *Impressors.* Even the word sounded sinister. She and Nin had been overhearing bits of news about them for a couple of years now. As the story went, boys were disappearing all over Kelanna's island kingdoms, too many to be runaways. There was talk of boys being turned into killers. You'd know them if you saw them, people said, because they'd have a burn around their neck like a collar. That was the first thing impressors did—brand the boys with red-hot tongs so they'd have that exact scar.

The thought of the impressors made Sefia hunch her shoulders, suddenly conscious of how exposed she was in this sea of strangers, these watchers and whisperers. Checking behind her, she caught sight of a flash of crimson among the stalls. Redcoats. They were headed her way.

As soon as the woman and her son left, Sefia dumped Nin's pelts on the counter. While the furrier thumbed through them, Sefia fidgeted impatiently, glancing around at the swirling crowd, reaching behind her every so often to reassure herself that the mysterious angular object remained inside her pack.

Someone tapped her on the shoulder. Stiffening, Sefia turned around.

9

Behind her were the redcoats.

"Have you seen this woman?" one asked.

The other held out a yellowed sheet of paper, curling at the edges. A fading sketch. The features of the wanted woman were hooded and indistinct, but there was no mistaking the slope of her shoulders, the matted bear-skin cloak.

Sefia felt as if she'd been dropped into dark water. "No," she said faintly, "who is it?"

The first redcoat shrugged and moved to the spices stall. "Have you seen this woman?"

The other smiled sheepishly. "You're too young to remember her, but thirty years ago she was the most notorious thief in the Five Islands. They called her the Locksmith. Someone a few towns over said they spotted her, but who knows. She's probably long dead by now. Don't you worry."

Swallowing, Sefia nodded. She recognized the story. The redcoats passed into the crowd again.

The Locksmith.

Nin's old moniker.

She agreed to the first price the furrier offered her and dumped the gold coins into her purse beside a piece of rutilated quartz and the last few rubies from a necklace she'd stolen in Liccaro. Was it enough? It had to be enough.

Stowing her purse, she brushed the bottom of her pack once more and plowed into the crowd, elbowing the other shoppers aside in her haste to leave town.

Once she reached the jungle, she began to run, breaking brush, catching on branches, made awkward and slow by the weight of her pack.

Was that crashing in the foliage the sound of her own passage, or the sounds of a chase?

She stole a glance behind her, imagining the creak of leather boots, the pounding of feet.

She ran faster, the hard rectangular object beating painfully against the base of her spine. The woods grew hot and humid around her.

Word travels quick. She had to get Nin. If the redcoats knew Nin was in Oxscini, there was no telling who else knew too.

The campsite was only twenty yards ahead when, without warning, the forest around her went silent. The birds stopped singing. The insects stopped buzzing. Even the wind stopped whispering. Sefia froze, all her senses alert, her breath sounding loud as a lumber saw in the unmoving undergrowth. Her skin crawled.

Then came the smell. Not the foul, rotting smell of sewage but a too-clean smell, like copper. A smell she could taste. A smell she could feel tingling in the tips of her fingers.

A smell she knew.

Through the trees, she heard Nin's voice, low and guarded, the same voice she used when she was facing down large game, all claws and tusks, ready to charge: "So. You finally found me."

CHAPTER 2

Worse Than Redcoats

S efia ducked into the nearest patch of ferns, trembling so violently the fronds began quivering at her touch. The stench of scorched earth and copper was so strong her insides hummed with it.

There was the sound of laughter, like ground glass. "I almost didn't believe it when we got word some redcoats nearly caught you in the Oxscinian backwoods, but here you are."

We. Sefia dug her fingers into the dirt. Her suspicions had been right. Someone—a group of someones—*had* been searching for them. And found them.

Because of her.

She began pulling herself along the ground. Spider-webs caught in her hair. Thorns pricked her skin. She gritted her teeth and kept going, inching closer and closer to the campsite.

"I've spent my whole apprenticeship hunting you. I wasn't even sure you were as uncatchable as everyone said you were—"

"Get on with it, will you?" Nin interrupted.

A quick, muffled snap made Sefia pause, eyes wide, in the brush. But through the huge, shovel-shaped leaves she could see nothing.

". . . or if you were dead."

After a moment, Nin grunted, "Still kicking."

"For now."

No. Sefia dragged herself through the brush. *Not again.*

Ignoring the spines of an overgrown rattan, she wedged herself up against a rotting log shrouded with moss and air plants. Branches caught at her clothing, but through the spiked leaves and dead vines, she could almost see what was happening in the clearing.

Nin was on her knees, gingerly touching the side of her head. A trickle of blood ran down the heel of her hand and dropped from her wrist.

A hooded woman stood over her. Clothed all in black, the woman was like a shadow come striding out of the forest, all violence and darkness. At her side, her right hand rested on the hilt of a curved sword.

Past the screen of leaves, Sefia could just make out the forms of two black horses tied among the trees. Two horses. There was someone else in the clearing.

"Search her," came a man's voice, dry and brittle as bones.

Sefia shuddered at the sound of it.

The woman in black knelt in front of Nin's pack and

upended its contents onto the forest floor. The pots and knives, the tent and hatchet, the collapsible brass spyglass, all of Nin's belongings came clattering out in a burst of noise. Sefia started. Rattan spines raked her cheek, drawing blood.

She barely noticed. A cold rivulet of fear ran down her spine. Sefia could see the woman clearly now. Her enemy had a face: ugly dishwater eyes and cratered skin, with a few limp locks of hair floating around her cheeks.

Was this the same person who had killed her father?

"It's not here," Nin said.

It. Sefia's hand went to her pack. Through the leather, the hard metal corners of the strange object dug into her palm. This *was* what they wanted.

The woman went rooting among Nin's things, tossing aside the patched shirts and hand-carved utensils with a carelessness that made Sefia's insides burn.

At last the woman in black straightened. The stink of metal grew sharper. It crackled and burned, until the air was buzzing with it.

She whirled on Nin. "Where is it?"

Nin glared up at her, bent forward, and spat in the dirt.

The woman struck her across the face with the back of her hand. In the bushes, Sefia bit down on her tongue to keep from crying out. Nin's lip split. Blood pooled between her teeth.

Sticking out her chin, Nin leaned over and spat again. "Gonna take more than that to make me talk," she said.

The woman in black let out a bark of laughter. "You'll talk. By the time we're done with you, you'll *sing*. You saw what we did to him, didn't you?"

Her father. Sefia fought back the memory of amputated limbs. Misshapen hands. Things no kid should see. Things no one should ever see. *Nin* hadn't seen the body. She'd spirited Sefia away into the woods as soon as she'd shown up, sobbing and bedraggled, at Nin's door.

But Sefia had seen it.

She knew what they could do.

Nin said nothing.

Beyond Sefia's vision, the man spoke again, his words like ice: "Let's go. It's not here."

"I already told you that," Nin grumbled. "For folks who're supposed to be so powerful, you aren't too bright, are you? No wonder it took you so long to track me down."

"You think that matters? You think that'll stop us?" The woman in black hit her again. "We are the wheel that drives the firmament. We'll *never* stop."

And again, her fist making wet smacking sounds against Nin's wrinkled flesh.

Sefia flinched. A branch snapped beneath her. She tensed.

The rhythm of the woman's blows didn't falter, but across the clearing Nin froze. For a second, her eyes locked with Sefia's, warning her to stay put. To keep quiet.

Nin crumpled at the next impact. Her face in the dirt, her flesh swollen and cut.

Stop them, Sefia told herself. She could go out there and give up her pack. Just give them what they wanted.

But fear roiled inside her.

A dismembered corpse. The sick stench of metal.

She'd seen what had happened to her father.

There was movement to her right. Sounds of footsteps in the dead leaves. Sefia went cold. The man was coming for her, stalking the underbrush like a predator. She still couldn't see him, but the tips of the ferns bent and tilted at his passage, sending ripples among the fiddleheads. He was getting closer.

The smell of metal was so sharp it made her teeth hurt.

"Wait," Nin coughed.

The man halted.

The woman in black paused, her arm drawn back.

Slowly, Nin pushed herself off the ground. Blood and saliva dribbled from her chin. She wiped it away, squinting up through her bruises. "If you want to do any real damage, you've got to get my good side," she said, tapping her other cheek.

The woman in black seized Nin's hand and twisted.

Nin buckled.

Her wrist snapped.

Sefia nearly lunged out from the brush to get to her, but Nin was watching her again. *Stay put. Keep quiet.*

"Enough," the man said.

The woman in black glared in his direction, but she grabbed the collar of Nin's cloak, hauling her to her feet. The horses were stamping and whiffling at the edge of the clearing.

Now, Sefia thought. *Before it's too late.*

But she couldn't move. She couldn't.

They bound Nin's hands and mounted, Nin letting out a slight *whuff* of air as they forced her up. Despite the thorns that caught on her hands and arms, Sefia pushed away the barbed leaves until she could see Nin's swollen eyes watching her from the back of the horse.

Nin.

The only family she had left.

Then they were gone, slipping away between the branches, which closed behind them as if they'd never been.

As the sound of the horses faded into the distance, the copper smell dissipated like mist, leaving that familiar metallic taste in the back of Sefia's throat.

Her breath came in ragged gasps. Hoisting herself over the log, she staggered into the clearing, where she fell forward among Nin's belongings. The sobs came suddenly up from her stomach, wracking her entire body.

Six years on the run from these people. A lifetime in hiding. And still they'd found her.

Sefia began gathering up Nin's things—an oversize shirt, the spyglass, her lock picks—as if the weight of them would be enough to hold on to, now that Nin was gone.

Of course it wasn't.

Sefia unfolded the leather case that held the lock picks, her fingers catching on the metal tips of Nin's most trusted tools. Her eyes blurred with tears.

Her mother and father were dead. And now Nin had been taken from her too. To be beaten and tortured and who knew what else.

No. Sefia twisted the leather in her hands. *Not yet.*

The woman's words came back to her like shards of glass, cutting into her: *We'll never stop.*

Not until they'd gutted everything she'd ever loved.

Not until they'd laid waste to everyone who stood in their path.

Sefia's hands burned, as if everything she touched would burst into flame.

They wouldn't stop? Well, neither would she.

Tucking the lock picks away, she jammed a bundle of Nin's things into her pack and shouldered it. Then, narrowing her eyes, she located the hoofprints in the soft earth and marched into the jungle.

They were faster than her, but Sefia was relentless. She tracked them through miles of rain forest, over fallen logs and into creeks, past gnarled thickets of thorns and stagnant pools buzzing with mosquitoes. By midafternoon, just as Nin had predicted, sheets of water began pouring over the rain forest, dripping from the canopy until everything was wet through. Grimly, Sefia pulled her rain cloak over herself and the pack, squinting into the rain.

As she slogged through the downpour, it became harder and harder to track the horses. But they didn't stop, and neither would she. She carried on, searching for crescent-shaped puddles and broken twigs in the failing light.

The rain fell, but she didn't stop.

Darkness fell, but she didn't stop.

But on the edge of a roaring creek, swollen with rain, she slipped. She slid down the muddy bank, clutching at loose roots that ripped away in her hands, and landed in the turgid water, tumbling over and over in the dark and the cold. Again and again, the current thrust her under, but every time she came up gasping for air, striking at the rapids with her arms and legs, searching for shore.

With nothing but her stubbornness and what remained of

her fading strength, she made it to the opposite bank and hauled herself out of the water on shaking limbs. The rain pelted her face as she lay gasping in the dark. How far had she come? She must have been miles downstream now.

Sefia pushed herself to her feet, gritting her teeth against a sudden pain in her ankle. She knelt, testing the swollen joint with numb fingers. It wasn't broken. At least there was that. Gathering her pack, she ran her hand over the outside to check that its contents were safe, and limped away from the water to set up the little tent.

The rain didn't stop. It hammered on the canvas as she hauled the pack after her and placed it in the space where Nin would have lain, though she couldn't fool herself into thinking the sodden lump was her aunt. Wincing at her scrapes and bruises, she struggled out of her wet clothes and climbed under her blanket, pulling herself into a ball with her hands clasped around her knees.

Dry-eyed, she stared into the darkness.

"Nin," she whispered.

CHAPTER 3

The House on the Hill
Overlooking the Sea

There were a few hours every morning when the house on the hill became a round island, cut off from the village below, floating in cold fog with views of nothing but birds, air, and an endless ocean of insubstantial white.

Hours before he was killed, Sefia's father walked her down the misty slope to the blacksmith's shop, as he had done every morning for four years, since her mother died. They'd go hand-in-hand through the grass, her father turning his head like a stag watching over his tiny herd, and when he said good-bye he always tapped her once, lightly, on the chin. Then he'd go back to the house on the hill to tend the animals or repair the fences or study the ocean through the telescope.

Sefia loved the workshop. It wasn't a shop, really, just a shed in the back of the blacksmith's house, with a dirt floor and blackened walls hung with hooks and tongs and hundreds of locks and keys.

Sometimes she brushed her fingers against the keys, making them clatter and clank until the small room was a cacophony of noise. Other times, like today, she simply watched the blacksmith's strong hands bend to their craft.

"Aunt Nin," she said, tapping the woman's round shoulder. "Will you teach me to do that?"

"Do what," Nin said, her voice like gravel.

Sefia put her hands on the tall counter. "Pick locks."

"I'm fixing a lock, not picking one."

"But will you?"

"Will I what."

"*Teach* me." She had perfected the whine of a nine-year-old.

Nin didn't pause in her work. "When you're older."

Sefia laughed. Nin's gruffness never bothered her; she'd known the woman all her life. When her parents had built the house on the hill, Nin had helped them. She'd fitted all the doors and windows with locks, and at their request, installed three additional, secret doors.

The first was hidden in the stones beside the hearth. You used the end of the fire poker to unlock it, and it opened onto a secret stairway that led to Sefia's basement room, just a small place for her bed and belongings. Her parents never let her keep anything in the house proper, though they never had visitors to notice. To anyone peering through the windows, it used to look as if there were only two occupants in the house on the hill.

Now it looked as if only a widower lived there.

They kept to themselves as much as possible, gardening, raising chickens and pigs and goats and even some sheep, only going down the slope to the village out of necessity.

Besides the small family, there was only one person allowed in the house, and that person was Nin.

Sefia had guessed a long time ago there was something different about her family—their secrecy, their isolation. Someone was after her parents. She didn't know why, but she imagined it was some shadowy figure with red eyes and sharp teeth, a monstrous villain come out of her nightmares with metal hounds to hunt them down.

Sometimes she pictured her mother and father as heroes. Keepers of some arcane knowledge. Her mother proud and small, her black hair twisted into a bun at the base of her neck, a silver star glinting at her chest like a sheriff. Her father with a shock of hair like a bristle brush stiff with shoe polish, rolling his large sleeves up to his elbows while the scar at his temple gleamed white.

Sometimes she woke screaming in her basement bedroom, knowing with absolute certainty that someone was coming for them.

"When you teach me, will I be able to pick any lock in the world?" Sefia asked.

"Only if you're very good."

"Are you very good?"

Nin didn't look up. "Don't be stupid," she said.

Sefia squinted. Her eyes turned to slits above the soft bump of her nose. "That's what I thought. Daddy said that's how he and Mama met you. Because you were the best."

"Is that what he said."

"Yep. He said you helped them. He said he wouldn't be here if not for you."

"Well . . . I wouldn't be here if not for them either."

Sefia nodded. Her parents must have been captured, once, held in iron cages above seething fire pits while their enemies gibbered around them. Nin must have freed them, with her slender tools and miraculous hands, and they'd all gone running into the sunset together.

Smiling, Sefia laid her head on her folded arms, watching silently as Nin's fingers worked and the little room filled with the clicking and jerking of teeth.

Under ordinary circumstances, Nin would break for lunch at noon and walk Sefia back up the hill to the house, but on that day there were horses to be shod, axles to be fixed, and all manner of locks and hinges and bolts to be repaired, so Nin sent Sefia scooting out through the back door with warnings to be aware of her surroundings and not to make too much noise.

"And go straight home, or your father will have my head," she added, giving Sefia one last shove.

Delighted with her temporary independence, Sefia skipped out into the fog. At first she cackled softly and ran at the indistinct shadows of barrels and wheelbarrows, pretending they were monsters rearing out of the mist, but she was too accustomed to caution to dally for long.

As she left the village and began climbing the hill to her house, the fog crept closer. Out of the corner of her eye, she spied swirls of golden light appearing here and there on the dewy slope, but when she looked closer, they melted into wisps of gray. Sefia's pace grew slower and more subdued. Moisture from the tall grasses clung to her shins and shoes, making her toes uncomfortably damp.

A breeze stirred the mist, and the faint scent of copper stung her nose. Sefia stifled a cough and shivered in the fog. It wound around her like a living thing.

After a moment the smell dissipated—so quickly she wondered if she'd imagined it. But as she inhaled the sweet scent of grass, she tasted metal at the back of her throat and knew it had been real.

In the mist, climbing the hill seemed to take hours, but finally she reached the top, rising out of the fog that lapped at the foundations of the lonely stone house, and stepped up to her front door. Above her, the sky was an empty unnerving blue.

Sefia took out her key—her father always locked the house—but the heavy wooden door on its well-oiled hinges swung silently open at her touch.

They say that fear is a pit in your stomach, but what she felt was a *dissolving*, as if the fog was burning off and frittering away, leaving behind only Sefia, bare and defenseless with nothing before or behind her but emptiness.

As she tiptoed into the house, even the walls themselves seemed to chip away. One by one went the boards and the beams, falling to pieces with tinny clattering sounds, littering the wooden floors, the broken chairs, the smashed vases and shattered lanterns. It looked as if a hurricane had torn the house apart. Nothing was in its place. Paintings slashed from their frames, her father's telescope missing from the east window. As she tiptoed through the debris, with every step realizing how silent the house was, how still, it was like the furniture began to crumble, the strands of silk in the rugs fraying and turning to dust, until everything in the house—the copper pots on the floor of the kitchen, the quilt on her parents' shredded mattress, the overturned dining table—had disintegrated, so by the time she reached the back room, it seemed as if all that remained on the top of the hill were Sefia . . . and her father's corpse.

She knew it was him without even having to look closely. She could not look closely. She knew it was him by the sheepskin slippers, by the shape of his trousers, by the oversize threadbare sweater. She knew it without having to see his face, because

Her father.

She staggered back, her insides like slush. It was so dizzyingly cold she couldn't breathe. She gasped, but no sound came out, and no air came in.

Her *father*.

She stumbled to the fireplace to unlock the secret door. There was a soft *click*, and a panel of stones slid back into the wall. She entered, pulling the door shut behind her, and descended the steep stairs to her bedroom, which, as her parents had planned, had gone unnoticed and untouched. There were no windows in the basement, so she groped her way among the chairs and toys that had once seemed so familiar—now riddled with the potential for bruised toes and dinged shins.

But she had been preparing for an event like this—just like

this—for years. When her mother was still alive, they had rehearsed the steps together; and when her mother died, her father had made her practice, and practice, and practice. Some days, Sefia ran through the steps so often that she dreamed of them when she slept. She had been drilled so many times that, as she was meant to, she had begun to implement the steps already.

Blindly, she fumbled for the knob of her bedpost and began to unscrew it from its wooden leg. Inside was a key—a shiny silver thing shaped like a flower, something that might be overlooked, mistaken for a child's plaything—that unlocked the second secret door in the north wall.

Sefia opened it and crawled inside, closing the door behind her, shutting herself into a room barely bigger than a travel trunk. And then she cried. She cried until her head ached and bright spots burst across her eyes. She cried loudly, hoping someone would hear, and quietly, fearing the same thing. She cried until she had almost forgotten about the mutilated body sprawled on the floor above her. And she cried again when she remembered.

Eventually she must have blacked out, because she awoke what seemed like hours later, with her eyes swollen nearly shut and her nose stuffy with snot. Gulping back a few dry sobs, Sefia uncurled, aching, from the floor and put her palms to the stone walls.

There was no key to the third door. Nin had designed it to open when the cobblestones in the wall were pressed in a certain order, and though Sefia's parents had rehearsed the series with her, they had always done it in the warm lamplight of her bedroom. Get to the tiny room, then wait for her parents to arrive. That had always been the plan. They had always known someone would hunt them down, eventually, but they had always thought one of them would survive.

Sefia remembered the sequence; her hands found the right river rocks by their contours—the first one in the upper left-hand corner, the second shaped like an owl, the third like a cabin, then a half-moon, two mice in a row, and the last a shaggy buffalo with a single stubby horn. As she touched them, they clicked into place. But what happened next was something her parents had never mentioned, had not warned her about or prepared her for, and it was perhaps the most important thing of all.

As the small door unlatched, something—some heavy rectangular *thing* wrapped in soft leather—fell out of the crack in the door. It must have been wedged there, stuck fast in the threshold.

Sefia ran her fingers over it and clasped it to her chest. She hadn't seen it once in all the years she'd been practicing for her escape.

She considered leaving it. The thing was so heavy and awkward in her skinny arms. She wished she'd thought to take something from the house before she left. Her mother's silver ring with the secret compartment inside, a painted hand mirror, one of her father's old sweaters—anything would have done. But they'd never taught her that. They never told her she might want a keepsake, a memento. And now all she had was this thing.

She gripped it tighter, until its edges dug into her palms and the flesh of her cheek, and then she took it with her.

She had to go on her hands and knees. The tunnel was a burrow of crumbling dirt walls, with some places so narrow she couldn't even crawl—she had to lie on her belly and *worm*, pulling herself along with her fingers, pushing with her elbows, the tips of her toes. She slithered for hundreds of feet in the unimaginable dark, an almost tangible darkness, blacker than night, blacker than closets with closed doors, blacker than closed eyes under bedsheets.

As she inched forward, not knowing how far she had come or how far she had to go, with nothing but the noise of her own body and the darkness, it was the very *thingness* of the rectangular thing, pushed before her as she slid through the tunnel, that assured her she was still alive, that she had not perished in the aboveground world with her father.

At last she reached the end, where the tunnel terminated abruptly in a wooden hatch. Sefia crouched beneath it, scuffling at the splintered ceiling, and unlocked the door. Pushing upward with what remained of her quavering strength, she heaved it open and emerged in a tangle of bramble with summer's last shriveled berries still clinging to the vines. She pulled herself through the hatch, clutching the rectangular thing to her side.

It was evening. The fog had burned off, and the cool air was clear, the shadows bruised and purple. She rubbed her arms. The entire afternoon had passed, sucked up by the darkness of the tunnel. For a moment, Sefia crouched, scratched and dirty, in the deep knotted safety of the thicket.

Her parents had given her three instructions: Use the secret doors. Go through the tunnel. Find Nin. She'd done the first two, and after she did the last, she'd have nothing left of them. Nothing but the strange object in her arms.

Sefia shut the hatch as quietly as she could and stood up. She recognized this thicket. Her father used to take her berry-picking here, and when their baskets were filled, they'd bring one to Nin. He'd always claimed these brambles had the sweetest fruit, but now she realized he'd been training her, showing her the way.

At the thought of her father, she began to cry again. Clutching the leather-wrapped object as if it were a blanket or a stuffed toy or a shield, Sefia stumbled out of the bushes and took off running through the dusk, ducking branches as they snatched at her hair. Saplings slapped at her face and arms. Ditches fell out from underneath her. But even though she sobbed and stumbled, even though her legs were weak and her body was shaking, she didn't stop.

By the time she got to Nin's back door, Sefia was lost and half-gone with grief, spitting, blind, blundering, falling into Nin's thick cushiony arms as if she were diving off a cliff.

Dimly, she heard Nin's voice: "It's finally happened, hasn't it? I'm sorry, girl, I should've been there. I should've walked you home."

She had done what she'd been told. Use the secret doors. Go through the tunnel. Find Nin. And now it wasn't her father's empty dismantled body that frightened her so much, but the silence, that unbreakable silence of the dead, because there would never be another reassuring word, no familiar gurgle from laying her cheek on her father's stomach, no sneezes, no coughs, no creak of tired joints, none of those everyday sounds of life. She had done what she had been told. And now there would be no further instructions, no way for another word to pass from her father's lips into the bright prism of the still-living world. He was dead. And gone forever.

CHAPTER 4

This Is a Book

The rain had not let up by the time Sefia awoke the next morning, and the little tent was filled with cold dingy light. As she lay there staring up at the stained canvas, she could have sworn she saw movement out of the corner of her eye: Nin stirring beneath the mound of clothing. Or there, Nin passing outside the tent. But it was just the water dripping out of her belongings, it was just a shadow falling across the canvas. Nin was gone. She had been cut out of the world like a paper doll, though Sefia could still see where she should have been, the vague outlines of her silhouette, the spaces echoing with the things she should have said.

Wincing at the pain in her ankle, Sefia sat up and stared at the unmoving tent flaps as the memories of the previous day washed over her again. The stench of metal. The pockmarked face of the woman in black. The *crack* of Nin's bones.

Nin had protected her to the last, and Sefia had done nothing to save her.

Twisting her damp hair away from her face, Sefia began digging her belongings out of the pack, laying them out in neat piles until her searching hands hit something flat and solid and firm.

This.

This was what they wanted.

She had kept it for six years, and though she remembered it often, she'd only taken it out once.

She'd been nine, and she and Nin had left the house on the hill two days earlier. Nin was off hunting, and Sefia had pulled it out of her pack. A heavy thing like a box, with dark damaged spaces along the edges that must have been for filigree and jeweled settings, though someone had torn most of that off a long time ago. The only gold pieces left on it were the caps on the corners and two tarnished clasps that kept it closed. She'd been on the verge of opening it when Nin came back.

"What are you doing?" Nin demanded. A dead rabbit dangled from her hand.

Sefia froze and looked up at her guiltily. "What is this?"

Nin stared at the thing like it was a bear trap, full of metal teeth. "I never asked," she snapped. "Put it away. I don't want anything to do with it."

"But Aunt Nin, it belonged to—"

"I'm not your parents." Turning her back, she began to skin the rabbit. Among the sounds of ripping flesh and popping sinew, her next words came over her shoulder, cold and final: "If I see it again, I'll throw it in the fire with the logs."

Sefia hadn't looked at it since then, but whenever she cleared out her pack, she touched it. Her hands knew the shape of the thing so well she could have recognized it in the dark.

The memories lanced through her chest again.

Her father.

Her aunt.

Sefia dug her fingers into the leather casing and ripped it away. Through bleary, angry tears, she stared down at the rectangular object in her lap.

The rich brown leather seemed to glow like varnished wood, and in the center was some sort of emblem, like the crests she'd seen over the shops in town, a circle inscribed with four lines:

The leather had been stamped and burned, so the lines were dark and sharp. A clue. As she studied the symbol, she tried to imagine what it was supposed to be.

A trident.

A rising sun.

A helmet.

Tipping the strange box on its side, she studied the gold clasps that held it closed. Whatever was inside must have been important. And dangerous.

Her mind flicked through the most dangerous objects she knew: guns, knives, poisons, magical items like the Thunder Gong or the Long Telescope that could see through walls, cursed objects like the Executioner or the Diamonds of Lady Delune.

Or maybe it would tell her where to find *them*—the people

who had taken Nin. And if she could rescue Nin, if she could get to her in time, maybe that would make up for letting them take her in the first place.

She hoped.

Sefia flicked open the clasps and raised the lid.

Inside was paper. Just paper, smooth and crisp as ice. She riffled through it, turning each sheet first one way, then another, expecting illustrations, but all she saw were patterns, line after line like ribbons of black lace.

Is this it?

Panicked, she dug through the paper, searching for clues, tearing faster and faster through the sheets until paper cuts crossed her fingertips and whorls of blood smeared the corners. Until at last she realized that no matter how far she flipped, she never reached the beginning or the end. There was always more beneath her frantic fingers.

She slammed the box shut and thrust it away. Her hands stung.

Paper. That's all they'd wanted. An infinite supply of paper, to be sure, but nothing more than paper, strewn with marks like debris from an explosion.

Tentatively, she lifted the lid again. With the tip of her finger she traced the strange markings: straight lines like beetle tracks through a dead log, or birds swarming in a white sky. Each tiny sign was perfectly formed, with little flags and short tails at the ends of each stroke, resting on invisible horizontal strings like pins perched on a clothesline. But they weren't guild signs or crests, and they didn't make pictures, like tiles in a mosaic.

They did repeat. She spotted individual marks recurring again and again on a single page, and found entire clusters replicated, sometimes ten or thirty times in perfect patterns.

But some figures stood alone, isolated by blank space like tents pitched on winter slopes or lampposts on white roads.

Sefia stiffened.

She'd seen these signs before.

They had been carved onto some of her toys, brightly painted wooden blocks, their sides engraved with symbols and simple pictures. There had been a whole set of them.

A mongoose.

An artichoke.

A ring.

She used to sit in the kitchen for hours, building caravans on the table while her mother sliced up garden vegetables or butchered hens at the counter, her knife quick and confident on the cutting board, her brown hands flecked with pale scars. Every so often she'd look out the window for Sefia's father, then turn back to Sefia and slide the blocks across the table—the snake, the elk, the feather—singing in her soft voice, "Ess-ee-eff-aye-ay."

"Essie effai yay," Sefia repeated, laughing.

"Yes." Her mother brushed her cheek with the curve of her finger. "Sefia, my little Sefia."

Sefia blinked tears out of her eyes and touched the mark, like she could impress it onto her skin.

"Ess," she whispered.

The symbol had a meaning, and a *sound*, as if it had been

plucked from the real world and pressed flat, like some strange dark flower, between the pieces of paper. And that sound was a hiss, like a sting or the sizzle of water on coals.

She scrubbed at her face. Her mother had been teaching her to decipher the symbols, before the fevers, the awful hacking and coughing and the blood-spattered handkerchiefs, the way her mother wasted away to almost nothing.

Her father had burned the blocks the day after her mother died. She remembered him crouched in front of the stone hearth, feeding her toys into the flames.

"Daddy, no!" She tried to stop him, but he caught her, drawing her flailing body into his arms.

"It's not safe. You weren't supposed to know," he said, murmuring into her dark hair. "It's not safe."

Sefia let out a wail, crying for her mother.

"Mommy's gone." Her father stroked her hair as the firelight flickered over the scar at his temple. "She's gone, Sefia. It's just you and me now."

She buried her cheek in the extra folds of his sweater and watched the paint curl as the fire consumed the blocks.

"We're a team, you and me," he said. "We're in this together, no matter what."

The sound of his weeping blended with hers, and she squeezed him tighter, like she'd never let go.

Sefia was crying again, her tears smudging the ink. She dabbed at the smears with the cuff of her shirt.

The strange symbols were *words*. The paper was filled with them. Were they messages? Magic? Some ancient wisdom entrusted only to her parents?

Why hadn't her father continued teaching her?

Why hadn't he given her anything to go on?

She narrowed her eyes and curled her lacerated fingertips into her palms.

It *wasn't* safe. He was right about that.

They wanted it, and they'd never stop until they had it.

They'd come for her father. They'd come for Nin. And they would come for Sefia sooner or later. No one was safe.

Unless she stopped them.

Sefia closed the lid and clicked the clasps back into place. She'd use it against them if she could, but they would never lay their hands on it again.

All these years, she'd had someone to protect her, but now she was alone, and *they* were still out there. With Nin, if she wasn't already . . . Sefia dug her fingers into the ⊜, hissing as the pressure stung her paper cuts. *No.* Nin needed her now. Needed her strength and her resilience, her cleverness and her resolve.

There was only one way to protect herself from the people who had destroyed her family.

She had to stop them herself.

She tried to pick up the trail again a day later when her ankle hurt less, but the rains had washed everything through, eliminating whatever footprints they'd left in the jungle. Though crowds made her uneasy, she scouted populated areas for signs of the woman in black and her mysterious companion, asking after them in nearby villages and in lumber encampments in the forest.

But no one had seen them.

No one knew anything.

It was as if they'd disappeared altogether, leaving her with only one clue: the strange box of paper with the symbol on the lid.

So she retreated into the thick jungles of Oxscini to sharpen her skills and study the object. She turned every hunt into a challenge now, made sure every arrow found its mark. She figured out how to throw knives and make poisoned arrows from the skins of frogs, to sneak up on prey twice her size and track targets in the dark.

Because she knew they were out there, the people who came for her father, who came for Nin, and who would come for her too . . . if she didn't get to them first.

Sefia spent weeks stalking around Oxscini's interior, poring over the papers, inspecting, searching, wondering. She took to making her camp in the trees, in a hammock fashioned out of rope, and when she took out the strange object, she felt like someone were peering over her shoulder, scanning the lines for secrets just as she was.

It didn't take her long before she could recognize different marks as easily as she recognized animal tracks—the empty gasp of an *O*, the murmur of an *M*—but it wasn't until a month later, on a night with a full moon shedding pale light over the canopy, while she was lying in her hammock with the object propped up on her knees, that she began to read.

A single line had caught her eye. Just a few markings clustered together, like the footprints of a sandpiper that has abruptly taken flight. They stood out because they were alone;

the other marks paraded on and on across the paper, but these ones were flanked by white space.

She leaned so close to the paper that the tip of her nose nearly touched it, and she inhaled its pulpy odor. Furrowing her brow, she fought for the right sounds, willing her tongue and teeth to work—the whispered consonant, the hiss.

This

Grinning, she smacked the paper with the flat of her hand. She said it once more, memorizing the order of the shapes: "This!" The next word was faster:

is

And the one after, even quicker:

a

The last one made her pause. She struggled with the pieces, trying to force them together, to make them make sense.

"B-buh . . . buh . . ."

Then it came to her, in all its clarity, leaping like light out of a prism, into bands of color:

book.

She said the whole thing again, more sure of herself this time: "This is a book." Her voice sounded awkward and resonant among the whispering trees, but she said it again, all together:

This is a book.

Like saying so made it true. She said it again, and again, not entirely certain that the final word meant anything, although the more she said it, the more it made sense. It was a *book*. This strange rectangular thing had named itself.

It had a name.

"Book." Sefia grinned.

For a moment, she felt as if the marks were bright and burning. Gold crept in at the corners of her vision. Then she blinked, and the whole world flooded with light, whirling all around her in wide interconnected circles, up into the sky and among the stars. She'd seen the light before, but this one showed her the world was *full* of little golden currents, a million of them and a trillion motes of light, all perfect and exact and brimming with meaning.

The sight of it all knocked her back in the hammock. The book fell from her hands.

Magic. It made her feel like she was peering past the edges of the stars into whatever lay beyond.

She could feel herself, dimly, still in her own body, still sitting in her hammock, but there was so much brilliant, churning light she felt like she could be swept away at any second, lost forever in the sea of gold.

It was terrifying to see so much. To drown, flailing, in light. Her stomach turned. Her temples throbbed. She clung to the side of the hammock, as if that would anchor her, as if that would stop the world from spinning.

Then she blinked, and it was gone, and Sefia lay there dizzy and gasping, trying to focus on the black forms of the trees, on a single star, to stop her vision from reeling.

What was this magic?

How did her parents come by it? And why did her enemies want it?

Did Nin know what it was for?

The unanswered questions wheeled around her as she

pressed her hands to her head to stop the throbbing in her skull. The trees hunkered in close around her.

She repeated the words:

This is a book.

They were so small. There were dozens of other marks, hundreds of other words, just on that one sheet of paper—and on the next, more marks, more words . . . and the next and the next and the next.

Sefia thought of her vision, that sudden dizzying feeling that everything was huge and connected. Were there signs for each of the stars, and grains of sand on the beach? For *tree* or *rock* or *river*? For *home*? Would they look as beautiful as they sounded, hovering in the air?

It was as if, all this time, she'd been locked out, catching glimpses of some magical world through the crack beneath a door. But the book was the key, and if she could figure out how to use it, she'd be able to open the door, uncovering the magic that lay, rippling and shifting in unseen currents, beyond the world she experienced with her ears and tongue and fingertips.

And once she understood them all—all the signs, all the words—she'd find out the meaning of the symbol on the cover, and she'd find out why her family had been taken, and who had done it, and how to hunt them down.

CHAPTER 5

The Apprentice

Two weeks ago, just days after his fourteenth birthday, Lon would never have believed his life could change so drastically or so fast.

There'd been the usual morning traffic at the south gate—farmers and merchants heading up to Corabel's tiered heights, sailors fresh from the sea, smelling of salt and mischief—but many of them were regulars, onto his tricks, so he didn't work particularly hard at coaxing them to his table.

He slid the small brazier of coals closer to him, then back, a little to the left, and again to the right. He'd been clinging to the dwindling hope that his parents would return for his birthday and whisk him away from the city on some fantastic voyage to a distant land, where he'd begin an apprenticeship with a great seer, only to be kidnapped by a sand pirate desperate to find the cure for the sickness that plagued his beautiful daughter.

But his parents had been gone for six months, traveling with a troupe of other acrobats and actors and street performers. They didn't make enough to hire messengers, so he had no idea when they'd be back. He didn't even know if they were still in the kingdom of Deliene or if they'd traveled south to the other islands.

Sighing, Lon sprinkled a pinch of incense over the brazier, and in the sweet-scented smoke that spiraled from the embers, he felt as if his life were unraveling before him: a string of days that would turn into years, each one the same as the last, telling fortunes by the city gate, until he grew too feeble to carry his table out onto the street.

As the smoke dispersed, he spied an old man wandering through the crowd, his graying shoulder-length hair uncombed, his eyes darting wildly from the terra-cotta rooftops and ornamented iron balconies back to the cobblestone streets as if it were his first time in Corabel. You could always spot visitors to Deliene's capital by their bewildered looks and crooked necks as they tried to take in all the busy sights of the city on the hill.

Squinting, Lon studied him carefully. The man's skin was dark and wrinkled as a walnut shell, though there was little sun damage on his face and hands. His sweeping velvet robes were ill suited to travel on the crowded streets, and as other passersby stepped on his trailing hems, Lon caught sight of his soft slippers, the uppers already splitting from the soles.

He must work inside, Lon observed, *but he left the house today without thinking to change his clothes.* In a hurry? Or just absent-minded? And if he was a visitor to Corabel, why did he look like he had just stepped out of his house in his dressing gown?

"Hey, grandfather!" Lon called. "Over here!"

Blinking, the old man looked up. He seemed to have trouble focusing.

He probably wears glasses. Lon stood, waving him over.

The old man made his way through the handcarts and fishmongers fresh from the sea, stubbing his toes on the cobbles and bumping into sailors on shore leave. He collapsed gratefully on the short stool Lon offered him, dabbing at his brow with the edge of his embroidered sleeve.

Lon grinned. After that, it only took a little prodding to learn the old man's name—Erastis—and a little more to get him to exchange a few copper zens to have his fortune told.

"Take a pinch of incense and sprinkle it over the coals," Lon explained, pocketing the man's coins. "I'll be able to see what's in store for you in the smoke."

Obediently, Erastis did as he was told. The fire crackled and through the smoke, Lon began scrutinizing him, mentally noting the callus on the middle finger of his right hand, the ink stains and the stray hair on his embroidered sleeve, the curve of his back and shoulders, the purple shadows beneath his eyes, the shallow indentations on the bridge of his nose.

But Erastis didn't bat an eye when Lon explained that he wore glasses, that he rarely went out but was on an important errand, that he spent most of his time hunched over a table, inking fine details with a sable brush.

The old man smiled, creasing his already wrinkled face. "Any con artist could tell me that. I heard *you* were special."

Lon balked. "From who?"

"You tell me."

Never one to back down from a challenge, Lon swept his hands through his dark hair, making it stand up at the ends. Inhaling deeply, he stared straight into Erastis's hazel eyes. He felt his awareness begin to split in two as the bright colors and the clatter of traffic began to fade, replaced by his perception of the world that went beyond sight and sound and smell. Usually, all it took was some observation and a few leading comments, and his clients would practically tell him what they wanted to hear. But when he needed it, there was always this double vision. He needed to concentrate to divide his consciousness between the physical world and the shining one beneath it, and he always came up sick to his stomach, as if he'd swallowed too much seawater, but in the worst of times this extra sense got him paid and kept him fed, and he was more than a little proud of it.

He could look at the detail on a patched sleeve and watch its history unfold before him in scattered images: old mottled hands sewing in the guttering candlelight, a grandfather on his deathbed, a journey to the capital to register his passing with the Historians in the Hall of Memory.

If he examined the empty setting on an old brooch, he'd see what happened to the missing gem: a miserly master, a midnight theft, a pawnbroker, ailing children, and draughts of foul-smelling medicine.

Lon blinked, and his extra sense swam into focus. Bands of gold flooded over the old man's head and shoulders, streaming down his arms to his slender hands, where they pooled with meaning.

And he knew why Erastis had come.

"This is only the third time in the past decade that you've left home, but someone named Edmon said it was important." Lon passed a hand across his face, surprised. "He said *I* was important. He said you'd want to meet me. 'Because the Library has been without an Apprentice for too long.'"

Lon blinked again, and his extra sense ebbed out of him. The light disappeared, leaving him swaying slightly as he fought off the dizziness, the nausea. "What's a Library? How'd he know where I was in the first place?"

"Your gifts." Erastis tucked his hair behind his ears and leaned forward. "Other people are born with talents like yours. You've heard of them, I'm sure: seers, conjurers, makers of magic weapons. Most legendary figures have some sort of ability that makes them noteworthy."

Lon beamed. "Like the man with the strength of an ox? Like the jeweler who made the Cursed Diamonds of Lady Delune?"

"They're amateurs compared to us. We can teach you to use your gifts with the precision of a scalpel."

"Who *are* you?"

"We are a society of readers." Erastis smiled. "People like you."

Readers. Lon tested the word on his tongue, though the reverence in the old man's voice kept him from saying it aloud.

"We were formed long ago," the old man continued, "before any of the Historians can remember, when each wave of history erased everything that had come before. All was chaos and darkness, and into that darkness we became the light, charged with the protection of all the citizens of Kelanna."

Lon frowned. Ever since the resolution of the blood feud between the Ken and Alissar provinces, Deliene had been doing all right, but every day he heard news of war in Everica, of famine and ruination in Liccaro, the Desert Kingdom. "You're not doing a great job of it, are you?"

"Eh, you try protecting an entire world from itself."

"Isn't that why you're here?"

"True." Erastis smiled ruefully. "We have great plans for you."

He described the wondrous feats of magic Lon could achieve if he joined them. They'd walk among the mountains and across seas, like the adventurers and outlaws that filled his daydreams, all oceans and sailing ships and *pop*s of gunfire. Their deeds would bring peace to an unstable world, preserved in legend among the stars.

"There's never been peace like that. Not once," Lon pointed out.

"There will be."

"How do you know?"

"We have the Book."

Lon hadn't known what the Book was, but he could feel his path forking before him: Down one path was the life of a street performer, spinning fortunes for spare change. Maybe one day his parents would take him with them. Maybe they'd never return.

Down the other path lay the unknown, with the promise of power and danger and the kind of great purpose he'd always imagined for himself . . . and he knew he had to find out what that purpose was.

He used his meager savings to leave a message for his parents at the main post and left Corabel with Erastis that night.

The next day, he entered into his new life as the Apprentice Librarian.

The Library itself was more than Lon could have imagined. It had been built into the side of a mountain, overlooking granite peaks and a valley carved by ancient glaciers. The north wall of the Library was made entirely of glass, with doors leading to a terraced greenhouse that refracted light like a prism.

The Library had a domed ceiling and stained glass windows and balconies guarded by bronze statues of past Librarians. The walls and marble columns were hung with electric lamps that bathed the rooms in plentiful golden light. Electricity! It enthralled him with its mystifying machinery; the rest of the world was still using candles and kerosene lamps.

A sharp *thwack* brought him out of his reverie, and Lon snapped to attention. Erastis, the Master Librarian, was tapping the chalkboard with the tip of a long stick. Lon had been right, of course: years of poring over manuscripts had given the Librarian severe myopia, and he wore thin half-moon spectacles on the end of his nose. Already, Lon had learned that when he rushed through his lessons, Erastis would glare at him over the rims of his glasses, stern and judgmental.

Just like now.

"Tee," Erastis prompted.

Lon was supposed to be working on his letters, though he'd

memorized the alphabet before the end of his first week, and now found these exercises dull.

"Tee," he repeated dutifully. His tongue tapped the backs of his teeth.

A slow, thin smile spread across Erastis's face. He tilted his head, as if he were listening to music. "Splendid, and . . . ?"

"Aitch."

"Aye." Lon's attention wandered again.

In the center of the main floor was a circle of five curved tables fitted with reading lamps, inkstands, and little drawers for pens, linen bags of pounce and sandarac, blotting papers, lead pencils, gum erasers, magnifying lenses, straightedges—anything you might need for writing or copying. Steps led to more tables at the edges of the room, where caramel-colored wooden shelves reached up to balconies furnished with velvet couches and more alcoves of bookshelves behind.

There were thousands of manuscripts in this room. Some of the oldest were in desperate need of restoration, their bindings fraying, their pages speckled with mold, and Erastis often spent his afternoons repairing torn pages and reattaching loose spines while the Library's blind servants dusted the shelves, though they never touched the texts themselves.

All the servants in the Main Branch, including the ones who served the Library, were blind. To protect the words, Erastis said. To ensure that the power they held would not fall into the wrong hands.

The manuscripts were divided into Fragments, texts copied out of the Book, word for word in painstaking script, by other

Librarians, long dead; and Commentaries, interpretations and meditations on the meanings of various passages, indexes and appendices and tomes filled with definitions and etymologies and cross-references. Masters and more advanced Apprentices used the Library's books to further their studies, to learn from the past, to plan for the future. But Lon wouldn't be able to examine them until the Master Librarian said he was ready.

Erastis was working on his own Fragments now, copying sections of the Book no one had read before, to preserve the writings in case the Book was lost—or worse, destroyed. Except for the missing texts that had been lost in the Great Fire, you could find enormous amounts of information from the Book on those shelves: records of noble lineages, histories of the provincial border wars, prophecies of things to come. Despite all this, Erastis estimated that they had reproduced only a small fraction of the Book.

"Much of it is useless," he'd said, idly waving a calligraphy brush through the air. "I've studied pages upon pages of the history of a single stone."

"Why bother copying it, then?" Lon had asked.

The Librarian had answered, "Because a single stone can alter the course of a river." And when Lon had rolled his eyes, he'd added, "And because it is written."

"Lon!" Erastis's voice brought him to his senses again.

S The boy jumped. Under Erastis's steady stare, he read the last letter from the chalkboard: "Ess." Out of all the letters, Lon liked the *S* best. The sound fit its shape, like the rasp of scales through sand. He smiled. "This," he said. "This. This. This."

The Master nodded approvingly. "It took me a month of studying the alphabet before I could string a word together."

Lon sat up eagerly. "So . . . can we do something more fun now? Rajar and the others are already so far ahead of me in Illumination."

Book magic. The ability to do miraculous things. He'd already begun to use the first tier of magic, Sight, when the Master Librarian found him, but with Illumination he could learn to do greater things than peering into people's histories—lift objects without touching them, create talismans that granted their bearers strength or invisibility, disappear from one place only to reappear in another.

"Rajar and the others have been here longer than you. And don't listen to Rajar." Erastis batted the air dismissively. "Soldiers think in terms of what they can maneuver and destroy and conquer. That's why they're only Soldiers."

"Yes, but at least they *do* things," Lon said.

The Master Librarian scowled at him.

"Okay, so how about the vault? I still haven't seen the Book."

Erastis glanced furtively over his shoulder. The movement was so quick Lon wasn't entirely sure he had really seen it. "We're the only division with the privilege of working directly with the Book. You'll see it when you're ready."

The order was composed of five divisions, each with a Master and an Apprentice, and a Director to lead them all. Soldiers studied battle strategies in the sand gardens. Assassins practiced tracking in the wilderness. But only Lon would handle the Book, one day.

He looked past the chalkboards to the round metal door

set into the stone of the mountain. The vault had a five-spoke wheel that controlled the dead bolts and two keyholes on either side of the handle. The Master Librarian had one key, which he wore on a long gold chain around his neck; Director Edmon, the leader of their order, had the other. No one knew where he kept it. Once you had both keys, you needed to perform a complicated sequence of turns and rotations to open the door.

Lon was dying to see the Book, though. He'd only heard about it from Erastis, who described it in numinous terms, as if the Book were made out of light and magic instead of paper and thread. Every day, Lon begged the Master Librarian to describe it, until he could see it when he closed his eyes— especially when he closed his eyes—the thin fluttering pages, the brown leather covers, the jeweled clasps and gold filigree on the corners. He swore to the other four Apprentices that he knew the shapes of the settings and the sparkling gems, and that sometimes when he was lying in bed at night, he could even smell it: mildew, grass, acid, vanilla. But not even Rajar believed him.

"No one gets to see the Book whenever he wants, including Edmon," Erastis admonished him. He tapped the board again. "Continue."

Lon sighed and tried to sit up straight. "Is," he read, skipping the spelling. "A. Book. This is a book." He rolled his eyes. "*This* isn't a book. This is a chalkboard."

"Is that what you think?"

Lon opened his mouth to reply, but shut it again after a moment. He tilted his head to the side, puzzled. *Could* a chalkboard be a book? Could anything be a book, if you knew how to read it?

"Again." Erastis raised the stick.

Sucking in another deep breath, Lon trained his attention on the letters. "Tee," he said. "Aitch. Aye. Ess."

• • •

If anything could be a book, there was no telling what you could learn, if you knew what to look for. Smooth river stones spelled out across a mossy floor. Lines drawn in the sand. Or inscribed on the side of a fallen log, half-obscured by twigs and mulch: *This is a book.*

Captain Reed
and the *Current of Faith*

S trictly speaking, there were several green ships in
Kelanna, but anyone who knew anything could
tell you that only one of them really mattered. Her
figurehead was a tree that seemed to grow out of the
hull itself, its branches winding up the proud spear of
the bowsprit, looking as if leaves would burst from their
stems in stunning helixes at any second. People said it
was a magic tree from the secret grove in Everica where
the trees walked, whispering to the witching woman who
lived among them.

They said this ship could outrun any other in the
Central Sea, her speed matched only by that of the
Black Beauty in the southeast. But everyone knew the
Current of Faith didn't run. She'd come face-to-face with
maelstroms and sea monsters, been in more battles than
ships twice her age, and survived them all.

When the ship was docked, and her crew spent their
evenings in dank taverns that smelled of sweat and ale,
they leaned conspiratorially over the tables to whisper
things like, "The *Current* will show you the way." Even in

the noise that swelled to the cobwebbed tavern ceilings, they spoke of her in hushed, reverent tones: "The *Current* will never steer you wrong."

Others said it wasn't the ship that was remarkable, but its captain. Cannek Reed was the son of a stonemason with rocklike fists, and he belonged to the water the way his father—a rare creature—belonged to the earth. They said Captain Reed surrounded himself with the finest crew in Kelanna. They worked for him—they'd give their lives for him—because he looked after them, made them legends, and treated them like brothers. He was always the first into danger.

Sometimes when the *Current* was in port, he'd climb the mainmast and stand in the crow's nest while the sun sank, and as the waters turned golden and dark, he'd listen to the sea. They said the water spoke to him. He knew all the natural harbors, the swiftest currents, how to avoid a squall even when it seemed intent on destroying him. Some people even said he could look at the pattern of the waves and tell you where they'd come from, where they were going.

Everyone in Kelanna knew about Reed and his ship. That's how it was. You lived among giants and monsters. People passed stories from mouth to mouth like kisses, or plagues, until they flowed down the streets, into gutters, streams, and rivers, down to the ocean itself.

CHAPTER 6

The Boy in the Crate

Although Sefia never left Oxscini, she spent the next year roaming the Forest Kingdom, searching in vain for signs of Nin or her kidnappers, growing tough and strong in her solitude. For the most part she survived on what she could gather, trap, and hunt; and when she wasn't setting snares, weaving lobster traps, or bow hunting in the woods, she was teaching herself to read.

It had been slow at first, one line at a time, until seeing the letters and understanding the most common words had become easier and easier. Still, it could take her minutes to make out the meanings of some words, struggling through the pronunciation, testing each sound on the edge of her tongue before stringing them all together. Other passages were so full of confusing, convoluted words that she ground her teeth at her own uselessness and skipped to something simpler.

She taught herself to read perched in treetops, in caves

carved by wind, overlooking surprising waterfalls crashing through the mountains, and every time she got the book out, every time she unwrapped it from its casing, she ran her fingers over the emblem on the cover, tracing the indentations.

It helped her conjure the people she'd lost. Her mother, features fading like watercolors in the sun. Her father, stiff and cold as wax. And Nin, staring at her through the leaves.

It became a ritual for her. Two curves for her parents, a curve for Nin. The straight line for herself. The circle for what she had to do: Learn what the book was for. Rescue Nin. And if she could, punish the people responsible.

But still the book gave her no answers, and however much she read, however skilled she became with a knife and a bow, she seemed no closer to fulfilling her vow.

Then, one day a couple weeks before she turned sixteen, everything changed.

As usual, Sefia was curled up in a hammock strung between two trees, eighty feet above the forest floor, with the canopy creaking and swaying above her and the mulchy ground far below. Soft whipped clouds drifted across the blue sky.

She had just settled down to read with the book cradled in her lap, and she unwrapped it in swift, smooth motions. There was the symbol, looking back at her like some dark eye. She traced its lines with the tip of her finger.

Answers.

Redemption.

Revenge.

Then she ran her fingers along the edges of the cover and flipped it open to a spade-shaped leaf she was using as a bookmark. The pages rippled beneath her hands, and she began to read.

The sound of snapping twigs interrupted her. Light as a bird, she closed the book and peered down through the leafy branches. There were more sounds: footsteps crunching through the undergrowth, groaning, the rattling of sword scabbards and gun holsters. Sefia listened intently. Judging from the noise, there were fifteen to twenty people trekking through the forest.

A minute later they came into her line of sight: dirty, sweaty men with sloping shoulders and stooped postures. They wore heavy boots, and their footfalls made great stomping sounds on the ground. A few of the men led underfed donkeys that towed rickety carts loaded with supplies. But the last cart carried only a battered crate, padlocked shut, with airholes punched in the sides, and branded on the back—a symbol she would have recognized anywhere.

She immediately thought of books, more books than she ever could have imagined existed, stacked one on top of another, and between their covers, millions upon millions of new words, new combinations.

She stared down at the book in her lap. A year of searching for the symbol and it had appeared not among the words but in the world, solid as the crate it was branded on.

A crate with airholes.

Sefia checked herself. *Books* didn't need air. She caught one glimpse of the crate before it disappeared around the next bend.

Nin?

Her hand went to her knife, and as the footsteps faded, she dismantled the hammock and shoved her belongings back into her pack. Checking for her bow and quiver of red-fletched arrows, she scrambled down the tree trunk.

Nin.

Before following the men north into the jungle, she dug her hands into the earth and narrowed her eyes, promising herself that this time she would not fail.

B y the time they stopped, the sun had already sunk between the tree trunks, casting slanted yellow beams and bands of shadow through the undergrowth. Sefia scurried up a nearby tree, where she could survey their whole camp. The cart with the crate sat at the edge of the trees. The men seemed to avoid it as they built a fire and cooked dinner, going out of their way to keep a good distance between it and themselves. While they ate, Sefia gnawed a few strips of dried meat, searching the men for weaknesses while the rumble of their voices drifted up through the trees.

A man paused in polishing his rifle. "I tell ya. I never get tired of it. I've never seen anyone fight like that. Kid's quick as a cat."

Beside him, his friend lifted his eye patch and scratched the skin stretched over his empty eye socket. "Mean too."

"Stop that." The rifleman swatted his friend, who laughed and straightened his eye patch. "You'd fight like crazy too, if you were in his place."

One-Eye picked his teeth with a sliver of bone. "You gotta watch his face, though. You know what I'm saying? His face when he's fighting, it's . . ." He glanced nervously at the crate and nodded again. "He's like a cat. One of them big cats, with the golden eyes."

Sefia scanned the campsite, but couldn't see anyone who fit that description. Disappointment flooded her. It probably wasn't Nin inside that crate.

Just beyond the ring of firelight, two men sat on a rock away from the others. While the bulk of the group ate and chatted easily, these two were watchful, calculating.

"A born killer," said one, smoothing his bristling red beard. "I think that's the third one he's done in by snapping his neck." His voice was deep and filled with the gravel of a life-long smoker, and there was a delight in his words that made Sefia's skin crawl.

The second man grunted and picked at a scab on his fleshy arm. "All that matters is that he won, and we got paid." He must have been Redbeard's superior. Sefia could smell his self-satisfaction from her perch above the clearing. She studied him more closely: watery brown eyes, sparse straw-colored hair, skin gone ruddy from a life on the road. He wasn't tall, but he had the beefy figure of a wrestler. Not a man you'd want to cross.

Sefia gripped her knife harder, its cold curves reassuring in her palm. She glanced at the crate, still untended at the edge of the clearing. The airholes stared at her like dozens of black eyes.

Impressors. The word trickled down Sefia's back and spread like ice to the tips of her fingers. Boys captured and forced to fight each other. Boys turned into killers. A wave of cold anger and confusion struck her. What were impressors doing with the symbol on their crate?

"And we're one step closer to the Cage," their leader added.

"You think we'll meet Serakeen, Hatchet?" Redbeard asked. "I hear Garula met him, when his boy won in the Cage."

The hair rose on Sefia's forearms. The Scourge of the East. Was he responsible for the kidnappings, the brandings, the killings? It fit with his brutality. But why here? Why pay impressors to turn boys into murderers when he had enough murderers in his fleet already?

Hatchet flicked the last of his scab into the dirt and squinted at the raw skin beneath. "I couldn't care less about Serakeen. It's been too long since we've even gotten that far, and I'm dying to find out just how much the Arbitrator pays." He stood abruptly and motioned to one of his other men.

Sefia watched one of the tallest men in the crew disengage from the rest of the group and trot over to where Hatchet and Redbeard sat.

"Yeah, boss?" he asked. When he spoke, the scar across his lower lip stretched and pulled, making his face seem crooked, like that of a clown.

"Get that mess cleaned up, Pal." Hatchet gestured to the

spit and carcass. "Bury it. Far away. I don't want scavengers to come nosing around here tonight."

Up in the tree, Sefia set her jaw. So the impressors were Serakeen's lackeys. How many boys did he have now? How many boys had died for this?

These men didn't have Nin. She doubted they knew anything about the book either. But they were connected, the book and Serakeen's impressors, by the symbol. And she had to find out how. She checked for Nin's old lock picks in the inner pocket of her vest and settled down to wait.

You'll get more than scavengers tonight, she thought.

One by one the fires became red pulsing embers, and the men settled under their blankets. Some of them snored, but most fell into the deep soundless sleep of the exhausted.

Sefia shouldered her pack and climbed down from her tree, alighting at the base of the trunk like a shadow. Unhooking the safety catch on her knife, she crept forward. The lone sentry, a young impressor with red hair, sat on one of the carts at the edge of the clearing, leaning against the sideboard for support.

She paused beside the cart wheel, watching the back of the sentry's head. The handle of her knife grew hot in her palm. She couldn't risk him alerting the others. She had the advantage. Easy. It would be quick.

Still she didn't move. The side of his face was silhouetted in the dying firelight, which passed through the fine fuzz on his jaw, illuminating each thin strand. He was barely more than a boy himself.

The sentry's head tipped forward. He began snoring softly.

Swallowing, Sefia released her knife. She slipped the lock picks into her hand and crept to the crate, looking forlorn at the edge of the clearing.

Running her fingertips along the splintery edges, Sefia searched for the heavy iron padlock and grinned. It was a simple lock, the sort you could commission from any common blacksmith. She'd been picking locks like this since she was nine. She took a deep breath and scanned the rest of the clearing, but no one stirred.

She traced the symbol on the corner of the crate. Two lines for her parents, one for Nin. One for her, and what she had to do next. Inserting her picks into the lock, she set to work.

After a few seconds of tinkering, she released the padlock and eased the door open with one hand. With the other, she grasped her knife. Deep inside, she was still hoping to see Nin, or at least books and stacks of paper, but she wasn't surprised when a battered-looking boy emerged from the shadows. He was laced with fresh wounds—cuts and bruises on his legs and arms, across his bare back. He peered out from under the crook of his arm, but she couldn't tell if he was afraid or ready to attack.

"Shh," she murmured, stealing a glance at the sleeping sentry. "I'm here to help you."

The stench was awful: a mix of blood and sweat and urine. But she gritted her teeth and whispered in the kindest voice she could muster, "Come with me." The boy cringed, but she said it again, though her hand didn't stray from her knife. "Please, come with me."

He began to crawl. As he crept into the light, she saw more

wounds, scars. The skin around his neck was puckered and white—a scar that encircled his throat like a collar.

At the sight of it, her sense of the other world washed over her and Sefia staggered back, blinking.

In an instant she had one of those dizzying visions, like the one she'd had the moment she learned to read. The boy was flesh and blood and bone, yes, but also pulsing with light. Little streams of light circling and expanding around him like a river. For a second, Sefia swore she saw storms, great roiling clouds rolling with thunder, and lightning cracking overhead. There was smoke. Hot wet blood. Teeth. Fists and feet.

Then, just as quickly, it was replaced by a sense of small-ness and quiet. Night. Kerosene lamps, reflected a hundred times. Walking alone on a rocky coast with white-capped waves thrumming against stone. In the dark, two pairs of hands gently exploring each other, roving quietly over knuck-les, cuticles, fingertips, the delicate details. Smiles like patches of sun.

Then it was gone.

Blinking, Sefia leaned on the side of the crate for support, digging the heel of her hand into the splintered edge, as if the pain would distract her from the upheaval inside her.

Nausea. That was familiar, at least. But the rest?

She'd done nothing different. But when she saw that scar, it was like her sense of the lighted world had boiled over all at once, rushing over her, revealing images, stories . . . or were they memories? History?

Was this magic something her parents had wanted to keep from their enemies?

Whatever it was, she was getting better at it.

The boy was fully out of the crate now. He was taller than her, maybe a year or two older. Looking wide-eyed at the shadows, he hugged his arms awkwardly, like he didn't know what to do with them. All he wore was a pair of ripped trousers, and his bare feet gripped tentatively at the ground. He was underfed, so skinny his bones protruded under his skin, and he looked so lost, standing there, clutching his own elbows. The scars at his neck glowed almost white in the moonlight.

Whatever it was she had seen in the flash of light, it had been real, she was sure of that. Somehow, she'd peered into him, like watching a frothing sea through the eye of a needle, all those images and thoughts and feelings at once, all part of him. She knew what he had done—what he had been made to do—but she couldn't forget how tenderly he had touched those other hands. She didn't know whose hands, and that didn't matter. It was that sense of calm and warmth. Blinking back a headache that had begun knotting behind her eyes, she fastened the safety on her knife.

But she couldn't leave yet. She crawled inside the crate, gagging as she riffled through the bits of straw on the floor and felt the walls for signs of safes or hidden compartments. There was nothing.

She could have sunk into the ground.

There was *nothing*.

The boy shifted hesitantly beside her, still looking around like a lost child. Gritting her teeth, Sefia got to her feet, clipped the padlock back in place, and tapped him on the shoulder to let him know they had to go.

Instantly, his hand snapped over her wrist. Sefia went for her knife. But he looked surprised when he saw what he had done, and quickly released her. There was a horrified expression in his eyes, like he couldn't believe that was *his* hand. He hung his head. She let the blade slip back into its sheath.

With one last longing glance at the crate and the symbol on it, Sefia headed off into the jungle. The boy fell into step beside her, strangely silent, and together they stole away into the woods.

They walked for hours without saying anything, picking their way over logs and under low-hanging tree branches. Their pace was glacial, slow enough to set Sefia's teeth on edge, to make her jump at every branch snapping, every rustle of movement. But she couldn't leave him.

The boy soon began shivering in the moist night air. He didn't complain. His teeth didn't even chatter. But he hunched his shoulders and rubbed his arms and Sefia knew he was cold. Pausing a moment to pry the blanket from her pack, she offered it without touching him. He looked at her warily, but she forced a smile, and he took it and wrapped it around his shoulders.

They continued walking. She stopped once or twice more to give him meat to chew and a few sips from her canteen, but otherwise, they walked without speaking, and almost without sound. Sefia was glad he didn't try to make conversation. She didn't want to get close to him. Those who were close to her always got hurt.

It was near dawn when they finally halted. They had crossed streams and doubled back on their own tracks more than once, just in case the men had a tracker among them, and Sefia was exhausted. She clambered wearily up a nearby tree and began slinging her hammock.

The boy followed, wincing, but he made it. Sefia gestured him into the hammock, where he fell asleep immediately. Settling herself on a wide limb, she leaned back against the trunk, knotting a rope around her so she wouldn't fall. For a while she tried to keep watch, scanning the ground for signs of movement, but soon she drifted off, frowning and fists clenched, as the night melted into gray predawn.

• • •

Once the door began to open, letting in a crack of moonlight so bright it was painful, the boy scuttled to the corner of the crate and huddled there, shielding himself from the light. He had been locked up for days, had been jostled, bumped, dropped. If he saw sky at all, it was only through the holes in the sides of the crate; everything else was dark and close, smelling of blood and waste.

He winced. Every extra breath of light and air meant fear and pain were coming. Fear and pain were coming soon, and it would hurt and someone would die. The sight of the trees and the forest floor made him cower and cringe. The moonlight was drifting through the door. Fear and pain were coming.

Instead, it was a voice that came to him—*Shh. I'm here to help you.*—like a soft dark tendril in the devastating light, stringing one word after another so, so gently, stirring inside him memories so deep that they had become like dreams: *Come with me.* A dark shape reached for him and he cringed, but the words were still there: *Please, come with me.*

He began to crawl, like an animal, out of the crate and toward the words, which fluttered before him like delicate shadows. He stood and blinked and looked around. Fear and pain were not here. They were not here. Only this cold, and this voice. But he remained alert. Because they were coming. They always came. And it would hurt, and someone would die.

• • •

Knife cuts in a tree trunk, high above the forest floor: *This is a book.*

CHAPTER 7

Born Killer

Over the spreading canopy of the Oxscinian forest, the clouds rolled through the sky, growing darker and darker with each wave. The night creatures returned to their hollows and grottoes, and the birds flitted nervously between the branches, twittering. Rain was coming.

It wasn't until well after noon that Sefia woke. The rope tying her to the tree dug into her waist, and she spent a few moments unknotting it while she studied the boy, asleep in the same position he'd been in the night before. His nose was crooked—it must have been broken in the past—and there was a slight powdering of nearly invisible freckles on his tawny cheeks. He looked more human now, less like a caged animal.

She wondered what her vision had shown her the night before. Moments from an ordinary life. His life? Did this magic allow her to see the past? Had her parents been seers too? Was that why the woman in black wanted them?

No, Sefia corrected herself. The woman in black had said *it*. She'd wanted the book.

Was she in league with Serakeen?

Sefia unhooked her pack as quietly as she could, but at the slight noise the boy opened his eyes. They trained on her, golden, or amber, with flecks of copper and mahogany in them. He seemed unafraid.

She'd never been this close to a boy her own age before. She hadn't been this close to *anyone* since Nin was taken. Coiling the rope into her pack, she averted her eyes from his bare skin. "You can go home today."

The boy didn't speak, but he crawled slowly out of the hammock, barely rocking it. He looked around him like a baby animal seeing the world for the first time. Even the leaves and the grayed-out light filtering through the branches seemed new to him. He rubbed his eyes.

As Sefia soon learned, the boy didn't speak at all. She didn't know if he *could* speak. He only watched her, mild and curious, as she stowed the hammock in her pack, and followed her down from the tree without a word.

She quickly grew irritated with his helplessness. He just stood there, waiting for her to do something. She had to press a tin cup into his hands just to get him to drink.

As he slowly chewed his breakfast, she sat opposite from him with her arms crossed over her chest, watching. The skin around his throat was pinkish white where the burns had healed unevenly.

His right arm had been burned too, with fifteen parallel marks the length of her palm and the thickness of a finger, from the oldest scars on his shoulder to the newest past his elbow, like the rungs on a ladder.

She didn't question him about them, but she did ask about the symbol, tracing it in the dirt for him: the circle, four lines.

He shook his head.

"Didn't think so." She dusted off her hands and pointed west. "There's a town a day's walk that way. Just keep going and you'll make it. Someone'll get you home."

Dutifully, the boy turned in the direction she was pointing, then turned around. His eyes were questions.

"I'm going to follow them." She pointed to the ⊖ on the ground. "Maybe I'll get some answers out of this yet."

The boy nodded as if he understood, so she put half her provisions into his hands—more than he would need for just one day. Then she shouldered her pack and began walking back the way they'd come. She hadn't gone ten paces before she heard his faint footsteps behind her. She turned, and the boy walked up to her.

"What?"

He cocked his head and blinked.

She scowled at him. "You're free now. Go home."

The corners of his mouth twitched. Maybe he almost smiled.

"Get moving." Sefia paused. "Before the rain comes."

When he didn't respond, she muttered a curse under her breath and began walking again. But the boy continued to shadow her, clutching a few strips of jerky and saying nothing.

Every so often, Sefia turned to see if he was still there. He always was.

"Go away," she ordered once. "What are you doing?"

The boy merely looked at her and put a narrow piece of meat in his mouth. He gnawed and stared. When she started off again, he followed, chewing slowly.

After an hour, Sefia took the meat out of his hands and stuffed it back into her pack. She gave him a drink of water and waited as he sipped. They had stopped beside a massive log, overgrown with moss and ferns. It had ripped a huge hole in the canopy when it fell, creating a clearing that let in the light. The sky was darker now, completely clouded over. The storm would break soon. Sefia sat down on the log and put her chin in her hands. They were losing time. It was already midafternoon. The boy stood awkwardly clutching the canteen.

"They're probably looking for you," she said, plucking it out of his hands. "You should get as far away from them as you can." She waved him away, trying to ignore the pained expression in his eyes. "Now."

The boy looked down at his bare feet.

"You don't understand." Her voice rose. She fluttered her hands uselessly at him. "I can't take care of you!" She was speaking too loudly. She wasn't listening hard enough. Behind her, footsteps crunched in the mulch. "It's too dangerous." She didn't hear the creaking of leather or the men's voices either. A last desperate hiss: "Just go!"

Two men stumbled into the clearing. Hatchet's men. Sefia recognized the young sentry, though now his hair had been roughed up on one side and there was a bruise soaking his cheek. The other man was already pulling out his sword.

Sefia jumped to her feet, swinging her bow from her back

and nocking an arrow in one smooth motion. The sentry cried out. Their swords flashed.

She let the arrow fly.

But the boy was faster than all of them. He was a golden blur leaping past Sefia, landing on the second man's chest, knocking him aside so the arrow struck his shoulder instead of his heart. The man let out a grunt as the air left his lungs, the boy on top of him like a jaguar on its prey. There was a brief struggle, fists and fingers. Then the boy grabbed the man's head and twisted. Sefia heard the *crack* and felt its tremors go up her spine.

The sentry backed away, turning to run, but the boy grabbed the man's sword. He was standing. The blade was leaving his hands.

Everything slowed.

The boy's arm extended, fingers empty.

The sentry's back exposed.

Sefia blinked.

Between them, the trajectory of the sword was outlined in rippling eddies of light. She could see them more clearly this time: each current was made up of thousands of tiny specks, all drifting and swirling.

The boy's hand—the sword—the sentry's back.

She blinked again, and the currents of light disappeared. Time snapped into motion again.

The blade went straight through the sentry's spine. Her bow clattered as it fell from her hands. She looked for the boy. He was just standing there, staring at the bodies.

The men were dead. The boy had killed them. They'd died so fast. She hadn't known it would be so fast.

Was that what it would be like to take someone's life away?

She clenched her fists at her sides, digging her nails into her palms, wondering if that was what had happened to her father when he died.

No. Her hands trembled. *They made sure to kill him slowly. It would have looked nothing like this.*

The memory of his corpse burned behind her eyes.

Next time, she'd be faster. She'd make the kill herself.

It started to rain. The drops pelted the canopy, filling the forest with the roar of water. Thunder rumbled through the sky like drums.

Sefia and the boy were drenched within minutes. Water dripped down their faces and puddled around their feet. The ground turned to mud beneath them.

Slowly, painfully, she uncurled her fingers. These men weren't the ones she wanted. She wanted the woman in black. She wanted the man with a voice like ice.

And if he was involved with them, she wanted Serakeen too.

There was a light touch at her elbow. Sefia hissed and drew her arm away. The boy backed off, looking at his hand as if it had burned her.

The *snap* of a branch burst like a gunshot through the jungle. She looked up suddenly. Amid the thunder, shouts sounded in the woods.

"Patar!"

"Tambor!"

The boy grabbed her bow from the ground, took her hand, and pulled her toward the nearest tree, where he climbed to the first branch and hauled her up after. Her hands clutched at the

74

wet bark. Their mad scrambling sounded so loud. The scratching and scraping. Blood came up on her palms.

"Where'd you get to? Boss wants us to head back!"

Sefia and the boy didn't have time to climb any higher. There were a few branches blocking them from sight, but Sefia had to hoist her legs up so that they wouldn't dangle beneath the screen of leaves. They were so exposed. She barely dared to breathe.

"Patar! Tambor!"

Two more of Hatchet's men appeared in the clearing below. The rifleman and the man with the eye patch. One-Eye knelt beside the first body he came to, felt his broken neck. The rifleman dropped to his knees with the gun at his shoulder.

"Dead?" he asked.

"Dead."

"The boy?"

"Probably. But he had a partner." One-Eye pulled Sefia's arrow from the body, its shaft glistening red. He squinted, blinking water out of his good eye. "Any sign of them?"

The rifleman swept the edge of the clearing. To Sefia, it was obvious where they had sat, where the broken stems and twigs and churned-up places in the mud revealed their passage, but the man was looking out into the trees, not at the ground.

Lightning flashed overhead, followed almost immediately by thunder. The rain came down harder. The branches felt slippery under Sefia's hands.

One-Eye pulled his gun from its holster. The *clank* of the cocking mechanism cut through the cascade of the rain. "Which direction did they go?" he asked.

"Do I look like I know?" The rifleman spat sideways and kicked uselessly at the ferns, dislodging raindrops. "Tracker's gone southeast with Hatchet." He made a disgusted noise deep in his throat. "Boy!" he shouted. "You better come on in before it gets real bad for you! Hatchet's mighty pissed about you running off!"

The two men stopped to listen. To Sefia it seemed like they stayed there for hours. *Don't look up. Don't look up. Don't look up.* Her skin was slick. Her arms and legs began to tremble. She tried to stop it, but the tremors increased. Her elbows felt like they'd give at any second.

The rifleman took a step forward. He was almost directly under them now.

Sefia's legs were spasming painfully; she couldn't hold them up much longer. Her arms shook. She gritted her teeth and tried to hold on.

Perched just above her on the branch, the boy leaned down—quietly, quietly—and took hold of her legs. She felt him take her weight. She stopped shaking.

The rifleman studied the corpses. "Should we go after them?"

An uncomfortable pause. The men chewed the insides of their cheeks. Sefia felt like every breath coming in and out of her lungs could rattle the entire world. The rain came down hard.

After a minute One-Eye shook his head and took a step back. "Nuh-uh. I don't care what Hatchet does to us when we get back."

The rifleman's gaze kept darting out into the forest, like he was expecting the boy to leap from the undergrowth when he wasn't looking. "Yeah," he said. "I say send the tracker after them."

Sefia held her breath. Hope flickered inside her.

The men looked at each other for a second longer before they put away their weapons and began fashioning a stretcher from long branches. They worked quickly and methodically, and soon they had piled the bodies on their makeshift stretcher. With a last nervous glance around the clearing, One-Eye tucked the arrow and the sword on the stretcher beside the bodies, and then he and the rifleman marched back into the woods.

Sefia eased out of the boy's grasp and settled more securely among the branches. But she did not speak, and she did not come down.

She and the boy waited while the storm swept over them, bringing more rain. In the late afternoon, when the deluge finally let up and the thunder became a distant echo, they descended from the branches with deep shuddering breaths. Sefia's legs and arms went limp as wet rags. She sank to her knees. The mud was cold and slick under her, but at least she was on the ground again.

The boy stood next to her, peering into the trees in the direction Hatchet's men had gone.

"I would have been caught if it weren't for you," Sefia said. After a moment, she added, "Thanks." The word felt clipped and unnatural on her tongue.

He looked down at her and nodded gravely. His hair was plastered to his forehead.

"I'm not after them, you know." She tried rubbing her

muscles to get them working again. "But I guess you'd come with me anyway."

The boy nodded again.

She sighed and got slowly to her feet. She was a little wobbly, maybe, but otherwise fine. "We can't stay here," she said, glancing at the bloodstain and the matted-down places in the ferns. "And we've got to be more careful."

He smiled then. A real, warm smile that seemed to surprise him, as if he hadn't known he could still do it. His smile was a soft buttery thing.

We.

"Yeah, yeah. Come on. They're bringing the tracker." She began hiking away from the clearing, taking care with her tracks. Placing his feet where her feet had gone, the boy followed, still smiling.

• • •

Brittle, brightly colored leaves arranged in a forest-floor collage: *This is a book.*

CHAPTER 8

A Good Day for Trouble

Captain Reed jogged across the *Current of Faith*, avoiding coils of rope and redheaded chickens that squawked underfoot. As he passed, his sailors pressed themselves against the rails then closed behind him like waves in a wake, the clicking and scraping of six-shooters and swords rattling at his heels.

Across the water, the *Crux* rode huge and golden on the waves, sea spray sparkling along her gilded figurehead—a wooden woman holding a diamond the size of a cow skull.

Out of the corner of his eye, Reed saw them lower a rowboat into the sea. Dimarion was coming. They had to be ready.

He slapped both of the chase guns at the bow—*nine, ten*—and turned down the starboard side.

By the carpentry workshop, he found Meeks, the second mate, lounging in the doorway while Harison sat outside, running a cleaning rag over his revolver.

"They say Dimarion killed one of Roku's last dragons for

it," Meeks said. The leader of the starboard watch was a short, spry man with neatly kept dreadlocks twined with beads and shells that winked like gems in black chenille. He was cheeky and liked a good story more than anything else. The rest of the crew enjoyed giving him a hard time, but they listened when he spoke. Even when he was supposed to be readying his watch. "The battle lasted an entire day, and when the dust settled and the smoke cleared, it was Dimarion who remained standing, and it was Dimarion who claimed the diamond."

"And Cap invited *him* onto *our ship*?" Harison's voice cracked on the last word.

Reed smacked one of the sixteen-pound guns on the starboard side—*eleven*—and chuckled. "Right, you weren't here for that bit with the Thunder Gong, were you? Must've been five years ago that happened."

Meeks grinned, showing the chip in his front tooth. "Cap stranded Dimarion in a maelstrom. Remind me to tell you about it when we're done here."

Harison shook his head. "Sometimes I still can't believe I'm on your crew, Cap."

Reed liked the ship's boy. He was a goofy kid with a broad nose and big wide-set eyes. Ears like a bush baby, but that didn't stop the girls in port from cooing over his smooth brown skin and short black curls. "Believe it, kid," he said. Then he jerked his head at Meeks. "Don't you got a watch to get in order?"

Meeks snapped to attention and tipped him a mock salute. "Yessir, Cap, sir!" Flicking his dreadlocks over his shoulder, he strode across the deck, calling orders to the rest of the starboard watch.

Reed rolled his eyes and finished his circuit of the ship, slapping the last sixteen-pounder—*twelve*—and taking the stairs to the quarterdeck two at a time. He liked eights best, but he'd settle for fours, sixes, twelves, sixteens, any even number, really. Made him feel like things were in order.

On the quarterdeck, Aly, the ship's steward, was busy arranging a table for two, laying out fluttering linens and gleaming silverware. Two long blond braids hung over her shoulders as she made a quick set of pleats in a napkin. "Before you ask," she said as he approached, "I already stowed my rifle under the gunwale."

Captain Reed grinned. Dimarion was coming. But they were ready. "You're as sharp as you are sweet, Aly," he said.

She beamed.

The chief mate had not stirred from his place at the rail. An old man with a lined rectangular face and a scar across the flat arch of his nose, he was the leader of the larboard watch and Reed's right-hand man. At the sound of Reed's footsteps, he turned, dead gray eyes probing. "Is it today?" he asked. The same question he asked before every adventure. Before every dangerous caper.

Reed ran his fingers through his thick brown hair, listening to the waves wash against the hull. "Nah," he said. "Not today."

The mate's frown deepened as he handed the captain his high-crowned hat. "How close is he?"

As much a part of the ship as the timbers themselves, the chief mate could see and hear anything on the *Current*—the face you were making behind his back, the state of the holds, the conversations of the crewmen in their bunks at night—as if the beams of the ship were extensions of his eyes and ears and nose and sense of touch; but anywhere except the ship he was blind, his milky eyes sightless. People said he never left the *Current of Faith*, and that as long as he lived, he never would.

The *Crux*'s rowboat was nearly at their hull now. Dimarion's back was to them, but there was no mistaking his mountainous form. Reed even fancied he saw four sparkling rings on the man's right hand.

"Close enough." He tapped his fingers along the rail. Eight times.

The mate smiled grimly. "Dimarion isn't a man for bygones. Do you think he's angling for a fight?"

"If we're lucky," Reed answered.

When Dimarion and the *Crux* showed up on the horizon that morning, well, the smart thing would have been to run. The *Current* was quick, and she didn't have the double gun decks and the heavy artillery of the *Crux*. But being smart was overrated. Being stupid and brave and curious? Now that's something stories are made of.

Dimarion's boat struck their hull with a dull *thunk*, and the chief mate grunted. "Get your guns up. Here comes trouble."

Meeks scampered by, his dreadlocks flying behind him. "It's a good day for trouble!" he cried.

Captain Reed laughed. The men were waiting for his signal to bring up their guests. The water was blue and the wind was fine and the smell of salt and tar was strong in his nostrils. They were ready.

∙ ∙ ∙

Cooky and Aly had done all he asked and more. In addition to the fine china and the shining silverware, they'd added crystal glasses, a bottle of deep-red wine, and a wide platter of delicacies. Eight slices of apple; sixteen grapes; four halved figs, their insides shining pink and gold in the sun; twenty-four slices of cheese; twenty-four round crackers dotted with herbs; and four squares of dark chocolate already softening in the sun.

Dimarion whistled appreciatively and seated himself. He was tall, taller than the legends said, so large his legs wouldn't fit under the table, and he extended one booted foot toward Reed. The gold tip glinted in the light. "I hope you didn't go through all this trouble for me." He chuckled. He had a deep melodious voice like a finely tuned instrument.

Reed sat in the chair opposite, one hand tracing interconnected circles on the tablecloth. "Nothing but the best for my old enemy," he said.

"Enemy!" Still chuckling, the captain of the *Crux* twirled his glass between his huge oak fingers. He had smooth brown skin that matched his powerful bassoon-like voice. "And I'd so hoped we could be friends."

"With respect, we been on the wrong sides too many times to be friends. Seems a shame to go and change all that now."

Dimarion tipped the wine into his mouth and swished it between his cheeks before swallowing. He smiled and selected a cracker and a slice of cheese. "I suppose that suits us, doesn't it? After all, you did steal my gong."

Reed crammed a cracker into his mouth. "What gong?" he asked.

"*My* gong."

"Oh, you mean the gong that by rights is mine, as restitution for the way you marooned me on that island?" He grinned slyly.

"Have you used it?"

Truth was, the thing didn't even work, but he wasn't about to tell Dimarion that. Instead he shrugged and countered with a question of his own. "How'd you get outta that twister?"

Dimarion smiled and drained the last of his wine. Aly, who was waiting nearby, refilled his glass and slipped away again. He didn't thank her, barely even glanced in her direction. Reed would have been insulted if her tendency to fade into the background wasn't so useful.

The large man nibbled a cracker and hummed with pleasure. "This isn't abysmal," he said. "What a shame for an artist like Cooky to end up a dough-slinger on a ship like yours."

"The chief mate don't settle for less than the finest grub."

Dimarion swirled the wine in his glass. The burgundy liquid swept up the sides of the bowl and dripped slowly down as he held it to the sunlight. No stranger to snobbery, he even wore a silk scarf tied around his head to keep off the sun. For an outlaw who spent his time pillaging merchant ships and taking the survivors as galley slaves, he was impossibly clean.

But the life of an outlaw attracted all sorts. For all the petty bickering of the Five Islands, the jurisdiction of a kingdom extended only so far as you could still see its lands. The rest of Kelanna was free ocean. Outlaws could be as good or as immoral as they pleased, and they didn't answer to any authority but the gun and the sea.

"But you didn't come here to jaw about Cooky's grub," Reed said.

Dimarion inspected his neatly trimmed fingernails. His four rings, tipped with sharp canary diamonds, flashed in the sun. If he ever got the chance, he'd use those rings on Reed. That was how the captain of the *Crux* marked his enemies; if he hit you hard enough—and Reed knew from experience, he hit *hard*—you'd have four star-shaped scars, one for each ring, for the rest of your life.

Dimarion took a fig from the glistening tray of fruit and popped it into his mouth. Its pinkish pulp squished between his teeth. "I have a proposition for you."

Reed watched as Dimarion's gaze flicked to his tattoos. They sprawled across Reed's arms, disappearing beneath his sleeves and reemerging at the parting of his collar where the top button of his shirt was missing—a sea monster with long sucking tentacles, a school of winged fish, a silhouette of a man with a smoking black gun. Every important thing he'd ever done was there, dark and permanent. If you looked closely, you could find the stories of the Lady of Mercy, the Rescue at Dead Man's Rock, and his love affair with the cold and perilous Lady Delune.

But Dimarion was only looking for one: in the crook of Reed's left elbow, a tiny tattooed ship perched at the edge of a spinning maelstrom—a reminder of their last encounter. Dimarion cracked his knuckles. "Treasure," he said.

"I got treasure."

"Not treasure like this."

In spite of himself, Reed sat forward in his chair. Only one treasure could ignite that deep greedy yearning in Dimarion's voice. "The Trove of the King," Reed whispered.

It wasn't only the size of the hoard that gave the Trove its allure, it was the mystery of its disappearance and the desolation of what had happened when it was lost. According to legend, Liccaro had been a rich kingdom once. Though much of its lands were sand and high desert, its mines had yielded more precious metals and gemstones than any other in Kelanna. With such fine raw material to work with, the Liccarine people became the best artisans in the world; travelers from all over came to see their work, and to buy it if they could afford it. And then one day, for no reason at all, King Fieldspar took all the scepters, the crowns, the jeweled cloaks and necklaces, the fine enameled vases, and he spirited them all away, deep into the labyrinth of caves beneath his kingdom, and was never heard from again. People said his ship sank in the Ephygian Bay on his attempted journey home, but no one knew for sure. The kingdom fell into disrepair. The mines dried up. Drought and famine struck. Divided and corrupt, the regents did nothing. The people suffered. The cities were abandoned, and shrank to a fraction of their original size, all their considerable wealth sold off to pay for seeds that didn't grow, for land they couldn't water.

"As long as there are people to hear it, they'll tell the story of the man who discovers it," Dimarion said, his eyes never leaving Reed's. "Another story for your collection."

Reed rapped the tabletop with his knuckles. Sometimes at night when he couldn't sleep, he lit a flickering candle and counted his tattoos. He counted them until he forgot the darkness looming at the portholes and the fringes of his life. Sometimes he needed more than one candle.

"Why you tellin' me this?" he asked.

"What if I told you I knew how to find it?"

"I'd say if you really knew where the Trove was, you'd already be on your way by now."

"Ah, but I need your help."

"For what?"

"I didn't come by this information on my own." Dimarion placed a hand over his heart, and said, his voice laced with venom, "I had a source in the employ of a certain captain we know . . . a fine woman dear to both our hearts."

Reed swigged his wine and wiped his mouth with the back of his hand. There was only one woman Dimarion hated as much as he respected her: the captain of the *Black Beauty*, the quickest ship in the southeast. Reed snuck a glance at the surrounding sea, but there was no sign of another ship. "That's what you need me for," he said. "Battlin' the *Beauty*."

"Our two ships against hers. If we combine forces in our search for the Trove, we can't lose."

"I wouldn't bet on that." Captain Reed drummed his fingers on the table. "Where is she now?"

"Oxscini."

"The old king of Liccaro hid his treasure on another island?"

"No. I believe she's hunting down a traitor."

Reed shook his head. *She* didn't tolerate betrayals. If she knew one of her crew had betrayed her secrets to Dimarion, it wouldn't be long before she found him. He shuddered, thinking of funeral pyres burning on the surface of the water, of red lights in the deep.

"Where's the Trove, then?"

"I don't know for sure. But I hear the first clue is in Jahara."

Reed laughed and sat back, eyeing the gold hulk of the *Crux*. Jahara was too far north for such a slow ship like the *Crux* to get to before the *Black Beauty*, even if she was making a detour to Oxscini.

Dimarion leaned forward. "She won't be expecting me to partner with you, not with our . . . complicated history." When Reed hesitated, he continued, "Think of what a story it will make: the three best ships in Kelanna engaged in a race for the Trove of the King! No matter who prevails, they'll continue to tell that story long after you die and your body returns to the water."

"The Trove's most likely buried somewhere in Liccaro, though." Captain Reed shook his head. "That means tanglin' with Serakeen, if we don't get caught in the crossfire between Oxscini and Everica first."

"Don't you fly the flags of an Oxscinian privateer?" When Reed nodded, Dimarion continued. "I do the same for Everica. They'll let us pass unmolested, if they know what's good for them. As for Serakeen." The captain of the *Crux* stood, and the deck seemed to bend beneath his weight as he crossed to the rail. "That man is a discredit to all our kind. How long has it been this way? Kings and queens can squabble for land, but no self-respecting outlaw says he *owns* the sea."

"Lack of self-respect don't make him less of a threat."

"Pah. Even the Scourge of the East would think twice about engaging both the *Crux* and the *Current*. He might even take out the *Beauty* and rid us of the competition."

Reed frowned. They might have been enemies, but the thought of a world without the *Beauty* in it made the seas seem a bit smaller, a little less grand.

Reed joined Dimarion at the rail. Though he was tall and tough as nails, he seemed almost fragile compared to the captain of the *Crux*.

For a moment, they both studied the stunning blue sea.

Captain Reed rubbed the sun-browned circle of skin at his wrist, the only empty patch of skin on his left arm. In a world where the only evidence of your existence was a body subject to decay and the works you left behind when the body was gone, you tried all manner of things to convince yourself that your life had some meaning, some permanence. But one day, even his tattoos would rot away—the images of horned whales, beautiful women, disappearing islands—and nothing would be left of him but the whispered legends of things he'd done.

He looked across the ship. His crew appeared busy swabbing decks and picking oakum, but their gazes kept drifting toward the quarterdeck. Harison, Meeks, Aly. Sailors who'd stuck with him for the past five years, after . . . well, after what had happened. Men and women who depended on him to keep them alive in legend even after they were gone.

"I'll tell you where to find the clue and we'll rendezvous in Jahara as allies and equals," Dimarion said.

Captain Reed counted to eight. He liked the number, how it cut when he said it, like biting off a piece of apple. He liked the length of time it took to count to eight, always the perfect amount of time to make a decision or take aim. He never missed when he counted to eight. It was a good number.

On the main deck, the mate waited at the rail, his dead eyes seeing everything. With his keen sense of the ship, the old man was probably listening to every word they said. Under Reed's scrutiny, he nodded, just once.

Reed played an eight-beat tattoo on the gunwale with the heels of his hands. This was what he needed. Danger. Adventure. Something to be remembered by. Because in Kelanna, if they didn't keep telling your story after you died, you might as well never have lived at all.

"For treasure and glory," he said, extending his hand.

Dimarion took it, grinning like a predator who knows its prey has been cornered. "With a little bloodshed thrown in for interest."

CHAPTER 9

Being There

To Sefia's relief, they hadn't come across any more men on the way back to Hatchet's camp, but she kept them off the trail and covered their tracks all the same. They breathed quietly and didn't speak.

The men had deserted their camp, but there were plenty of signs of their passage: upturned earth, broken twigs, crushed leaves. The crate was gone, and where it had lain were the remains of a funeral pyre. White ash and charred cinders, with bits of blackened metal and chips of bone protruding from the ruin.

Sefia skirted the clearing while the boy stood beside the ashes, staring at the smoking mound as if he couldn't quite understand what it was.

"There's nothing we can use," she said after a few minutes, "but I found their trail. Are you sure you want to do this?"

The boy nodded. The movement of his hair sent a whiff of foul odor in her direction. Sefia wrinkled her nose and tried not to cough. "Fine. But . . . look at you." She gestured at his torn pants, the dirt and straw embedded in his sandy blond hair, the mud—or worse—that hadn't been washed away by the rain. "Get yourself together."

He looked down at his ripped clothes, picked at one of his scabs, then looked up at her again.

She moistened a cloth with water from her canteen and tossed it to him. "I'll steal you some clothes and shoes next chance I get. Just get cleaned up, will you?"

As they walked, the boy dabbed at his cuts with the wet rag, picked bits of straw out of his hair, and ran his fingers through the tangles. He even stopped downstream at their next water crossing to rinse off in the creek.

At one point during the evening, Sefia found another, narrower trail. She lifted her face to the wind and sniffed deeply. "Get undercover," she said, and disappeared into the brush.

By the time Sefia returned with a bundle of clothing, the boy had curled up between the roots of a banyan tree to wait. "I don't know how much of it will fit," she said, thrusting the clothing at him, "but some of it's got to."

She turned her back as the boy abruptly pulled off his pants. When he was done changing, she made him bury his old clothes. The boots she'd found were a little large, the pants a little short, but the shirt was broad enough for his shoulders, and at least the garments were clean and whole. He smiled, barely, and plucked tentatively at his new clothing.

Sefia looked him over critically, but he didn't look half-bad. "Could be worse," she said grudgingly.

But when he grinned at her, she turned her back again and stalked away. After a year on her own, it was strange to be traveling with someone again, to have someone *be there* at all. Strange, and comforting, and dangerous.

She'd lost everyone she'd ever cared about. If she didn't stop herself, she'd end up caring about this boy too.

And she knew if that happened, she'd lose him.

After a wary week of circling, watching for signs of an ambush, Sefia realized that the men had spent a few days rooting around the forest, leaving some trails that struck out among the trees at awkward angles only to reappear a few hundred feet away, but they hadn't mounted any real search for the boy. Maybe they'd been scared, like the rifleman and his friend, not wanting to be out in unfamiliar territory with the boy on the loose. Maybe they were afraid of retribution.

From the look of their footprints, one small group had headed west in the direction Sefia and the boy had gone. But when she saw the tracks of the group rejoin the others, she knew she'd done all right covering their trail. After that, the men had continued marching north, and Sefia and the boy followed them.

This part of Oxscini was filled with tall elegant trees with leaves the size of their fists, and there was nothing but air between the canopy and the ferns on the jungle floor. There were birds too: red- and yellow-breasted, blue-winged, with long teardrop tails or orange feathers like lace cuffs around their necks. They dipped and flitted, chirping, making the little pointy sounds of small birds. Sometimes Sefia would stop in the middle of the path to look up and watch them flickering between the tree trunks, and the boy would pause by her side, looking too.

To keep him from being useless, she taught him the survival skills Nin had taught her: how to spot signs of prey in the undergrowth, how to stalk game, how to shoot.

The first time Sefia let him handle the bow, they used trees for targets. She showed him how to creep soundlessly forward, knees to the ground; pushing the bow out in front of her to minimize her movement, she took aim.

But she never saw trees. She saw killers. A woman in black with ugly blue eyes and a curved blade. A faceless man with a voice like ice.

Answers. Redemption. Revenge.

She released the arrow, and the tree shuddered when it struck, its metal point buried in the bark.

Sefia flexed her fingers and gave the bow to the boy.

He nodded and took it carefully, running his fingertips over the heartwood, testing the strength of the string. Then, without further coaxing, he mimicked her steps perfectly, and crouching low, nocked an arrow, drew back, fired.

He missed.

The boy looked at her and shrugged, the bow limp in his hands.

"Eh," she said. "You'll do better next time." Pushing her way through the saplings and fallen branches, she found the arrow thirty yards into the trees, its red fletches bright against the mottled green understory. When she drew it out, there was a wood quail pinned to the other end, shot through the skull.

Sefia pivoted slowly. The boy stood beside her, looking shocked. "Have you done this before?" she asked.

He shook his head.

She wasn't surprised to discover he could also handle a knife with ease. He could turn anything—a stick, a handful of mud, a shred of clothing—into a weapon. He was slower with the skinning and dressing, the cooking, the fire starting, and even with the stealing, as they got him better-fitting clothes and a blanket of his own. But he used a bow like he'd been doing it for years, and soon he was throwing knives farther and more accurately than she. Any technique he could use in a fight, he absorbed like a sponge.

But Sefia wasn't afraid of him. She would watch the way his head went back with surprise when he killed something—a fly with the tip of a knife, a fish with an arrow—and how he took the greatest care when approaching his kills or retrieving his weapons. He would hang his head and cradle the fly or the fish in his long hands. If he could have said he was sorry, she was sure he would have.

Still—and it was so quick that she had to be looking for it in order to see it—just as he flung the knife or released the arrow, he smiled, and it wasn't the tender hesitant smile she had come to know, but the smile of a wild thing, starving, slack-jawed, with a desire to kill in its eyes.

As the days passed they began to develop their own way of communicating. Soon all it took was a quick gesture for him to understand that she was searching for a place to camp. Or another few hand motions to show that the men they were tracking had stopped at this very spot the night before.

Sometimes he would mime the shooting of a bow and slip soundlessly away into the forest, and she would know he'd spotted quarry between the tree trunks. She'd continue walking, and fifteen minutes or half an hour later, he'd appear by her side again, with a quail or a pheasant dangling from his hand.

One time, as Sefia dressed a kill and set it on a spit over the fire, she narrowed her eyes at him and said, "You need a name."

The boy looked up at her. There were dark flecks in his bronzy eyes, but they were only visible when you were close to him like this. He seemed wary, but expectant.

"I have to call you *something*." She prodded the coals with the tip of a stick. "You can't just *not* have a name."

Sefia examined him for a long moment. He was peering at his hands and, with the pads of his fingers, touching each one of his scars. Every so often he would frown, as if he were trying to remember how he'd gotten them. But when he looked up at her again, his expression had not changed, and she knew he hadn't remembered.

"Archer," she said. "Your name's going to be Archer."

Archer smiled and pointed to the scar at his neck. His sign for himself.

Sefia tried not to smile.

By the time they tracked Hatchet to the base of the Kambali Mountains in northern Oxscini, after two weeks on the trail together, they had developed an informal partnership.

Archer watched for game; Sefia watched for tracks. He hunted and fetched water; she cooked. Sefia set up camp; Archer packed it away in the morning. She spoke; he listened. The only thing they didn't share was the pack, which Sefia insisted on carrying herself, though every morning Archer offered to carry it for her.

One night, they camped inside a small cave. Formed long ago by the collapse of two rock pillars, the rubble had created a little enclosure, barely big enough for two people, hidden by a tree perched at its entrance. It was one of those high, out-of-the-way places Sefia liked, one of the few places where she felt safe enough to sleep on the ground. The other side of the cave looked out over a waterfall cutting through the forest, with the rushing and crashing of the water tumbling over the bedrock.

Neither Sefia nor Archer could sleep. The cave was so narrow they nearly brushed shoulders as they lay on their stomachs, chins propped up in their hands, staring out over the waterfall into the star-dashed sky. But they didn't touch.

"It's my birthday," she said quietly. "I turned sixteen today."

Archer smiled at her, but as soon as he saw her face, his expression changed. He touched his temple, asking what was wrong.

She looked away. "Did you have birthday parties, before all this?"

He opened his mouth, but no sound came out. He tapped his throat a few times and shrugged.

"I've never been to a party. My parents never let me have one. They didn't even let me have friends." She paused, thinking of their lonely house on top of the hill, her basement bedroom, her parents' insular lives. "Sometimes I wonder what it would have been like, growing up normal."

Archer shrugged again.

For a second, she closed her eyes. A real birthday party. There would be bright paper lanterns and streamers cascading from the branches of trees thick with summer fruit, and below, on picnic tables covered with colorful cloths, all her favorite things to eat: pear salads, roast duck with crispy red skin, dinner rolls with oozing pads of cinnamon butter, and little white buns with sugary decorations and sour lemon curd centers served on delicate saucers with silver forks. There would be minstrels and a band, and embarrassing stories told by her parents and her oldest friends—one story for each year of her life—and on a wooden platform there would be dancing: couples kicking up their heels and spinning 'round and 'round like dandelion fluff, people laughing and the music swirling in between them. She'd have catty friends who whispered about her at the edge of the dance floor, and baby cousins who danced on her shoes, and some boy who'd never spoken to her before would ask her to dance, his sweaty hands at the small of her back, his face tense and nervous. Maybe, since she was sixteen, there would even be a kiss.

But this was not her life. It had never been her life, and after what had happened to her father, to Nin, it never would be. Her life was solitary, carried around on her back with all that she had of the people she loved.

Answers. Redemption. Revenge.

When Sefia opened her eyes again, Archer was watching her. She unclenched her fingers. "Sorry," she mumbled.

But Archer only smiled and handed her a long green feather. It had a magenta rachis down the center with soft green vanes that shimmered yellow and purple and blue depending on how you turned it.

She twirled the feather between her thumb and forefinger. It cut the air. "Where'd you get this?"

He flattened his hand and waved it this way and that, as if mimicking the movements of a feather falling from the sky.

"Thank you," she said.

He nodded.

Sefia ran the feather across her cheek, feeling its softness. The first birthday present she had gotten in six years, since her father was killed.

She was suddenly aware of how close they were. She could feel Archer stretched out beside her, his shoulders and elbows and feet, the quiet calm of his breathing.

She sat up abruptly and wrapped her arms around her knees. "What do you think the stars mean?" she asked, babbling in her discomfort. "There's so many. I think they must mean something. Sometimes I lie here and think that if only I could understand what the stars mean, I'd understand why things happen. Why people do the things they do. I mean, what they did to you . . . What makes people so cruel? Or . . ." She was silent for a long while, looking up into the night.

"Why people are born," she said. "Or why they die. Sometimes I feel like our stories are all up there, in the stars, and if only I knew how to listen, I'd understand things more. You know?"

He looked back at her, the low light touching on his scars and healing wounds, the marks of the impressors written all over his body. And she knew she couldn't let him continue to travel with her, not unless he knew the whole story. Not unless he knew what he was getting into.

"Archer." Sefia pulled her pack toward her. "I'm going to show you something I've never shown anyone before. I don't even think Nin knew what was in here." She dug through her belongings until she found the book, which she hadn't removed in two weeks. Withdrawing it carefully, she put it on the ground in front of them. "This is a book."

Archer looked up at her, and in the candlelight she began to read, her words mingling with the sounds of falling water outside: "It had never been done before . . ."

Captain Reed
and the Maelstrom

It had never been done before.

It would never be done.

Every ship that had tried to make it to the western edge of the world had been lost at sea: the *Domino*, the *Gambler*, the *Rocinante* . . . all good ships, now rotting somewhere at the bottom of the ocean.

They didn't understand. Why risk a ship like the *Current of Faith* on a voyage from which it would never return?

It was a waste, they said.

A fool's errand, they said.

And if you began this story with the day they set sail for the wild blue west, you'd be inclined to agree.

But to truly understand why Captain Reed took his ship to the Red Waters, and what happened to him and all his crew when they got there, you'd have to begin before the beginning.

You'd have to begin with the maelstrom.

The walls were already starting to tip and shake

by the time Captain Reed reached the seafloor. The maelstrom roared around him, up and up like the walls of a green well, with the bright eye of the sky and the silhouettes of the *Crux* and the *Current* circling far above. Under his hands, the sand was damp and soft as powder.

Dimarion pivoted, his huge bulk framed by foam and spinning water. His clothes were soaked, and the tail of his head scarf snapped behind him like a whip. Between them, the contents of the broken treasure chest lay exposed in the sand: The mallet and brass disc had gone green with age, half-corroded by time and salt water, but the gong was unmistakable. Carved figures paraded around its edge, screaming or singing, holding weapons or ancient instruments, calling for the storm in the center—roiling clouds and lightning.

"How did you—" Dimarion's deep voice was barely audible in the howling of the twister.

Sea spray struck Reed's cheek as he stood, testing the shifting sand with his toes. He grinned. "You think there's a body of water in Kelanna I can't cross?"

"Hah." Dimarion's gaze darted to the ancient copper coin in the sand. As long as it spun, the whirlpool would remain open. But it was beginning to tilt and wobble, its gleaming faces oblong and unsteady. The maelstrom was coming undone, with little twisters coiling sideways out of the water. Soon the ancient coin would fall, and the walls would cave in, and the water would crush them in seconds, their broken bodies chewed up inside it for the scavengers. "I don't suppose you have any bright ideas?"

Reed tapped nervously at his thighs, where his guns should have been. His fingers inched toward his knife. "I just landed myself at the bottom of a twister with a man who's tried to kill me twice. Don't reckon any of my ideas are too bright."

Dimarion drew his revolver. "What good are you, then?"

There was a gunshot. An explosion of light and smoke, and the quicksilver of the bullet splitting the distance between them.

Reed dodged. Sand kicked up behind him as he sprang forward, knife extended.

Blood. Dimarion released the gun and Reed kicked it aside, where it was sucked up by the spiral of water and flung into the sea.

What a sound the water made as it roared around them! The ocean's wordless calling.

Something collided with the side of Reed's head. A fist—a foot—a sledgehammer? Lights popped in his skull. He staggered sideways.

Dimarion caught his arm and twisted. The knife dropped.

Then Reed was being lifted. His feet left the ground. That roar. That voice of wind and water. He got in a hit, maybe two, before Dimarion flung him to the ground. A cringing crater in the sand, and the sea screaming around him.

Dimarion was on top of him. Bare fists like avalanches pummeling him in the face, the arms and hands, ripping away bits of flesh, bringing up bruises and blood. It was a good thing he didn't have his rings yet, or that would've been the end of Captain Reed.

Reed wriggled sideways and scrambled to his feet, panting. He wouldn't survive if they went to blows again.

Dimarion laughed, heaving himself up like a giant out of the earth. "There's nowhere for you to go."

Captain Reed shook his head and circled warily, counting his steps. *One, two, three, four...* "Don't you remember what I said about water?"

As Dimarion opened his mouth to reply, Reed lunged across the sand, grabbed the gong, and dove into the curving wall of water.

His breath left him. The sea tumbled him over and over like a stone, seeking out his eyes and nose and throat. His leg broke. He couldn't hear, couldn't see, but he felt it snap. Felt the bones splinter. He tried to swim, to kick, but in the maelstrom there was no up or down. Only the spinning and the savage water.

Captain Reed clung to the gong. Things were going hot and dark, but when they found his body washed up on some distant shore, they'd know he'd gotten what he came for.

And when he was sure he was going to die, swept up

forever into the boundless blue ocean, that's when the water spoke to him.

No one knows for sure what it said, but some people think it told him how he was going to die. Some people think he saw it all in a flash, fast and full of light: One last breath of salty wet air. A black gun. A bright dandelion on the deck.

And the timbers of the ship bursting.

And darkness.

For a moment he fought against it, as if he could strike at the vision with his hands, his flailing legs, but soon he was overcome by a sudden and intense peace. It spread through him as blood spreads through cloth, saturating his every fiber.

He was going to die, all right, but he wasn't going to die today.

And that's when he decided to take his ship to the western edge of the world.

Because there were thousands of adventures still to be had, and only a limited number of days left to have them.

Because it was out there.

And why not?

With that thought, he smiled, and closed his eyes, and let the water take him.

CHAPTER 10

The Beginning of
a Powerful Friendship

Sefia squinted at the darkened page in front of her. The candle had burned low while she read, and now its blackened wick began to smoke out on its own. Sitting back, she placed the green feather between the pages and closed the book. Her eyes were dark and serious in the dim light.

Sometimes she felt like the passages she read in the book had been written just for her, as if they were leading her to some greater understanding, like they'd done the day she learned to read. And there were clues even in old stories of outlaw heroes she'd been hearing about her whole life. But as she traced the symbol on the cover, she couldn't help but wonder: If the book was supposed to be *teaching* her, why didn't it give her the answers she needed? Why didn't it tell her how to find the people who'd destroyed her family?

"What would you do if you knew how you were going to

die?" she asked. "Would you run toward it like Captain Reed, or run from it?"

Archer fingered the edge of his throat and shook his head.

"I'd make sure I finished what I started. If that meant running toward it, well . . ." She shrugged. For a second she wanted to scratch the entire cover away, and the pages beneath, as if destroying the book would destroy her need to understand it. But she couldn't do that.

"I'm willing to do whatever it takes," she said. "But you don't have to. In fact, it might be better for you if you didn't."

Archer's eyes widened with hurt and surprise.

She should have told him sooner. Told him who she was and what she had and how no one she knew was safe because of it. She'd tried not to like him, tried to pretend he was nothing to her.

But that wasn't true.

She told him everything—about her father, about the house on the hill overlooking the sea, about the book, and about Nin's disappearance. Because he was in danger. Everyone she came into contact with could be taken, tortured, killed.

"You can get out. You can go home," she said. Her words wavered. "But this is it for me. I have nothing else."

His fingers tapped at the uneven edge of his scar, and she held her breath, afraid to disturb the stillness that had settled between them.

Would he leave her?

Did she really want him to?

Outside the cave, the waterfall roared beneath them, growing louder in his silence.

Finally, he raised his hand. She could just make out the shapes of his fingers against the starlight. As she watched, he crossed his middle finger over his index finger, twining them together.

He'd never used this sign before. But as she caught on to his meaning, a sad sort of warmth washed over her.

He was with her.

Not just there with her in the cave, but *with* her in all the ways that mattered.

A smile spread across his face.

She gripped her knees and felt her eyes glittering in the low light. They'd do it together, then, she and Archer.

Learn what the book was for. Rescue Nin. Find the people who'd ruined their lives and exact their revenge.

• • •

After she had learned to decipher that first simple sentence, it didn't take Sefia long to realize that she would never be able to master the words unless she could reproduce them. She had to make the symbols herself, so that she would understand them, their curves, how to use them and make them her own.

She started by making the same marks over and over again, repeating them aloud as she did: *This is. This is. This is. This is this is this is this.*

At first the letters were shaky and uncertain, poor imitations of the crisp lines she saw in the book, and she'd wipe them out with the toe of her boot or the broad blade of her hand. She practiced harder.

Later, she wrote with the blackened tip of a stick on the

smooth backs of leaves: *This is a book. This is a book. This is a book.* When she was finished, she thrust them into the fire. Clouds of smoke unfurled beneath the wide green rims as the leaves darkened and withered in the flames, their words becoming faint distorted lines before they turned to ash.

She wrote other things too, words with smooth bell-like syllables, passages she wanted to memorize, but she always returned to the same sentence. The first sentence she ever learned.

As she became a better writer, Sefia stopped erasing her words. She didn't leave them where anyone would find them, but making them wasn't enough anymore; she wanted them to be permanent, like the words in the book, signs that she had been there, that she had existed. She began carving with the tip of her knife on the highest branches of the tallest trees in the most unreachable regions of the forest: *This is a book.*

Or, on the stones of her buried campfires: *This is a book.*

And, traced invisibly on her inner arm, on the round of her knee: *This is a book. A book. A book. A book.*

What she did not know was that the people hunting for her would look *everywhere*: in the tallest trees, on sunken stones. They craved the book the way starving people crave food. Sick with longing for it, they followed her. And every word she wrote, every letter she left behind was a trail, with tracks as clear as footprints.

● ● ●

The flesh of the skull had been removed long ago, leaving behind charred bones like burned pieces of driftwood in an ocean of blue velvet that lapped at its empty eye sockets, the unnerving hollow of its nose, the protruding teeth fixed into a permanent grin by the attached mandible.

Lon glared at the skull, its silent mocking laughter, and rolled up his overlong sleeves. "I already know how to do this," he grumbled.

"Then prove it," Erastis said. He sat at one of the long curving tables, poring over manuscripts laid out like patches in a quilt. His gloved hands cradled the pages as if they might crumble at his touch.

Lon glowered at him. But when the Master Librarian didn't look up, he sighed and focused his mind. In the year since his induction, he'd read every esoteric word, every mundane passage Erastis had thrown at him. In fact, he'd mastered reading and writing so quickly he'd begun training in Illumination three months earlier than any Apprentice before him. Tapping into his extra sense, he searched for the shifting points of gold glimmering just beyond the physical world.

Then he blinked, and the Illuminated world rose around him. He was simultaneously aware of his body, of the Library around him and the skull sitting before him, and of the magnificent tapestry of light that was always there, behind the world he could smell and touch and taste. By accessing the Sight, he could sense both worlds at once.

The Illuminated world was a web of all the things that had ever been and that would ever be done. That's why it nauseated untrained Illuminators: it was an ocean of history, full of eddies and heaving tides, and it would rip you away down the slipstreams of memory. To keep yourself from being swept away, you needed a mark or a sound or a smell, some referent in the physical world to anchor your awareness to this moment, right here, so your split consciousness could later become one again.

Lon shuddered. Erastis had warned him about the dangers of losing your referent. Of being batted about in the Illuminated world by all the dizzying currents of light, so lost in all the things that had happened before that it would feel like drowning, casting about vainly for a shore you would never see again. Illuminators who lost their referents collapsed, their bodies empty and catatonic, eyes open but not seeing, breathing but not living, until their organs slowly stopped working and they died.

Buffeted about by the spirals of gold, Lon concentrated on the scorch marks. The currents of history spun around him and came into focus, and he knew what had caused them. Heat and smoke, flames so bright they nearly blinded him, and a lone figure treading into the fire, pulling smoldering books from the shelves.

"His name was Morgun," Lon said, watching the ancient Librarian's robes catch and flare, listening to his screams. "He was the Librarian during the Great Fire, and he died trying to retrieve Fragments out of the flames."

This was the link between literacy and Illumination, why Erastis had insisted on teaching him to read before teaching him to use the Sight: reading was the interpretation of signs, and the world was full of them. Scars, scratches, footprints. If you could tap into the Illuminated world, you could read the history of each mark as clearly as you could read a sentence from a book.

"That's one thing you can learn from this skull. There are two more."

Lon blinked again, and the Illuminated world faded. "C'mon, give me a challenge."

"This is a challenge," Erastis said calmly. "You're already farther along in your study of Illumination than I was at your age."

"But it's not a challenge for *me*." Lon ground his teeth in frustration. "Did you know Rajar got his first commission today? He's out there sailing with his Master right now!"

"Rajar is six years older than you."

Outside the Library, dark clouds crouched on the glacial peaks, and the wind blew fitfully past the windows. "I'm wasted in here," Lon said. "I should be out there. In the world. *Doing* things."

"Nonsense." Erastis flicked his fingers at him dismissively. "Nightfall is in a few hours."

Lon tossed his head impatiently as if to buck off Erastis's words. "That's not what I mean! You promised me when I joined you that we'd do great things." He began quoting from the oath he took on the day of his induction. " 'Protect the Book from discovery and misuse and establish stability and peace for all the citizens of Kelanna.' "

"And so we are. I told you the Master and Apprentice Librarian are the most powerful positions in our order, aside from the Director. Without us, there would be no one to interpret the Fragments. There would be no one to investigate prophecies or develop new techniques for Illumination. It's because of us that Edmon and the others can do what they do."

"But I'm not *doing* anything!" Lon was about to continue when he saw the girl at the threshold of the Library. He didn't know when it had happened, but as if out of thin air she had appeared in the doorway, clutching two blue-bound volumes in her arms.

His face reddened.

She was small and thin, with big dark eyes and black hair knotted in a bun near the top of her head, exposing her neck. Lon's heart pattered around in his chest. She was arrestingly beautiful. Sometimes when he saw her he forgot to breathe.

She was the Apprentice Assassin, but she didn't have a name. Assassins didn't have names. Assassins knew the hunt and the kill, and nothing else. Instead, she was known as the Second; her Master, the First. Like the other divisions, there were only ever two.

The Second was a few years older than him and had been there longer, so she had more privileges, like being able to check out Fragments from the Library and return them at her leisure. In the year since his induction, she'd never said more than a handful of words to him. Not that she was always around. Like Rajar and the Apprentice Administrator, she and her Master frequently left the Main Branch on errands for Director Edmon. It was only Lon who was stuck here.

But he knew she was talented. Without meaning to, he kept turning toward her, to see her better, to see what she would do.

She moved with quick, delicate motions like a bird or a dancer, shifting from foot to foot in a silent, complicated shuffle, as if she were practicing choreography. A kick, a slide, a tap of her toe on the tile. Then she looked up, saw Lon staring at her, and stopped. Her eyes bored into his, daring him to keep looking.

He blushed and turned away.

Finally Erastis noticed her by the door. "Come, come in, my dear!" he said, motioning her over to the table. His gloved hands fluttered like large white moths. "You've completed your reading of the Ostis Guide to Talismanic Blade Weapons, have you? What did you think?"

She crossed the tiled floor soundlessly and set the volumes on the table beside the Librarian. "Thank you. I have what I need."

"Excellent!"

Lon approached the table too, his frustration with the Master Librarian momentarily forgotten. He tried not to look directly at her. "For what?" he asked.

He felt the Second staring at him silently, but Erastis beamed. "The Second will be forging her own bloodsword soon."

"What's a bloodsword?"

The Second glanced at the Master Librarian, who gestured for her to explain. Frowning, she pressed her fingertips to the edge of the table. "A bloodsword is a weapon that's undergone Transformation. You've heard of those?" When Lon shook his head, she tried again, "A *magic* weapon? Like the Executioner?"

A black gun cursed to kill every time it was removed from its holster, and if you didn't pick your target, it would pick one for you.

"Oh. Yeah."

"According to Ostis, you can use Transformation to imbue a

sword with 'a thirst for blood,' so when it comes time to kill, the blade itself seeks out its targets."

"You mean the sword kills on its own?"

"No. It becomes a more accurate and deadly tool for a skilled swordsman. In the wrong hands, it would likely injure or kill the bearer."

"Oh."

"It will also soak up the blood of its targets, giving blood-swords their distinctive ferrous odor," Erastis added helpfully, "and making for easy cleanup."

"Wow . . ." Lon paused. For a moment he was more impressed than ever with the Second, with the things she could do, the things she was learning, but then his jealousy and frustration returned. He whirled on Erastis. "She gets a *bloodsword*? Why don't I get a bloodsword? Or whatever! A . . . a bloodpen!"

Suddenly the Second was in motion, all curves and violent grace, striking him in the chest so hard he stumbled back into the chair she'd somehow slid out from under the table. He plopped down, dazed.

She was so fast.

She had *touched* him.

He could feel her handprint like a burn throbbing against his collarbone.

"This is your *Master*," the Second snapped. "You don't speak to him that way."

Erastis chuckled. "Oh, he does this all the time. I don't let it get to me. I went without an Apprentice for decades. I wouldn't have chosen him if he wasn't worth it."

She made a disgusted sound in the back of her throat.

"Hey!" Lon glared at her and rubbed his chest where she'd hit him.

The Second met his gaze. It was strange: When he was a kid, he'd made a living off his ability to read people. But he couldn't tell what she was feeling now. Annoyed? Scornful? Likely. That's how she always looked at him. But as she closed her fingers, he couldn't help but wonder if she felt the same warm pulsing in her palm as he did in his chest.

Lon glanced away. "I *am* worth it," he declared, standing. "I'll show you."

Without waiting for her to respond, he looked over at the skull and blinked. The Illuminated world burst to life before him, an interconnected web of brilliance.

There was a hairline fracture in the jawbone. He followed it back through the glinting threads of the old Librarian's life. "When Morgun was an Apprentice, he was walking down the stairs when the Apprentice Soldier shoved him."

Beside him, the Second added, "Morgun fell forward, cracking his jaw on the banister. Stupid. Soldiers have no restraint."

She must have been reading the skull too, as quick to rise to a challenge as he was. Lon glanced at her, and his heart dropped.

In the Illuminated world, she was *radiant*. Like a comet. Like devastation and loneliness. All fire and white heat, blazing defiantly across the black.

"That's two out of three," Erastis said, sounding amused. "You have one more."

Lon searched the skull for another mark, another referent,

but found nothing. He walked over to it and picked it up, turning it in his hands, peering into its darkened crevices.

That was when he saw it: protrusions deep within the temporal bone, where the ear canal would have been. He would never have seen it with his eyes alone, but in the web of light he could peer past the bone into the hollows of the skull. He laughed.

"You've seen it," Erastis said.

"He was deaf!" Lon crowed. "Morgun was deaf. These bony growths closed his ear canals when he was an infant."

He blinked, and the light faded from the world. "See?" He turned to the Second, grinning, chin thrust out.

But the Second frowned and shook her head. Her pupils were pinpricks, barely visible in her dark brown eyes. She must have still been using the Sight. "Where?" she asked, all her annoyance with him gone.

Another time, he would have wanted to gloat, but not now. Not to her.

Lon gave her the skull, feeling her open palms slide over the backs of his hands, and pointed to the cavity in the temporal bone. "Here."

Her eyes widened, and he knew she was seeing Morgun as a child, holding his ears and crying with pain. She was seeing a doctor strike a tuning fork and hold it up to the sides of his head. She was seeing Morgun rubbing his fingers by his ears, listening for a whisper of sound, and slowly growing accustomed to a life lived in silence.

The Second blinked again, and her pupils returned to normal. "How'd you even know it was there?" she asked.

"He has a good teacher," Erastis said, returning his spectacles to his face.

Lon laughed. The Second was watching him, her mouth pulling slightly upward at the corners. A smile. In the whole year he'd known her, he'd never seen her smile. It was a magical thing. When she caught him looking at her, her smile widened. And this time he didn't look away.

Chapter 11

The Folded Page

Tanin fed leaf after leaf into the campfire, where they curled inward like blazing tongues before they shriveled and turned to ash. Around her in the smoke, the trackers laughed and told ribald stories that would have made a lesser woman flush with embarrassment. Tanin, however, smiled tolerantly at their jokes—she liked to consider herself above such petty emotions. On another night, she might even have joined them; after all, she could tell a dirty story as well as the rest of them.

But she was in no mood for it tonight.

Tanin trailed her finger through the leaves at the edge of the campfire, tracing the letters arranged there:

S A BOOK

She frowned. It had taken them three months to learn the girl even existed, and another two to figure out she was still in

Oxscini, but they were close now. Close enough for Tanin to abandon what she was doing and join the Assassin in the humid jungles of the Forest Kingdom. Close enough that she could almost feel the draw of the Book like the draw of a magnet on iron dust.

They would catch up to the girl in three days.

She plucked up a leaf with deep purple veins and spun it between her fingers. The girl must have written this sentence hundreds of times by now. As Tanin and the trackers closed the distance between them, the words became more and more obvious—carved into logs, scrawled onto stones with charcoal—as if the girl were deliberately leaving a trail for them to follow.

To the trackers, the words were as meaningful as scat or broken twigs, signs of the girl's passage but nothing more, and Tanin kept it that way, eliminating every letter they found.

And if a tracker's curiosity overcame his discretion, she eliminated him too.

More than anything else, the girl's recklessness bothered her. If the girl's parents had taught her to write, they should have taught her to be more careful. They should have taught her that words were dangerous. That if they fell into the wrong hands, it could be the undoing of a plan that had taken generations to put in place.

She gathered the remaining leaves and flung them into the fire, where they caught, flaming, and drifted upward like burning black pages. Sitting back, she watched the leaves flicker out in the understory.

Beside her, the Assassin glowered at the trackers, the darkness of the jungle rising behind her like two black wings. Like her master, who had been called away on a mission in the Oxscinian capital, she wore all black, and from beneath her hood, her eyes darted from one man to the next as their jokes grew more and more vulgar.

Nudging her with his elbow, a stout man named Erryl winked sloppily at her and extended a flask. "Hey, you're awfully quiet. Why don't you loosen up?"

The Assassin's pale blue gaze roved once over his hands and face before flicking away again.

Erryl laughed. His oily cheeks gleamed in the firelight. "Come on, you're making the rest of us look bad."

Hesitantly, the Assassin took the flask and lifted it to her lips. A second later, she thrust it away from her again, coughing. When the trackers laughed, her porridge-like skin flushed with shame. She seemed to wilt into the shadows.

Erryl snatched the flask out of her hands, guffawing.

Tanin narrowed her silvery eyes at him in warning, but he was too drunk to notice.

"You can always judge a woman by how she takes her moonshine." He chortled. "Does she swallow or—"

"You can always judge a man by his talk." Tanin's words were as precise as a blade parting skin. "The more he has to say, the less he knows."

The others laughed as Erryl sputtered.

"In fact, judging by how very much you talk, I'd say you know very little about anything." Her voice dug into him again. "Better you keep your mouth closed for the duration of your time with us, I think. Maybe you'll learn something."

"I was just trying to have a little fun—"

"At the expense of my lieutenant?" Tanin laughed coldly. "Let me make this profoundly clear: You are expendable. She is not. As such, you will treat her with respect and deference to the point of obsequiousness. If you do not, she has my full permission to dismember you as quickly or as slowly as she pleases."

The man blanched; his bloodshot eyes darted to the Assassin's sword. The black scabbard was embossed in intricate detail—mere designs to the uninitiated, but readers like Tanin and the Assassin could pick out hundreds of tiny words hand-tooled in the leather: spells of protection for the bearer, curses against her enemies. As if responding to his fear, a tangy copper smell snaked out of the sheath, pervading the air.

Dusting off her hands, Tanin stood. "With that, gentlemen, I bid you good night." She twisted her graying black hair away from her face and left the ring of firelight. Behind her, the trackers began speaking again, their voices more subdued, and as she hiked into the shadows, she glanced once over her shoulder at the Assassin, who smiled back at her.

Darkness hung from the canopy like black curtains, and as Tanin's eyes adjusted, she picked her way among sprawling roots and rotting logs until she reached a clearing.

Under the light of the stars, she drew a folded page from her vest. The paper was old and creased, no longer stiff to the touch but pliable as cloth. The writing was hurried and cramped, the margins overflowing with questions and hastily jotted notes, but she could have recited every phrase and placed every punctuation mark with her eyes closed.

A copy of a copy. Most of the original Fragment had been

destroyed by the fire, the burning pages flapping and frittering away into ash, all their words turned to dust. She had ordered what was left to be locked safely in the vault, but not before she copied this one page.

It was maddeningly incomplete—paragraphs scorched at the edges, whole words blotted out by fire—and over the years her notes had overwhelmed the actual text with conjecture and half-completed sentences until it was unreadable to anyone but herself.

Suddenly, she looked up. The stars had changed positions in the sky. She must have been standing there, studying the page, for hours. "I don't know why you let them get to you," she said to the darkness.

The Assassin stepped forward, materializing from the tree line as if out of thin air. "Easy for you to say. They like you."

Tanin smiled as the sweet coppery smell wafted around her. She had learned a trick or two from the Assassins over the years, but she'd never be able to disappear into the shadows the way they could.

Just as well. She had no interest in being invisible.

"They fear me," she said, "as they should you."

"They *do* fear me." The Assassin picked at the frayed cuff of her blouse.

"If they feared you, they'd respect you." Tanin sat down on an overgrown log, patting the damp wood beside her. "And I wouldn't have to intervene on your behalf."

"You didn't have to," the Assassin muttered, joining her.

"Of course I did."

Although the vows of her order forbade her from having a

family of her own, Tanin still remembered younger sisters from her life before her induction: awkward, unpopular, willful, like less-beautiful versions of their older sisters, who they followed around like puppies. But you loved them—didn't you?—for their nerve, their loyalty, and because they were your family.

And though Tanin wasn't related to her by blood, the Assassin *was* family.

Tanin glanced down at the paper, as if the words might have rearranged themselves when she wasn't looking. But they hadn't, and she tucked the folded page back into her vest. She could never figure out the specifics, but the one thing she had always known was that she would get the Book back.

And now she knew when.

Three days.

The Assassin laid her head on Tanin's shoulder. "Anyway," she said, "thank you."

Tanin pressed her cheek to the top of the Assassin's head, her senses filling with copper. She closed her eyes, sighing. "Anytime."

CHAPTER 12

The Boy in the Cabin

Sefia and Archer had reached the cloud forests of the Kambali Mountains, the last range before the land sloped sharply toward the north coast of Oxscini. In the alpine jungles, lakes and little rivers drew herds of deer and the big cats that hunted them, making for plentiful game. Three summers ago, she had come here with Nin to trade with the hunter-trapper families who lived in the cabins peppered throughout the mountains. Having been a loner all her life, Sefia hadn't known what to do with the other children, so while they were playing Ship of Fools and gambling for copper kispes, she stole their most valuable trinkets.

A branch snapped in the woods—something large, from the sound of it—and Sefia and Archer dashed off the path, hunkering down among the leaves.

From down the trail, voices drifted toward them.

"That's the problem with the wasting disease. The whole

forest was littered with carcasses that year, just rotting away. We couldn't do anything with them. Their meat and hides were useless."

"What did you do?"

Two people appeared around the bend. The boy was a teenager, a little younger than Archer but not by much, with roasted-chestnut eyes and small-boned hands. The man was tall and thin, with a round face and laugh lines at his eyes. He carried the carcass of a deer over his shoulders, its legs stretched awkwardly, head lolling, and under his arm was a hunting rifle. He and the boy wore matching short-billed caps. "Your granddad used to say, 'We'll do better tomorrow.'"

"And did you do better?"

The man chuckled. "Sometimes yes, sometimes no. Times were hard. Then he'd say the same thing. 'We'll do better tomorrow.' For some reason, I always believed him."

They passed Sefia and Archer, concealed in the undergrowth, and continued north along the trail, their voices growing fainter and fainter in the jungle.

"Why? If you knew it wasn't true?" said the boy.

"It's not really a matter of doing better, is it?" answered the father. "It's a matter of doing the best you can and believing you can keep improving."

Their voices faded as they took the bend in the path and vanished among the brittle vines and green ferns. They must have been heading home.

While she waited for the father and son to gain a little distance on them, Sefia pecked at the ground with her fingertips, plucking up twigs and brown leaves. Something about the boy unsettled her—maybe his small hands or the way he tilted his head when he was listening to his father's stories—and she glanced at Archer again, but he was watching her fingers hop and dance in the mulch, and he didn't seem at all disturbed by seeing the boy and his father, so she didn't say anything.

A s the afternoon stretched toward dusk, Sefia and Archer reached the top of a ridge overlooking a small round lake. The water was green with plant life, and the trees hung over its glassy surface. From the crooked stone ridge, they could see for miles.

They sat on some rocks, dangling their legs over the edge, and shared a few sips from the canteen while the sun sank closer to the mountaintops and the clouds turned from white to pink. An orange light flickered to life at the northern end of the lake. Hatchet's camp. Sefia narrowed her eyes.

In the east, a few miles down the ridge, a trail of smoke drifted out of the canopy. Archer pointed at it and tilted his head, touching his temple with the fingers of his other hand.

"Probably that father and son we saw earlier," she said.

Archer nodded. The light caught in his eyes, turning them warm and golden. A faint smile passed over his face.

As the shadows lengthened across the water, Sefia sighed and stood, hefting the pack onto her shoulders again. "Come on. We need to find a place to camp."

Archer tapped her on the arm.

"What is it?"

Squinting, she caught a flicker of movement in and out of the trees—figures stalking along the lake's shore. Burrowing into her pack, she grabbed Nin's old spyglass. "Get down."

They dropped to their bellies on the ground.

Sefia propped herself up on her elbows and peered out over the lake again, putting the glass to her eye. Six people were heading east through the jungle. Her breathing quickened. She recognized that heavy walk. Five carried rifles, but the last held a long pair of tongs with tips that formed a large black circle at the end.

"Hatchet's men," she muttered, passing the spyglass to Archer. "Where are they going? Are they hunting?"

Without warning Archer dropped the spyglass and scrambled backward. His hands dug into the dirt, pulling at roots and handfuls of earth.

"What's wrong?"

He backed into a tree. The whites of his eyes flared in the low light.

Sefia scanned the valley again. "What did you see?"

Archer brought up his shaking hands and put his fingers to the base of his throat, where his scar began, and spread them around his neck like claws.

The tongs.

Big enough to encircle a boy's throat. Hot enough to burn him.

"The boy," Sefia muttered. She sprang to her feet and searched the valley. The cabin was two miles from Hatchet's camp at the lake, but three from the ridge. They would have to run.

Sefia snatched up the spyglass, pulled on her pack, and returned to Archer's side. He hadn't moved.

"Get up," she said. "We're going to warn them."

Still he could not stand. He was pressed so hard against the tree that the rough bark tore his shirt, the skin beneath.

Sefia knelt at his side and laid her hand on his shoulder. It was the first time she'd tried to touch him since she'd cleaned his wounds two weeks before, and his shirt was damp with sweat, his skin hot under her palm. She held up her other hand. Deliberately, making sure he saw, she crossed her middle and index fingers.

A sign.

Their sign.

"You won't ever have to do that again," she said, locking eyes with him.

Archer watched her, wide-eyed.

She was *with* him.

"I promise."

He shuddered once more and then was calm. His mouth closed. He pushed himself to his feet.

Then they were running. The sky had turned to fire, smoky and orange. In the darkness, the trees loomed close and menacing. Bats flitted through the canopy, and the night birds screamed.

They ran. Skidding down the slick slope and leaping sharp switchbacks that twisted among the trees. The ridge disappeared in darkness behind them as the terrain flattened out.

Along the trail, the moon rose round and pale through the leaves. The trees shone silver where the light struck and the ground was as blue as water.

129

Still they ran. Their legs burned. Their feet throbbed. They ran faster. Arms pumping, feet pulling at the ground. Their lungs ached.

At an intersection, they took the eastern trail. Hoping it was the right one. Knowing they wouldn't get a second chance if they were wrong. Shadows raked their arms and faces. They were running so fast they seemed about to explode. Even the air in their chests was full of fire.

They burst into a clearing with a cabin at the center, surrounded by drying racks and clotheslines that made strange cobwebbed formations in the yard, where the glow from the windows touched the tips of the tools and the stretched hides. A rack of antlers adorned the apex of the roof, and smoke rose from the chimney like a signal tower. Sefia and Archer stumbled to the door, doubled over, breath squeezing in and out of their beaten lungs.

Sefia knocked. The hollow sound of her knuckles on wood echoed in the clearing, but the cabin was silent. She knocked again.

There was a scraping sound inside, like the dragging of a chair across the floor, followed by a scuffling. The curtains twitched in the window.

"Who's there?" a woman demanded, her voice harsh and suspicious.

"Open the door." The words rushed out of Sefia like water. "You're all in danger."

The latch clicked and the door creaked open. A woman in high-waisted trousers and suspenders stood in the doorway. She held a rifle, her finger resting next to the trigger. She had small, delicate hands, like the boy's.

Behind her, a woodstove crackled merrily, and through the doorway Sefia could see the corner of a dining table stacked with plates, cups, and a steaming pot of stew, but there was no one else in sight.

"What sort of danger?" the woman asked. The tip of her rifle rose a few inches.

Sefia brushed her hair out of her face impatiently. Her hand came away wet with sweat. "Impressors!" she snapped.

The woman staggered back as the door was thrust open. The round-faced man they'd seen earlier that day stood there, framed by the doorway. He squinted at them, deepening the wrinkles around his eyes.

"Impressors?" His voice was deep and full of questions.

"Just a story," the woman said.

"No." Sefia pointed at Archer's throat. "Real."

The boy crept up behind his parents. "Look at his neck, Mom."

Archer feathered the edge of his scar with his fingertips.

"Come into the light, boy," said the woman.

Sefia held her breath as Archer took a step forward. He raised his chin so the firelight reached his scars. Instinctively, the woman hefted her rifle. The man cursed.

The boy paled. Sefia could read the thought on his face as plainly as if it'd been written there: *That could be me.* She glared at him. He was so small. Nervous. Soft. He wouldn't survive a day if their places were switched, if she got a nice comfortable cottage and two loving parents, and he had to fend for himself in the wilderness. For a second she hated him.

Archer stared at the boy and extended his hands, palms up. The boy's eyelid twitched.

"He wants to help you," Sefia said.

"Help him what?" the woman asked. She still hadn't lowered her weapon.

"The people who did this to him are coming *here*. Right now. They're going to kill you and take your son unless you leave."

The man pulled a rifle from behind the door. "This cabin's been in my family for generations," he said.

"Six impressors are coming for you," Sefia snapped. "You won't have any family left if you stay."

"And if we leave, who's to say we won't be robbed?" The woman looked her up and down: the pack on her back, her dirty sweaty face, her wild black hair.

For a moment, Sefia was speechless. She felt like she'd been slapped. Archer kept making that gesture, with more and more urgency. But no one moved.

Then the boy patted his father's elbow. "Pop . . ."

The man ignored him. "Even if they do come, we're not scared of a little bloodshed."

Sefia found her voice again. "It won't be a *little* bloodshed. It'll be yours, and hers, and his." She pointed at each one of them in turn, her finger landing at last on the teenage boy, who gaped at her. "Is that what you want?"

She glanced over her shoulder into the silver woods. How much time had they lost, standing here arguing?

Slowly—much too slowly—the woman lowered her rifle. "How far behind you?"

Relief spread through Sefia like ink in water. "They'll be here any second."

The man and woman stared at each other. Sefia could almost see their conversation passing between them like arrows.

How far would they get if they ran?

What should they take?

Did they trust the girl?

The boy stared at Archer, taking in the size of his arms, the set of his feet, the scar at his neck. Archer fingered the hilt of his hunting knife and cocked an ear toward the jungle.

The moon rose higher. Sefia fidgeted with the straps of her pack. Hatchet's men were coming. They would arrive soon.

Finally, the man and woman began opening wardrobes and pulling on coats. The whole family was a flurry of movement, grabbing jackets, guns, cartridges.

"We have a hunting blind in the mountains. Hard to find." The woman stuffed a revolver in the band of her pants. "What are you two doing?" There was no invitation in her voice.

Sefia hadn't expected them to take her and Archer along. She wouldn't have gone even if they had invited her. But venom crept into her words anyway. "Saving your family. Then running too."

The woman looked at them pityingly, but didn't say anything more.

The man was the last one out of the cabin. He locked the door behind him and pressed a leather-wrapped package into

Sefia's hands. "My knives," he said quietly, with a glance at Archer. "Good balance. Good for throwing."

They nodded.

The man tugged at the short bill of his cap so only the lower half of his face was visible, like a crescent moon, and he turned away.

As she followed him around the side of the cabin, she deeply missed her own father. He would have taken two stray kids with him to safety. She shook her head, thinking of their house, its secret rooms, its isolated location on the top of the hill, the way they never had company. *My father would have taken us, wouldn't he . . . ?*

Behind the cabin, the woman was already passing into the forest, but the boy paused. He waited for Sefia and Archer, fretfully drumming the barrel of his rifle.

"Clovis," the woman hissed from the shadows.

The boy took Archer's hand. Archer was so anxious that he nearly recoiled, but the boy held on, his small fingers tightening over Archer's. He tried to smile, but it came out as a grimace. "Thank you."

Archer swallowed, making his scar shift over the motion of his throat.

The boy dropped his hand and followed his mother into the jungle. The man went last, and he didn't look back when he melted into the darkness.

Archer closed his fingers over his palm where the boy had touched him. His mouth twisted.

Sefia slipped the package of knives to him. "We did a good thing," she said. She meant it, but she also felt angry and hollow inside, with this hot buzzing like bees. No one had warned Archer. No one had warned her.

Voices from the trail dragged her out of her anger. She and Archer ducked. The yard blazed with light from the cabin. You could see everything. They scrambled behind a woodpile at the far end of the clearing and breathed quiet.

She tugged at his arm and pointed into the woods. They could still get away.

Archer ignored her. He was already taking out the knives, testing their weight. The moonlight glanced off their polished bone handles.

Maybe he hadn't understood. She pulled at his arm again, but he shrugged her off. His hands flashed through a series of signs: the collar he'd made on the ridge; his sign for hunting; three fingers for the family. He was going to fight. He was going to give the family time to get away.

Sefia was about to protest when Hatchet's men reached the clearing.

There was a sudden crash as the door of the cabin broke in. Boots beat on the floorboards like drums.

"No one's here!" A few seconds later: "Food's still warm. They can't have been gone long."

Another voice answered, deep and gravelly. Sefia remembered that voice. It belonged to Redbeard, the one who loved violence, the one carrying the tongs. "Check the woods," he growled.

Shadows shifted across the ground as two figures appeared around the side of the cabin. They carried rifles.

Archer looked back at her. His eyes seemed to glow eerily

in the darkness, like those of an animal. He pointed into the woods, away from the clearing, and he didn't need words to communicate what he meant.

Hide.

Sefia scrambled away into the trees, dirt flying from beneath her hands and feet. She found a small hollow in a stump and squeezed inside. Rotten pieces of wood crumbled around her ears and shoulders, into the collar of her shirt. Spiders or beetles crawled over her skin. She'd barely gotten herself inside when she heard the first scream, cut off at the end. It came from her left, closer to the clearing.

She listened hard in the dark.

"What was that?"

Muffled cursing. "It's Landin. Throat's been cut."

She tried to calm her breathing. The seconds lengthened into minutes. She heard the rustling of clothing and the quiet creaking of leather. Someone pulled back the hammer of a revolver. She cursed herself for picking a hiding spot with such terrible visibility. She could only imagine what was happening.

Where was Archer?

Her legs were cramping, begging to be moved. Sefia switched positions as quietly as she could, but her bow and quiver rubbed against the inside of the stump. She winced as the log crumbled around her, sounding like an avalanche to her heightened senses.

She paused. She had her bow.

She slid out of the stump and unhooked the bow and quiver from her pack. She listened for any change in her surroundings, but the nearby trees were silent, their leaves motionless.

Nocking an arrow to her bow, she peered over the stump. The orange glow from the clearing silhouetted a man at the edge of the yard, searching the trees with a rifle at his shoulder. After a few seconds, he pivoted away from her and began pacing the perimeter of the clearing.

When she was certain he wasn't looking, Sefia stalked forward, keeping low, like she would if she were hunting. She hardened her jaw. She *was* hunting.

Silently, she crept forward, pausing outside the ring of light. The man was rounding the drying racks on the opposite side of the clearing. As Sefia raised the bow, she recognized him: it was One-Eye, who'd built a stretcher for his dead friends and carried them away into the jungle to be burned. If she loosed the arrow now, it would strike him. She'd hit birds at farther distances than this. But she hesitated. The string cut into her fingers.

Do it, she told herself. He was an impressor. He deserved it, for what he'd done to Archer.

You can't fail again.

Her fingers twitched. Across the clearing, One-Eye circled around to the front of the cabin and disappeared.

A heavy hand descended on her shoulder and yanked her off her feet.

Her body left the ground and collapsed in the clearing. The impact knocked the bow and arrow from her hands. Her head spun. She tried to sit up.

A huge, hulking man stood over her; he was so big the revolver in his hands looked like a toy. Catching sight of her red-fletched arrows, the man grinned, stretching the crooked scar on his bottom lip. That scar. She recognized him from the first night—the man who'd had to remove the remains of the impressors' meal.

"So you're the one who caused all this trouble." His voice was hot and dry as embers, but it made her shiver.

A gunshot rang out from the other side of the cabin. No screams. She twisted, trying to see what had happened. She kept picturing Archer lying on the ground. Archer motionless. Archer dead. She glared at the impressor in front of her. "Yeah," she spat. "*I'm* the one."

The man cocked his pistol.

A round black eye and the moonlight on a silver barrel.

A smile warped by a scar.

Sefia took one last breath. The sound was sucked out of the clearing. She didn't even hear the dirt scatter beneath her as she scrabbled backward.

She blinked.

Then her vision took over.

The man's lips parted, and his mouth, his chin, the veins in his neck, the joining of his bones, his shoulder and arm and wrist all turned into light. Bands of it flooded his body, twisting around his torso and crossing his limbs, spiraling down his legs and over his boots.

He pulled the trigger, but it wasn't a bullet that came out at her. It was a band of light.

She'd seen the light before, but she'd never seen it like this. Strings of it radiated from his body, twining and intertwining, on and on, back and back, whirling around this moment. The world spun.

In the spirals of light she saw him trip. Just a kid, he lost his footing on the slippery dock. His face splitting on the splintered edge. That's how he got his scar.

The currents shifted, and she saw his birth. His mother had been a woman with curly hair and a mole on the side of her neck, and she'd named him Palo, after her father. Palo Kanta. That was his name. She saw his sisters and half brothers and the raggedy old cats he rescued from the streets, fistfights, blood, the smell of sewage, the first time he ever held a gun, his first murder, the women he'd loved or thought he'd loved and really just wanted to own. She saw a recurring nightmare in which he tried to outrun a rising tide but no matter how fast he ran, no matter how hard he pumped his arms, it caught his feet and legs and body, and it always swallowed him up.

Nausea struck her, and she gasped. She saw his death: knifed outside of a bar, past midnight with no witnesses.

She could see all the interconnected ways his life was knotted up, and how it had led here—to her own death. She could see it coming, the whole thing: the moon and the trail of smoke leading into the sky, the bullet speeding toward her, the light streaming out behind it like waves. It would puncture her. The cords of her life would snap.

She didn't want to die. She had so many questions left to answer. She was suddenly filled with hot, biting anger. She hated this man with the scar on his mouth, this man who was preventing her from doing what she had vowed to do.

Sefia found her feet. She put all her strength in her legs and lunged, swiping her hand through the streams of light. She felt her muscles burn, her bones buckle under the pressure. But the tides shifted. A wave of gold roared away from her, sparking with whitecaps.

This wasn't her death anymore.

Maybe there was thunder. Or was it the sound of the bullet exploding from the chamber—delayed?

The man ripped.

His threads snapped.

Making fragments.

The sound came rushing back into the world.

She looked down at her arm, expecting to see ruptured flesh and broken bones, but it was unharmed. The world was spinning, twisting tighter and tighter around her skull. She looked wildly for the man with the gun, but he wasn't there. He was on the ground, gasping. With a hole in him.

He was just a man now, no longer filled with light. The light was leaking out of him, growing dimmer and dimmer. The scar on his mouth no longer looked menacing. His face was crooked, yes, but sad, like the reflection in a cracked mirror.

He looked at her but didn't speak. Maybe he couldn't. Maybe his words were leaking out of him too. He looked at her . . . and then he wasn't looking at her anymore. He wasn't looking at anything anymore.

Sefia fell to her knees and pressed her hands to his wound. His blood was slick and lukewarm between her fingers. Her hands turned red.

This was what it meant to kill someone.

She looked up and saw Archer standing at the corner of the cabin, staring at her.

She looked down again. The world had gone wet and blurry. Was she crying?

Palo Kanta. That had been his name.

Then Archer was beside her, pulling her to her feet. He took her hands unflinchingly and held them in his own. He put his forehead to hers. He didn't speak.

She tried to jerk away. "Where are the others?"

He pulled her back to him and shook his head. Holding up three fingers, he pointed northwest toward Hatchet's camp.

Only half of the impressors had survived the encounter. Archer must have killed two of them.

"They ran?"

He nodded.

"Because of me?"

He nodded again.

As he led her to the cabin, she tried to explain. The man had shot her. The bullet had come at her. And she didn't know how, but she had turned it back. She'd seen his story—and then she had violated it, changing the man's death.

Changing everything.

He sat her by the front door and brought her a pot of water and poured it over her hands. The liquid splashed over her skin and onto the ground, creating a small puddle of mud. Archer gently rubbed the blood away. The color. The stickiness. Sefia let him.

While he raided the cabin for supplies, pulling open drawers, grabbing things out of the cabinets, she sat dumbly in the doorway, rubbing her fingers one by one. She had killed a man. She kept picturing the vacant expression, the slack jaw. Her head ached.

"I didn't want to kill him." She found the words, feeling for them like foreign objects in the dark.

Silence inside. Then Archer sat down beside her. His fingers strayed to his neck—the scar. He understood that sometimes you did things out of necessity, things that were horrible, or underhanded at best, things you wouldn't do if you had a choice.

"I always knew I wanted to kill *someone*," she said. "But not him . . . and not like this."

Whatever *this* was.

Archer put his hand on her shoulder. He had a pack now, filled with items. A dark ribbon of blood caked his left temple. The gunshot she'd heard earlier. The bullet must have grazed him.

"You're hit," she whispered.

He touched the side of his head with his fingertips and showed them to her. The blood was already drying. Then he collected her bow and helped her to her feet. He led her around the side of the cabin, past the body of the man he'd killed. One-Eye. His throat had been split, and the dirt was dark beneath him. Sefia tried to focus on where she placed her feet.

They crossed into the trees. The silver leaves rustled. The loam was soft and spongy beneath their feet. Archer got Sefia to direct him to her hiding place in the stump, where her pack was still stashed, and then they walked into the woods—Archer leading, Sefia following.

CHAPTER 13

There Are No Coincidences

I t was all so quick, so improbable, that if she hadn't seen it before, if she hadn't done it herself, she never would have believed it.

There was a gunshot.

A burst of smoke and a lashing of fire.

And the girl sent the bullet spiraling back into the man's chest.

Crouched just beyond the reach of the light, Tanin fought to steady her breathing. She was suddenly aware of her body, her lungs, the ache in her chest. Behind her, the trackers hefted their rifles and watched for her signal, but she didn't move.

The girl dropped to her knees by the man's side. Tanin marveled at her. She was so young, but she had the same lamp-black hair, the same dark eyes.

And she knew Manipulation. If she had already mastered

143

the second tier of Illumination, there was no telling what else she could do.

"Now," the Assassin said. She blended into the darkness so neatly that even her voice was a shadow, like the breath of a nonexistent breeze.

"Not yet."

The girl was trying to stanch the wound. She was going to fail.

She looked like *her*. Tanin hadn't been expecting that. Hadn't thought it would matter so much.

There was a crackling in the undergrowth, and a man burst from the trees behind them, his round face twisted in anger. He took one look at Tanin and the trackers and raised his rifle.

This she could handle.

A glance at her men, a flick of her fingers.

The lead tracker ran his knife across the man's throat and caught the corpse as it slumped to the ground. The man's head lolled forward, his short-billed cap tipping over his lifeless eyes.

The Assassin edged forward, toeing the pool of light. "Why not?"

"You didn't know . . . her." Tanin grimaced. Even after all this time, she still couldn't bring herself to use her name.

"It's not *her*."

No, *she* was dead. And Tanin hadn't even been there to see it. To hold her hand or wipe her brow or whatever you did when your loved ones were dying.

She had to do something now. This was what she'd come for, wasn't it? Tanin scanned the clearing, her gaze skimming over the cabin, the fallen bow and arrows, the bodies. "She doesn't have the Book on her."

"You could make her tell us. It would be easy."

Tanin watched the boy help the girl up. The light from the cabin flashed on his collar of scar tissue.

He was a candidate.

Tanin shook her head. Out of all the companions the girl could have chosen, she had picked a candidate.

"Look at his neck," she whispered, her voice trembling. When was the last time it had done that?

The Assassin didn't take her eyes off the girl. "So what?" Her voice dripped with condescension. "Serakeen's dogs bring another one to the Cage every few months."

Tanin passed her hand over the hidden pocket of her vest where she kept the folded page. "Edmon used to say there are no coincidences, only meaning."

Ten years, Serakeen had been paying impressors to fetch him scarred young killers.

Twenty years, she had been searching for the Book.

And now here they were, both of them together.

It had to mean something.

"We can take the boy too, if that's what you mean." The Assassin slid her sword an inch out of its sheath. The smell of copper bloomed around them.

Tanin caught her by the elbow. "I said no."

The Assassin glared at her, but Tanin's attention had already moved on.

The boy took the girl in his arms and led her back to the

cabin, where she collapsed on the steps, all knees and pointy elbows. Awkward. Vulnerable.

The Assassin wrenched her arm from Tanin's grasp. "This is what we came for. Capture her. Take the Book. It has to be now."

"If he's the one, you couldn't take her with a hundred swords."

"I only need one."

With a wave of her hand, Tanin directed the trackers back into the jungle, where they slipped away like eels in black water.

She turned on the Assassin. "You will obey me in this, or you will be removed from this assignment." Her voice cut. "I have no use for subordinates who can't follow orders."

The Assassin balled her fists until the leather glove on her left hand creaked. "You never trust me," she said. "Not like you trusted her."

"You're not her."

The Assassin's eyes widened at the sting of Tanin's words, and she whirled away, darting soundlessly into the under-growth.

The girl was sitting on the cabin steps, rubbing her fingers as if she could erase what they had done. For a moment, Tanin wanted to go to her. Hold her, maybe. She didn't know.

Slowly, she backed away from the clearing, fading into the shadows beneath the trees until she could no longer see the girl.

Sefia.

A reader and a killer.

CHAPTER 14

Doubt

S efia felt the warmth of the breeze and the swaying of the hammock before she was even fully awake, and for a moment she was couched in the gentle cocoon-like space between being asleep and awake, completely content. All was warmth and light and cottony softness.

But then she woke.

She opened her eyes and found herself staring up into the treetops. The events of the previous night flashed through her mind.

Palo Kanta.

Sefia untangled herself from the blankets and sat up. Archer sat across from her, legs swung over the branches for balance as he sharpened his new knives. All around him, suspended from the tree like misshapen fruit, were other new items: stolen shirts, socks, a length of rope, a tin cup, an extra blanket, sacks of food.

Seeing her rise, he wiped down the knife with a cloth and sheathed it.

"You did all this?" Sefia asked weakly.

Archer's gaze skimmed over the little encampment he'd made in the trees. He nodded.

"You did good."

Looking down, she noticed traces of dried blood in the creases of her hands and the U-shapes of her fingernails. Grimacing, she dug her thumbnail into the cuticles of her other hand. It came away with rusty specks underneath.

Her face twisted. Palo Kanta. He'd had a whole *life* behind him . . . and he could have had a whole life ahead of him . . . but she had taken that away. She had taken the threads of that moment and changed them, reversed the trajectory of the bullet so that it wasn't coming for her—but for him. And the bullet had entered him, made a hole in him, and he had not survived it.

She had killed a man.

Tears spattered her arms.

There was a movement in the branches, and then Archer was taking her hands, wiping each of her fingers with a clean wet cloth.

"I'm sorry," she whispered. Not to Archer but to Palo Kanta, though he couldn't hear her, though he would never hear anything again. "I'm sorry." That it had come down to this. Kill or die. Him or her. A choice you couldn't unmake.

Archer squeezed her fingers once and let go again, tucking away the cloth.

Sefia pressed her fists to her eyes and shook her head. "No.

No, no. What am I saying?" She'd been so sure this was what she wanted. Answers. Redemption. Revenge.

But this hadn't been revenge.

"He would have killed me." She bared her teeth. "He was an *impressor*. The world's better off without him. Why am I *sorry*?"

Archer tapped his chest, over his heart, and smiled sadly.

"I am *not* a good person. All these months, all I've wanted . . . A good person wouldn't have . . . I just let them *take* Nin." The last words came bursting out of her. "It's my fault she was captured. If only I hadn't gone into town alone . . . If only I'd come back a little sooner . . . I was *right there*, Archer. All I had to do was say something. It's my fault. It's all my fault, and now . . ."

She beat her own thighs. Pain blossomed beneath her fists. Archer tried to catch her hands, but she jerked out of his reach. "I was *supposed* to do this. For Nin. For my father."

We're a team, you and me. That's what her father had said to her. *We're in this together, no matter what.*

But when it had mattered most, she hadn't been there for him. He'd died alone in that empty house while she played, stupidly, ignorantly, in the village below. She'd been the only one he had left, and she had failed him.

Frantically, Sefia dug through her pack for the book. She needed it in her hands, this thing, the only thing she had left of her father. She needed it to remember. To remind herself. She flung off the leather wrappings and traced the brand on the cover.

Two curves for her parents. A curve for Nin. The straight line for herself. The circle for what she had to do.

"Learn what the book is for." She flubbed the words. "Rescue Nin, if she's still alive . . ." Sobs choked her voice. Her vision had gone wet and blurry.

But try as she might to reach for that anger, that rage that had sustained her all these months, whenever she grasped for it, she saw Palo Kanta.

Saw the bullet strike him.

Saw the blood drain out of him.

Saw him dead at her feet.

Sefia clutched the book in her arms and cried. Hating herself for this weakness.

"I don't think I can do it," she whispered.

Then Archer crawled into the hammock and took her in his arms. She felt the pressure of him on her shoulders, the plane of his cheek on the top of her head, his hands holding hers. The kind of contact she hadn't had in years, wrapping around and around her like a bandage, until all the broken things inside her were held fast, secure in the loop of Archer's arms.

Captain Cat
and Her Cannibal Crew

After the *Current of Faith* fished him out of the maelstrom, and Captain Reed announced his intention to sail for the western edge of the world, there was some consternation among the crew.

He'd cracked, they said.

Something had happened to him, down there in the wild water.

This was going too far.

Some of them left, of course, but for the most part they stayed. Perhaps they'd grown so used to hearing the tall tales of their own adventures that they truly believed they would survive when all others had failed. Perhaps they thought Reed and the chief mate wouldn't let the *Current* disappear into the sea like the rest. Perhaps they knew she was the only ship in Kelanna with even a shred of hope of making it.

Whatever their reasons, they took their considerable earnings, loaded up with provisions in the Paradise Islands off the coast of Oxscini, and set a course for the blue and boundless west. All was smooth sailing till eight weeks into their journey when, on the verge of uncharted waters, they came across the longboat filled with human bones.

Pelvises, scapulae, ribs.

Among the skeletons, two survivors stared up at the curving hull of the *Current* with sunken eyes. Their lips drew back from their teeth, revealing swollen tongues.

"It ain't right," said Camey, one of the sailors on Meeks's starboard watch. He was new, someone they'd picked up in the Paradise Islands, and a bit of a rabble-rouser, but no one contradicted him when he said it again, louder: "It just ain't right."

While the crew shifted uneasily at the rails, Captain Reed waited, counting out the seconds, weighing his choices. Take them in or let them die? It happened that way, sometimes on the ocean.

Of course he took them in. He was Captain Reed. He went down himself.

One of the survivors fainted as soon as Reed landed in the longboat, but the other backed away, scrabbling for purchase in the piles of bones. She had a fine velvet coat and felt hat, but her clothing was in tatters, and her long red hair had begun to fall out in clumps. She clutched at a splintered femur and sucked it greedily.

Reed sat down beside the mast and unscrewed the cap of his canteen. The woman looked at it curiously, like she'd forgotten what it was for.

"Who are you?" he asked. "What happened to your ship?"

A flicker of understanding passed over her face. Her mouth worked; her tongue came unstuck from her teeth. "Catarina Stills," she croaked. "Captain of the *Seven Bells*."

You've heard of the *Seven Bells*, of course. She was known for exploring the deep south, venturing farther and farther beyond Roku into the Everlasting Ice. Captain Cat had inherited the ship from her father, Hendrick Stills the Southern Explorer, who died of pneumonia on his last voyage.

What no one knew was that since her father passed, Captain Cat had been quietly exploring the west, sailing closer and closer to the edge of the world.

"I'm Captain Reed," he said. "You're safe now."

She let the bone fall from her hands, and Reed went to her, cradling her stinking emaciated body, and put the canteen to her lips, letting drop by drop slip into her mouth, wetting the cracks. Wide-eyed as a newborn babe, Cat stared at him, wondering, disbelieving, as he signaled to the crew, who began hoisting the survivors onto the deck of the *Current*.

The survivors remained in the sick bay with the doc for the rest of the day, but the crew couldn't stop talking about them. They kept sneaking glances toward the main hatch, where the sick bay lay belowdecks, though they never looked directly at it. Sailors are mighty superstitious, and as they went about the day's business, they were careful to avoid it, as if they'd catch cannibalism, or bad luck, if they strayed too close.

Against the doc's advice, Captain Cat insisted on eating dinner in the great cabin that night, though her man Harye was still laid up in the sick bay. "Delusional," Doc said, polishing her glasses. "I caught him hoarding bones, you know. Aly and I thought we'd gotten them all, but I found them stuffed up his shirtsleeves. I don't even think he knows he's been rescued. In his mind, he's still out on that boat." She ran her dark fingers over her close-cropped hair and sighed. "I'll be surprised if he makes it another day."

Captain Reed asked Meeks to join them in the great cabin. A teller of tales if there ever was one, the second mate could soak up a story and wring it out later word for word, and he was always happy to oblige. He sat across from Captain Cat, toying absentmindedly with the ends of his dreadlocks as he committed her tale to memory.

Cat had been cleaned up, her wounds washed and bandaged, but she was skinny as a beanpole, and her hands shook when she picked up the silverware.

"Believe me or don't," she began, "but this is how it happened..."

The chief mate leaned in, examining her with his dead gray eyes, scanning for falsehoods the way he'd scan the *Current* for leaks.

But she didn't lie. Sometimes truth is more gruesome than fiction.

The *Seven Bells* had been at sea one hundred and twenty-two days searching for the western edge of the world, when a long crack appeared in the black sky, drowning the stars and the dark seas with cascades of light.

"Lightning?" Reed asked.

Captain Cat shook her head. "It was like the sky had split open at the seams, revealing some bright world on the other side. As we approached, the whole sky grew pale, and the *Seven Bells* was lit up, clear as morning. I never felt so tiny. A speck of dust in an infinite ocean. And there was something so beautiful about that, it nearly brought me to my knees."

But then the light went out, and it went out with a *bang*, and it let such a storm loose upon them as they'd never imagined in their darkest dreams.

Captain Cat was shouting orders, but the noise had deafened them all. The wind churned up the waters, snapped the masts. The *Bells* was breached, taking on water so fast they barely got out with half of what was in the holds . . . and that wasn't much, not after sailing out there so long.

The men were scattered. The wind had ripped some of them right off the yards. Others went down with the ship. Out of a crew of forty-two, only eleven of them survived.

At this point in her story, Captain Cat was silent for a long minute. When she spoke again, her voice was harsher and more brittle than before.

She described the dehydration, the cotton-mouth thirst. Under the beating sun, their bodies blistered, and soon they were so wasted away that even sitting was agony.

Slowly, painfully, the remaining members of her crew began to die.

At first they tried to use the bodies as bait, chopping them up and trolling the pieces behind them. But they were attacked by a monster with milk-blue eyes and sawtooth skin and teeth like spears jutting from its lower jaw. Bigger than a whale, meaner than any shark. Within seconds, it had killed half the remaining crew, and, well, they didn't bait any lines after that.

Captain Cat paused again, panting. Sweat shone on her brow. The words tumbled out, faster now, as if a dam inside her had broken, and the story was roaring through her.

In the fifth week their provisions ran out, and it was decided they would cast lots. They tore up scraps of canvas, placed them in a hat, and drew, one for each sailor.

The black spot meant death. It marked you. It meant you were going to die.

When Farah drew it, they killed her and ate her heart immediately. The rest of the meat spoiled in two days, and after that they only had bones to pick at.

A week and a half later, they drew lots again, and

the black spot came to Waxley. He lasted them another twelve days, until it was time to draw again.

And so it went.

It had to be one of them, so the others could live. You do things to survive that you never would've done otherwise, just to keep going another week, another day.

"I don't regret doin' what we did," Cat said, "but I regret takin' my crew so far west in the first place. I regret bein' so scared of the south, after it took my dad, that I couldn't go back. Maybe if I hadn't been so scared, they'd still be alive. Maybe they would've been the first to cross the Everlastin' Ice to whatever lies beyond."

"I don't reckon they blamed you," said Reed. "They chose to follow you."

For the first time, Captain Cat looked at Meeks, whose dark skin went ashen under her gaze. "How much choice do our men have?" she asked. "They're *our men*."

She was growing weaker and weaker with the effort it took to continue speaking, but the story inside her was bubbling up again. It wouldn't let her rest until she'd finished telling it.

Eventually, there were only two left: Captain Cat and her man Harye. Two scraps of canvas, and one would kill you. Either one of them could've drawn it, but the black spot came to Harye. He was marked. Their seventieth day since the wreck, and he was going to die.

But then the *Current of Faith* came along, and for the first time the black spot didn't mean death.

"Forty of my crew died," she said. "Only two of us survived. Forty men … Forty of my men … Forty …"

She was shrinking back into her emaciated body, shoulders slumped, wrists limp. She seemed to have deflated with the telling of her story, as if for a little while the story had filled her out and held her up, but now that it was gone, she had collapsed, and there was no more strength in her.

At length she said, "We're in debt to you, Captain, for returnin' us to civilization."

"What?" Meeks blinked, looking from Reed to the chief mate and back again. "Cap, we ain't—we're turnin' back?"

Reed sucked in a long breath and tapped his forefinger on the table. Eight times. He could feel Cat watching him with her yellowed eyes.

"No." He sighed. "We ain't turnin' back."

CHAPTER 15

Stories and Stones

Sefia slammed the book facedown in the dirt. The pages bent. She didn't care. Standing, she drew her knife in one smooth movement and flung it at the nearest tree, burying it point-first in the trunk.

Archer looked up from where he stood waist-deep in the water, washing their clothes in a pool rimmed by flat stones.

She ignored his doe-eyed expression and stalked over to the tree, wrenching her knife from the bark. Flipping it in her hand, she pivoted and hurled it again.

The blade lodged in another tree.

Ignoring the pain in her bare feet, Sefia stomped through the undergrowth. Yanking her blade out of the wood, she closed her eyes and exhaled through her nose, conjuring up the memory of dishwater eyes and a stippled face, the metallic sting in the air, and a voice like smoke.

She opened her eyes, took aim, and flung the knife.

But as it left her fingers, her memory of the woman in black was replaced by the crooked face of Palo Kanta. A man who feared the ocean. A boy who rescued cats.

Her knife clattered off the bark and landed sideways in the mulch.

Cursing, Sefia went to retrieve it, but Archer got there before she did. He rubbed the dirt from the steel and pressed the cold handle to her open palm.

She took it, but she didn't throw it again.

Archer touched his temple with his fingers and held the blades of his hands together, opening and closing them like the covers of a book.

Sefia closed her fingers around the knife. "Because Captain Cat was a coward," she said, "and her men paid for it. She said it herself: If she hadn't been so scared of the thing that killed her father, she never would have put them in danger. They died because she was *afraid*.

"I could have stopped them from taking Nin. I was right there. But I'd seen what they did to my father . . . and I couldn't move." She looked away. At the ground. At the waterfall trickling into the pool. Anywhere but at Archer. "I don't even know if she's still alive. But if she is . . . I have to stop them. I can't let them hurt her anymore. I can't let them hurt anyone anymore." Tears sprang to her eyes as she sheathed the knife.

Archer nodded, and she followed him back to the edge of the pool, where he picked up the book, smoothed its wrinkled pages, and placed the green feather between them so she wouldn't lose her place.

Sefia curled up by the edge of the water and he sat beside her as he dried in the sun. He had gained some weight in the past couple of weeks, but his back was freckled with scars. It would take years for some of them to disappear—and others would never fade.

Hatchet's men had left the lake three mornings ago, and she and Archer had continued following them north. They were probably heading for the port city of Epidram, situated in the northeast corner of Oxscini.

Since that night with Palo Kanta, she'd been practicing her vision. She could feel it all the time now, shimmering beneath the surface of things. If she focused just right, and blinked, then it appeared before her. But every time she entered that world of light, she was overwhelmed with images, memories, history, until she was flailing through the endless fragments of time, fighting off headache and vertigo and nausea.

It felt like drowning. Sometimes she got so lost in the flood of sights and sounds and infinite moments in time that she wasn't sure if she'd be able to find her way back to her own body again.

She looked over at Archer. She'd been able to see all of Palo Kanta's life in one quick blur. Maybe she could find out who Archer really was. His story must have been lurking inside him, caged by his silence, even though the marks of it were all over him: the scars at his throat, at his back and chest and arms.

She narrowed her eyes and felt the vision rising around her.

Fifteen burns, lined up like ridges on his right arm.

Fifteen marks.

She blinked, and the golden world unfurled around her.

Fifteen counters.

161

Threads of light rippled around his arm. They pooled and swirled, sparkling with thousands of tiny motes of light. She fought for control of her vision as images rushed past her in a slipstream of history.

Then she saw the fights.

They had been held all over Oxscini: in circles of hard-packed earth cleared of brush and rubble, outlined with torches that stained the undersides of the leaves black; in basements where the floors smelled like clay; in cages of iron bars through which the spectators prodded the fighters with sharp wooden poles, jeering and shouting.

They always fought in a ring, and someone always died.

Sefia saw them flash before her eyes, quicker than she could follow, making her dizzy and sick: boys with snapped necks; boys skewered by spears; boys bleeding from dozens of deep gashes, dying on the ground; boys with bashed-in, unrecognizable faces.

And Archer standing over every one of them. Archer holding the spear, the dagger, the rock. Archer wrestled to the ground by men twice his size and pinned in the center of the circle while someone burned him with a blazing-hot iron. It happened over and over again. Archer's body hitting the floor. The side of his face in the dirt. The stink of sizzling flesh. His right arm collecting burns like trophies. The pain. The cheers. A mark for every fight he won.

He'd been branded because he survived.

Sefia blinked again, and the light washed away, leaving her gasping. The fights were a blur inside her, but she had seen enough to know what had happened to him, what he had done,

162

why the story was locked up inside him like an animal. She felt like she had been inside his skin, and his blood was her blood—his heart, her heart—a closeness she'd never felt before, and hadn't earned.

It was a cruel kind of thievery, stealing into someone's worst memories. She held her aching head in her hands, fighting back the throbbing at her temples and behind her eyes. She wouldn't do that to him again.

But she understood now, some of it anyway. Digging into the pocket of her vest, she fished out her coin purse and dumped its contents into her palm: some gold colbies, an uncut tourmaline, and a piece of rutilated quartz as long as her thumb.

The crystal was shot through with streaks of black and gold like shooting stars, and when you held it to your eyes the whole world seemed to be blasted with fireworks.

Archer looked on with interest as she held out the piece of crystal in the center of her palm.

"I want to give you something."

He touched the quartz with his forefinger.

"Nin gave me this when I was younger," she explained. "She called it a worry stone. And whenever I got caught up, remembering all the bad things that had happened . . . my mother dying . . . my father . . . You rub it with your thumb and it reminds you that you're safe. That you're not back there anymore."

As he took the crystal, his thumb brushed her palm, leaving a drop of water in the creases of her hand. He held the stone to the light, where it sparked black and gold, and rubbed his thumb across it once before tucking it deep in his pocket.

He grinned at her. He had a huge, handsome smile, with sharp canines.

Sefia was suddenly aware of his skin, of the dips where the water pearled and the sheen of bronze on his bare arms. And she didn't know what to do with her hands, so she hugged her elbows and smiled awkwardly back. She could still feel the water in her palm like a tiny gleaming star.

Archer made the sign for the book, flapping his open palms like wings.

She rolled her eyes. "Yes, I'll read now. But if Captain Cat continues to act like a yellow-bellied coward, we're skipping it."

Captain Cat
and Her Cannibal Crew
(Continued)

He saw the news go through her like a bolt of lightning. *Not turning back?* Captain Cat gaped at him, thunderstruck.

Before she could respond, there was a crash from belowdecks.

"Help!" The cries exploded across the ship. "Help!"

Reed was at the door before the other three had even left their seats, out of the great cabin and onto the deck, where the crew had gathered around the main hatch.

"It's the captain," they murmured, parting for him. "The captain's here."

As he descended into the hold and approached the sick bay, a deep sense of dread rose up in him. He began tapping his fingers together—thumb and forefinger, thumb and middle finger, thumb and ring finger, thumb and little finger. *One, two, three, four* . . .

He reversed the order, starting with the little finger. That made eight. Eight taps. He reached the door.

The doc looked up from where she knelt beside a

huge man cradling a limp, skeletal body in his massive arms. It had lost most of its hair, and its hands were thin and overlarge on its wrists.

Harye. He barely looked human.

Doc closed Harye's eyes with two long fingers.

The man holding the body was Horse, the ship's carpenter. He had broad shoulders and bulging arms, hands like hammers, and the leathery skin of a man who'd been sunburned so many times his naturally creamy complexion had grown tough and brown as rawhide.

"I came to check on him." Horse nodded at the large flask lying on the floor next to him. Sniffling, he pulled the yellow bandanna he wore on his forehead down over his eyes. "You know, maybe give him a little pick-me-up. But when I came in, he took one look at me and charged. I didn't know what was happenin'. He came at me outta nowhere. He was crazy, screamin' something . . . I don't know what. I—I hit him. To get him off me, you know? But he's so light. He went flyin' across the room into the wall."

There was blood on the wall next to him, but not much. Maybe Harye didn't have much blood left in him.

"He wasn't gonna last the night anyway," Reed said, squeezing his shoulder. It was never easy, taking a life. Especially for a man like Horse, the kind of man who'd drop in on a total stranger to cheer him up. "Right, Doc? We took him off that boat too late. He wasn't gonna make it."

Doc nodded.

Horse slid his bandanna back up to his forehead. "But why'd he do it?"

There was a scream—a keening animal sound. Captain Cat shoved her way past Reed and into the sick bay, where she fell next to the body, her hands fluttering uselessly over his withered limbs.

"I'm sorry, Captain," said Horse. "I didn't mean to."

As she looked on the giant who'd killed her last crewman, Cat's eyes widened. "The black spot," she muttered, pointing a trembling finger at his hands.

They were speckled black with pitch.

She recoiled, baring her teeth. "You've been marked," she said. "You're the next to die."

"What?"

Outside, the men were whispering among themselves. "It ain't right," said Camey. He rubbed his hawklike nose and glanced around to see if he'd garner any support from the crew. "I tell you, it ain't right."

Greta, a stout woman with sallow skin and black hair that seemed to drip down her head like candle wax, tutted her tongue disapprovingly.

Camey elbowed the cabin boy who'd come aboard with them in the Paradise Islands. "It ain't right, is it, Harison?"

Jigo, the oldest man on the *Current*, shoved him from behind, growling, "Shut it," from beneath his bushy whiskers.

Camey fell silent, but Greta clicked her tongue once more.

"Enough," the chief mate snapped.

Meeks watched them all with interest.

"Horse is our carpenter," Reed explained to Cat. "His hands always look like that."

Captain Cat backed up against the bunks. "It wasn't Harye's fault. He didn't know. You don't understand. You weren't out there with us . . . All those endless days . . . You don't know what it was like."

"You ain't out there no more," Reed said.

She looked at him sadly. "I'm *always* gonna be out there. If you don't want to be out there with me, you've got to turn back."

Reed shook his head. "Beggin' your pardon, but we set out to accomplish something, and we ain't turnin' back till it's done."

Her fingers were claws. Her teeth were fangs. "Didn't you listen?" she snarled. "You're all gonna die out there!"

The crew was whispering again.

"Did you hear what she said?"

"I don't wanna end up like that."

"Captain," Reed interrupted, silencing the others. "I'm gonna give you a choice. We're goin' to the edge, with or without your permission. If you like, you can come with us—we'd be glad to have you. Or you can get back in your longboat and take your chances with the sea. You might make it. There's a shippin' route a coupla weeks east of here. But I won't make you go any farther'n you want to."

Her jaw went slack, her breathing heavy. "I'm—not—goin'—back—in—that—boat," she said. "And I'm not goin' with you either."

He studied her thin face, her ragged hair, the way her skin clung to her bones. It only took him a second to understand what she meant.

In her mind, she was still out there, surrounded by the bones of her crew, and no matter how healthy she got or how much distance she put between herself and the sea, she was always going to be out there.

"Captain, you can't—"

"I can," she said. "I'll do it anyway, if you don't help me."

She'd used up the last of her life telling her story, and with Harye gone, she was ready to join her crew. To make it forty-two. Forty-two dead. An even number.

Letting his hands fall to his sides, Reed drew the Lady of Mercy.

In the faint light of the sick bay, the revolver seemed to glow. Its long silver barrel was embellished with cottonwood leaves and clusters of seedpods, its ivory handle inlaid with mother-of-pearl. Some said it was the most beautiful gun ever made, crafted by a Liccarine gunsmith for her lover, and never a more perfect expression of yearning and devotion had there ever been.

Gasps went up among the crew. But the other gun remained in its holster, with only its black grip showing beneath Reed's restless thumb.

As Captain Cat rose, she lifted her chin, walking out of the sick bay with as much dignity as she could muster. The crew parted for her. Some of them bowed their heads as she climbed the steps to the main deck. In the moonlight, she looked like a corpse already, with shadows in the pits of her eyes. She climbed the rail, refusing assistance when the crew tried to help her, and clung to the rigging, her body wavering in the cool air.

"This is it, Captain," Reed said. "You're sure?"

"Never been more sure of anything in my life," she answered. Gripping the line in her blistered hands, she was fragile, but proud.

Every man and woman on the crew watched as the captain raised the weapon. He pulled back the hammer, and the sound struck the ship like thunder.

"Last words?" he asked.

Captain Cat stared at him. Facing down her own death, with the hissing of the sea behind her and the night spread out like a cape, she seemed to have grown taller, haughtier. Her voice rang out like a bell. "Maybe they'll remember you, Cannek Reed," she said, looking at each of the crew in turn, letting her gaze come to rest, finally, on Camey, who scratched his hooked nose uncomfortably. "But who's going to remember your crew?"

Reed pulled the trigger.

There was a flash and a *bang*, and then the body of Captain Cat was tumbling away from the ship, her hair streaming out behind her, her arms and legs splayed. She fell into the water with a splash, and then Catarina Stills, daughter of Hendrick Stills the Southern Explorer, last captain of the *Seven Bells*, was gone.

But her words remained. Meeks was already repeating them to himself, staring at the blank space she had occupied mere moments before. They were words Reed never forgot.

Who's going to remember your crew?

CHAPTER 16

Trickery

The east side of Epidram was a maze of shacks and narrow alleys cluttered with old lobster cages and lines of damp laundry. Along the dirt roads, the gutters were filled with small rivers of filth and debris that smelled of rotting food and rank liquids. New wooden fortifications topped the old stone walls on the outskirts of town, and watchtowers had been built along the shore, but the war had not touched Oxscini's forested lands yet.

Sefia and Archer crept uneasily through the streets, searching for signs of the 🌐 carved into lampposts or above doors, but there was no trace of the symbol. Earlier that morning, they had watched Hatchet's men slink into the outskirts of town, but now the impressors were nowhere to be found.

"They came this way, I'm sure of it." Sefia glanced up and down the road and cursed. "I can't track on streets like this."

A few small businesses were open, with awnings erected

over their wide windows or tables set out on the street. Down one way, a man was puffing a pipe under a tent, and curls of sweet-smelling smoke rose from the gnarled twigs of his beard. He was surrounded by apothecary drawers, separated into little square compartments into which he occasionally dipped his fingers for a pinch or two of pipeweed.

She'd never felt so conspicuous as she stepped out onto the street. Her boots creaked. Her pack rattled. Everything she did seemed too loud, too out of place. She'd never been in a city this big.

In the shadows beneath an awning, Sefia dimly made out the figures of five old people, as thin as skeletons, sitting in rocking chairs. The wisps of their clothing rose and fell with their rattling breaths. She shuddered. She had the eerie feeling she and Archer were being watched.

Archer followed her, keeping a careful eye on their surroundings, glancing up to the rooftops and around corners.

They hadn't gone far past the next intersection when a familiar figure strode out of an alleyway in front of them. The soles of his boots were caked with dirt and there was trail dust on the hem of his long jacket. He had gray hair and a red beard.

Sefia pulled Archer behind a set of crates. "That's one of Hatchet's men," she whispered, pointing.

He nodded. Redbeard had been carrying the tongs when they attacked the cabin. Archer gripped the handle of his hunting knife.

They waited until Redbeard had gained a little distance on them, and then they struck out after him. He led them up and down the streets, deeper into the city. Sefia and Archer followed

173

him, ducking into alleys and waiting, half-hidden, behind lampposts or clusters of barrels.

Sefia didn't take her eyes off the back of his head. They were close now. She could feel it.

Redbeard led them to a small street market jammed with people. There was too much to look at. Stalls and shoppers, pickpockets and rag-tag bands of war orphans. The sounds and smells swelled around them in a dizzying cloud. But while Sefia hesitated, Redbeard charged into the crowd without a backward glance.

She raced in after him.

Halfway down the street, he slipped into a building with grimy windows and a swinging metal sign overhead: a frothing mug surrounded by a circle of twisted rope. The mug signified that it was a tavern, but the noose . . .

Sefia staggered backward. She'd seen this place before: dirty windows and flaking green door flanked by a candle-maker's workshop on one side and a kitchenwares stall on the other.

Palo Kanta was supposed to have come here. He was supposed to have sauntered right through that crooked door and into the bar with the rest of Hatchet's men.

Suddenly light-headed, Sefia stumbled sideways into Archer, who caught her by the elbow. "He should have been here," she said, dazed. "Palo Kanta should have been here."

He nodded.

"I stopped him."

Archer didn't look at her. He toyed with the votives on the table outside the candle-maker's workshop. Sefia wondered what Palo Kanta would have been doing inside. Drinking, probably. But what else? Laughing? Telling stories with his friends?

"Do you think Hatchet is in there too?" she asked.

Archer peered at the dingy windows and shrugged.

The candle-maker paused in his work and sneered at them. Two half-finished candles dangled from his battered hands. "You kids gonna buy something?" he asked.

"What's that place called?"

"The Hangman's Noose?" The man's lips twisted into a wicked grin. "You don't want to go in there. It's not a nice place for little girls and boys."

Sefia shifted uncomfortably. They moved to the shop on the other side of the tavern, where they fidgeted with some dented pots.

"What can you tell me about the Hangman's Noose?" Sefia asked the vendor.

The woman tucked a dry gray curl back under her bonnet. "They hang folks who can't pay."

"Does a man named Hatchet ever go there?"

"It's none of my business, girl. All *my* customers pay up front."

Sefia gripped the straps of her pack and took a few steps to the side. "Where's Redbeard?" she muttered.

Archer tapped his collarbone and shrugged helplessly.

As the sun rose higher in the sky, Sefia grew more and more nervous. Jumpy. She started at every loud noise, every sudden movement in the crowd. Again and again, she reached for her knife.

At last she couldn't wait anymore. She crept up to the windows of the tavern and rubbed at the grime with the side of her fist. Cupping her hands against the window, she peered through the glass.

Feeling for the golden streams of history simmering beneath the everyday world, she blinked. Light seeped through the cracks in the floorboards, pooling around the tables, washing against the walls of the tavern until even the dangling ropes were soaked with gold.

Her head swam. There was so much to see—bar fights and broken glasses, cockleshells collected by a broom, whispered words, drunken songs, and among it all Palo Kanta, standing by the bar, raising a glass, slapping someone on the back—but none of it would remain still long enough for her to get a good look. Someone crossed her vision—*Redbeard?*—and she whipped her head around to follow him, but the world spun with her. She couldn't see where he'd gone. The light was a vortex, thrashing, bellowing, threatening to swallow her whole.

Sefia blinked, and the world again became dank and brown and foul.

Her own saliva tasted sour. She couldn't do it. Her magic had failed her.

Gently, Archer squeezed her arm.

Meeting his gaze, she shook her head. It was all there, the information she wanted, but she couldn't find it. She wasn't good enough.

"We have to go in." Sefia stood, staring down at the dirty glass. With tiny strokes of her pinkie finger, she traced the letters in the grime of the windowpane, mouthing the sounds as she wrote. Just a few marks in the corner, so you'd barely notice, unless you were looking for them:

Palo Kanta

He couldn't be there—she had made sure of it—but his name could, at least for a while. At least she could give him that. Sefia wiped her finger on her pant leg.

"His name," she said.

Archer nodded again. Together they entered the tavern.

It was a grubby sort of place with dark stains and bits of shells and sawdust on the floor. The walls were hung with orange lamps, old rusted anchors, and thick ropes. There were a few other patrons in the tavern—a hooded woman nursing a glass of amber liquid in the corner, a man with one arm sitting at the bar, picking at peanuts—and they glanced up as Sefia and Archer entered, but Redbeard was nowhere to be seen. Sefia searched the darkened corners for a back door. Where had he gone?

Polishing glasses with a soiled rag, the bartender was in no better shape than the rest of his establishment; there was dirt under his fingernails and his hair hung around his shoulders like the braids of a wet mop. His face, however, was the most distinctive: his left cheek was marked with a row of four star-shaped scars, white and puckered around the edges.

Those scars meant something, the kind of marks that showed who you really were. Sefia had heard about them, or maybe even read about them, somewhere. But she couldn't quite remember.

The bartender grinned when he saw Sefia looking at him, and his teeth seemed oily in his mouth. "Now, now, children," he said, "what are two upstanding young creatures like yourselves doing in a place like this?"

As Sefia approached the bar, the man with one arm tipped toward her. His eyes were unfocused and he had the sickeningly sweet smell of liquor on him. His fingers scrabbled with the peanut shells on the bar top. Her lip curled in disgust.

"We're looking for a man with a red beard," she said. "Have you seen him?"

The bartender's smile was a crooked, wily thing that made the scars wrinkle in his cheek. He tilted his head and tapped his chin with a dirty forefinger. "Perhaps, perhaps," he said, smiling, "but I see lots of folk. Hard to remember them all."

"He was here not fifteen minutes ago. We saw him come in."

Archer shifted behind her. She could sense him glancing around, searching for threats.

"I suppose my memory just isn't what it used to be," the bartender said. "Sometimes all it needs is a little something to get it going."

Nin had always said that there were four ways to get information out of someone who didn't want to give it: bribery, fear, force, and trickery.

Clenching her jaw to keep herself from snapping at him, Sefia took her coin purse from the inner pocket of her vest and withdrew the uncut tourmaline. Holding it up, she let the dingy light shine through its watermelon reds and deep greens. Then she plunked it down on the bar top and stuffed the purse back in her pocket.

The bartender shrugged.

"Are you kidding? That stone's worth more than a little information."

"Doesn't look like much to me. It isn't even shiny." He shrugged again, but the deadness in his eyes told her he was lying. He wanted more.

Gritting her teeth, she reached for her purse again.

Then Archer pulled out the piece of rutilated quartz she'd given him.

"Archer, no," she said, trying to push it away. "Let me do this."

But the bartender nodded and licked his lips. "Well, well, now we're talking."

Archer gently brushed her hands aside and deposited the stone on the bar. Even in the low light, the streaks of gold and black seemed to spark. The bartender touched an edge with a dirty fingertip and rocked it slightly back and forth.

"This is something," he said, "but it won't buy you much."

She glared at him with a look that could have liquefied burning blackrock. If bribery wasn't an option, she'd have to outwit him.

"Then how about we play a little game?" Sefia snatched the quartz from under his fingers and grinned with a confidence she didn't feel. "I'll give you the tourmaline just for playing."

"What's the game?" He looped his greasy hair back around his ears and leaned forward eagerly.

It was a foolish gamble. Her vision was fickle and wild as the sea, and it had already failed her once today. Nin would have told her to find another way.

But Nin wasn't here. And Sefia had to know where Redbeard had gone.

She took a deep breath. "You ask me one question—any one question—about your life. If I answer correctly, you tell me what I need to know."

He grinned. "And if you answer incorrectly?"

Sefia held up the rutilated quartz. "You get this."

The bartender crossed his arms. "Now, now, that doesn't seem fair. Anyone can get a lucky guess." He looked slantways out of the corners of his eyes. "Make it *five* questions, and you've got yourself a deal."

"Two," she countered.

"Three."

Sefia stuck out her hand and placed the quartz back on the bar top. "Don't lie to me when I get them right."

"On my honor, I will not lie."

They shook. Her palm came away clammy and cold.

"First question," he said, sliding the tourmaline into a fold of his apron. "What's my name?"

She studied his face: the wrinkles, the aquiline nose, the mumbling mouth. But she needed to see more than this. She focused on his scars, like four stars in his cheek. She willed herself to decipher them the way she would decipher an unfamiliar four-letter word, each symbol lined up one after another.

Then she blinked, and the light flooded over her. Four star-shaped scars on the left cheek: *Liar. Traitor.* She could see the lines of his life leading backward from this moment, through time. She saw his loneliness, his poverty, his fear. Years and years of it stretching back and back until he was just a young man, serving on the deck of an enormous golden ship. He'd gotten greedy. Then he'd gotten caught.

"Farralon Jones." She swallowed. "Your name is Farralon Jones."

The bartender laughed. "Well, well, that's some trick! Who told you?" He pointed at the one-armed man. "Was it you, Honeyoak? You dirty old bastard."

The man sipped his drink and chuckled. His speech was slurred. "Wasn't me, Jonesy. Never said a word to this girl in my life."

Sefia's eyes unfocused as she slid, dizzy and nauseated, through the currents of his life. The pounding had begun in her temples and the pain was radiating behind her eyes. She put a hand against the bar to steady herself. "That's one," she said. "Ask me another."

Jones tapped his chin again. "Interesting, interesting. That's a nice trick. I've got to think of a harder question this time."

"Don't be all day about it," she snapped. Her insides lurched. "I'm in a hurry."

"All right, I have it." The bartender pointed to his cheek. "How did I get this scar? Don't leave out any details, now."

The light spun around her in gut-churning spirals. She swayed. "You betrayed your captain."

"Now, now, girl." He rubbed his cheek. "You've got to do better than that."

She narrowed her eyes. A sour taste washed over her tongue. "You were a common sailor on the *Crux*, serving under Captain Dimarion. Things might have turned out all right for you, if you hadn't gotten so greedy. But you were passing through

181

Oxscinian waters, and there was a bounty out on him. They'd increased it since he'd been attacking ships in the Bay of Batteram. The money was too good. You turned him in. You thought you could get away with it, but he caught you."

Honeyoak laughed, and the bartender glared at him. "All right, all right. That's two."

Sefia was sweating. The room heaved and swelled around her. She could feel the heat of Archer's hand on her elbow and tried to focus on that instead of the dizziness, instead of the breaking and splitting inside her head. "Ask me another," she said.

Farralon Jones stared at the piece of quartz and passed a hand over his face. Then he narrowed his eyes and said, "What's the one thing I value most in this world?"

Sefia grasped for answers, her vision flooding into the darkest corners of his past, invading his history. She saw too many things to name; sights, sounds, smells washed over her again and again like cruel gold waves, but among them, as if she were thrusting her head above water, gasping for air, she saw flashes of the answer. The captain had a fist like a sledgehammer, and on it he wore four vicious jeweled rings. She felt the pain in her cheek, like it was her own flesh being ripped to pieces. No one would hire him after that. No one wanted to hire a marked man. Not even his own wife trusted him. And Sefia could see how much that meant to him, losing his wife, his daughter, the only two people he'd ever really cared about, besides himself.

She flailed in the light, choking on it as she tried to return to herself. Her body. Somewhere out there in the riptides of gold and light.

Then she felt it: the warm pressure of Archer's palm on the point of her elbow, reeling her back to him. Back to herself.

She blinked, and her awareness came barreling back into her body. Her knees buckled. But Archer caught her.

"You want me to say it's your wife and daughter," she gasped. Her insides were heaving, her mouth dry. But even the seasickness was welcome, this being wholly herself again. "But that's wrong. You never looked after them the way you looked after yourself. If you loved them at all, you never would have done it. You only ever cared about yourself. That's your answer."

Everyone in the bar was looking at them.

"How did you—?" His eyes flicked nervously back and forth. "I never told anyone . . ."

"I *see* you," she said. She put the heels of her hands to her temples and squeezed, as if that could stop the awful pounding. She remembered his wife's words, the last words she had ever said to him, and Sefia repeated them one after another. *"You're a greedy little coward, Farralon Jones, and now everyone who sees you will know it."*

He dropped the glass he had been polishing. It hit the bar top, chipped, and fell to the floor, where it shattered at his feet. He backed away. The shards crunched under him. "I didn't— How did you know—"

"I told you," Sefia said. *"I see you."*

She felt breathless and dizzy and sick inside, but she had won. She snatched up the quartz and handed it back to Archer, who pocketed it solemnly.

Honeyoak was still laughing, tipping drunkenly on his stool. She dipped her finger into his glass and traced the ⊖ on the wooden bar, its wet edges wavering under her trembling finger. "This symbol," she said. "Do you recognize it?"

Jones peered at it dumbly. "Never seen this brand before."

Sefia nodded. Except for Archer's crate, she'd never seen the thing in all her travels either. "Tell me about the man with the red beard, then." She breathed fast through her nose and tried to ignore the nauseating stink of sopping sawdust rising from the ground.

"He works for a man called Hatchet."

"I know. Where did he go?"

"The back door." Jones pointed to a corner of the tavern, where a small door was hidden among the darkened tables. He smiled an oily smile, though Sefia wasn't sure why. "He and Hatchet are leaving port this morning on a ship called the *Tin Bucket*. She's docked at Black Boar Pier now."

"Where are they headed?"

He shrugged. "Don't know. The *Bucket* can go just about anywhere in the Central Sea from here."

"When do they set sail?"

He knelt to pick up the pieces of glass on the floor, his voice rising from behind the bar like smoke: "Half an hour."

She looked up at Archer, who nodded grimly. "We don't have much time." She headed toward the back, still unsteady on her feet, pulling Archer after her. He closed the door behind them just as she flung herself to her knees and threw up in the gutter.

Over and over she vomited, her body shuddering and heaving.

Archer sat beside her and rubbed her back, his palm making

smooth up and down motions along her spine, over her shoulder blades. The touch comforted her, helped to subdue the nausea and the blistering headache.

When she finally sat back, he offered her the canteen. She took it weakly and washed out her mouth a few times. They were in a little alley cluttered with trash bins and old fishing nets.

"I thought I was lost back there. Like I was going to be swept away, my mind, my memories, all picked apart and dissolved into nothing." She shuddered. The last vestiges of headache still throbbed between her eyes, and the shacks and streets wouldn't stop swaying, but she struggled to her feet.

"But you brought me back," she finished. "Thank you."

Archer smiled.

"Let's go."

He nodded and took the canteen from her. They left the alley as fast as Sefia's wobbling legs would let her.

Down by the shore, the piers were crowded with rowboats, sailboats, and other small craft. The merchant ships were flagged with the colors of their home kingdoms—white-and-gold for Liccaro, black-and-white for Deliene—but there was no trace of Everican blue-and-gray. To fly Blue Navy colors in Oxscini would have meant certain death. Beyond the arc of the harbor, a flotilla of Red Navy ships patrolled the shore—a sash of crimson in the deep blue sea.

Dockworkers scrambled up and down the gangplanks as they loaded great nets with cargo and hauled them over the rails, and Messengers in black armbands scurried here and there among the passengers, rattling off their messages. Gulls wheeled over-head like vultures or perched ominously on barnacle-encrusted stumps peeking out of the green water.

"News from the Northern Kingdom!" a newsman called as they raced past. "No word from the Lonely King in months! Sir Gentian to return to Deliene!"

Sefia tipped a copper into his collection tin as they passed, and the next bit of news only dimly reached her over the noise of the port: "Blue Navy strikes the Oxscinian shipping lanes again! Queen Heccata sends more ships north from Kele-brandt!"

At the entrance to each pier was a tall wooden pillar, and at the top of each pillar was a sculpture. Sefia and Archer raced past Crown Pier, Canary Pier, Red Barrel Pier, dodging scrawny war orphans and wagons and sailors unloading crates. When they finally reached Black Boar Pier, with a snarling steel razor-back at the top of its pillar, they found it bustling with activity, so jammed with dinghies and little sloops and sailors that it was hard to walk. Peering through the crowds, Sefia spotted a few tall ships at the end of the dock. Men swarmed around them like black ants.

She tugged the sleeve of a nearby sailor. "Can you tell me where the *Tin Bucket*'s headed?"

He snatched his arm out of her reach. "Get lost, kid. I don't work here."

While Archer kept a lookout for Hatchet and his men, she tried again and again to find someone who knew the *Bucket*'s destination, even attempting bribery with a few copper kispes, but no one would tell her.

"If that greasy backstabbing coward lied to us . . ." She fidgeted with the ends of her pack straps. "C'mon. We'll see for ourselves."

Archer nodded. Together, they snuck along the crowded pier, hiding among groups of passengers, but they saw no sign of the impressors.

As they neared the splintery gray ship that must have been the *Tin Bucket*, they ducked behind a stack of crates to survey the dock. On her hands and knees, Sefia peered around the corner, her quick eyes picking out stevedores milling about on the decks and gangways.

But none of them were Hatchet and his men.

Sefia cursed again and crept forward, through the clusters of barrels and old nets and other miscellaneous cargo waiting to be loaded. She glanced over her shoulder at Archer, but before she could say anything, Redbeard leapt out from behind a crate and grabbed her by the collar, dragging her painfully to the center of the dock. Struggling in his grasp, she watched in horror as the rest of the impressors appeared from their hiding places.

"No!" Sefia kicked and flailed, bit and screamed. "Archer, run!" She got one good look at his frightened face before Redbeard struck her in the side of the head.

The world spun, and she remembered the bartender's greasy smile. He'd tricked them. And she hadn't seen it.

Hatchet and his men closed in around Archer, weapons drawn.

CHAPTER 17

Fear and Pain

Archer dashed forward. He had to get to her. Four men surrounded him. There were others behind him; he could feel them blocking his way off the pier. His knife was in his hand. He had to get to her. He kicked the first one he reached, slammed his foot straight into the man's gut. The man toppled backward. Another came at him. Archer dodged and slashed him across the throat. Blood. That familiar gurgling sound— surprised. They always sounded surprised.

A shot, like thunder. He lunged. He had to get to her. Someone tackled him. He was on the ground. The man was heavy, all arms. Archer fought for air, searching wildly for Sefia.

The man with the red beard was laughing as she flailed in his arms. He spun her around. A knife at her throat.

"Thief!" he spat.

Her hands went to her neck, but he was too strong.

"At least you brought back what you stole."

Sefia stamped her heel down on top of the man's foot. His grip loosened. She jammed her elbow into his stomach. The wind went out of him. And then she was free.

"Archer!"

Archer raised the knife and stabbed the man who'd tackled him. The blade slipped between the ribs, up to the hilt. He shoved the body away from him. The man with the red beard kicked him in the side. Again and again. To keep him down.

Archer slashed at the man's ankle. There was a *pop*. Redbeard crumpled. Archer was on his feet again. The others were closing in around him, but he was only looking for Sefia.

She had been caught, lifted up by the throat. She gasped for air, fingers clawing at the hand that held her. Hatchet's hand. With his other hand, he jammed a gun into her cheek. "Enough," he called. His meaty face was red, his brown eyes slitted dangerously. "Be still, boy."

He couldn't throw the knife faster than Hatchet could pull the trigger. Archer dropped his hands. There was blood on them. There was blood on the dock. The men were limping out of his reach. Two weren't moving, stretched out on the ground.

"The blade too," said Hatchet.

Sefia was going red in the face. Archer let the knife fall from his fingers and felt the men around him breathe sighs of relief.

"Look at you, boy! Well-fed and fattened up. I bet this little thing has been treating you *real* nice." He leered at her. "And thank *you* for returning him in such excellent condition. He's in even better shape than when you stole him." He put his face close to hers. "You think I didn't know I was being followed? You think I'd just let him go? He's the best fighter I've ever seen. I wouldn't be surprised if he *is* the one Serakeen's been looking for all this time. A great soldier to lead his army."

Archer calculated the amount of time it would take him to reach Hatchet. Too long. Sefia's eyes were closing. The color in her face was growing darker.

Hatchet holstered the gun, but didn't loosen his grip on her throat. "You were a fool to come here, boy. You could have gotten away with your freedom if not for her."

It was happening again. It was going to happen again. The packed, blood-muddied earth. The fists and knives and chains. The crate. The stinking darkness. Not that. Anything but that. He'd run. He'd die first.

But he couldn't let them kill Sefia.

He steeled himself for a blow, but it didn't come. There was another gunshot. Hatchet hissed and dropped Sefia as bits of flesh and bone shattered in his arm. The crate behind him splintered. Sefia fell to the ground and didn't get up.

They all looked to the man standing, gun smoking, across the dock. He was tall and lean, with his hat pulled low over his eyes. A normal-looking sort of sailor. But it was his gun they were staring at: silver filigree, and an ivory grip inlaid with mother-of-pearl. One of the two most famous guns in the world. The other was still in its holster.

"I heard you was traffickin' kids," the man drawled. "Didn't want to believe it, though."

Hatchet gritted his teeth and held his wounded arm. "This isn't your business, Reed. Just let me take my property and—"

Another shot grazed his ear. There was a little blood, and a tuft of hair fell to Hatchet's shoulder. He flinched, but didn't cry out.

"People ain't property," Reed growled. Beneath the brim of his hat, his blue eyes flashed.

"We're headed to Jahara, out of your hair," Hatchet called, undaunted. "You can have the girl, if she's alive."

Archer stared at Sefia. She wasn't moving.

"Kid." Reed nodded at him. "Best get your friend and high-tail it outta here."

"Maybe all that fame's going to your head, Captain," Hatchet sneered, "because you seem to think you can waltz in here and get what you want with one gun, when the truth is you're out-numbered." Hatchet's men cocked their guns. There was the insect-like clicking of hammers being pulled back.

Reed chuckled. "I can count."

Behind him appeared the crewmen of the *Current*. They seemed huge, standing there, grinning and gunning for a fight.

Hatchet's men lowered their weapons. Archer shoved his way past them to Sefia's side. She was wheezing, but she was alive. He touched her gently on the shoulder.

"Move it, kid," Reed called.

Archer scooped her up. She was so light. Like a feather, or a fledgling. He grabbed her pack. She wouldn't like it if he forgot her pack. He carried her, softly, like she'd break in his arms. Hatchet's men parted for him.

The captain hadn't lowered his weapon. "I got people all over this kingdom," he said, "and if I hear one more word 'bout you capturin' children, I'll take my ship, and I'll hunt you down like an animal. No matter where you go in this big blue world, I'll find you."

Archer was out of earshot now, so he couldn't hear what Hatchet said next, but he heard the gunfire. He heard the scream, and the clash of swords.

Sefia wasn't doing well. There were ugly red marks all around her neck. He swallowed compulsively, feeling the scar tissue around his own throat contract. He reached the beginning of the pier. It was deserted. All the people had fled. He didn't know what to do. This wasn't like in the forest, where she'd been able to show him where to go. She hadn't had time to teach him what to do.

All the docks looked the same—all the boats and ships and piles of cargo. He couldn't stay. He had to go somewhere.

He began running. He had to find help. There were still people on the other piers. Maybe they would be able to do something.

Archer dashed in among them. He opened his mouth.

But the words did not come. They were not in him. He could feel the place where they should have been, like a black hole inside him, but the words themselves were not there.

"Boy, are you all right?"

Their faces loomed huge in front of him. Their hands were reaching.

"What happened to the girl?"

They clustered around him. They all looked the same. His head spun. He didn't know where he was, how far he had gone. Sefia was breathing shallowly in his arms.

There were too many people. They were too close. Their

hands were grabbing at him, reaching for Sefia. Their words became gibberish. They were loud, circling him. He had to get away. He had to go somewhere safe.

Darkness. That was what he needed. Someplace small. A place where they couldn't get to him, where he would be safe.

Fear and pain were coming, and this time Sefia's soft dark voice wasn't there to stop them. The livid marks on her neck had stolen her voice away, and now she lay unconscious in his arms.

So he did the only thing he knew how to do. He hid. He found an empty cargo crate on one of the piers, laid Sefia inside, and crawled in after her, pulling the crate closed behind him. And then there was nothing but black and the sounds of footsteps and voices outside.

His hands were sticky with blood, but he set down the packs and did his best to brush the hair out of her face before propping a pack behind her head like a pillow. Then he sat down against the side of the crate, arms around his knees, listening to her breathing, listening for sounds of pursuit, and waiting for her to wake.

CHAPTER 18

The First Adventure of Haldon Lac

Petty Officer Haldon Lac was annoyed. It was too early—or rather, if he was being honest with himself, which he was not, he had woken too late. And why not? He was a maturing young man who needed his sleep, and this new early schedule didn't suit him at all. He hadn't had time for his usual cup of coffee with cream and three lumps of sugar, so to him the sun through the clouds was too bright, the sea breeze in the air too chilly, and the smell of fish too overpowering for his delicate olfactory senses. He pouted his perfectly formed lips and surveyed the splintered shingles and abandoned nets from which the unsavory fishy smell arose. Lac put his sleeve to his nose and coughed.

"Breathe through your mouth, sir," said Hobs, his subordinate, who grinned at his discomfort. Hobs was a funny, slant-eyed fellow with a nearly spherical head. Punctual and thorough, he had a good work ethic and absolutely no ambition, which suited Petty Officer Lac, who had plenty of ambition but no work ethic to speak of. They made a good team.

"Shut up, Hobs," said Fox. She was another matter entirely. Though she was a rank beneath Lac, she was the perfect combination of diligence, talent, and drive. They were all new additions to the city's naval complement, soon to be sent to sea and to war, but if the rumors were to be believed, she'd already made a name for herself in Epigloss, Epidram's sister city to the west. Moreover, as Lac had observed frequently since she had been transferred to his unit, she was gorgeous. She was sharp as smoky quartz, with perfect teeth and eyes that cut. She combed an unruly lock of hair back into place behind her ear. "How much farther to the Eastside Market?"

Lac glanced up and down the alley and shrugged. They were supposed to relieve another patrol, but who knew where anything was in this rat's nest of a sector? Dried brown weeds wilted in the windows of the house nearest him, and barrels of stagnant water and discarded crates filled the alley. The chatter of vendors and the rattle of carts swarmed in the air, though the market was nowhere to be seen.

A pair of slender young men in stained smithy aprons passed, their shirts open at the collars. One ignored Lac's staring, but the other, who had a slightly crooked gait that made him hop-skip every few steps, met his gaze. Lac smiled. He had faith in his smile. It was a perfect, moon-shaped crescent that had cooled more tempers and earned him more favors than he could count.

The boy laughed and walked away. Oh, he had *excellent* shoulders. Lac stared after him wistfully.

"I think we're lost again, Petty Officer," Hobs said.

"Are we?" He groaned and turned back the way they'd come. "I'm never going to get used to this city."

"Hopefully we won't have to," Fox said. "I want on a ship as quick as possible. That's where all the action is."

"I couldn't agree more." Puffing out his chest a little, Lac leaned on the nearest barrel. It sloshed, spilling foul-smelling liquid over his bright red coat. "Ugh!" Thick brownish-green ooze was seeping into the fabric. Haldon Lac gagged. "I just had this cleaned!"

"Looks bad, sir," Hobs added helpfully.

Fox stared down her nose at him and sighed. "They warned me about coming to Epidram. But did I listen?"

"Why *did* you transfer?" Hobs asked. "You never said."

She hesitated so long that Lac glanced up from the stain on his coat to study her face. She seemed . . . sad. She'd never looked anything but impatient or focused. Her sadness was quiet and brittle, like a fallen leaf.

Before Lac could say anything, the back door of the one of the buildings swung open, and out stepped a man with an overgrown red beard. Lac recognized him immediately. He'd never seen the man himself, but he'd seen the Wanted sketches tacked up on base. According to the rumors, Redbeard and a man called Hatchet were mixed up in some sort of human trafficking outfit, though no witnesses had ever come forward and no one ever seemed to have proof. They had been evading the Oxscinian Navy for years, always slipping in and out of the city before anyone noticed, stirring up trouble in their wake.

Lac grabbed Fox and Hobs and dragged them behind the trash bins. He held a finger to his lips.

Petty Officer Haldon Lac was lazy, and if he was being honest with himself, which he definitely was not, he had been riding for a long time on his good looks and natural charm, but deep down under his flawless skin and perfect bone structure, he did have some real talents—among them, a nose for important situations. And he could tell that this, as innocuous as it seemed, was an important situation.

He turned to Fox, who nodded in agreement.

They slipped out from behind the bins and followed the man with the red beard to the mouth of the alley, where he was joined by another man. Lac, Fox, and Hobs ducked behind a pile of fishing nets to watch and listen.

"Hatchet was right," the man with the red beard mumbled. "Once I let them see me, they followed me all the way to the Noose."

"Good," said the other. "Does Jones know what to do?"

"He's a greedy one. He'll try to get a bribe out of them, if he can."

"But will he do what he's told?"

"Yeah." The man with the red beard looked over his shoulder and pulled the collar of his jacket higher around his neck. "Let's get to the *Bucket*. I don't like being followed by that boy . . . or the girl, for that matter."

Lac's head swam. It must have been the lack of coffee. What bucket? What boy? He was acutely aware of Fox's presence next to him, and if he was being honest with himself, which he

certainly was not, he secretly hoped that she was paying attention to how well he was handling the situation.

"The *Tin Bucket* docked at Black Boar Pier two days ago,"
Fox whispered. "It ferries back and forth between here and
Jahara."

Haldon Lac realized dazedly that she must have been keeping track of all the ships coming in and out of Epidram. She
was just as ambitious as Lac was and probably hoping for a promotion as well.

At the entrance of the alley, the man with the red beard and
his companion slipped around the corner and out of sight.

Haldon Lac stood and smoothed his hair. "Look," he said as
Fox and Hobs got up. He could feel that this was his moment.
He, Petty Officer Haldon Lac, was having a moment of greatness, and he wanted everything to be perfect. "We're going to re-
connoiter this situation for ourselves. Black Boar isn't far off and
once we see what Hatchet's up to, we can send someone back to
base with concrete information." He grimaced at the brown spill
on his coat, which was the one stain on his moment of greatness,
but it was quickly drying in the morning sun and he couldn't do
anything about it now. At least it no longer smelled.

They left the alley and headed north along the twisting
streets, making a few accidental detours and wrong turns that
Lac hoped no one else noticed. Had he mentioned that he *hated*
this side of the city?

But Fox was grinning. Her grin was a devious, feral thing,
like that of a coyote.

"You wonder how that guy gets his red beard?" Hobs asked
suddenly.

"What?"

"His hair's gray, right? You think he dyes it that color? Or does he dye his beard?" Hobs nodded and pulled at his lower lip.

"Shut up, Hobs," Fox snapped.

"Maybe he dips it—"

"Shut *up*, Hobs!"

As they neared the docks, Haldon Lac rehearsed what he would say when they brought in Hatchet and his men. "Just doing my duty, sir!" He'd smile there, to give his superiors the full effect of his charm. "A promotion, ma'am? Well, if you insist! I'll chase those blue Everican bastards out of our trade routes! King Darion's going to learn what it means to mess with the Oxscinian Royal Navy!" He was so busy practicing speeches that he forgot to pay attention to where they were going and Hobs had to tell him they had completely bypassed the cart road to the port and were now heading in the wrong direction.

When they finally reached Black Boar Pier, Lac groaned. There were so many *people*. It would take an age to find Redbeard.

Suddenly, they heard a gunshot. Screams broke from the crowd. Lac jumped. He glanced around to see if anyone had noticed.

They hadn't.

People fled past him, elbowing others out of the way.

"Easy now," said Hobs in that unhurried way of his. "Not to worry. Royal Navy, here. Royal Navy, coming through."

Nobody paid him any attention.

Another shot rang out.

Fox darted through the press of people, dodging dockworkers and leaping crates. Haldon Lac followed in her wake. If he was being honest with himself, which he absolutely was not, he may have messed this one up. He could feel his moment of greatness slipping through his fingers.

The three of them arrived at the end of the pier in a few minutes and ducked behind some crates for cover. Fox had the better vantage point, but Lac saw a boy about his age scoop up a slight, black-haired girl and go running past them down the dock. He felt faint. The girl was unconscious, and the boy's hands were covered in blood.

Raising his eyebrows, Hobs pointed after them, but Lac shook his head. Fox flashed a series of hand signals at him as he struggled to remember what they meant. They were numbers, but he didn't know which ones. Five? Fifteen? Twenty? Her fingers moved so quickly they were like hummingbirds flicking from one meaning to another.

A voice carried over the pier: "I got people all over this kingdom, and if I hear one more word 'bout you capturin' children, I'll take my ship, and I'll hunt you down like an animal. No matter where you go in this big blue world, I'll find you."

This was Lac's moment. It was a shame that he had already missed the initial confrontation, but now his duty was to stop it from continuing. There was no time to send for reinforcements. Lac took a deep breath and stepped out from behind his crate, shooting his pistol once into the air. "That's enough now," he announced. "We'll take it from—"

A bullet struck him in the arm. He felt the pain first, then heard the shot. Where had it come from? He screamed in a particularly unattractive way and fell back.

The pier erupted into violence. Bright *crack*s of fire burst from pistols and rifles. Steel flashed in the sun. Lac leaned against a barrel, clutching his gun in both hands. His shoulder was bleeding. It *hurt*.

Fox and Hobs were fighting against a handful of solid, mean-looking men on the pier, but they weren't fighting alone. They had been joined by some sailors who were whooping and hollering gleefully as they slashed with their swords and fired their guns.

Haldon Lac blinked. He recognized them as you'd recognize a character who's climbed out of his story and into yours. The giant with the yellow bandanna. The quick one with the dreadlocks. They fought with a wild abandon he'd never seen before, never even imagined, driving Hatchet's men toward the edge of the pier and into the water. Hatchet himself was retreating as well, clutching a wounded arm, staggering back under their onslaught. He shot a venomous glance into the melee and dove into the stinking dock water. Despite the pain in his shoulder, Haldon Lac felt disappointed. His moment of greatness was escaping into the green foam.

The fighting was already over. He struggled to sit up, but the pain in his shoulder was too much. One of the sailors approached him. Petty Officer Haldon Lac cringed and squinted up at him.

The man leaned down. He had the brightest blue eyes—even prettier than Lac's, if he was being honest with himself, which he was not. He felt himself hoisted to his feet and dusted off.

"It weren't your brightest idea, bustin' in here, guns blazin'," the man drawled. "But it worked out all right."

Gesturing with their guns and laughing, the other sailors corralled the remainder of Hatchet's men. Only three were left, bleeding freely from their wounds. Four were dead. Redbeard, whom Lac had seen less than an hour before, lay on the dock, blood at his ankle and at his chest, staining his scraggly beard a deeper shade of red. His eyes were open, his mouth fixed in a silent snarl.

Fox passed Hobs a length of rope and said, "Make yourself useful."

Hobs knelt to tie Hatchet's men's hands. "Where's the petty officer?"

Haldon Lac felt himself pushed forward by a steady hand. "Reckon that's you," the man said. Lac stumbled forward, dimly aware of his blood and the brown stain on his jacket.

Fox looked past him. "Thank you, Captain Reed," she said. "You've helped us apprehend three associates of the criminal known as Hatchet."

Captain Reed? Lac blinked again. That's who this man was? He tried to smile, but no one was looking at him.

Reed chuckled drily. "Just doin' my duty to the kingdom."

Just doing his duty. Haldon Lac's smile wilted.

"I'll make sure my superiors know it was you who helped us," Fox continued.

"I'd appreciate that, ma'am." He tipped his hat toward her

and sauntered off, leaving Petty Officer Lac standing dumbfounded on the dock. Laughing and talking, the other sailors followed. Lac recognized the crew of the *Current of Faith* now: Horse, the enormous carpenter with the bandanna tied around his forehead; Meeks, the dreadlocked, story-loving second mate . . .

Hobs looked up and grinned. "There you are, sir. I thought you'd missed all the action."

Haldon Lac shook his head.

"Put some pressure on that wound," Fox said.

Obediently, he pressed his hand to his shoulder and looked at the blood on the dock, the corpses. This was not a moment of greatness at all, he realized. They had gone in without orders, and they didn't even have Hatchet to show for it. Someone else had swooped in and taken all the glory, which Fox was going to give him—rightfully so, if Lac was being honest with himself. No, this was a chapter in someone else's story, probably not even a very important one, and he hadn't lifted a finger to take part in it.

Well, he'd lifted an arm. And look how that had turned out.

"Hatchet got away," he said.

Fox shrugged. "We have prisoners. We'll get him next time." Was she smiling at him? Her leg was wounded, and blood was smeared across her forehead, but yes, she was smiling at him. That wild coyote smile.

Haldon Lac smiled back.

CHAPTER 19

The New Crate

When Sefia awoke, it was so dark she wasn't sure if she had opened her eyes at all. She heard footsteps, hoarse voices, the creak of ropes. The warm, close air pressed in around her like a blanket. She coughed and stirred, croaking, "Archer?"

Something cool was pressed into her hands, and her fingers flitted over his as he raised the canteen to her mouth. Water trickled past her lips and down her throat. She sat up and spoke again: "Where are we? Did they get us?"

His hand squeezed hers. They were safe.

"Thank you," she whispered.

As he sat back, he took something from his pocket and began turning it in his fingers. She reached out, and in the darkness found the worry stone resting in his hand.

Outside, waves murmured in the slow breath of the tide. They were near the water, maybe on one of the piers. Their hiding place was small, with hard wooden sides, barely big enough to fit the two of them.

"A crate!" Her fingers brushed the folds of his clothing.

His hand found hers and he held up two crossed fingers in the dark. They were sticky—with blood?—but she knew what they meant.

She was with him. They were together. So he was okay.

She sat back again, but Archer's hand remained over hers. In the darkness, the pressure of his fingers seemed like the only real thing in the world, and if she let go, all the pieces of her would scatter, spinning wildly into the black. They'd touched before, but it had never felt like this.

She didn't pull away.

"What's out there?"

Archer's shoulder lifted and fell. She took another sip of water. "I'm sorry," she said, her voice low and cracked. "I should have been more careful. I should have noticed . . . I just couldn't control my vision . . . ." She trailed off. "Hatchet said you were supposed to lead an army."

He didn't answer, but she knew he was still rubbing the worry stone. Serakeen had already claimed vast stretches of ocean. Now he wanted land too. Liccaro, with its corrupt regents and impoverished people, would be easy pickings.

Was that why he needed boys? For his army? But the way Hatchet talked about Archer on the dock made it seem like he thought he was special. Not cannon fodder, but a leader. A captain. A conductor of violence. Archer had already killed fifteen boys, but still Serakeen wanted more. Legions more.

"Never." She gripped his fingers tighter. "You'll never have to kill for them again."

He leaned down and touched the top of her head with his cheek.

After a moment, Sefia reached out, feeling the familiar shape of her pack and the book inside. "We didn't even find out where they were going."

Archer tapped the back of her hand excitedly.

"Did they say something?"

He nodded, and she began guessing. Corabel. Kelebrandt. "Roku!" She laughed. The littlest of the kingdoms was a steaming volcanic island that smelled of sulfur and ash. Although it was once an Oxscinian territory and still exported blackrock and gunpowder to its former sovereign, it was too small and isolated in the deep south to be of much consequence. "I know. No one goes to Roku."

Still, it didn't take her long to land on the right answer. "Jahara," she whispered. "They were going to Jahara."

It seemed like Archer was about to respond when they heard footsteps echoing outside: quick, nimble beats like those of a bird. Inside the crate, they froze. Pressed against Archer's shoulder, Sefia could feel her own pulse drumming in her neck. The footsteps grew louder, then halted. Someone was close, separated only by a few wooden boards.

There was a scratching noise, like burrowing, like fire on dry wood. It rumbled and crackled around them, filling the crate with noise.

Then, a rough voice: "You there!"

The noise ceased, and they heard someone scurrying away.

"Hey, wasn't that the girl who—?"

"Nah, too old. She was just a slip of a thing."

The voices drew nearer, and someone slapped the side of the crate. Sefia shuddered.

"After that brushup on Black Boar, everyone's behind schedule. Cap wanted us back at sea an hour ago."

"Even an hour ago wouldn't have been soon enough for the captain."

They laughed.

Archer's hand tightened over hers.

The crate shook. Something large and heavy was being slapped against it. Ropes. The crate was being tied up like a present. She braced herself against the walls. She'd been on ships before. She knew what was coming next.

She felt as if the ground had dropped away beneath her. Her stomach lurched. They were aloft, swinging through the air, listing this way and that. She tumbled into Archer as the packs struck her back. They fell over each other, all elbows and heads and knees and flailing straps.

Then they were dropped. Sefia bit her lip to keep from gasping at the impact.

They were surrounded by hollering and rumbling and things moving into place. Sefia and Archer lay motionless at the bottom of the crate, curled up where they had fallen. His arm along hers. Her shallow breaths in his tousled hair. In all the commotion, he had not let go of her hand.

There was a great *thud*: a hatch being closed on top of them, and then they were alone. The voices were distant above.

They had been loaded onto a ship.

Sefia shivered. They were stowaways now, and stowaways were expendable. She'd heard the stories. If the ship was on a short journey, between the kingdoms or down the coast, they might be enslaved and sold at the next port. If the ship was on one of those long sea voyages, they'd be killed immediately, their bodies left in the open ocean without ceremony.

The crate, which had only moments before seemed safe and warm, now closed in about them like a prison.

Archer was shaking. His breath came too fast. Under her hand, she could feel him dragging his thumb over the worry stone again and again. She curled around him and pressed her cheek to his hair, muffling his trembling with the pressure of her body on his. "It's okay." Her words were barely audible as they whispered past his ear. "It's okay."

How much food did they have?

"It's okay."

How much water?

"It's okay."

How long could they last in the bowels of the ship?

"It's okay."

CHAPTER 20

Her

Tanin leaned against the bulwark of the ship as if she belonged there, propped up on her elbows with her hands crossed loosely at the wrists. It wasn't her ship, of course, and she *didn't* belong there, but from the deck of the old cutter she had a clear, unobstructed view of the dock and, fifty yards away, the crate that contained the boy and the girl.

Beside her, the Assassin was trimming her fingernails with the tip of her knife, flinging little white slivers into the frothy green water below. Under their boots, the decks were slippery with the blood of the watchman, who now lay dead at the bottom of the main hatchway.

"I still think we're wasting time," the Assassin said.

Tanin didn't take her eyes from the crate. "And that would matter, if I cared what you thought."

The Assassin said nothing, but her frustration radiated from her in waves.

Tanin sighed. "I'm sorry. I know you're impatient. So am I. But if we act before we have all the relevant information, we may lose the Book, and that's not a risk I'm willing to take."

"How is watching them sit in a box relevant?" The Assassin sheathed her knife.

"If they're as important as I think they are, everything is relevant."

Tanin's eyes narrowed at a flicker of movement on the dock. A slender figure darted from behind a set of crates, her long black hair tied back. She moved with the quick steps of a thief, or a blackbird hunting insects, so sure and elegant that Tanin's breath caught in her throat.

No. It can't be her.

Tanin was too far away to see her face clearly, but as she watched, the woman paused beside the crate. A knife flashed in her hands. She glanced around to make sure no one was looking and then she began to carve.

Tanin straightened suddenly. She would have recognized that posture anywhere.

The woman was writing.

Vaulting over the rail, Tanin ran down the gangplank to the dock. Through the crowded pier, she saw two men approach the crate. The small dark-haired woman looked up once—too far away for Tanin to make out her features—and ducked into the crowd.

Tanin's gaze skimmed over beggar children and sailors, servants and merchants, messengers running this way and that in their black caps.

The Assassin joined her on the pier. "Is that—"

The woman sprinted out from behind a cluster of passengers and raced away. Tanin ran after her.

She could see the Assassin out of the corner of her eye, running beside her as they dodged through the throng, narrowly avoiding pull-carts and men rolling kegs across the wooden planks. Ahead of them, the woman leapt over piles of nets and slid, legs kicking, over the tops of wooden chests, squeezing between plump businesswomen and groups of confused travelers.

As she ran, Tanin kept hoping—*hoping*—the woman would turn, even if only for a second. Just long enough for Tanin to get a good look at her. To see that it was really her. Even if it was impossible.

But the woman didn't look back once.

They chased her to the end of the pier, and without breaking her stride the woman bounded up a set of crates and took a flying leap over the water, arms outspread like wings.

The Assassin raised her knife. It flashed in the sun.

"No!" Tanin shoved her aside as the blade left her hand.

It slashed through the woman's arm just before she disappeared. The blade dropped into the water, but there was no other splash. It was as if the woman had winked out of existence entirely.

Tanin halted.

Teleportation. That tier of magic was so far advanced that even Master Illuminators rarely attempted it. But the woman couldn't have been . . .

The Assassin skidded to a stop and slammed her gloved fist into one of the crates. It burst apart, its boards breaking like kindling. A few nearby dockworkers started toward her, but she

211

glared at them with such malice that they raised their hands and backed away, shaking their heads.

"Why did you stop me?" she demanded.

Tanin stared at the space where the woman had been moments before. "I didn't want you to kill her," she said faintly.

The Assassin kicked at the bits of splintered wood on the dock. "I wouldn't have killed her. Stopped her from teleporting, yes. Gotten you the answers you wanted, yes."

"I couldn't take that chance."

"Was that even *her*?"

Tanin turned away as tears distorted her vision. "I don't know," she whispered. Her words cracked as her voice, always so under control, split and fractured like ice.

The Assassin snorted. "Why do you care so much?"

Another few tears spilled from the corners of her eyes, and she wiped them away hastily, straightening her clothes. "Because she was family."

"We don't have families. We swore to it." The Assassin spat sideways. "Sometimes it's like you don't even want the Book back."

All traces of Tanin's disappointment vanished in an instant. She snapped her hand over the Assassin's wrist and gave it a vicious twist.

Crying out, the Assassin dropped to one knee, her hand caught fast in Tanin's viselike grip.

"I like you, Assassin," she said sweetly. Her regular voice had returned, as supple and sharp as a fencing foil. "Under ordinary circumstances, I even like your obstinate braying and your mulish devotion to the cause." With every word, she put

212

more and more pressure on the Assassin's wrist, until the joint began to buckle and tears welled in the younger woman's eyes. "But these are extraordinary times, and if you can't stop yourself from sounding like a shortsighted nag every time you open your mouth, I will ship you back to the Main Branch to let the Administrators break you like the wild ass you are."

She gave the Assassin's wrist one last wrench and released her.

The Assassin gasped, cradling her injured hand to her chest.

Tanin smiled down at her. "Now, let me spell this out for you: That woman—whoever she was—*transformed* that crate. She's *protecting* them. If someone that powerful is watching over these children, they must be important. You'd be a fool to try to capture them now."

Despite the pain in her wrist, the Assassin's eyes flashed at the challenge.

Straightening, Tanin threw back her shoulders and lifted her chin. The sea breeze caught her silver-black hair, whipping it away from her face. "At any rate, we know where they're going. We'll follow the ship." She paused. "They'll be safe enough, if they're careful."

At her feet, the Assassin looked like she could spit venom, but she said nothing.

"Come." Tanin took her arm and helped her to her feet, brushing splinters of wood from her black sleeve. "I owe you a new knife."

CHAPTER 21

What the Stars Mean

L on stood by the glass wall of the Library, looking out over the mountains. Gray fingers of moonlight parted the clouds, touching on blue ridges and black trees dusted with snow. Taking a deep breath, he blinked, allowing the Illuminated world to swim before his eyes.

Under the blanket of winter white, the boulders and trees glimmered with golden threads of light, swirling and shifting with the passage of time.

He watched the growth of the trees and felt wildfires burning across the landscape, experienced lightning strikes on the granite domes, and suffered the slow inevitable advancement of glacial ice. Entire lifetimes revolved before him while he stood there, dimly aware of the passing minutes, his breath fanning against the glass.

Erastis had always said he would need a referent, something in the physical world to anchor him in the seas of light that spanned all of history. But Lon was better than that. It had taken him months of training, but now he could absorb decades of information without falling ill or losing himself in the waves of light.

"I thought I'd find you here."

Lon blinked, and the Illuminated world drained away. He turned to find the Second standing beside him, smelling of metal. She was dressed in her black Assassin's garb, with frost still clinging to her dark hair. Her curved sword hung at her side.

"You're back," he said. Even though he spoke softly, his voice still echoed faintly in the marble hall.

The Second didn't look at him, but she nodded. There was something different about her now. After their encounter in the Library, they'd spent six months becoming friends—as she forged her bloodsword and he trained in the Sight—and then one day, over five weeks ago, she and her Master had disappeared. No one would say where they'd gone, and Erastis, when pressed, had only shaken his head and said, "I told you not to get too attached to her, Lon. Assassins don't form ties they can't break."

And now, she seemed almost as distant as she had the day they'd met.

"Where did you go?" he asked.

"I was on another mission." Her words were a thread of condensation, fading quickly against the glass.

"Oh."

For a whole minute, nothing moved but the snowflakes outside.

"How long are you going to be back?"

"As long as I'm ordered to."

"Oh." Lon watched her intently. She'd been on missions before she'd gotten her bloodsword, before they became friends. But he didn't remember her coming back like this, cold and remote as the frigid Northern Reach.

The Second slid her sword a hand-span out of its sheath, her gaze passing over the copper-colored steel, which had been inscribed with hundreds of words, swooping up and along the blade in perfect spirals. After forging the blade, she had spent another three months using Transformation to engrave the weapon, imbuing it with its magical properties. In the moonlight, the letters seemed to glow.

He tugged awkwardly at his huge sleeves. He didn't like thinking about it, but Apprentices were assigned to their divisions for a reason. At eighteen, the Second had already had at least a dozen missions, each one of them a kill, and as she grew more powerful, she would begin operating on her own, separate from the First, doubling their deadly reach. One day, Rajar, his bighearted, bigmouthed best friend, would hold the lives of hundreds of soldiers in his hands. The Apprentice Administrator, who was almost as old as her dying Master, had been chosen long ago for her aptitude for poisons and torture.

Lon was still anxious to prove himself, but he no longer envied his fellow Apprentices.

"Do you want to talk about it?" he asked quietly.

The Second hesitated a long moment before sliding her sword back into its scabbard with a definitive *click*. "What were you doing in here?"

He swallowed. "Watching the glaciers."

There was a flicker of their old friendship in her eyes. "You must have improved since I saw you last."

He shrugged. "I still can't see the future, though."

"Only one seer in a thousand can see the future."

"That's what Erastis says too." Lon slowed his voice and clipped his words in imitation of the Master Librarian. "'It takes a rare talent to see the stories yet to be told, my Apprentice. How can you see them when you don't know what they will be?'" He rolled his eyes. "But that doesn't mean I can't try."

The Second raised an eyebrow. "I suppose you'll want to teleport to the future too, in a few years."

"Why not?"

"Because *that* has never been done."

"That doesn't mean it can't be done."

A light bloomed in the corridor at the other end of the Library, and the Second grabbed his hand, pulling him to the glass doors of the greenhouse and into the warm soil-scented air inside.

Easing the door closed again, she crouched with him behind an array of papery poppies as they watched Erastis enter the Library, an oil lantern dangling from his hand. He claimed it was a waste of power to use the electric lamps just for him.

Lon grimaced. "I thought he'd be asleep for longer tonight."

"Shh."

At night, the Master Librarian wore the same long velvet robes he wore during the day, and they swished and slithered across the floor as he ascended the steps to one of the alcoves.

The lamplight wavered as he disappeared behind the book-shelves.

"He scolds me for sneaking in here at night, but he brings *lanterns* to the stacks," Lon grumbled.

"He's in charge of the Library. He makes the rules."

"But I'll be the Master Librarian one day. And I won't burn it down then either."

Erastis emerged from the shelves carrying a red-bound volume under his arm. He padded out of the Library again, the light batting at the ceiling as he withdrew down the hall.

"You're lucky to be a Librarian. The rest of us"—the Second paused for a moment; her mouth twisted, and the rest of the sentence seemed to change direction abruptly—"can't come in here and take whatever we want. Not even the Director can do that."

Lon's powers of observation, honed during his time as a street performer, told him something was wrong. That her latest mission had been different, had shaken her somehow, so that the pieces of her had been dislodged and were now rattling around inside her. But he didn't dare ask about it again. Instead he said, "Neither can I."

"But you will someday." She smiled sadly, but he knew from the pain in her eyes that her sadness was not for him.

When he didn't say anything, she clasped her hands around her knees and looked up at the sky through the glass ceiling. There, between the clouds, they could see the constellations—each set of stars a story, spelled out in needlepoints of light and the imaginary threads that connected them.

"Do you know the story of the great whale?" the Second asked.

Lon nodded. "When I was a kid, and my parents tucked me in at night, they used to tell me all sorts of stories about the moon and the stars and the shapes of the trees. When they were home, at least. Before their troupe was called off again to who-knows-where."

"Tell it to me." Her voice shivered, like a ripple in the still surface of a lake.

He looked at her for a moment, but she wouldn't meet his gaze. So he found the stars that formed the shape of the whale, inhaled the deep scent of earth that surrounded him, and began, his voice falling easily into the cadence of the old stories.

"Once there was, and one day there will be. This is the beginning of every story.

"Once there was a great whale, as large as an island kingdom and as black as the night itself. Every day, the whale would swim across the oceans and rise up out of the sea at sunset, making a great leap into the sky with drops of water still clinging to its skin. All through the night it swam across the sky, and when dawn came, the whale dove into the sea again to repeat the cycle: through the water by day, through the sky by night.

"At that time there was a famous whaler whose name has been forgotten, though his deeds have not. He had killed more whales than any man who ever lived or has lived since. They said his ship was made of whale bones and he drank from cups of whale teeth. Every night, he watched the great whale swim through the sky, and he knew that no matter how many ordinary whales he killed, he would never be the greatest whaleman until he had killed this one.

"It took many long years of preparation, but eventually he was ready. At dawn, when the sparkling black whale dove back into the sea, the whaleman released his harpoons. The great whale was caught! But it was so strong that it kept swimming. All day it swam across Kelanna, pulling the little whaler behind it.

"As night approached, the whaler prepared his ship for flight. But as the whale leapt into the sky, the lines snapped. The ship slammed back into the water. Many men were cast overboard and lost in the dark seas. But the whaler would not be stopped. He and his remaining crew sailed the ship into the air . . . but it was too late. The great whale was already halfway across the sky, and though the whaleman pursued his quarry through what remained of the night, the sun caught up to him, and he and his ship disappeared into the light.

"The next night, a new set of stars appeared: it was the whaler, doomed to chase after his quarry for the rest of time. And the great whale swam freely through the ocean and the sky, untroubled by men."

As Lon finished his story, the Second's hands drifted to her bloodsword, and the scent of metal bloomed in the greenhouse.

"Your parents told you this?" she murmured.

"Didn't yours?"

Her gaze fastened on him. "I have no parents," she said.

"Right. 'I shall forsake all ties to kin and kingdom.'" Lon rattled off the words of their oath. "But you *had* parents, at one time anyway."

As her fingers tightened on her scabbard, he could see the scars and nicks on her skin shifting over her tendons.

Finally she released her grip on the sword. Her shoulders drooped and she hugged her knees to her chest. "Will you tell me another?" she asked.

For a moment, Lon studied her. She had closed her eyes, and the blue-gray light edged her forehead, her lashes, her nose and lips. He'd never seen anyone look so vulnerable and so impenetrable at the same time.

"Do you know the story of the bear man who split the Gorman Islands?" he asked.

Almost imperceptibly, the Second shook her head.

Leaning back on his hands, Lon stared up at the sky. "Once there was, and one day there will be . . ." he began.

He told her story after story, skipping them one by one like stones into the darkness, where they disappeared without a splash. She didn't say anything about her mission, and he didn't ask again, but they spent the rest of the night in the greenhouse, until the sky lightened and the smell of green and growing things overpowered the scent of blood and iron.

CHAPTER 22

The Stowaways

Sefia didn't know how much time had passed since Archer had fallen asleep, but judging from the way the sounds of the ship had gradually faded—the voices, the footsteps, the sudden unfurling of sails like turning pages—it was night by the time Archer stirred.

He woke as quietly as he did everything else, with the barest twitching of his fingertips. She felt him sit up.

"We have enough food and water for three days, if we're careful about it." She began feeling along the edges of the box. "We need to find a way out."

After a little pushing and prodding, one side of the crate cracked open. Fresh air came streaming through the opening and they breathed deep, happy breaths. Their relief lasted only a moment, however, because as they shoved harder against the wall, it jammed and wouldn't open farther.

Archer slammed his shoulder into it, pushed, feet and hands

and body. Sefia crawled out of his way. He flung himself at the walls, fists and head and legs. The crate seemed to shrink around them. The imaginary smells of blood and urine, old straw and fouled floors enveloped them.

"Archer, please!"

He ignored her. He shoved his whole weight against the side of the crate. She could feel his panic as palpable as sweat.

Then, with a scraping noise, the wall gave way. Archer wriggled out into the hold at the bottom of the ship. He crouched there for a long moment in the semidarkness, listening. Sefia held her breath.

But there were no signs that anyone had heard—no sound of the watch, no footsteps.

Soon Sefia crawled out and stretched her legs. The rest of the hold was stocked with crates, barrels, burlap sacks. Archer inspected the hatchway that led to the lower deck above them, but there were no signs of movement.

Near the fore of the hold, Sefia picked the lock to the galley store and found potatoes, salted beef, carrots, hard cheeses wrapped in cloth, butter, suet, eggs, and in the corner, an unlit lantern with a cracked glass globe.

She blinked, and the history of the lantern swam before her eyes: the rough seas when it broke, where it had come from, images so quick and confused that she couldn't focus on them. Nausea washed over her and she stumbled, banging the backs of her legs on a nearby crate.

Why did her vision work sometimes but not others? Shaking her head, she blinked and tried again, but still she found herself floundering in the sea of hands, faces, glimpses of dark places.

Her vision leapt from the past to the future: she saw herself lighting the lantern, the shadows of Archer's face, and then she was slipping through history to a glassblower's workshop, with the heat on her face, watching globes of glass spin on iron rods like enormous globs of crystal taffy.

Then she blinked and returned to the present, where Archer stood in front of her, a smile lighting up his eyes. Sefia's stomach flipped, and not just because of the nausea. How long had he been watching her? What did she look like? She almost laughed, and nervously clamped her hand over her mouth to silence herself.

Archer's smile widened.

Busying herself until the heat in her cheeks subsided, she collected the lantern and rummaged around until she found oil to light it. Then she and Archer retreated silently back to the crate.

Over the course of the next few days, they ate their own food first, but when their stores ran out, they started stealing, always taking a little less than they needed: half a handful of peas, a scoop of water, a small wedge of pork. They were always hungry. Their stomachs grumbled. But they couldn't afford to be full.

They learned to recognize night from day by the way the sounds of the ship faded away, keeping time by the sudden eruptions of noise at the changing of the watch, and only came out after the rest of the ship had gone to sleep—just a few minutes to stretch and gather supplies.

Once they were sneaking crumbs of cheese when footsteps

sounded on the deck above. They ducked behind the nearest crate as lantern light flooded the dark hold. There was a sound of rats scurrying away into the corners.

A long shadow crossed the hold to the galley store, where the ship's boy unlocked the door and began poking among the barrels, a silhouette of long limbs and curls on the curving timbers. "Butter," he said. "Butter, butter, butter. I'll never get used to it. We oughta get a cow and make our own, at the rate he's usin' it." He found it bundled in the corner of the hold, took a hunk, and stomped back up the stairs, still grumbling under his breath.

They didn't take any butter after that.

It turned out that trips to the hold were fairly regular, occurring a few hours before each meal, with only occasional unexpected visits, and Sefia and Archer grew accustomed to the boy's comings, goings, and mutterings.

They slept during the day, curled up next to each other, waking only at the sounds of footsteps above, holding still and barely breathing, until the footsteps faded and they were alone again.

In the hours they spent awake, through the darkest, safest hours of the night, Sefia practiced using her vision. Sometimes it worked. Sometimes she saw old Delienean pastures, rolling green hills with black-and-white cows grazing in the shadow of Kozorai Peak, where overgrown trenches and stone walls served as reminders of a siege that had occurred hundreds of years before, in the heat of the Ken-Alissar blood feud. Sometimes she saw rough hands picking apart ropes and twining them together again, with salt in the air and a breeze in the sails. But every moment of seeing brought headache and vertigo and nausea, and she couldn't maintain her vision for long.

Other times, when she deemed it was safe enough, she lit the lantern inside their little crate. Archer leaned in close, the light playing across his chin, his cheekbones, his golden eyes. And she read. Her voice surrounded them with stories, until they were saturated with the world inside the book, breathing it in, hearing not the creaking of their own ship but that of the one in the story, the one with the green hull, sailing for the western edge of the world.

The *Current of Faith*
and the Floating Island

Leaving Captain Cat and the bones of her cannibal crew behind, they sailed on. By the time they found the floating island, it had been over six months since they left the Paradise Islands, and they were feeling the effects of starvation. Even Cooky, for all his tricks with vegetable peelings and bone broth, couldn't ease the twinge in their guts. Some days Captain Reed sacrificed one of his meals to Harison, the ship's boy they'd picked up in the Paradise Islands, or Jigo, the oldest man on watch, but they were all going hungry.

So it was no surprise that at the sight of the island, the crew raced to prepare for landing. Reed stood at the prow while they flurried around him, with Jigo and the chief mate at his side.

The mate lifted his weathered face to the wet breeze. "Judging by the wind, I'd say we're headed straight into that storm," he said.

Beside him, Jigo nodded and rubbed his hip with his knotty old hands. "It's a real beast, all right. Gonna last through the night." After a hard fall from the rigging twenty years before, he'd claimed he could predict the duration of a storm by the ache in his bones. As far as anyone knew, he'd never been wrong.

Reed squinted at the clouds, bristling with rain. "I don't like bein' moored in a storm any more'n either of you, but we ain't gonna last if we don't find something on that island."

Jigo grunted and hobbled off to join the rest of the larboard watch.

The mate's dead gray eyes were unblinking. "Is it today?"

"Not today." Reed took off his hat and ran his fingers through his hair. "I'll leave Aly with you. Send her if you get jumpy. That storm comes down on us, and everyone better be back on board—and our cargo too."

They were close enough to the island now to see it was teeming with plant life: trees twice the size of the ship and an understory of bushes and tall grass.

"You'll be cutting it close."

"Ha!" Reed jammed his hat back on his head and grinned. "I've shaved closer'n this."

The island was moving fast, but the *Current* was a match for it. They drew up alongside the shore, skimming past mottled beaches and fields of grass. Tiny horned deer loped through the bushes and birds like jewels flitted through the air. The wind kissed their faces and swirled around their arms. And suddenly, all across the ship, the sailors let out whoops of delight, their laughter filling the sails.

The island was not an island at all. It was a giant sea turtle with a broad shell that rose a thousand feet out of the water, its enormous flippers churning the waves in great up-down motions like slow wing beats. Its massive head rose above the waves on a long white neck that gave way to smooth brown scales, ancient heavily lidded eyes, and a sharp beak that could snap a man in two.

Horse adjusted his bandanna. "Well ain't that something."

Beside him, Harison murmured in the same awestruck voice: "That's something, all right."

At a nod from the captain, Jaunty, the helmsman, began racing the *Current* against the turtle. He was cackling like a madman. None of them had ever seen Jaunty so excited about anything—head thrown back, molars showing. And the whole crew clinging to the rails, whistling and cheering.

Captain Reed scrambled up the bowsprit and stood there, poised over the hissing sea, howling for the pure joy of it.

And for a moment, they forgot how hungry they were. Because experiences like this were better than all the provisions they could have hoped to rustle up.

As they drew near enough to use their grapples, the captain mounted the rail. All around them was the sound of water—the murmur of waves onshore, the cacophony of water falling from the turtle's enormous flippers as they dipped and rose in and out of the sea.

To be boarding a creature as old as that! Older than all the stories they'd ever heard. Older, maybe, than all the words in the world.

It was something, all right.

As soon as they landed, the captain sent them off. "Take what we need, but don't take it all," he said. "This place is too pretty to be ruined by the likes of us."

Pairing up, they spread across the island in search of provisions. The undergrowth was lush with tubers, wild onions, and spicy lettuce; the forest, with green and yellow fruit. Large rodents nosed among the roots and munched contentedly on fallen nuts.

In the underbrush, Harison bent to the ground and picked up a green tail feather with a curious curlicue at the end. Twirling it between his fingers for a moment, he tucked it into the top buttonhole of his shirt.

"My ma's been collectin' feathers since she was a little girl," Harison explained. "She's got at least a hundred of 'em, but she can tell you the story of how she got each and every one. When I left, I promised to bring her feathers from all the places I'd been."

The captain clapped him on the back. "I'll keep an eye out."

As he and the ship's boy continued digging for roots, Camey and Greta stomped toward them. He had a boar slung over his shoulders, and she clutched three dead birds in her hamlike fist.

Harison made a face as they approached. Reed chuckled.

Neither Camey nor Greta had made themselves popular with the rest of the crew. They kept to themselves for the most part, did only what was asked of them and no more. But they were his crew, and Reed treated them fair.

"Seems this job'd be easier if we could flush 'em out with fire," Camey said, slapping the boar on the haunch. He was a good marksman: the animal had been shot clean between the eyes. "We done it plenty of times back home. Right, Greta?"

"Vacated their hidey holes right quick, the vermin did." Greta grinned, her teeth yellowed from years of smoking. She ran her free hand through her greasy black hair, and a flurry of dandruff settled on her broad shoulders. "Like shootin' bottles off a fence line."

"This ain't like back home," Reed said. "The island's a livin' thing, and livin' things protect themselves. You start a fire here, the island goes under, and you get nothing but a watery death."

"Either the sea or the sword, eh, Captain? That's what we got to look forward to." She clicked her tongue ruefully and, noticing the dandruff on her shirt, began flicking away the largest flakes with her thumb.

"Only a fool runs toward death," Reed murmured,

more to himself than to Greta. "Even if we run from it, we all lose that race eventually."

"I ain't a fool," Camey grumbled. Taking hold of the boar's legs again, he continued downhill toward the beach, muttering, "It ain't right, treatin' us like that."

Clicking her tongue as if to say, *What can you do?* Greta followed, the dead birds flopping awkwardly in her hand.

"How long they been like that?" Captain Reed asked, looking after them.

Harison shrugged sheepishly and ran a dirty hand through his thick curls. "Since I can remember, Cap."

"They're gonna be trouble if we don't reach the edge soon."

After two hours, the rain began. The crew raced back and forth from the trees to the ship, bringing meat and eggs, heads of wild cabbage and casks of freshwater. Huge drops pelted the grass and the surface of the sea. The game disappeared, taking shelter from the rain, and the men began foraging for whatever they could find: blood-drop berries, hard-shelled nuts, flightless birds with white-and-gray wings.

Overhead, thunder rumbled. Lightning flashed deep in pockets of the sky.

Captain Reed began touching each of the crates and water casks before they were loaded. Even over the din of the storm, they could hear him counting: *six, seven, eight* . . .

Harison and Jigo went off searching for more tubers in the woods.

The rain came down harder. Lightning lanced through the sky like a trident, and for a second the entire island was lit up in brilliant blinding light.

Drops of rain sparking in the black sky.

The turtle's fins like giant moving stones, coursing with water.

Dead deer shot and waiting to be loaded—sodden fur and limp legs.

Thunder. An orange blaze and a trail of smoke in the forest.

The lightning had set fire to the trees.

Reed gave the order to load up the remainder of the cargo and then raced up the hill and into the brush, searching for the rest of the crew.

Jules and Goro.

Theo and Senta.

Pair by pair, he sent them running back to the ship, until the only crew left unaccounted for were Harison and Jigo.

The rain came down in bullets, but it didn't quench the flames. Leaves fell around him like hot fluttering moths while branches withered to embers and ash.

"Jigo!" Smoke burned his throat as he dashed through the tangled bushes. "Harison!"

All around him the trees were alight. He could no longer hear the water—not the rain or the charging of fins through the sea—only the snapping of flames as they gobbled the ancient trees and tender saplings.

He nearly stumbled over Jigo in the chaos. The old man was on the ground, trying to splint his leg with a wet branch. In the firelight, he squinted up at the captain, his eyes red from smoke.

"Fell." He grunted. "This cursed hip."

With quick fingers, the captain tied off the splint. "Where's Harison?"

The old man pointed up the hill with a gnarled finger. "Said he couldn't let 'em all die."

Reed cursed. "Get home. I'll find the kid."

As Jigo hobbled off toward the beach, Reed thrashed deeper into the forest.

The air flickered. Fire leapt from one tree to another, igniting the crowns of leaves. Branches snapped and fell, sending up clouds of sparks.

"Harison!"

"Cap!"

The boy was standing in the center of a clearing, his black curls streaked with ash. In his arms, he held his hat like he was carrying something precious inside. An empty burlap sack was draped over the opening.

Captain Reed grabbed Harison's hand—ignoring the boy's cry of alarm at the sudden movement—and yanked him out of the clearing. The fire licked at their hands and forearms. They raced out of the trees through bursts of smoke and sparks. As they broke from the woods into the open field, lightning slashed across the clouds.

Together, Reed and Harison stumbled through the field. The slope was slick with wet grass, and they slipped and skidded, their feet sliding out from under them. When they reached the beach, the entire island lurched sickeningly beneath them.

Over half the cargo had been loaded, but the waves were pitching and the *Current* was straining at her moorings. The crew rushed over the beach, hauling the water casks and sacks of vegetables on board.

"I remembered what you said," Harison croaked, folding the burlap back from his hat. Four sets of beady eyes gleamed in the shadows, and there was a soft fluttering of feathers.

Birds. Harison had been collecting baby birds. "I couldn't just leave 'em, sir."

The island heaved again. They were loading the cargo as fast as they could, but they weren't fast enough. Even Camey and Greta, unusually silent, did their part. Loading and lashing. Bundling and tying. The shifting of the island grew worse as the fire crept closer.

All of a sudden, they heard the chief mate cry out over the storm: "Time to cut her loose!"

You didn't argue with the mate when it came to the *Current*. They grabbed whatever they could carry and clambered up the grappling lines to the ship.

Reed was the last man aboard. As he hauled

himself over the rail, the ship pitched sideways. The final mooring line broke. They drifted wide, the winds pushing them one way, the turtle swimming another, tipping sideways in the waves to quench the fire at its back.

The captain squinted into the rain. The deck was chaos. Some of the crew were on the yards, furling the sails; some of them, down below. Had they all made it?

As if in answer, the mate appeared at his side. Water ran into his cloudy gray eyes, and when he spoke, his voice was hollow: "Jigo isn't here."

Reed flung himself against the rail, searching the waves for signs of his crewman. The last time he'd seen Jigo, the old man had been a bent silhouette limping into the flaming brush. He was supposed to have made it back. He was supposed to be here.

But he wasn't.

The island was already disappearing into the rain, the skeletons of trees smoking against the sky. In the water, the lost animals paddled their little paws and searched for land, but one by one, they went under.

Jigo was out there somewhere. Drowning in the water or stranded on the island. Maybe he was watching them sail away at that very moment, gut-sick and full of dread, knowing he'd die out there alone, with no one to burn him or remember his name.

Harison was crying. He still held his hat with the four little birds inside.

Reed wiped his eyes. "I saw him. I sent him back to the ship. I *saw* him."

Lightning lit the sky and flashed on the serrated sea, but Jigo wasn't there, and the water revealed nothing.

"She warned me," Reed said.

CHAPTER 23

Assassin on the Ship

I would never leave you behind." Sefia placed the green feather between the pages and closed the book.

Archer prodded the edge of his scar. In the lantern light, a smile passed across his face like a wisp of smoke.

It was still a couple hours before dawn and the air was cold and calm, filled with the dreams of sleeping men. Soon, the cook would send the ship's boy to the hold to fetch a link of sausage or a slab of pork. His approach meant that it was time for Sefia and Archer to put out the lamp, pack themselves back into the crate, and will themselves to sleep until night came again. They had lived this way for five days and were determined to continue doing so for as long as they could. Neither of them complained. It was better than death or slavery.

Archer pulled the door of the crate into place and curled up. In the close space, they lay face-to-face, knees touching.

Sefia ran her hands along the edges of the book, fingering

the leaves that protruded from the pages, until she found the soft blade of the feather Archer had given her. A green feather, like the one Harison had picked up on the floating island, for his mother.

Her own mother had had no interest in collecting anything of any sort—not shells or buttons or shiny stones. No, her mother loved things that lived. She used to spend long hours in the garden, weeding and sowing, pruning and picking, her neck arched elegantly as a bird's, with her black hair coming loose around her face. She often smelled of damp, rich earth.

Once, when Sefia had asked why she loved gardening so much, her mother had sighed and sat back on her heels. Her shoulders slumped, as if she were tired, though they were only a few hours into the morning. After a while, she answered, "There's enough death in this world. I want to help things grow." For a moment her brown eyes were radiant in their sadness. Then she smiled and brushed Sefia's cheek, smudging her with dirt.

It had been eleven years since she died and sometimes Sefia couldn't remember her face, but she remembered the texture of the needle-fine lines on her mother's hands, the smell of the soil.

She wiped her eyes and smoothed the tip of the feather until it was a sharp point. The book always stirred her up inside, dredging her memories. It brought them back. It made them real.

While her mind wandered, she began to tremble. She was cold; her skin, clammy. Her breath came faster. Something was wrong. Her fingers groped through the darkness; her legs twitched. Everything inside her was screaming, *Run! Run! Run!* All of a sudden she felt small and afraid.

Because she could smell the spiteful scent of hot metal.

A bright, tangy smell that buzzed between her teeth. She saw flashes of the day Nin was taken: The woman in black. The shadow of a voice. Nin staring at her through the leaves.

No, she told herself. *I am not there. I am on a ship. I am with Archer. I can feel him next to me. I am with Archer.* As the flashes faded inside her, she opened her eyes and sat up.

Archer was awake too, sitting upright, tense and alert. But he didn't know. He hadn't been there. She thrust the book into her pack and shoved past him into the hold. The smell was worse. It made her head ache. The yellow light of a lantern flickered on the crossbeams. On the stairs, someone was muttering, "If it's not butter, it's bacon." The ship's boy. "Bacon, bacon, bacon."

Couldn't he smell it? Couldn't he sense it? Someone was going to die.

But she could stop it. She had to try.

Drawing her knife, Sefia dashed out from between the crates in time to see the ship's boy at the foot of the stairs, holding a lantern, his mouth opening as he saw her appear, and then the black shape behind him, the flash of a blade.

"No!" she screamed.

The ship's boy turned—too late. A strangled cry, cut off at the end. Blood spurted onto the floor.

He crumpled like a piece of paper.

Behind him on the steps was the woman in black.

The curved sword.

The cratered face.

The ugly dishwater eyes.

Her.

The woman smiled in recognition and opened her arms wide, beckoning to Sefia with her gloved left hand.

Sefia tightened her grip on the knife. *Do it,* she told herself. *For Nin.*

But while she hesitated, the ship's boy lay on the floor clutching the side of his neck, red leaking from between his fingers like water from a broken dam.

Kill or die.

Him or her.

A choice you couldn't unmake.

Sefia fell to her knees and pulled the bandanna from her hair, pressing it to the boy's neck. He clasped at her hands and gulped. His eyes were wide and scared.

Archer lunged past her, drawing his knife. He almost reached the woman, but her blade flicked out. He jumped back, bleeding.

Sefia could hear them moving, the quick impacts of their arms and hands. But the knives made no sound. Blood pooled through the cloth, between her fingers. "I'm Sefia," she said. His mouth moved, but no sound came out. The blood came quicker. "Shh," she said, "it's okay. I'm here with you."

The tempo of the fight changed. She glanced up. Among the stacks of crates and kegs, the movement of it was so fast it looked like a dance, a complicated quickstep of feints and counters, with the blades flickering like sparks between them.

There was a shout from the landing above, something unintelligible, a kind of animal cry filled with anger and fear, and then someone was kneeling beside her. He smelled like spices and cooking grease. "Press hard, girl," he said. The man ripped off his apron and bundled it under her hands. "Harder."

She was pressing so hard she was afraid she might strangle the boy, but the blood was coming up too fast.

"He needs the doc. Stay with him." Then the man was gone. Red seeped into the apron. She pressed harder.

"It's okay," she said, looking deep into his glassy, fearful eyes. She could see golden ripples of light pooling around him. They dripped from the corners of his eyes onto his cheeks, leaked through the folds of cloth at his neck. She blinked and began to skim through the chapters of his life. The churning spirals of memory made her sick, but that didn't matter. What mattered was that someone knew him, understood him, was with him.

His childhood flashed past her, his adolescence in the Paradise Islands sailing skiffs and spear hunting with his friends, the birds whistling on his mother's porch, and then—

She knew who he was.

For a second she wondered if she'd slipped into the book, if she and Archer were now bound for the edge of the world and the strange starving days ahead.

She shook her head.

The ship's boy was older than he was in the book, but he had the same black curls, the same wide-set puppy-dog eyes. But this was not the book. This was real. And he was dying. And then she saw something darker, colder, with red lights blinking in the deep. It loomed up out of his life like the shadow of a building falling over you in the cold afternoon—a building you do not want to enter, though you know you must. The boy was afraid. And she was afraid for him, afraid of the dark and the cold and the red lights. She blinked and came out of her vision gasping.

The ship's boy stared up at her. The corners of his eyes were wet.

"Don't die." She brought her mouth close to his ear and willed the blood to stop streaming out of him, to turn back, to stay inside him where it belonged. "Don't die, Harison." Then even his blood was golden and glowing, filled with little pinpoints of light, like stars, slowing down, trickling out of him like the turn of constellations across the sky. She watched each bead of light fall leisurely out of him, with aching slowness. Each bead of his life.

• • •

Across the hold, Archer slashed at the woman's face, his knife flickering in the lantern light. The woman deftly stepped aside and cut him across the back of the arm. He retreated. His arm stung. His head was buzzing with the hot smell of metal. The lowest deck was packed with cargo, forming narrow walkways in the hold. Not much room to maneuver. Easy to get trapped.

Then the woman was attacking, slashing, stabbing, Archer just barely evading the seeking blade. It whispered past his skin.

They parted.

The woman waited, her knife hooked downward, her gloved left hand raised to protect her neck.

He attacked again, stabbing this time, but she trapped his

wrist with her knife and pinned his arm, slashing him once across the abdomen. Blood spilled out of him.

He pulled, pivoting away, his wrist twisting in her grasp. His blade flashed out, cut into her skin. And then they were facing off again. The black sleeve of her blouse was torn. He checked his arm, the gash across his stomach. Twice. She had cut him twice. He couldn't be sure, but it felt like a long time since anyone had done that.

The woman's pale gaze flicked past him to the crate where he and Sefia had been hiding. She wanted the book. He flipped the knife in his hands, copying her, holding it like an ice pick. He wouldn't let her past him. In the background was the reassuring lull of Sefia's voice. "Shh," she was saying, "it's okay. I'm here with you."

But it wasn't okay. He recognized a wound like that when he saw it. The boy wasn't going to make it.

The woman attacked. But just as she had done to him, he hooked the dull edge of his knife over her wrist, trapping her arm, and twisted. Her eyes widened. He got in a slash across her stomach before she bounded out of his reach again.

Her mouth split open, revealing small white teeth. She was laughing: a soft, breathy "Ha-ha-ha . . ." like puffs of smoke.

Then they were engaged, knives flicking in and out, parrying, dodging, opening little slits on each other's hands and arms and legs. It was the quickest fight he had ever been in; each attack came faster than he could think, and it was only the swiftness in his limbs that allowed him to keep up with her.

They paused, facing each other, breathing hard. How long

had it been? Minutes? A few seconds? Someone else came running down the steps, footfalls like hammers. "Press hard, girl," came a gruff voice. "Harder."

The woman ran in again, slashing sideways at his knife hand. He parried, but the next attack didn't come from her blade. She brought her gloved fist crashing into his rib cage. He had expected the blow, but he didn't expect it to knock him to his knees. Something broke. The wind went out of him. He lashed out with the knife as he hit the ground. The woman danced out of reach. The floor spun beneath him. He'd never been hit so hard. He pushed himself to his feet.

The woman flexed her fingers; the leather glove creaked.

She rushed forward, attacking again, furious and impatient. A slash nearly got his knife hand as he stepped backward. Another almost took out his leg. His back hit something hard and unmoving. Barrels. He had been driven up against them by her attack. Then her gloved fist was coming at him and he knew if it struck him the bones in his face would shatter. He ducked. A barrel splintered behind him. A great crashing sound filled the bowels of the ship. For a second her entire left side was exposed. He slashed at her neck. The tip of his knife nicked her throat, but she didn't retreat. She attacked again. And again. And again.

He barely had enough time to react. The injury to his ribs slowed him down. She kept landing her knife. He lost count of how many times she'd cut him.

Again.

And again.

And again.

She was so fast he didn't realize until too late that she'd dis-
armed him. His knife clattered to the floor. She could have finished him off then, but the entire ship was waking up. Time was
running out. Soon the rest of the crew would swarm belowdecks
and then it wouldn't matter how fast she was. There would be
too many.

He got one good look at her face; she was bleeding, bright
red spilling from her brow down into her eyes. And then she
was running, leaping up the steps, disappearing into the shadows of the deck above.

He grabbed the knife and leapt after her—over the boy's unmoving body and up the steps. Maybe Sefia called after him. He
didn't hear.

There was a shout above him, but he couldn't identify the
words. He reached the lower deck. Through the slats of the
stairs he saw a huge figure charging toward the woman in black.
She raised her knife arm. She was going to attack. Archer recognized the downward slash of her arm.

His knife was solid and well-balanced in his hand. *Good for
throwing.*

He flung the knife.

It sank into her forearm, mid-swing, lodging deep in the
muscle. She didn't scream.

In the second it took him to dash around the hatchway, she
pulled the knife from her arm and struck at the big man, who
staggered back. She darted past him into the open air.

Archer paused to grab the man by the forearm and haul him

to his feet, and then he leapt up the steps to the main deck, where he got his first breath of fresh air in days. It was cold, and the ship was wreathed in fog. Men swarmed out of the forecastle. Their cries were sharp in the night.

The woman in black drew a sword. The scent of metal fanned out as it hissed through the cold air. He gagged. The steel smelled of blood. The sword swung outward in a copper-colored arc, daring him to approach.

He heard the shot almost as soon as he saw the flash behind her. The woman spun. He had never seen anyone react so fast. Blood fountained from her shoulder, but she was still on her feet. The shot would have killed her if she hadn't twisted out of the way.

Then, in one smooth movement, she flung herself over the rails of the ship. Arms out, her body poised like a diving bird, she was just a shadow against the swirling mist.

There was another shot. It hit her on the way down, right through the head. Her arms and legs went limp, and she plummeted into the water like a stone.

Silence. A tall, lean figure crossed the deck, holding up a smoking gun. The man paused by the rail, looking down into the water, but there was only the murmuring of waves on the hull.

Even in the dim light, Archer recognized the weapon: all black, with engravings of scales and dull gold inlay. The Executioner. A cursed weapon. Over the years the Executioner had traded hands so many times no one remembered who had owned it first. But everyone knew who owned it now.

Archer swayed on his feet, watching the man come closer.

Now the Executioner belonged to Cannek Reed, captain of the *Current of Faith.*

Archer felt the crew members turn on him. They hadn't put their weapons down. Eleven of them, and him alone. Didn't they recognize him? Didn't they know him from the pier? He wished Sefia were there. She'd be able to explain it all. He was keenly aware of his bleeding, the way his skin had been opened up by the woman's knife. He poised for a fight.

"Lay off," someone said. The big man Archer had helped on the stairs pushed through the ring of sailors—Horse, the ship's carpenter. "The kid saved my life."

They hesitated, but Archer did not relax. His gaze flicked over them, counting weapons, checking for weaknesses.

Captain Reed looked over Archer's shoulder at the chief mate, who stood beyond the circle of the crew. "Well?" he asked.

The mate nodded. "Horse has a nose for these things. There's a girl belowdecks too . . . with Cooky and the doc." He sighed. "Harison's dead. Knifed in the throat."

The crew began muttering and Archer raised his hands defensively, but Reed silenced them. He still held the Executioner. "This ain't the first time we've had trouble on our own ship, and it ain't gonna be the last. Horse, take the boy to the great cabin."

Archer felt the big man's hand on the crook of his arm, but he tugged away. The captain was giving orders so rapidly that Archer, dizzy with blood loss, was having a difficult time following, but he fought off light-headedness until he heard him mention Sefia.

"—fetch the girl and bring her to the cabin too."

Archer started forward, blinking rapidly to clear his vision. His legs wouldn't seem to carry him. But he wasn't going to let them take her.

"Easy, kid." Horse put his hand on Archer's shoulder.

The rest of the crew had dispersed. Reed came up to Archer then, walking softly, keeping his distance. The Executioner seemed to absorb all the light that struck it, like a shadow in the captain's hand. "I remember you," he murmured. "I don't know how you got on my ship or what you're doin' here, but best not stir up any trouble, if you and the girl want to get through this alive."

Archer nodded and let Horse take him by the elbow, leading him across the main deck. He got one last glimpse of the sky before the door closed behind him.

CHAPTER 24

As Blind as Ever

As the chief mate and the other members of the larboard watch descended the main hatchway to the lowest level of the ship, the hold filled with the thudding of footsteps and the creaking of lamp hinges. While the men searched for signs of the stowaways, the mate wandered among the stores, checking the insides of a crate, lifting the lid on a barrel. Though he was blind, he could tell the slabs of salted meat had small chunks carved out of their undersides, and some of the oldest and hardest fruit was missing—not so much that you'd notice, but enough to confirm that the kids from Black Boar Pier had been hiding there since they'd left Epidram.

It troubled him. With his acute sense of the ship's inner workings, he should have been able to sniff out two stowaways as soon as they boarded. With the rats taking bits of their stores every day, it was easy to hide a little thievery here and there, but hiding two people altogether—it had never been done. Not on the *Current*.

Jules had found something near the center of the hold. The chief mate knew it the moment her shoulders straightened and her cheeks warmed with a sense of satisfaction. Before she'd even called out, "Found it, sir," he was already making his way toward her.

The mate wound expertly through the stacks of foodstuffs and spare parts until he reached Jules. The others gathered around.

"Well?" he demanded. "Where is it?"

Jules hesitated. That was unusual. With her counterpart on the starboard watch, Theo, she led chanties while the crew raised the sails, while they sweated and heaved at the capstans. She was reliable and decisive in a position where rhythm mattered most. She rarely hesitated.

There was an indistinct murmur from the other sailors.

They were surprised.

The mate must have been joking.

"Sir?" she asked. Her ordinarily strong voice wavered like silk in water. "It's right in front of you."

The mate had inherited the ability to communicate with the trees from his grandmother's grove in Everica. Near the end of the Rock-and-River Wars, when the Everican provinces fought each other for land and resources, the lumber from the grove had been used to build a sleek ship with a tree for a figurehead. Now the timbers of the *Current* told him what was happening on the ship so clearly that he often forgot he no longer had the use of his eyes. But now, for the first time in a long time, he remembered that he was blind—well and truly blind. And from the sounds of their voices, the crew had remembered it too.

Aware of the growing sense of alarm in Jules and the others, the mate reached out and took a few halting steps, adopting the bent shuffle he'd never thought he'd have to use again. He felt old, hands groping at the air, feet sliding across the floor until his fingertips brushed the hard edge of a crate.

"Well, I'll be—" He ran his hands over it, not entirely convinced it was there at all.

But his inability to see it was not the cause of the deep disquiet within him. Something even more troubling was inside.

"Jules, is there anything peculiar about the contents of this crate?"

Jules's surprise flitted across her broad face like a bat at dusk. "No, sir," she said, reaching inside.

The mate gulped. Inside the crate, Jules's strong tattooed arm had completely vanished. That must have been how the stowaways had escaped his notice; everything inside it was invisible too. But only to him.

"Just packs and some bedding." Jules stood, pulling two packs from the crate. To the mate they seemed to have materialized out of thin air.

A wave of vertigo struck him. His knees felt weak. The smaller pack, more worn than the other, dangled from Jules's hand like offal. Something inside it made him feel dizzy and small—very, very small—a diminutive speck no bigger or more significant than a mote of dust. It reeked of magic.

He scooped both packs out of Jules's grasp. Though it was

lighter than he expected, the smaller pack gave the impression of being heavy and unwieldy, like a brimming bucket of water in danger of overflowing.

"Keep searching," he said, heading for the stairs. "Make sure there aren't any more surprises down here."

The others stared after him, wondering what was wrong.

Why he had shuddered when Jules took out the packs.

Why he was afraid.

"And bring up that crate," he called over his shoulder. "The captain will want to see it too."

He found Reed on deck with the starboard watch, prowling the perimeter of the ship. The night air was cool and thick with moisture.

"Can't see a stone's throw in this fog," the captain said as he approached. The man hefted the Executioner in his hand and continued pacing. "You find out where them kids was hidin' all this time?"

The mate trailed one hand over the rail as he walked. The curve of the wood grounded him to the ship, and his senses spread to the timbers and the sails and the running lines, down to the sick bay where Cooky stood vigil over Harison's body, and up to the crow's nest where Aly crouched, peering into the cold.

The packs hung loosely from his other hand. He told Reed what he had found.

"Dangerous?" the captain asked.

"More strange than dangerous." With his keen senses, he riffled through the contents of the packs without opening them, carefully avoiding the thing at the bottom of the smaller one.

Reed eyed the packs. "Never thought we'd see them kids again, after the brushup on Black Boar. When we interrogate 'em, put the packs on the floor," he said. "I wanna see how they react."

Jules and the others brought the crate from the hold and heaved it onto the main deck before the mate dismissed them. Taking one of the lanterns from a nearby sconce, Reed approached the crate cautiously—or at least the mate thought he was approaching it. He made a face, hating his inability to sense where it was.

The captain chuckled at his discomfiture and extended his hands flat into the air. "I never thought I'd see the day you'd be blindsided by something on the *Current.*"

"Guess it's up to you, then," the mate answered sourly. "Be my eyes."

Reed laughed softly and got on his hands and knees, disappearing up to his waist. The mate grimaced, sensing only half of the captain's body, unattached to a torso but still moving, still alive. The rest of him reappeared a few minutes later, removing a couple blankets, which he folded neatly and placed aside. Then he stood and bent at the waist as if he were bowing.

He set the lantern on top of the crate—to the mate it seemed to float eerily in midair—and peered at one of the corners. He must have seen something—and whatever it was drained all the humor from him. He tapped his chest and stood upright again.

"Captain?"

"C'mere," Reed said. As the mate approached, the captain took his hand and drew his fingers to the corner of the crate.

Scratches. The splintery carvings bit into his skin, but he could not make sense of them.

"Means nothing to me," the mate said, "but I don't like it."

The captain straightened and looked toward the stern, where the stowaways were waiting in the great cabin with Doc and Horse. He spun the cylinder of his revolver with his thumb over and over—a sound like chattering teeth.

Reed hadn't been this angry in a long time. It emanated from him like currents of heat, so loud and blistering that without even probing him, the chief mate could sense flashes of pain in his chest, visions of black and amber liquid, shame. The mate winced but didn't pry any further.

"What're you planning on doing with them?" he asked.

Reed didn't answer.

In the silence, Cooky poked his head out of the main hatch. His narrow eyes were puffy with crying and as he sniffled, dozens of rings tinkled along the lobes of his ears. "Cap," he said, walking toward them. His voice was thick and wet. As he came up to the rail, he rubbed his nose. "I'm glad I caught you."

In the face of Cooky's grief, Reed shook himself, and the edge of his anger dulled. "How're you doin', Cooky?"

The man rubbed his hand over his smooth scalp. "I'm doin' all right, Cap, thanks. Doc's tendin' to the boy now, but she wanted me to tell you somethin' before you went in there." He sniffed. "She said . . . she was surprised Harison lasted long enough for me to fetch her. I guess with wounds like that, most folks bleed out in a few minutes. She said it was mighty peculiar."

Now that was something. Doc had seen her share of battle wounds and mystical ailments. She wouldn't have mentioned it unless it was worth noting. Somehow, the girl had given Harison a few extra minutes, though it hadn't been enough to save him.

Reed nodded curtly. "Thank you, Cooky."

The cook shifted on his feet and rubbed his nose. "Uh, one more thing, Cap?"

"Yeah?"

"Go easy on 'em, would you? They seem like good kids."

The captain pulled the brim of his hat low over his eyes. "That's what I thought too, when we rescued 'em from Hatchet. But then they ended up stealing onto my ship."

"Yes, Cap."

As the cook trudged away, Reed shook his head. "I don't like killin' kids . . . but we could strand 'em. There's a coupla islands out here. They might get picked up."

The islands between Oxscini and Jahara were bare sand-swept places with little cover and no freshwater. "Picked up by whom? Dimarion's behind us somewhere. You know what he'll do to them if he finds them." The mate grimaced. "Aren't you even going to question them first?"

"'Course I am. I got too many questions that need answerin'." His anger burst from him again in hot sparks, though the only outward sign was the tightening of his fingers on the Executioner. "One way or another."

CHAPTER 25

A Story to Save Your Life

While Archer lay on the cabin's long table with the tattered remains of his shirt sheared away, Sefia watched Doc tend to his wounds. The woman's brown eyes swooped over his body, searching out injuries like an owl hunting in the night. Then her hands flicked open the metal fastenings on her black bag and began plucking out clear bottles of liquid, bandages, gleaming silver scissors, forceps, curved needles, and thread. She made each suture perfectly—one neat stitch after another—until they were lined up across Archer's wounds like sharp black letters, as if every set of stitches was a healing word Doc had written to keep his skin together.

There was a crash outside as a heavy wooden object hit the deck. The floorboards rumbled.

Sefia started up, but Archer caught her hand and held it fast. He stared at her, pleading with her to stay. There was so much blood—on the table, on the floor, on his face and hands and chest—and when he moved, the cuts on his arms and legs opened up like narrow red eyes. She sank back onto the bench.

There had been no word on where the woman in black had come from, and no word on whether others would follow her. How had she found them in the first place? How had she known Sefia even existed? There was only one—

"So you were with him—Harison—when he went?" A voice startled her out of her thoughts. At the end of the table, Horse, the ship's carpenter, looked up from the enormous flask cradled in his shovel-like hands. He'd drawn his yellow bandanna low over his brows.

"Yeah," Sefia murmured. "I talked to him."

Tying off a tidy row of sutures, Doc made a small *hmm* sound.

Horse wiped his cheeks. When he looked up again, his eyes were bright with tears. "I'm glad you were with him, kid."

Sefia nodded . . . more because she had to than because she wanted to. It was hard to be glad when she'd watched someone die. When he'd been crying and breathing raggedly in her arms one second and then . . . not.

And then . . .

. . . nothing.

Like Palo Kanta.

"It don't make no sense, though," Horse added, turning the flask in his palm. "Why was that woman in the hold in the first place? There ain't nothin' of value down there."

Sefia and Archer exchanged glances. *They* had been down there. The *book* had been down there. She looked toward the

258

door again. It might still be hidden in their crate, but with all that had happened, it wouldn't remain hidden for long.

Archer's hand clinched around hers, his face contorting, as Doc began stitching a wound on his right hand. He grimaced as she raised the edge of the cut with a pair of forceps.

"It's not too late for that drink," she said, though she didn't stop suturing.

He pressed his lips together.

"Suit yourself."

Slumped in his chair, Horse let out a weak chuckle and took a long pull from his flask. "Harison never liked drinkin' much either, not after the first time." He didn't seem to expect a response, so Sefia kept silent.

The ship's carpenter was just as she'd imagined him: the round mountains of his shoulders; the brown, sun-lined face and the bandanna tied around his forehead; the splintery abused hands spotted with scars and pitch. He even smelled right—like oakum and wood shavings.

As if sensing her watching him, Horse looked up, bleary-eyed. "What?"

Sefia felt her cheeks go hot. "This is really the *Current of Faith*, isn't it?" she asked. "You and Doc . . . everyone . . . you're all really here?"

"For now," Horse murmured.

She looked around the room. It was exactly as the book described it, down to the way everything came in even numbers: the hooks on the door, the chairs, the cabinets on the walls. The glass cases contained dozens of keepsakes: a ruby the size of a man's fist, a wedge of gold shaped like a sandwich, even the

Thunder Gong she'd read about in the book. She felt like she'd been dropped onto the page, among the letters, or like the book had somehow drawn the *Current* to them, as if it were all preordained. She swayed.

Archer blinked at her, and the corners of his mouth turned upward, dimpling the skin of his cheek. *They* were here, and they were still together.

At his forearm, Doc's hands wove in and out of each other, swift and silent as shadows.

"Can't believe I didn't see it before." Horse coughed. "You're the kids from Black Boar."

"You were on the pier?"

Horse bobbed his huge head a few times. "Funny little world, ain't it?"

"Yeah," she said faintly. Her gaze was again drawn to the objects on the shelves: A rusty iron key. A black box inlaid with ivory. A necklace, its square blue sapphires girdled by glittering diamonds coated in dust, except where a few fingerprints allowed the light to strike through. She blinked, and in her vision she caught glimpses of Captain Reed fingering the necklace. A cloud of ash. And the most beautiful woman she had ever seen, wearing the necklace like a collar, gaining eternal youth. That was what the necklace did. And if you were beautiful, well . . . it let you keep that too. No matter how old she was, the woman was always surrounded: by men, by flowers, by laughter, by children . . . and then by disease, by screams, and smoke.

"The Cursed Diamonds of Lady Delune." Closing her eyes, Sefia rubbed her aching temples.

"As the story goes, the captain was the only man to ever get her out of those diamonds. She turned to dust as soon as he'd unhooked it." Horse sighed. "I reckon that's what she wanted, in the end. The Lady didn't live a very happy life."

Sefia thought of the woman from her vision: Though she never grew older, she became colder and colder as the years passed, as her parents and husbands and children and grand-children were struck down by plagues and fires and cart acci-dents and suicides and withering old age.

"There's more to life than being young and beautiful . . . or happy, for that matter." Sefia thought of her own life. She wasn't living to be *happy*. It had been a long time since she'd wanted something as simple as *happiness*.

"Ain't that the truth, kid."

"My name is Sefia," she corrected him.

Horse nodded and sipped at his flask. "Right. Sefia. You're quite the pair, the two of you. I hope—"

The door swung open, and cold air flooded the great cabin, making Sefia shiver. Horse sat up straight, tucking away the flask as the chief mate entered, dangling their packs from one hand. Sefia looked eagerly for the familiar rectangle of the book and was relieved to see its outline straining against the leather. The mate dumped their packs casually in the center of the floor, but she noticed the way his arm jerked back, as if he could not wait to be rid of them. She resisted the urge to gather her pack up in her arms.

Then the captain entered. She recognized him by his bright blue eyes, his air of command, and the black gun he held in one hand. She had been excited to see him—the real Captain Reed!—but at the sight of him her excitement congealed in her stomach. He was angry. His anger seethed under his skin and behind his teeth. This was not the Reed from the stories.

"What's the damage?" he asked.

Archer pushed himself into a sitting position, wincing a little. The doctor sighed and began stitching a deep cut on Archer's shoulder. "Eleven wounds total, six needing stitches, two broken ribs. I think even you'd be proud, Captain."

Reed ignored the humor in the doctor's voice. "And the girl?"

Sefia spoke up for herself. "Fine, sir. Archer did the fighting, not me."

The captain stared at her for a long moment—long enough for her to wish she could swallow her words and disappear into the floorboards—but she did not look away.

"Horse?"

The big carpenter waved him off with a meaty hand. "Nothin' more than a bruised backside, Cap," he said.

Reed jerked his head toward the door. "Get goin', then."

Horse stood instantly, though he winked at Sefia. As he passed the captain, he leaned over and whispered, just loudly enough for her to hear: "They're good kids, Cap. If it comes down to it, you can count on my eatin' a bit less and workin' a bit more. I'll even kick in my wages if it comes to that."

Sefia smiled faintly.

If the captain was surprised, he gave no sign, and Horse put his large hand on the doc's shoulder, where she laid her dark cheek against him as she continued stitching Archer's wounds.

A touch so small that communicated so much.

He squeezed her shoulder once and withdrew, slipping out the door into the cool night air.

The captain sat down in the chair Horse had occupied and placed his black revolver on the table. Sefia watched it warily. While the chief mate stood behind them, Reed unrolled a leather packet and took out a set of tools, lining them up in neat rows. Without a word, he began cleaning his gun, opening it up and removing the bullets, checking the cylinder. He attached a small square of cloth to the end of a metal stick and began jabbing it down the barrel and through the chambers—eight times. It was clear that no one was going to speak until the doctor had left, so Sefia simply watched.

The black gun was beautiful, all gold inlay and ebony carved like dragon scales, but up close she could see how damaged it was: pitted and scratched, flecked with age and long-forgotten acts of violence. The entire length of the grip was cracked, with a deep seam visible where it had been glued back together.

She narrowed her eyes, feeling for the lights that simmered beneath the physical world, and then she blinked, slipping into her Vision, which she'd begun thinking of as having a capital V. As Reed began scrubbing the Executioner with a small brush, the history of the black gun rushed over her.

A flurry of gunshots, a spray of blood, and the wet *crack* of a body hitting the water. Then her Vision shifted, and she saw the former captain of the *Current*, a man with a kind face and a bulbous nose, put the Executioner to his temple.

An explosion—fire and flesh and bone.

The black gun hit the deck, its grip fracturing on impact.

Moments later, Reed heaved himself onto the deck, dripping with seawater that made his shirt cling to his chest, revealing the landscape of musculature and black ink beneath. The ocean puddled at his feet as he reached for the broken gun.

She gulped and sat back, blinking rapidly. Her gaze darted once to the packs.

The doctor finished bandaging Archer's wounds and snapped her black bag closed. Standing, she pushed her glasses higher on the flat bridge of her nose and focused on the captain. "Cooky told you?" she asked.

Reed flicked his eyes at Sefia and nodded.

What had Cooky said? Did he blame her for Harison's death? Because she hadn't pressed hard enough, hadn't stopped enough of the blood? There had been so much blood, going so fast. She chewed the inside of her lip.

The doctor nodded at Archer, then at her. Sefia wanted to thank her, but the stony silence of the room was forbidding, so she only nodded back. The doctor left the room, and then Sefia and Archer were alone between Captain Reed and the chief mate.

Reed finished wiping down the Executioner and began applying drops of oil to its moving parts, working the action a few times. He did everything in even numbers, just as the legends said. Then he rolled up the cleaning kit, set the gun on the table, and lined up the remaining rounds in a neat row of four.

"I remember you two from the dock," he said, tracing two interconnected circles on the tabletop, his finger leading into one and out of the other, over and over. "Didn't expect to see you again, though."

"No, sir," she said.

"You know who I am and what ship you're on?"

Sefia nodded.

"Then you know how peculiar it is for us to see intruders here. Tonight, I caught three of you, and one of my crew died. Now, that raises some questions. Dependin' on how you answer 'em, I might kill you, or if I'm feelin' lenient, drop you on a deserted island to get picked up by the next ship that comes by. You understand?"

Sefia looked back over her shoulder, and the mate turned his cloudy eyes on her. With a start, she saw the gray in them was from scarring: punctured places in his eyes that had healed over time. She swallowed. All the stories said the mate could sniff out lies like a bloodhound. She'd have to tell the truth. A truth that wouldn't get her and Archer killed.

Then she looked at Archer, who was sitting beside her, cradling her hand in his bandaged one.

He nodded, his golden eyes never leaving hers.

Whatever she said next, it was going to determine whether they lived or died. He had kept them alive on Black Boar Pier, and now it was her turn. She took a deep shuddering breath and looked back at Reed.

"We understand."

The captain spun the cylinder of the Executioner once, then fired his first question: "Who are you?"

"I'm Sefia and this is Archer," she answered.

"He don't answer for himself?"

She glanced at Archer, who shook his head. "He can't speak," she said. "I don't think he remembers how."

Reed's gaze flicked over her shoulder to the mate, who must have nodded. "How'd you get on my ship?" he asked.

"We've been here since Epidram, when we accidentally stowed away in one of your crates."

"Accidentally?"

"We didn't know it was yours. We just needed a place to hide."

"How many more of you are out there?"

She shook her head, confused. "It's just us, sir."

"How did Harison die?"

"The woman knifed him in the throat. I tried . . ." Tears rose in her eyes and she rubbed them away. But she couldn't help thinking of the way he had gone so still. "I tried to save him, but by the time the doc came, he was already dead."

"Who was the woman?"

Sefia went cold. Her hands clenched into fists. "I don't know. But she kidnapped my aunt." She didn't mention the scent of metal, or how the air had been laced with it the day her father died.

"What for?"

Her gaze flicked to her pack. Should she tell them about the book? It would be worse to be caught in a lie.

"She wanted the book." Sefia felt the color drain from her face. The only person who knew she had the book was Nin. Did that mean . . . She thrust the thought away immediately.

"What's a buck?" Captain Reed's voice interrupted her thoughts.

"A *book*. It's . . . it's this thing I have." Sefia grabbed her pack from the floor and began rummaging around inside it, her fingers groping for the shape of the book. She pulled it out; after the bewildering events of the past hour and the sudden intersection of her journey and the *Current*'s, it felt solid and familiar in her hands. It made her feel real. As she folded back the leather wrapping, the chief mate grunted behind her, like he'd been punched in the stomach. Archer turned, and Reed frowned at him, but no one said anything.

"This is a book."

She held it out to the captain and in one swift movement he was on his feet, hand outstretched, fingertip brushing the edge of the cover.

But he didn't take it. He looked at it suspiciously for a moment before unhooking the clasps and lifting the cover—as if it were a box and he were expecting to peer inside at whatever magical object it contained—

Reed turned on her. Before she could even react, the Executioner was pointed between her eyes.

Archer shoved her out of the way. The book flew from her hands, pages splayed, bookmarks scattering. She hit the floor. Behind them, the chief mate had drawn on Archer. The boy froze.

Sefia sat up, rubbing her elbow. Only three rounds remained on the table. The captain had loaded and cocked the weapon in less than a second. "Archer, don't," she said. Then, to Reed: "It's not dangerous. It won't hurt you."

The chief mate shifted. "The boy saved Horse," he said.

Captain Reed set the Executioner back on the table and sat down again. "That's why he's still breathin'."

Archer bent down to help Sefia to her feet, but she

motioned for him to sit. She began collecting her bookmarks from the floor: the green feather, the pressed leaves. She would never be able to find her place again now—all the stories she had been reading were lost among the infinite pages. Gingerly, she gathered the bookmarks into the book and put it on the table.

"Why did you do that?" She studied his face, the lines of confusion and anger. He didn't like what he'd seen. Distrusted it, maybe even feared it.

Reed scratched his chest. "What are those marks?"

"Words."

"Words are things you speak, not things you see."

"These are words too. Just . . . in a different form."

Reed narrowed his eyes. "What's so special about them?"

"I don't know."

The mate made a small movement behind her.

"That's the last time you lie to me." This time the captain didn't pull his weapon on her. Instead, he slid the remaining three rounds into the empty chambers and filled the rest from a pocket of his cleaning kit. He flipped the cylinder back into place and holstered the weapon. She realized why he had been cleaning it: he could only clean it after he'd killed, because every time the Executioner came out, someone died. At the same time, she understood that if he drew on her again, he was going to kill her.

"I mean—" She fumbled the words. "I don't fully understand it yet, but there's something magical about them. I can see things . . ."

"Like the mate?"

"No, not exactly." She tilted her head, thinking. "Or . . .
maybe? I can tell where something's been, who had it. That sort
of thing."

"And this magic is what hid you from the mate?"

"I don't know. We spent most of our time in the crate. We
tried not to make much noise."

Reed waved her theory off. "He shoulda been able to sense
you either way." He eyed the book. "So this is what that woman
wanted, huh?"

She traced the ⊖ on the cover. "Yes." The word was barely
more than a whisper.

"Why?"

"I think my parents were protecting it from her."

"Why?"

"I don't know. I didn't even know they had it until I was
nine . . . when my father was killed." She continued tracing the
symbol. Answers. Redemption. Revenge.

"By that woman?"

Sefia shrugged, though she didn't have the courage to look
up, to admit that she had failed again. If the woman in black
had found her because Nin had revealed her existence, Nin
might be dead already. Sefia might be too late. She balled her
fists and dug her nails into her palm, wanting the pain, wanting some punishment, wanting something to be different because she could never do what had to be done. "I think so," she
whispered.

"And how does Hatchet figure in to all this?"

She studied her palms, the four perfect crescents in her flesh.
"He wanted Archer, and I . . . It's a long story."

Captain Reed stared over her shoulder at the mate, and after a moment he sighed. "Well, kid, I'll say this: I don't believe you're out to harm me, my ship, or my crew, so I ain't gonna kill you. Now that gives you two options: either I drop you off, like I said earlier, or I take you with us."

Sefia straightened at his words, but Reed was still speaking. "Cooky and Horse've already vouched for you, and Doc . . . Well, I still got questions that need answers. Here's the deal: you tell me your story—who you really are, what you're after, what you know about this buck—and the strength of your story'll determine whether you stay or go. Them terms acceptable to you, little lady?"

Sefia nodded and lifted her chin. A story to save their lives. She could tell a story. She could at least do that. "My name is Sefia," she began.

The Place of the Fleshless

In Kelanna, when you die, they put your body on a floating barge. They place you on a pile of logs and blackrock, dry brush and kindling, and they send you burning onto the ocean.

They don't light candles. They don't burn fragrant sticks of incense or stacks of paper to send you on your way. They don't put coins over your eyes so that you will be able to pay the ferryman. They don't believe in a ferryman. In Kelanna, there is no afterlife to ferry you to.

In Kelanna, when you die, you're gone. They don't believe in souls. They don't believe in ghosts. They don't believe in calming spirits that walk by your side after your friend or your sister or your father has died. They don't believe you get messages from the dead. The dead no longer exist.

In Kelanna, when you die, they don't say prayers for you, for they have no heaven and no gods to pray to. There is no reincarnation; you will not return. Without a body, you are nothing anymore, except for a story.

In Kelanna, when they mourn, they tell stories—as if the stories will keep you close to them. Believing that if they tell them often enough, for long enough, you won't be forgotten. Hoping that the stories will keep you alive—if only in memory.

But some of them, a sad and hopeful few, talk of a dead sea. In the far west, in the wild waters beyond all the known currents: the place of the fleshless. They say that at night, when the sky is darkest, the waves glitter like rubies. They say that these are the thousand red eyes of the dead—though there are more than a thousand, and they will not always be dead.

• • •

Deep below the surface of the sea, far beyond the warm reach of sunlight, it will be a blind world, with no difference between night and day. There will be no color, no shape, no shadow. They will be suspended in the void, unable to tell if they are fixed or moving because there will be no landmarks for them to recognize. There will be nothing to tell them where they've been or where they are going. They will be alone.

This will be the wild black world at the bottom of the sea, a place meant only for monsters and ghosts.

But then, at last, after endless years of waiting, they will hear the call. They will rise, shooting upward through the darkness like bolts of light. They will come to the deep blue, where the whales sing their sad songs and starving sharks swim for miles in search of prey. They will stream by squid, sea turtles, clouds of shrimp, schools of shimmering fish, and enter the vivid turquoise world just below the surface. The white flashing underside of the sky and the sun striking the water.

Like spears they will burst into the air. They will remember how bright the world is, how the waves sparkle, how the sky is so unforgivingly blue. They will remember the way the wind pulls them, tugs them, scolds, and carves them. And the *sound* of it all: the slap of waves on a wooden hull, the creak of timber, the calls of gulls, the rough salted voices of sailors and the clatter of activity on deck, hammers clanking on distant shores, children laughing, swords crossing, guns firing, people speaking, shouting, singing.

They will have returned.

is this a book

CHAPTER 26

Ships in the Fog

It was past dawn by the time Sefia and Archer were let out of the great cabin. Captain Reed had not said he was going to let them stay on the ship, but there was a funeral to attend to, and some other business the captain and the mate would not discuss. Though the sun had risen, the fog obscured much of the morning light, and to Sefia's sleep-deprived brain, they seemed to be floating in a liminal space between night and day, here and there, reality and fiction. Beside her, Archer yawned and winced, patting his injured ribs.

The rest of the crew had gathered on the main deck, where a makeshift raft loaded with blackrock waited to be lowered into the sea. On top of the pyre, Harison's body lay with a single red feather between his stiff fingers.

For his mother.

"Looks like he's sleepin', don't it?" Horse murmured.

Sefia set her jaw. He looked *vacant*, not like a person but a person-shaped mound of flesh, and whatever had made him Harison, whatever had made him cringe and mutter and laugh, was gone. Her eyes were dry as she watched the fog churn over the gray waters.

As a rule, funerary rites on the sea were quick affairs, and most of the mourning was done in the weeks afterward, as those who knew the deceased told and retold the stories of his life. So there was little ceremony: the tolling of the ship's bell, the torch, and the lowering of the pyre into the sea.

Two crewmen pushed the burning raft away from the ship, and Jules stepped forward, twisting her cap in her hands. Sefia recognized her from the legends about the *Current*: a stalwart sailor with skin like sunlight on honey and arms tattooed with birds and flowers. She was in charge of leading the work songs for the larboard watch, singing out line after line for the rest of the watch to repeat as they hauled sheets or turned the capstan. Her voice was strong and fine as silk, rustling at the edges, and it rose over them as the pyre floated into the fog, fire and black smoke melting into the mist.

> *Soft as an echo, I feel I am fading—*
> *Fading until I am gone.*
> *Still I remain. I am listening and waiting—*
> *Waiting for you to go on.*

> *Once more, once more.*
> *Tell me my story once more.*
> *Swiftly repeat it before I'm forgotten—*
> *Pleading, O tell me, once more.*

Theo, the chanty leader on the starboard watch, added his haunting baritone to the chorus, and one by one, the other sailors joined them, until the song was a tapestry of sounds layered one on top of another in startling seamless harmony. The music made Sefia think of the way a city disappears, smaller and smaller on the horizon, as a ship sails away from it, until it is nothing more than a vague shadow . . . a smudge . . . an imagined point on the wide blue sea.

As the last notes faded, Horse murmured, "You miss a man so much."

And the rest of the crew echoed him.

You miss a man so much.

Then it was over, and the crew dispersed to their watches. Sailors scattered to the forecastle, the galley, the crow's nest. Sefia was handed a steaming mug and a bowl of rice porridge while Archer was whisked to the sick bay. She barely got the chance to tell him it was going to be all right before he'd disappeared belowdecks.

Sefia stumbled up the steps to the quarterdeck, clutching her breakfast. Her crate lay on the deck, its broken side splintered where Archer had shoved it open. Behind it, Captain Reed prowled back and forth at the rail, looking into the mist, then turning around again to stare with equal intensity at the crate. She wondered why it upset him so much. The chief mate simply stood beside it, brushing his fingers against it every so often, as if to reassure himself it was still there.

Hastily, she took a swig of coffee and gobbled down a few spoonfuls of the rice, which was light and creamy and fluffy as clouds, with a hint of ginger and red chunks of sausage. Even a few mouthfuls of Cooky's food warmed her insides, and she instantly felt more awake.

Reed gestured for her to eat faster. She shoveled a few more spoons of porridge into her mouth obediently.

"What can you tell me about this crate?" he asked.

Sefia swallowed. The wooden box was stamped with the insignias of all the ships it had traveled on: each stamp was painted with a black slash after the crate was dropped off, and then it was stamped again before being loaded onto the next ship. But that was nothing unusual. She crept closer, and what she saw nearly made her drop her breakfast.

There, in the upper corner, scratched into the wooden boards, were words.

Words!

She grasped for them. Their small splintery edges cut into the tips of her fingers.

ENTIRELY INVISIBLE

The letters were so precise they must have taken years of practice to perfect. There were other writers, then. Other readers.

Sefia swayed. The scratching sound they'd heard back on the docks—someone had *carved* these words into the wood while she and Archer were inside.

She had the sudden feeling that something was wrong with the crate—or no, not *wrong* exactly but *strange*, so that it flickered in and out of her vision, as if it were made of something more than planks and iron nails. She put out a hand to steady herself, to reassure herself that the crate was still there.

She drew back. That was what the mate was doing, brushing his fingers against the crate because *he couldn't see it*. It was *entirely invisible* to him, who could see everything on the *Current*. But how? Was it the words that had done it?

As she explained what the words said, Captain Reed glanced at the mate, whose brow furrowed, deepening the lines on his wrinkled face. "But I didn't know words could do *this*," she added.

Reed flicked open a knife.

Sefia tensed and glanced at the mate, but his grim face was impassive.

The captain offered the knife to her, handle first, and held out a scrap of wood. "Try. Let's see if you can make something disappear."

She only hesitated a moment before she took the knife and began to carve. She'd told him everything the night before, everything she knew about the book and the symbol, her parents and the impressors, Archer and Serakeen, what it meant to read and how she'd taught herself to write. She dug the tip of the knife into the wood, scoring it, chipping away at the curves of the letters, until the pale wood beneath showed.

ENTIRELY INVISIBLE

She grimaced at her own imperfect writing, the letters tipsy and mismatched.

"Well?" the captain asked.

The chief mate plucked the block of wood out of Sefia's hands and dappled his fingers over her hastily carved letters. "Nope," he said.

Reed took back his knife, blew the last splinters from its blade, and folded it up into his pocket again. He tapped his chest thoughtfully, and seemed about to speak when something on the water caught his eye. He pressed himself against the rail, his gaze traveling back and forth across the waves, tracing their shapes.

Sefia knew that look as soon as she saw it. He was *reading*. Maybe he couldn't read words, but he could read the water. He could navigate it effortlessly, as if the oceans were splitting into glossy liquid roads for him. *No one* knew the sea like him.

"Something's out there," he muttered.

"The ship that woman came from?" the mate asked.

"Don't know."

Sefia glanced down the stairs to the main deck. If more people were coming for the book, they had to get away. Archer was in the sick bay; the book, in the great cabin. She wouldn't leave without them.

"Sail off the starboard beam!" Meeks shouted from the crow's nest.

Reed stared into the fog. "What sort of vessel?"

"Don't know, Cap. She was gone before I could tell."

From behind them, the mate spoke up: "Is it today?"

Sefia glanced at the captain, who shook his head. "Not today," he said.

Pigtails flying behind her, the ship's steward, Aly, raced up to them and passed a spyglass to Reed. He put it to his eye.

All across the deck, sailors peered into the fog. For a moment, nothing stirred except the roiling mist.

Sefia edged toward the stairs, ready to run.

The mate caught her by the back of the neck. She struggled briefly, but his hand tightened like a vise and she went still. "Don't think so, girl."

She glared up at him.

From above, Meeks called, "There she is again, Cap!"

A ship appeared in the mist, little more than a shadow with tendrils of fog twisting around its hull. Reed passed the spyglass to Aly. "I need your eyes, kid. Who's out there?"

The tall steward raised the glass. After a moment, she lowered it again and shook her head. "Too much fog to tell, sir."

Reed cursed.

The mate's hard fingers pinched the back of Sefia's neck. "You said you could see things, girl."

She tried to pull away, but he hung on, and she looked toward the ship, steeling herself against the pain and the nausea. Then she blinked, and streams of golden light rippled outward from the shadowed vessel. She saw flashes of uniforms, rocky shores where Evericans once fought Evericans, before King Darion united them against their Oxscinian colonizers. She lurched forward, blinking.

The chief mate hauled her upright again. "What's wrong, girl?"

"It's from Everica." She grimaced as the vertigo struck her. "The navy."

A muscle twitched in the mate's jaw. "Are you sure?"

She rubbed her temples. "I'm sure." She'd heard attacks on

the shipping lanes were getting more and more frequent. Lots of people were scared to leave their own kingdoms. Even outlaws like Captain Reed skirted the battle zones in the Central Sea.

Meeks let out another cry from above. "It's a Blue Navy vessel, Cap! She's headin' our way!"

Reed's eyes widened with surprise. "That's some trick, kid."

"Is that where the woman came from?" Sefia asked.

"The Blue Navy don't make killers like that," Reed muttered. "Least, they didn't used to."

Sefia eyed the ocean. The ship was drawing closer, growing larger and larger in the mist like a shadow at dusk.

Suddenly, there was fire in the fog. Two explosions of orange lit up the mist like firecrackers.

"Get down!" Reed yelled.

Sefia was thrown to the deck. The chief mate's body landed on top of her, shielding her from the blow. The sounds of distant cannon fire reached them, but there was no splintering of wood, no splash of iron in the water. She scrambled out from under the mate and hauled him up after her.

The captain was already at the rail, staring out over the ocean. "That wasn't meant for us."

The mist rolled back, unveiling a second ship, its shapes blurred at the edges, its colors dimmed by fog. The Everican Navy vessel came about to meet her.

"Can you see who it is, Aly?"

The steward put the glass to her eye. "Sorry, Cap."

Sefia ran to the rail. "Is *that* where the woman in black came from?"

Reed nodded. "Maybe."

She straightened her shoulders and narrowed her eyes. The two ships were tilting at each other like jousters with spiked lances, the fog wafting around them as they prepared for battle. If that was the assassin's ship, she could find out where it had come from. Who else was on it. She blinked, and her Vision filled with gold.

She saw cannons. Powder kegs. Chain shot. Then a mirror. Echoing marble corridors and a round vault door of burnished steel. A keyhole like a star, with sharp points and birds in mid-flight etched around the edges.

Waves of light cascaded across her Vision, tearing at her focus. The fog was closing over the two ships, curling over their sterns and sails. She saw storms, rain, water droplets forming and falling and breaking apart as they struck the surface of the sea. She thrashed in the Vision, searching for the ship, but it was gone. The gold currents washed over her, pushing her deeper into the depths of light and memory. Stretches of blue. Heat. The white disc of the sun. The light spiraled around her, dragging her farther and farther from her own body, until she could feel the edges of her consciousness beginning to unravel, dissolving into the endless sea of light.

And then.

Someone grabbed her. She felt it distantly. Hands dug into her arms. The pain spread to her elbows and up to her shoulders, down to her hands and into her chest. She felt herself being drawn back into her body, slicing through the golden seas until she found herself again.

She blinked, but she saw nothing but thick clots of mist.

And then she was coughing, choking, leaning out over the water with Archer's arms around her, his wounds bleeding through his bandages as he tried to hold her back.

Sefia shook with anger and exhaustion. "No . . . !"

But the ship was gone. They heard the muffled thunder of cannons, saw blossoms of flame in the fog.

She slumped against Archer.

"It was *them*, I know it was!"

The wood bit into her skin as she pounded the rails.

Archer caught her hands and pressed them flat, holding them hot and bruised in his own.

Turning, she buried her head in his chest. "I'm sorry," she said. "I tried."

The doc was standing by the stairs at the edge of the quarterdeck. "We heard the cannons," she said. "He wouldn't listen when I said you were safe with the captain and the mate."

Behind them, the mate murmured, "The *Crux* couldn't have gotten here so soon. Think it was the *Black Beauty*?"

"She ain't gonna pick a fight with the Blue Navy when she wants that treasure as much as we do," Reed replied. He tapped his belt buckle. "I ain't gonna wait around to see which one comes outta this alive. Get the men on the yards."

"Wait!" Sefia pulled out of Archer's grasp as the mate strode toward the main deck, shouting orders. "They might know where Aunt Nin is. She might even be on their ship!"

The captain shook his head. "It ain't worth the risk, kid."

"They killed my father! They killed Harison!"

"You think I don't know that?" he snapped. "That boy was my responsibility. I'm the one who's gonna have to tell his ma that her baby is dead. I ain't gonna do the same for anyone else on my crew. Not today."

He turned his back on her, and Sefia fell silent as sailors began scrambling into the rigging. There was a great creaking of ropes and sails and the *Current* picked up speed. Doc tugged Archer back to the sick bay to re-bandage his injuries, and Aly slipped away so silently Sefia didn't even realize she was gone. And then Sefia was alone with the captain.

The far-off rumble of cannon fire faded into silence, replaced by the hissing of the ship on the waves. They stood at the rail, Sefia fighting the urge to empty her stomach overboard.

"What happened back there?" the captain asked.

Sefia held her throbbing head between her hands. "I thought that was my chance. To get the answers I've been looking for."

"You looked like you were dyin'."

She bit her lip. "I think I was."

"And your boy saved you."

"He's not . . ." Her voice trailed away. "Yeah. He did."

The captain's blue eyes flashed in the shadow beneath his hat. "You kids are lucky."

Sefia traced the ⊜ on the rail. "I wouldn't say *lucky*."

Reed was silent as he studied the steel-gray sea. "You said you were goin' to Jahara," he said finally.

"That's where Hatchet was going. I thought we could find the symbol again once we got there."

Reed peered down at her. A piercing blue search. "You ever been to Jahara, kid?"

She shook her head. "No, sir. Aunt Nin always said it was too dangerous."

"She was right." He stared at the waves and tapped his chest. "You'd do better to forget about it. Hatchet's one thing, but Serakeen ain't a man you wanna cross paths with."

The wind whipped at her hair, stinging her neck and cheeks as they skimmed over the white-capped water. "I need to save Nin."

"If she's still alive."

"Yeah."

"And then?"

"Stop them. For good." She glanced back toward the main hatchway and the sick bay below. "Or no one I care about will be safe."

Reed drummed his fingers. "And what if you fail?"

Sefia turned to the crate and dug her fingernail into the letters, pulling up splinters and flicking them into the sea. "I've already failed," she said.

He traced the blank circle at his wrist. There was a maelstrom at his elbow, followed by a skeleton eating its own bones, trees on the back of a turtle shell: all the stories of how they got to the western edge of the world, but no story about the edge itself.

"Sometimes you get what you want," he murmured. "And sometimes you wish you hadn't."

"Maybe." As she bit off the word, she pricked herself on a sliver of wood. Blood beaded on her fingertip, and she sucked it away, spitting it into the ocean. "But I have to try."

CHAPTER 27

In This Web of Light and Shadow

As the lamplight flickered off the portholes, the walls of the tiny cabin seemed to close in about her. In the web of light and shadow, Tanin hunched over the desk, smoothing the edges of the paper over and over until her fingertips were red and raw. She had cried so much in the past few hours that to cry any more seemed impossible.

Her mouth twisted as pain lanced through her face. Tears flooded her vision.

She had one more letter to write.

Tanin dipped her pen in a bottle of ink, and every movement felt heavy, as if her limbs were made of stone, and bits of bone would explode into bursts of powder at the slightest shifting of her joints. Across the top of the page, she wrote, *Dear Erastis*, in crumbling script.

Tanin brushed her fingers across her eyes, spattering black

ink over her blouse. She cursed and dipped the nib again. The words blurred on the page as she wrote:

The Second is dead.

She paused, her gaze straying to the four sealed letters she'd already prepared: one for each of the Masters, to inform them of the events of the previous night, and of her failure. Five times she had written these words now, and still they weren't enough. They didn't describe how the world had been *diminished*, as if the Assassin's absence had snuffed out all the lights in all the cities across Kelanna, and objects that had been sharp and solid moments before were now dim, halfway to disappearing themselves.

She pressed her pen to the page and continued to write, remembering the anger she'd felt when the ship's lieutenant had told her the Assassin was missing. The hurried search of the decks, her frustration ceding to worry and abyssal panic when she realized the Assassin was no longer on board. The creaking of ropes as the crewmen hoisted Tanin in her longboat over the side of the ship.

The night had been black and gray as the fog crept over the rowboat, winding along her arms as she strained at the oars. Blisters formed on her palms.

Then she heard the shot, followed quickly by another, like thunder in the dark.

She froze.

The chill of the night touched the tips of her toes and fingers, creeping up her limbs to her chest. She began to shiver.

Then the splash.

A body striking the water.

Somewhere in the mist, there was the sound of voices murmuring indistinctly, all round shapes and half-formed words. In her little boat, Tanin clutched her stomach, rocking herself back and forth as the tears coursed down her cheeks, past her open mouth, her lips forming the words but not saying them.

No, no, no, no, no . . .

They had killed her.

They had killed her.

And it was Tanin's fault.

If only she'd allowed the Assassin to act sooner . . . If only she hadn't been so harsh with her . . . If only she hadn't allowed herself to be so distracted by that little girl . . .

There was a knock at the door.

Bleary-eyed, Tanin looked up from the page. What had she written? She could barely read her own handwriting. Dashing tears from her eyes, she pulled the carved cylindrical lid over the desk, hiding her writing instruments.

She cleared her throat. "Come in."

The door swung open, and in strode the ship's lieutenant. Escalia was a formidable woman, broad as a man across the shoulders and chest, with an upright bearing that made every room seem to shrink as soon as she entered.

She flicked Tanin a smart salute. "The Everican ship is gone, ma'am. Limped off into the fog and left no trace." Her voice was bold and roughened by weather, but it still retained a brassy shine.

Tanin nodded. "Thank you, Lieutenant."

"Shall we mount a search?" Escalia's gold teeth flashed in the lantern light.

Tanin had known it would happen eventually, this conflict between Darion's Blue Navy and herself, with his Stone Kingdom at war with Oxscini, and her ship caught out in the open like any other outlaw. But that didn't make it less of a nuisance. She didn't have time to fight off the Blue Navy when she was chasing the *Current of Faith*. "No," she said. "Continue on course to Jahara."

"Yes, ma'am."

Tanin eyed her for a moment. "Is that it?"

The lieutenant cocked her head. "Is what it, ma'am?"

"You're not going to argue with me?"

"No, ma'am."

"Well that's refreshing," Tanin said wearily.

Escalia shrugged. "I follow orders. I don't question."

"What about your own opinions?"

"I'm a simple woman, ma'am. I leave the opinion-having to minds greater than my own." The lieutenant paused, thumbing one of the metal bands she wore on her upper arms. "I know there's always a reason you do what you do. Things always turn out."

Tanin pressed the pads of her fingers to her paper cuts. "Do they?"

"Yes, ma'am, I believe they do. Even a tragedy such as this."

"Thank you, Lieutenant. You're dismissed."

Snapping Tanin another salute, Escalia squeezed out of the cabin and shut the door behind her with a *click*.

Tanin stared at the back of the door. The entire thing was

a mirror with a silver frame of pages and waves—the letters spraying upward into frothy whitecaps, with riptides and whirlpools of words below—details so exquisite it seemed as if the frame were made of liquid metal.

She had always believed that coincidences didn't exist, that everything that happened, happened for a reason. But what reason was there for the Assassin's death?

They could have retrieved the Book at the cabin in Kambali. The Assassin had wanted to do it, but Tanin had stopped her. Because of the girl.

Sliding back the top of the desk, Tanin skimmed the letter, her gaze hovering on the words:

The Second is dead.

But now she felt numb, as if by the fifth time repeating it, throwing herself against the rocks of her grief, they had finally eroded, leaving nothing but smooth cold emptiness behind. Grimly, she folded the paper with crisp movements and ironed the creases.

It all came back to the girl. She had the Book. She knew Illumination. She had somehow freed a candidate, and together they had discovered that the final test lay in Jahara.

And she was a killer.

With a match, Tanin heated a stick of wax until molten pearls began to drop one by one onto the paper, creating an inky black pool. She flicked her tongue over a brass seal to moisten it and pressed the stamp firmly into the wax.

A reader *and* a killer.

The idea spread through her as the wax cooled and hardened beneath the pressure of the seal.

Was *this* why the Assassin had died?

So they would have an opening in their ranks?

The seal had left an impression in the wax, and Tanin traced it with raw fingertips. A circle inscribed with four lines, as familiar to her now as the shape of her own face.

It fit. It was almost perfect. The girl was a little old to be inducted, but exceptions could be made. After all, she already had no one. No family. No existing ties.

She'd make an excellent Assassin.

Everything under the sun came full circle—the seasons, the stars, the cycles of life itself. It was like poetry.

Carefully, Tanin gathered up the five letters, shuffling them into place between her hands, and approached the mirror. Her face, normally pale and smooth as chalk, was pink and bloated with crying. She studied her own reflection with disgust.

She was the Director—the leader of their order, the one to whom all the Masters and their Apprentices looked for protection and guidance—and the Director did not show weakness.

Edmon had been weak. And his weakness had cost them all.

She stared into her gray eyes and tucked a strand of black hair behind her ear, summoning the words of her oath as if they were an incantation.

"Once I lived in darkness, but now I bear the flame," she whispered. "It is mine to carry until darkness comes for me again . . ."

She straightened the collar of her ivory blouse, redid the buttons of her vest, regaining her resolve as she recited the words.

"It shall be my duty to protect the Book from discovery and

misuse, and establish stability and peace for all the citizens of Kelanna."

Running the blade of her finger beneath her eyes to remove the last of her tears, she sniffed a few times and raised her chin.

"I shall fear no challenge. I shall fear no sacrifice. In all my actions, I shall be beyond reproach."

Tanin's gaze roved over her reflection. "I am the shade in the desert," she murmured. "I am the beacon on the rock. I am the wheel that drives the firmament." With every sentence her voice grew stronger, until it rang like steel and glittered like ice, and anyone who heard it would know in their bones that she was as hard and impenetrable as armor, and she would not be moved from her course.

Harison Saves the Main Royal

It's the same with stories as it is with people," Meeks said, his brown eyes gleaming in the dwindling light of the sunset, "they get better as they get older. But not every story is remembered, and not all people grow old.

"It was thirty-two days since we left the turtle island, and the night was still as death. I remember the stars had a particular brightness to them, like snowflakes on a black table. You could see the whole blasted sky reflected in the water, and us too, all our sails and the lights of the watch, like we was in two places at once: aboard the *Current* cuttin' through the sea, and below the surface, upside down and starvin' for air.

"We felt the breeze first, and scrambled to bring in the sails, but we were too slow. The wind came bellowin' great guns out of the northeast, the waves washin' over the bow, beatin' against the hull like the hands of giants come risin' out of the sea.

"Then the sky opened up, all jagged along the edges, and the light just pourin' through it, bright as dawn. What an uproar! We were on the yards, and the winds were battin' us about like leaves. There wasn't no time to stare into that hole in the sky like Captain Cat and her cannibal crew, or all our sails would be torn to shreds and the masts snapped in two.

"Then came the thunderclap, and the world went dark. The sound of it knocked all the noise right out of our ears, and we were workin' in complete silence—couldn't hear the wind, couldn't hear Cap or Jules or Theo callin' out, couldn't hear nothing.

"The ship was plungin' into the troughs one after another, the sails gapin' in the wind. The staysail was blown to ribbons; the main topsail, split earing to earing. We was all scramblin' to the bowsprit or up the mainmast, the wind slashin' at us, roarin', though we couldn't hear it. I was sure the whole blasted ship was gonna be shaken apart, and us dropped into the waves like fish bait.

"Then the main royal came loose from her gaskets, flappin' and makin' the mast quiver like a bean stalk.

"Cap was shoutin' orders. I could see his mouth wide open and his eyes wild. The mainmast was gonna snap if someone didn't take in that royal or cut it loose.

"Somewhere in all that chaos, it was only Harison who knew what to do. He sprang aloft, gatherin' the sail with his long arms. There was times the wind was so bad he was nearly shook off the mast, but he kept at it. Through the pitchin' of the waters and the impossible soundlessness of the night. All by his lonesome, he sent the yard down. Saved the mainmast—saved the ship—all on his own.

"It was bold moves like that one that got us through the night, till the winds lost their spite and the waters cooled down. We had a job the next few weeks, fixin' all the damage those winds had done, but thanks to Harison we had another few weeks to do it.

"That boy earned his place with us that night, all right."

CHAPTER 28

It Is Written

Things were good.

The sun was blazing down upon the ship, and the clouds were puffs of cotton in the sky. The *Current of Faith* was clipping along at tremendous speed, smooth as silk through the water. At this rate, they'd reach Jahara in ten days.

In exchange for their assistance with the woman in black, their honesty in retelling their remarkable tale, and the assurance of their continued services, Sefia and Archer had been granted passage to Jahara under the provision that Sefia's book and lock picks be kept in a safe, with special dispensation for reading when she wasn't on watch, until she disembarked, at which point they would be returned to her in their original condition.

Until now, she hadn't had time to read. There was no shortage of duties for her and Archer to perform—scrubbing decks, scouring pots, trimming artichokes for Cooky, who shouted at them if it wasn't done quick enough—and they were kept so busy that when she did have a free moment, she would fall exhausted into her hammock and sleep until her next watch.

But after three days of backbreaking work, she was finally adjusting to life at sea, and today she was going to see the book again. Sefia prodded the calluses forming on her hands and waited on the quarterdeck.

Above her, Horse and Archer were on the yards with little wooden pails, tarring down the rigging. Their hands moved along the lines, stiff-bristled brushes dripping. Every so often, the acrid smell wafted over the ship.

These past few days on the *Current*, Archer had looked happier and more relaxed than she'd ever seen him. His smile was broader and he was quicker to laugh—a sort of silent breathy laughter that showed in his eyes.

As if he could sense her watching him, Archer looked down. Silhouetted against the flat blue sky, he rested easily on the yard, as nonchalant and perfectly balanced as a cat. Though at this distance she couldn't see his eyes clearly, she felt his gaze on her, probing, questioning, lingering on her eyes, her lips, her face.

Sefia blushed and glanced away. For some reason, she couldn't stop smiling.

The sound of footsteps on the stairs startled her, and she looked up to see the chief mate crossing the quarterdeck, his arms outstretched, holding the book as if it were a live and dangerous thing, like a snake. She laughed as he dumped it into her waiting hands.

Gathering the book to her chest, Sefia inhaled its familiar smell, felt its edges on the insides of her arms. "Why do you hold it like that?" she asked.

The mate shook himself like a dog and crossed his hands behind his back. "Don't know what's inside it," he said. "The farther it is from me, the less likely it'll get me, if something comes crawling out."

"All that's inside it are words," she said.

"Have you seen everything that's inside it?"

She shook her head.

"Then how can you be sure?" His tone was quiet, matter-of-fact.

Sefia peered up at him. The chief mate was a handsome figure, with his square jaw, his wide mouth, though the skin around his neck was beginning to sag, and the wrinkles in his face were like ravines. As she studied him—the gray of his hair, the notch across the bridge of his nose—she felt the world of gold and light swirling just beyond her line of sight—

"You're a nosy one, aren't you?"

Her sense of the Vision faded, and she sat down abruptly. "I didn't mean—"

"Sure you did."

Sefia swallowed. "I'm sorry."

"Don't do it again."

"No, sir."

He sighed. "I see things too. Anything that happens on this ship." When she nodded, he continued, "I recognized what happened to you the other morning. You almost lost yourself."

"Yes." She leaned forward. "Although my Vision works differently, I think. I can't see the present like you, but sometimes I'll catch a glimpse of what's happened before." Even after finding Archer, she'd been so alone in this, muddling through the words, struggling to control the Vision, with no one to help her understand what was happening, what it meant. "And history is huge," she said faintly.

"When I first joined the crew, I used to get seasick, not from the rocking of the ship, mind you, but from pure sensory overload. I can sense everything on the *Current*, not just the people, but the cargo too. And the rats." He grimaced. "People aren't meant to take in so much."

"How'd you learn to control it?"

He shrugged. "Same as you control anything else. Practice."

"But only the ship, nothing else?"

A flicker of grief crossed the mate's face. "No, nothing else."

Sefia peered up at him. "Why?"

"It's the trees," he murmured. "The trees tell me everything."

They were silent, listening to the stretching and groaning of the timbers, the hissing of the wind in the sails. Setting the book securely inside a coil of rope, she climbed to her feet and dusted off her hands on the thighs of her trousers. "Will you teach me?"

He stared down with his gray eyes, and she felt like he was peering inside her. What did he see? Was she as brave, or as good, as she hoped? Or did he see a stupid, reckless girl who'd gotten Nin kidnapped? Who'd killed Palo Kanta? She straightened her shoulders and met his unnerving dead gaze.

Finally he nodded. "All right, girl. Pay attention and do as I say."

She grinned. Normally she hated it when people called her

that, but the way the mate said it reminded her of Nin, who'd rarely used her name. But every time Nin called her "girl," it meant she was cared for. It meant she wouldn't be left behind.

"How about we start with this scar?" The mate tapped the dent on his nose.

She nodded.

"Don't let yourself look at the whole thing. You'll make yourself sick doing that, and you won't be able to make sense of anything when you're flat on your back trying to keep down your breakfast. Just focus on my scar. Tune the rest out."

She blinked, and the world filled with gold. Trails of it wove across the chief mate's square features, in and out like sparkling currents. She saw his childhood, before his sight was taken: the rocky Everican shore, an old woman laughing, the tangy smell of mulch, and trees, trees, trees whispering and creaking and laughing and speaking. The sights and sounds and smells churned around her, blurring into one bloody streak of memory.

"It's like picking out one person in a crowd." The mate's words cut through the chaos. "One voice. The one you're listening for. Let everything else become background noise."

The dent in his nose. All the threads of his past spun around her, faster and faster the longer she looked, but that one gleamed more brightly than the others.

"Do you have it?" he asked.

His grandmother had been able to talk to the trees. She had lived her whole life among them, in the green-gold light and the minty fragrance of their bark. And when his parents were killed in a mining accident, the mate went to live in the grove with her, learning to nurse the tender shoots into towering giants with rustling fan-shaped leaves.

When he was eleven, the men came. They came with saws and axes and rifles and carts. They came accompanied by soldiers in blue uniforms with silver epaulets. The navy needed ships, they said, and it didn't matter what his grandmother said or how she begged—they cut the trees down. The chewing and hacking of their axes. The mate saw one of the oldest trees in the grove topple, groaning, branches grasping at its neighbors as if they could stop it from falling.

His grandmother spat at the soldiers, cursing them. Her fingernails dug thick gouges in their skin. But she couldn't stop them. They barricaded her inside her own home and set it on fire. The *crackle* and *hiss* of burning wood. The smell of singed hair and blistering flesh.

The mate ran after her, but the soldiers caught him before he could enter. He thrashed at them with his scrawny fists. One of them raised a rifle. The butt end came smashing into his face. Explosions behind his eyes. Blood. Smoke.

When he awoke, he was blind, and the trees were gone. He couldn't hear the whispering of their leaves or smell the medicinal scent of their bark. All he smelled was ash and upturned earth.

Someone—a man with a voice like suede—adjusted the bandages over his eyes and nose. "They didn't have to blind you," he said sadly, "but people are cruel."

The mate nodded. His face burned as he tried to stop himself from crying.

"You have a choice now," the man said. "Come with me, and

you'll be safe. You'll have a good life in the Library." He described all the ways the Library was suited for the blind—the
routine, the unchanging furniture, the textured knobs and cup-
boards in the kitchen. He'd be given a home, and all he'd have
to do was care for it. Dust the tables. Tend the garden. A simple
life, away from the cruelty of men. "Or you can try to make it
on your own," the man said finally, "but the world will have no
pity for a blind boy."

"Now you know," the chief mate said.

Sefia blinked as the lights whirled and faded away. Swallowing tentatively, she waited for the nausea, the headache, but
none came. She beamed. "Who was that man? Did you go with
him?" The questions bubbled out of her in her excitement. "To
the Library? What's a Library?"

The chief mate shrugged. "I never found out."

"You turned him down? Why?"

He rubbed his hands over the smooth woodgrain of the rail.
"I was in no shape to go with him then, so he left me in the care
of a family from a nearby town while I recovered. I don't know
if he came back, because as soon as I was well enough, I left."

"Why?"

"When my grandmother died, she must have passed her
power to me, because I could hear her trees calling to me,
faintly at first, then louder and louder. Across the entire kingdom, I could hear them calling my name." The mate closed
his eyes, and Sefia realized he was listening to the ship, to the
very timbers it was made of. "And I had to go to them. I had
failed them once, but I couldn't let them be taken from me
again."

This wasn't the same magic as her Vision, but it was closer than anything she'd found yet. Maybe the mate could help her master it, so she'd be good enough to catch the answers she needed, next time.

Sefia twisted a couple of locks of hair in her fingers and looked to the book, where it lay in the nest of rope like an egg, ready to hatch. "Let's get to work," she said.

The chief mate made her practice for hours: sinking into the Vision and spinning out of it, studying the capstan, the chase guns, the amber ring he wore on the little finger of his right hand. She needed a mark. A dent or a crack or a scratch. Something to focus her Vision on so she wouldn't get swept away. By the time four bells struck, Sefia was exhausted, but she could wield her Vision with the precision of a filleting knife. If she'd wanted to, she could have seen the history of the sixteen-pounders at the gun ports, the ship, maybe even the sky, the sea, the very air that whipped around her.

"Not yet, girl." The mate grunted. "Not by a long shot."

She laughed.

"Get out of here. Go bother someone else." He dismissed her with a flick of his fingers, and she gathered up the book and wandered down to the main deck.

Stumbling a bit on the last step, Sefia waved to Jaunty. A gaunt man of fifty, the helmsman never left the deck. No matter the weather, he'd be out there in furs and oilskins, only leaving his post a few hours each night to sleep in a tiny closet on the quarterdeck, a few feet from the wheel. He'd never done more than grunt at her when she greeted him, and none of the crew much enjoyed his company, but he could steer a ship better than anyone in Kelanna.

On the main deck, she plunked herself down among the spare ropes and buckets of tar Horse and Archer had left on deck. Hugging the sun-warmed book to her chest, she leaned back.

Archer was on the mainmast, and the sun shone through the brittle sticks of his hair, turning them gold as sheaves of wheat. She watched him for a moment, painting the rigging black, his brush moving quick and sure on the ropes while the shadows shifted along his arms.

There was such grace to his movements; she wondered why she'd never noticed it before.

Smiling, she flipped open the book.

Her bookmarks were piled in one place between the pages, their stories gone. She picked up Archer's feather, gleaming iridescent green and fuchsia, and ran it along her cheek before tucking it into her hair.

The letters crackled with a sense of possibility. What would she read next? What grand adventure would come to her now? Leaning over the book, she began to read.

As she sank into the page, submerging herself in the words, at first all she saw was fog—thick fog, like snow, that shut out the sounds of the everyday world—and the noises of the wind and the waves seemed to fall away around her.

She shivered, delighted, as the words began to form images in the mist. Fence posts. The indistinct shadows of barrels and wheelbarrows. She imagined dew-dampened grass batting at her shoes and the legs of her trousers.

The sunlight seemed to dim as she read, sinking deeper and deeper into the silent world inside the book. A chill crawled up her back as a house appeared above her. At first it was just a shadow in the mist, but as she approached, she made out the muted shape of a grassy hill, a stone foundation, and white walls. At either end of the house, a stone chimney rose from the slanted rooftop.

Sefia gasped. She knew where she was—where the book had taken her. And she knew what she would find inside the house. She knew what she would see, and she went cold the moment the door swung open, and she was faced with the fragile silence inside.

But part of her, deep down, a part of her she could not quite subdue, wanted to see. To see him again, though it would not be him, not really, lying on the floor of the kitchen.

She kept reading. She couldn't stop. She watched the house break into tiny pieces and drop away. She watched the girl in the book step inside, trembling, her wet shoes leaving mud and bits of grass on the carpets. She watched her pass through the living room and the dining room—the rugs unraveling and the table splintering and the paintings on the walls turning to dust.

She reached the kitchen, and it was just as she remembered: the whitewashed cabinetry, chipped at the corners; the tile countertop; the wooden cutting board scored and nicked with age. Even the crumbs in the floorboards were the same, from the egg-and-vegetable tart they'd had the night before.

She was there.

There on the page and there in her memory, seeing it twice, seeing it all over again. Wanting to look away and desperately needing to read on, needing to see him again. But she knew **it was him without having to look closely. She could not look closely. She knew it was him by the sheepskin slippers, by the shape of his trousers, by the oversize threadbare sweater. She knew it without having to see his face, because she could not see his face anymore. There was—**

Sefia grabbed a bucket of tar from the deck beside her. She could barely see. Her eyes filmed over with tears. She raised the brush.

—no face left.

She dragged the bristles across the page, eclipsing the words.

Her father's killers had done more than kill him.

Every word.

They had destroyed him.

Every image.

They had taken his fingernails, his kneecaps, the lobes of his ears, his eyes and tongue.

Every memory.

The sentences grew dark and indecipherable under her brush. The smell of smoke filled her body. She thrust the bucket away from her, and it spilled over the deck, black and sticky. She dropped the brush. Specks of tar spattered her clothing, her hands and arms, her chin.

Were there footsteps? Was she retreating into the living room, to the fireplace and her secret staircase?

Someone took hold of her. They had her! This wasn't how it had been. She writhed in their grasp. She hadn't made it to the tunnel in time. They were going to take her away. They were going to kill her. They had killed her father and now they were going to kill her too. She screamed.

"What's wrong, Sef?" A voice like the bellows of a forge. Large arms and hands like hammers clasped her from behind. "What happened?"

Someone else knelt in front of her, his hands on hers. Two crossed fingers. Strong like twine. She blinked. Archer's face swam into view. Archer. Yes, Archer. She was with Archer, and Horse was behind her, asking what was wrong. She was on the ship. She was in the wind. There had been no wind that day. Tenderly, tenderly, Archer swept a lock of hair away from her forehead, along her temple, and back behind her ear. Archer. She clutched at his arms.

"I'm in the book," she whispered.

She looked down at the disfigured page, with its hideous black marks, and the words came lunging out at her, empty eyes and open jaws. She was caught. She was being sucked down with them, into the book, down into that darkness, into that cold cube of darkness in the walls of her basement bedroom, where she crouched, sobbing into the cold clay floor.

Her father was dead. He was dead. And gone forever.

CHAPTER 29

Tonight a Kiss,
Tomorrow a Lifetime

Lon crept through the corridors, his bare feet achingly cold against the snowy marble. He gritted his teeth against the chill and passed under the domed mosaic arches as quietly as he could. He would never master the Second's eerie stalking silence, and he could hear his shallow breaths and the slippery shifting of his feet in the vaulted stone hallways.

From the walls, the painted eyes of former Directors seemed to follow him, their faces austere, their lips unmoving. Their countenances were so lifelike that sometimes he was sure they would leap out of their frames in the deep of night, flat hands grabbing, clothes rippling behind them in unseen winds.

In the Library, the long curved tables were bare; the reading lamps, unlit. The bookshelves with their neatly ordered manuscripts slumbered in the shadows, while overhead pale moonlight wafted through the stained glass windows, lighting on the bronze statues of past Librarians standing vigil over the galleries.

Lon hesitated at the threshold, but there was no sign of movement. He had at least two hours before the Master Librarian woke from his fitful sleep and came padding among the bookshelves to check a cross-reference, a footnote, a scribble in the margins. Lon slipped into the Library, clinging to the walls as the Second had instructed him, pretending that he too could melt seamlessly into dapplings of light on the marble floor.

He passed the vault, trailing his hand along the steel spokes, the keyholes like compass roses, and he pressed his ear to the door, as if he could hear the rustling of pages inside. But, as always, he heard nothing, and continued to the shelves beyond. Lon tapped his fingers against each of the spines and slipped one of the books into his arms. The scent of leather, paper, and glue drifted around him, making him smile. There was only one smell he loved more than the smell of a book.

As usual, the Second had arrived before him, and the faint scent of metal still lingered in the air. She'd left the doors to the greenhouse ajar, with just enough space for him to slide through sideways, and he inhaled deeply as he stepped into the garden.

Outside, flecks of snow spiraled out of the black sky, landing on the glass walls and melting instantly, but the air of the greenhouse was warm and damp and smelled of earth. Lon walked quietly into the center of the indoor meadow and looked around. White primroses huddled beneath the trees, and cyclamen with their green and silver leaves were scattered among the hedges and outcroppings of rocks like strange cups of snow.

"You're late." The Second's familiar voice slid from the shadows.

Lon grinned lopsidedly at her. She was so silent that he was never quite sure where she would appear, like a fish breaking the surface of a black pond, and every time he saw her he felt like a witness to some rare creature that would disappear again if he blinked.

"Not by much." He handed her the book.

The Second wore dark green pajamas, and her black hair flowed loosely around her shoulders, blending into the curves of her back. Her feet were bare, and the cuffs of her pajama pants rose past her ankles as she sat in the grass, settling the book in her lap. She ran her fingers along the edges of the cover and peered up at him. "What is it?"

Lon plopped down beside her. "A manual on the Transformation of water into ice. I think you'll like it. In the winter of the Northern Wars, General Varissa ran out of ammunition, so she began making ice spears to launch at enemy ships. You're not a Soldier, but I thought maybe you could apply the same principle to something smaller."

The Second smiled. "And untraceable."

"Yeah."

She pulled a set of throwing stars from the folds of her clothing. They were made of some mysterious metal with no shine to it, some material developed especially for the Assassins. She held them up and grinned. "Are you still bored with juggling?"

Lon was nearly seventeen now, and three years since his induction, he'd finally graduated to the second tier of Illumination: Manipulation, a more complicated magic that involved directing the currents of light in the Illuminated world to maneuver objects from one place to another.

After four weeks of slow, painful drills in the practice room,

Erastis had still only allowed him to manipulate one object at a time. So he had started meeting with the Second in secret. Although at nineteen she was away from the Library more often and their lessons were infrequent, under her tutelage, he finally felt like his progress matched his ambition.

But at the sight of the throwing stars he grimaced. He had done juggling drills with her before, but those had always been with palm-sized beanbags that he could catch if he faltered. There would be no catching tonight. He didn't even like paper cuts, and shuddered to think of what it would feel like if one of the throwing stars nicked him.

"Stand over there." She pointed to a clear section of grass. "You can start with one, and I'll toss in the others if I think you're ready."

Lon took a deep breath and stood where she told him, allowing his sense of the Illuminated world to rise up inside him. Then he blinked, and the entire greenhouse began to glimmer with golden threads of light, swirling and shifting and moving with the slow growth of the trees, the upward inching of flowers.

"Ready—"

A throwing star whirred at him through the dark. He barely saw it coming. At the last second he found the golden thread of its trajectory and swept his hands through the air. The star went spinning upward into the darkness.

"Not so high," the Second said sharply.

The weapon was headed for the glass ceiling. Before it struck, Lon raised his hand and waved it down again. It hung in the air for a second and came looping back toward him. Up and down, he whirled the star, hands pushing and pulling at the golden currents as if they were streams of water. Up and down, over and over, while the Second pored over the Commentary he had brought for her, her hair falling down around the sides of the book, her fingers dipping and flexing in the air beside her as she practiced the techniques described within the pages.

Just as his movements became automatic, she threw another star at him. Instinctively, he dodged, but it grazed his shoulder.

"Good thing I wasn't aiming for you," the Second said without lifting her head.

Lon didn't have time to respond. It was heading for the glass wall. Struggling to keep the other circling in the air, he found the blazing course of the second star and pulled it back toward him. The pain in his shoulder was quick and clean, but it continued to sting long after he'd gotten both throwing stars under control. He tried to keep them together, sifting through his Sight and moving his hands up and down, up and down, over and over.

Eventually the Second helped him get all five throwing stars zipping in circles overhead, their strange dark shapes flitting like bats. Then she gradually whisked them out of their orbits and back into her waiting hands. He didn't know how she caught them without cutting herself; it must have been an Assassin thing.

Panting and sweating from the effort, Lon collapsed on the grass beside her. Out of the corner of his eye, he could see her close the book and brush her hair over her shoulders.

"Erastis thinks I'm not ready, but look at what I can do!" he crowed.

The Second raised her eyebrows skeptically. "With my help."

"Of course." He grinned up at her and waved airily at the darkened Library. "When I'm the Master Librarian, I won't spend so much time cooped up there. To make any real changes, you have to be out in the world. I've read about former Librarians who traveled across Kelanna, solving border disputes. Others spent their careers studying the natural world, making scientific breakthroughs. Did you know that's how we got electricity? Not from the Book. From the *world*."

"Hasn't it occurred to you that that's exactly how Erastis contributes to the cause? By remaining in the Library, studying the Book?"

"Of course it's occurred to me. But that's not enough. Not for me." Lon gazed through the ceiling. "When I'm the Librarian, I'm going to do great things. Things that would seem impossible to anyone else."

The Second's laughter swirled around him like flakes of ash. "I can see it now. You'll be the one responsible for this long peace Edmon is always talking about."

"Yes. Why not?"

"Because you're sloppy." She aimed a finger at his torn sleeve, the slender scab beneath.

"I'll get better." He chuckled. "Erastis isn't going anywhere; I've got time."

The Second tucked her hair back, exposing the perfect folds of her ear.

"Did you like the book?" he asked.

She nodded. "Watch."

Lon sat up as she raised her fingers. Drops of moisture rose from the grass beside her, gleaming like pearls as she transformed them into bullets of ice. She twirled them in the air for a second and snapped her fingers forward like she was shooting marbles. They flew outward and were gone, lost in the darkness of the greenhouse.

"All right, and . . . ?" he asked.

The Second tilted her head at him and set the book down. Then she rose gracefully to her feet, walked across the grass, and came back with a single cyclamen pinched between her thumb and forefinger. Sitting down again, she held it out to Lon, who began laughing quietly.

Each of its folded papery petals had been pierced by a small dart of ice, leaving behind tiny perforations that winked like fireflies in the light.

"You're amazing," he said.

She stopped smiling instantly and looked away. All he could see of her was the back of her head and the slope of her shoulder. Their friendship functioned when they were working, when she was tutoring him or he was finding Fragments for her to study. But if he tried to ask her who she was, how she felt, what things were like for her, she locked herself away. It wasn't her fault. She was the Apprentice Assassin—known only as the Second—and beyond that she didn't get to have an identity, or opinions, or feelings.

"I'm sorry," he said, knowing he shouldn't. She didn't like apologies. Apologies made things worse.

The Second was still. In the dark of the greenhouse at night, she seemed to dissolve into the background.

Which is about right, Lon thought. It was her job to kill, and then to vanish as if she had never been. *Being there*—having family or friends, forging the human connections that made your life meaningful—was a privilege for others, not for her. Erastis had told him this was required of all Assassins, if they were to master their art. To be a perfect killer, you couldn't really exist.

"Lon?" she said. His name floating out of the darkness.

"Yeah?"

"I want you to read me."

"What?"

She turned around: the corner of her eyebrow and the curve of her cheek, the wet shine to her eyes, the tip of her nose. "Read me."

He blanched at the thought. You didn't read other people. As soon as he had learned the Sight, he had learned this. Reading someone was more than rude. It was an intrusion into the very core of a person, deeper than any needle or spear could go. Maybe they did it to their enemies, but never to each other.

"But—"

"I want you to see."

Lon swallowed. He was repelled by the thought even as he was drawn to it. To read *her,* who so entranced and delighted and challenged him? To *really* see her?

He tried focusing on her face, on the spilling of her hair over her shoulder, on her razorlike movements, but his vision seemed to roll off her like beads of water over feathers. Was this something Assassins did to themselves? Something that made them impenetrable, even to the Sight?

His gaze fell to her hand. It was covered in scars. Notches in her skin. Welts. Nicks and pink punctures. Glittering with history. He blinked, and all of a sudden he saw her practicing, her movements like a dancer around the polished wooden floor. The cracks to her knuckles. Red blood welling out of her.

He saw her childhood. Her mother sweeping her into her arms, giggling, fingers running like spiders over her tummy. The shrieks of her laughter rippling through the kitchen with its wooden table and cast-iron pots, and her father standing at the stove grinning, a spatula raised above a sizzling pan.

She used to watch her parents tending to patients in the front room of their house. Mine accidents. Burn victims. Stained sheets and clear glass bottles. Sometimes the smell of rubbing alcohol and blood lingered for days afterward.

When her parents noticed that she was unfazed by their work, they were delighted. *It's no wonder!* they said. It was a sign that she wasn't sick at the sight of a little blood. She was going to be a doctor just like her mommy and daddy!

The currents of light shifted, and Lon saw her initiation ceremony. The swearing in. The stealing of her name, like a wind howling out of the north, whipping the syllables away into nothingness.

He saw her kills, one after another, the way the light went out of them, the way they collapsed as if they were sacks of stones.

He saw her at age eighteen, clutching the hilt of her newly formed bloodsword as she crept up the flagstone steps to a little cabin. She entered the front room, her memory of the place washing over her. There was the same operating table, the same glass syringes.

Her parents' house.

She drew her bloodsword, and the blade flashed. Blood coated the steel.

First her father.

Then her mother, who cradled her crying daughter even as she died, murmuring soft and close into her hair, "Mareah. Mareah. My little Mareah."

Lon blinked, and the lights of the Illuminated world faded away. The Second was watching him, the moon of her face rising in front of him.

She'd killed her parents.

That's the first thing she'd done with her bloodsword?

That's what her master had made her do?

To forsake all ties to kin and kingdom. To ensure—to test—her loyalty. It was unthinkably cruel. And yet someone had thought of it. Their order had thought of it.

He lifted his hand. He cradled her face, with his thumb just brushing the point of her chin. "Mareah," he whispered.

The word pooled in her eyes. She smiled—a twisted smile, with a knot of pain at the center. She had a name.

And then he was holding her. He was brushing his mouth against hers, tentatively at first and then, when she pushed back, harder, as if the pressure of his lips could for one moment make her forget her grief and horror and regret. Strands of her hair caught in his fingers, tangling them up. Her mouth was soft—softer than he could have imagined—and when he blinked he saw bursts of sparks like fire and gold. Flashes of their entwined lives. Stolen kisses. Heated breath. The *future*. They would do great things together. Magic no one had ever dreamed of.

And then he shut down the Sight so all he felt was the movement of her lips, and all he smelled was the wind and copper of her skin, and all he saw when he opened his eyes was the shadows of her cheeks, her eyelashes like scythes, and the glass ceiling peppered with snow.

CHAPTER 30

The Book of Everything

When Sefia awoke, she found herself in a bed. It had been so long since she'd slept anywhere but on the ground, in trees, trussed up in a hammock in the bowels of the ship, that she spent an entire minute memorizing the firmness of the mattress, the prickling of the feather pillow. If she kept her eyes closed, she could almost fool herself into thinking she was nine years old again, curled up in her bed with her stuffed crocodile tucked in beside her.

Tears trickled down her cheeks.

Her father.

She opened her eyes, squinting in the light that filtered through the portholes. Around her, bottles of medicine, jars of ointment, and half-mended sails lined the walls. Bundles of dried herbs hung from the ceiling, filling the air with the mixed aroma of feverfew and bitter orange.

"Look who's awake."

At the sound of Reed's voice, Sefia sat up. Her body felt heavy and cold, as if she had been sleeping in snow. She wiped her cheeks with the backs of her hands. "What happened?"

"You tell me." He was perched on a stool at the foot of the bunk, one tattooed arm slung over his knee. He extended a tin cup toward her. "Doc said you should drink this when you woke."

Sefia brought the cup to her lips. The liquid was acrid and citrusy, but as soon as she swallowed it, she felt less hollow, less iced over on the inside.

The captain leaned against the wall, tracing two circles over the curve of his knee, in and out of each other like snakes. "Your boy's on watch, but he'll be down at eight bells. The kid's hardly left your side."

Sefia tipped the tin cup in her numb hands. "How long have I been out?"

"Half a day. Whatever you saw shook you up good."

She looked away, and that was when she noticed the book on the sideboard. Someone had closed it, penned up all the ages of history between two gold clasps. It was a wonder it didn't sink the ship, taking everyone on it to the bottom of the sea.

"I saw myself," she murmured, "the day my father was murdered."

Captain Reed sat forward, his blue eyes burning. "You're in the book?"

Sefia nodded. "We're all in the book. That must be why they want it so badly—the people who did this. I think the book contains everything that has happened or will happen. All of history. All knowledge. Everything."

Reed's eyebrows went up past the brim of his hat. "I thought you said they were just stories."

"I thought they were." She took another sip. "But now I think they're a record. Of everything we've done and have yet to do."

"Me?"

"You. Me. Everyone."

"I'm in the book." He blinked a few times and passed his hand across his face, repeating, "I'm in the book. Can you show me?"

Leaning over, Sefia set the cup down and pulled at the book until it came tumbling into her arms, feeling so familiar and so utterly alien at the same time. If she used her Vision now, she knew what she'd see: a bundle of light so dense it would be like staring into the sun, as all the blinding currents of history spiraled in on each other.

This moment was in the book too. For a second she hesitated, afraid that when she opened it, she would be there—right there—looking down on herself as she read the book. She could see it, over and over, as if reflected between two mirrors, in a never-ending corridor:

Reading herself in the book.

Reading herself reading herself in the book.

Reading herself reading herself reading herself . . .

Maybe someone was reading her right now, and if she looked up, she would see their eyes staring down at her, following her every move. Maybe someone was reading the reader.

She shuddered.

But when she popped open the clasps, nothing peculiar

happened. She leafed through the pages, skimming for signs of Reed's name among the dusty paragraphs and disjointed phrases, but the stories were gone. "I'm sorry. It's too big. I could spend a lifetime looking and never find you."

The captain sighed and sat back. "Too good to hope for, I reckon."

"What d'you mean?"

"If I was in the book—permanently, y'know—and there was a place for me to rest, where I could exist, even after I died . . . maybe I wouldn't have to do all this."

"All what, sir?"

"Everything." He shrugged. "This treasure hunt Dimarion's got me on. The Trove of the King."

Piles of gold so high you could climb them like mountains and slide back down, trailing tinkling sounds and flashes of light.

"So that's why you're going to Jahara," she said.

He smiled sadly. "I been promised a good story."

Sefia closed the book. From the cover, the ⊖ blinked up at her like some cataractous eye. "Learn what the book is for," she murmured. "Rescue Nin." She paused, her fingertip at the apex of the circle. "I had the answers I was looking for the whole time."

"Sef—"

"If you knew how to use it, you could know what someone would do before they even had the idea to do it. You could find out the locations of treasures or the secrets of kings. You could even know where to find your enemies, and how to kill them." When she looked up, her dark eyes were bright with

322

desperation. "They're in here somewhere. If I find them, I'll know who they are. I'll know where they'll be, and then I can—"

"Sefia."

"What?"

"You said yourself you could spend your whole life lookin'."

In her mind's eye, Sefia saw herself hunched over the book, growing frail and nearsighted as the years piled up around her and the lights of her life burned low. She dug into the pages, as if they'd squeal beneath her fingers.

"After the maelstrom . . ." The captain looked thoughtfully at the book, though he didn't move to take it. "After I learned how I was gonna die, I coulda stopped sailin'," he said, still tracing those interconnected circles on his knee. "I knew it'd happen at sea. Coulda lived forever if I'd stayed on land."

"Why didn't you?"

"Swearin' allegiance to lords and fancy ladies? Carvin' out my survival from trees and stone? I'd rather rot in the ground." Captain Reed regarded her levelly. "You got a choice, Sef. Control your future, or let your future control you."

Above, the ship's bell began to toll. Once, twice . . . eight times. The sounds echoed inside her icy chest.

Then Archer appeared in the doorway, sweat gleaming at the edges of his face, his hair and clothing damp, and Sefia smiled—a real smile. He seemed to radiate heat.

And he didn't seem to notice when Sefia passed the book to Reed, golden clasps gleaming, begging to be opened.

She almost snatched it back.

But the captain gently drew it from her fingers and as he

323

took it down the hall, she felt its pull on her growing weaker and weaker, until she could barely feel it at all.

Archer knelt beside her, tracing the edges of her face with his fingertips.

Everywhere he touched seemed to glow with warmth, and cracks appeared in the bleak cold of her heart. She caught his hand with hers and held it to her cheek, skin to skin. "I saw my father," she whispered.

"The Boy from the Sea"

HARISON'S FAVORITE SONG

It was years ago now, on a warm summer night,
    When the boy came out of the sea.
His skin was blue and his hair was white,
    And he was in love with me.
He was wild and true, and right then I knew
    That he was in love with me.

In our ship we sailed for years on the ocean,
    Unfettered and totally free.
And he gave all his days to his endless devotion,
    For he was in love with me.
I called it a phase and made endless delays,
    Though he was in love with me.

One day the waves swept him right off the ship
    And dropped him into the blue.
As his skin turned to water, his hair into fish,
    He asked if I loved him too.
Too late I called through the wind and the water,
    "I was always in love with you."
    I was always in love with you.

CHAPTER 31

The Red War

Later that evening, while Sefia was supposed to be resting, Meeks, Horse, and a couple members of the starboard watch crowded into the sick bay to play Ship of Fools, bringing coins and dice cups and a gaming table that Meeks and Theo wrestled into the cramped cabin.

Freckled and bespectacled, with unkempt cinnamon-colored hair, Theo was something of an amateur biologist, and had recently adopted Harison's red lory, a small parrot with blue-tipped wings, which could now often be found perched on his shoulder. Sometimes he'd sing to her in his fine baritone voice, and she'd whistle back. As he grappled with the table, the brilliant red bird bobbled slightly and raised her wings for balance, chirping irritably.

Archer crawled onto the bunk beside Sefia, his knee resting against hers. Lifting a finger, he touched the green feather she'd tucked into her hair, and she watched the smile light up his face like a candle batting against the night.

"Here, Sef. Make yourself useful." Meeks dropped a square of canvas in front of her, and Theo placed a brush and a small jar of black paint on the table.

"Hey!" She laughed. "You said you came here to play!"

Meeks grinned, revealing his chipped tooth. "Yeah, yeah. We're here to play. But we *also* heard what you told Cap this afternoon, about us all bein' in the book and such."

"Yeah?"

"And we were wonderin' if you'd write our names."

Marmalade slid into the space beside the head of the bunk and tucked her honey-red hair behind her ears. She was Harison's counterpart on the starboard watch, the ship's girl, and not much older than Archer. She smiled hopefully, dimpling her cheeks.

"Of course," Sefia said.

"Great!" Meeks clapped his hands. "Start with Harison."

She nodded. She'd been hearing about Harison for days now, and finally she could contribute something to remember him by, something that might last beyond their words or their memory.

Too big to fit in the sick bay with the rest of them, Horse pulled up a stool and wedged himself in the doorway, his bulging muscles pressed against the walls. He winked at Sefia as she uncapped the jar of paint and dipped the brush.

While she wrote, the others leaned in, watching her sculpt the letters, each one a shivering architecture of dashes and curves. When she finished, she showed the scrap of cloth to Marmalade on her left before passing it to Archer on her other side. After a moment, he handed it to Theo, who slid it over to Meeks, who stared at it a long time before giving it to Horse.

The carpenter held the name between his thick tarry fingers and murmured, "You miss a man so much."

The others nodded.

You miss a man so much.

"Now mine!" Meeks cried.

Archer winked at Sefia. She felt her cheeks go hot.

Rolling her eyes, Marmalade pulled a pile of canvas scraps from a pocket of her loose patchwork jacket and slapped them onto the table.

Sefia bent over her work while the others anted up coins of varying sizes and degrees of cleanliness: loys from Deliene, caspers and angs from Everica, someone even had a single squint coin from Roku. It was these tiny details that showed the littlest kingdom's deep-rooted ties to its Oxscinian colonizers: it looked almost exactly like a copper kispe, except squints had square holes through their centers. Digging into his pocket, Archer added a few coins too.

"Where'd you get those?" Sefia asked.

"He won them last night! From me!" Theo exclaimed, upsetting the bird on his shoulder. "I loaned him some to get him started, but boy, was that a mistake. He's nearly as good as Marmalade."

Archer grinned.

Together, they rattled the wooden cubes and upturned

their cups. Ship of Fools was a simple game played in seafaring vessels all across Kelanna. Players had five dice and three rounds to earn points, with betting before each of the rounds.

First, players tried to roll a six, a five, and a four in descending order. Each number represented something different: the six, a ship; the five, a captain; and the four, a crew. You couldn't keep a crew without first having a captain, and you couldn't keep a captain without first having a ship. Or so the logic went. Archer set aside two dice—a six and a five—and swept the other three off the table.

Sefia watched the fine hair on his forearms gleaming in the lamplight. Every short strand was pointed perfectly in the same direction, and for a moment she wanted nothing more than to trail the backs of her fingers along his arms, seeking out the shapes of muscles beneath his skin.

Her hand slipped, and a fat blotch appeared at the end of Meeks's name. Blushing, she crumpled the piece of canvas in her hand and reached for another.

Horse leaned over the table. "How're you feelin', Sef? After what happened today?"

She shrugged as they bet and rolled their dice again. After you had a ship, captain, and crew, you rolled for cargo: three for a crate, two for a keg, and one for a gunnysack. Points were awarded for bigger cargo, and the best you could hope for was two crates, or six points. The trick was in deciding when to stop rolling and stick with your dice, because there was always a chance that you'd end up with nothing. Archer picked out a cube with four pips, dropping the last two in his cup and placing a copper coin in the pot.

"Okay, I guess," Sefia said.

Meeks shook his head. "Must be a strange thing, seein' your past."

"Yeah . . ." She finished the *S* at the end of his name with a flourish and set the piece of canvas aside.

"You ever seen your future in the book?"

"What? No."

They rolled for a third time. Horse grimaced at his dice and dumped them all back into his cup. Theo cursed and did the same. The bird chirped. Marmalade lined up a six, a five, a four, a three, and a one, glanced at Archer's dice, and laughed gleefully, gathering up the coins in the center of the table and stacking them into neat piles in front of her.

"But Cap said the book had the whole history of everything inside it," Meeks said, scratching his head.

"Yeah, but I haven't seen it all."

"So Cap's still the only one I ever met who knows his future." He shook his head incredulously. Then, to Archer: "'Sides you, of course."

Surprised, Archer touched the ring of white skin around his neck.

"Yeah. You know—the boy with the scar."

Theo and Marmalade glanced uncomfortably from Meeks to Archer and back again.

"We know the story," Sefia said wearily. "Serakeen wants him to lead a great army or some such."

Puzzled, Meeks sat up a little straighter and cocked his head. "What about the rest?"

"Let it go, Meeks," Horse warned.

"What do you mean?" Sefia asked.

The second mate frowned. "There's more to the story, Sef."

Theo adjusted his glasses uneasily. "It's just a story, though. No point in tellin' it if you haven't heard it."

"Right," Horse growled.

The bird bobbed its head.

Sefia looked to Archer, who nodded. "No. We want to hear it."

Meeks sighed heavily and tucked his dreadlocks away from his face. "They say he will lead a great army, and he will overcome many foes. He will be the greatest military leader the world has ever seen, and he will conquer all Five Islands in a bloody altercation known as the Red War." His voice grew softer and softer as he spoke, and the last sentence came out as little more than a whisper. "He will be young when he does it, but . . ."

Archer had gone a sickly greenish-gray. They'd heard the part about the army, but none of the rest. *The Red War.* An escalation of the war between Oxscini and Everica? Or some new horror? They hadn't known. He hunched over, one hand tap-tapping at his scar.

"But what?" Sefia demanded.

The second mate's dark eyes gleamed sadly. "But he will die soon after his last campaign—alone."

There was silence in the cabin.

"I'm sorry, Archer." Apologetically, Meeks reached across the table, but Sefia smacked his hand away. Paint spattered over the gaming surface.

"I don't believe that and you shouldn't either," she snapped.

"*He* isn't *that* boy. And don't you ever say anything like that again."

If Meeks hadn't already been pressed against the surgeon's workbench, he would have taken a step back. As it was, he nodded miserably. "I'm sorry," he repeated.

Sefia thrust the brush back into the paint and crossed her fingers, one over the other. "I meant it when I said you'd never have to fight again," she said to Archer. "Never."

He traced the backs of her fingers and nodded.

She wrapped her hand around his and squeezed once before turning to Meeks again. "How d'you know all of this anyway?"

The second mate tugged sheepishly at the ends of his dreadlocks. "I collect stories."

Horse leaned toward Archer, tipping the table so the coins and dice began to slide toward him. The others scrambled to stop them. "It ain't you, all right?" His voice was low and deep and urgent. "It ain't you."

"I don't *want* it to be Archer, Sef. But I'd be lyin' if I said I didn't want to be part of that story." Meeks didn't look at her as he studied the scrap of his name. "We got such a short time in this world, you know? Cut shorter by the blasted foolishness of men. Tavern brawls, rival outlaws, wars that claim the lives of thousands. Our existence is so small that most of us only matter to a handful of folks: the captain, the crew, maybe a couple others. But bein' part of a story like that? A story that'd blow all others outta the water in its greatness and scope? It wouldn't give me more time here, but if I was part of something like that, maybe my life wouldn't be so small. Maybe I could make a difference before my time ran out. Maybe I'd matter."

Sefia wanted to stay mad at him, but there was such sad desperation to his words, the same desperation she'd seen in Captain Reed when he asked to see himself in the book, the same desperation she'd heard at Harison's funeral when they sang his body into the sea, that her anger evaporated like water. She took up the brush again and met Meeks's gaze across the table.

He smiled sadly.

"But Serakeen isn't mentioned in the prophecy?" Sefia asked.

Meeks shook his head. "Just the boy."

"But if he controls the boy, he wins the war," she said.

Theo made a disgusted sound in his throat. "Outlaws used to have principles. You could claim your ship, you could claim your spoils. But the ocean was for all of us."

"Serakeen wants more than the ocean, though," Sefia said. "Why else would he be kidnapping all those boys? He wants the kingdoms as well as the seas."

To her surprise, the others laughed.

"No one would stand for it," Marmalade said. "No way, no how."

Theo nodded so vigorously the little lory raised her wings and scuttled sideways down his arm. "Oxscini and Everica'd even set aside their differences to put him in his place," he said.

The bird climbed from Theo to the table and onto Archer's hand. He straightened with surprise.

"But all those boys—" she began.

"They don't even come close to what the other kingdoms got," Theo said.

"Yeah," Meeks added, "and if you think Cap or any self-respectin' outlaw would bow to *any* man, you got another think comin'."

Theo adjusted his glasses. "You don't have to worry, Archer. Like Marmalade said, no one would stand for it. The Red War's a myth."

Horse nodded. "Got that, Meeks? A *myth*."

The second mate raised his hands. "I hear ya, Horsey. But Serakeen believes it's true. He ain't gonna stop just because someone tells him he's chasin' a lie."

Marmalade rattled her dice cup impatiently. "We gonna play or what?"

While they rolled their dice, Sefia looked to Archer, who met her gaze. A muscle twitched in his cheek.

"No," she murmured. "But someone has to stop him."

CHAPTER 32

Outlaws

Tufts of Jaunty's straw-colored hair stuck out around his ears and under the brim of his hat like tussocks of dry grass. He scratched the side of his face, his fingernails scraping along the patchy stubble of his jaw. The planes of his lined, wind-hardened face were dark in the afternoon sun.

Captain Reed stood beside him, tall and lanky, with his hat shading his ocean-blue eyes from the sun. Deep creases curved around his generous mouth, showing signs of humor, though he was studying the sea, and not smiling now.

Swaying slightly at the gentle rocking of the ship, Archer watched them both. Jaunty never said much to him during the long, four-hour watches, and when the captain joined them, he didn't add much to the conversation either, but that was all right. Archer didn't mind silence.

He scanned the deck, as he did every few minutes, and picked out Sefia perched on the edge of the quarterdeck, hunched over the book in her lap. Her long black hair was in a ponytail, but the wind kept whisking locks of it across her face, into her eyes. She drew it back with her fingers, but she was so engrossed in the reading that soon her hand dropped to the page and her hair escaped again, flying wildly in the wind. Archer smiled.

Jaunty turned the helm three spokes to the port side, going hand over hand on the wheel. A minute later the breeze grew stronger, filling the sails with the huge rippling sounds of stretching canvas. The ship began to speed faster and faster through the sea, pushed along by the new wind.

The old helmsman winked at Archer.

"Been a week since we met with the assassin and we still ain't found the ship she came from," the captain said abruptly, his voice coarse as sandpaper. "That strike you as peculiar?"

Archer nodded. Something should have happened by now. If whoever sent the assassin had been desperate enough to send someone onto the *Current of Faith*, they shouldn't have given up so easily.

"Makes you wonder, don't it?" Captain Reed said. "You reckon you scared 'em off?"

Archer shrugged.

Jaunty laughed. Even his laughter was gruff, more like a bark than a laugh.

The captain chuckled. "Don't be modest, kid. Horse said you flung that knife straight through the steps into that woman's arm."

Archer tapped the edge of his scar uncertainly, prodding the uneven, knotted skin.

"I heard Meeks stuck his foot in his mouth again, tellin' you about the Red War."

He nodded.

Captain Reed sucked at his teeth. "Did you know about it, before he told you?"

Archer shook his head. His memory only really began the night Sefia had opened the crate. He remembered the light on the floor, the cool biting air, and her voice: *Come with me. Please, come with me.* But before that . . . flashes. Different flavors of pain. Shouting. Darkness. Whatever his life had been before she rescued him, it hadn't been worth remembering.

"D'you think it's about you?" the captain asked.

Archer rubbed his arm, counting the burns. Fifteen. And then he'd killed those men in the forest, two more on the dock. But he was afraid he'd killed more than that. He was too good at it. But he didn't like it. He did it only because he had to.

"I saw you fight on Black Boar Pier. You coulda killed 'em all."

Jaunty grunted in agreement, but Archer shook his head. He wouldn't have been fast enough to save her, to stop Hatchet from killing her. He'd dropped the knife.

He stuck his hand into his pocket and grasped the piece of quartz Sefia had given him. With slow, deliberate strokes, he began running his thumb over the crystal's faces, once across each plane before rotating it and beginning again.

Captain Reed eyed him thoughtfully. "I built my whole life around the stories they tell about me. You know what I learned?"

Archer shook his head.

"What you do makes you who you are. If all you do is kill, then you're a killer."

Archer nodded and pointed to his neck.

The captain snorted. "I seen you do more than that, kid. You saved Horse. You protected your girl. A killer woulda let her die on the docks so he could get at his enemies. But you didn't."

Archer turned toward the quarterdeck, where Sefia was sitting. She'd barely moved—her hand was slightly off center on the page, and more of her hair had come loose from its ties, but she had that same familiar crease to her forehead, that same purse of her lips he'd come to know so well: pressed together lightly at the corners, making them a little rounder in the center. Slowly, he let the worry stone go, and felt it fall to the bottom of his pocket as he withdrew his hand.

"I ran away from home when I was sixteen," the captain said. He frowned at the water, and the lines on his forehead and under his eyes became more pronounced. "I reckon you know that from the stories about me."

Archer nodded. Jaunty adjusted his grip on the wheel, extending his index finger ever so slightly to feel the wind.

"I was just a stupid kid," Captain Reed continued. "I didn't have anyone like Sefia to look out for me—and I got caught as soon as I left Deliene. That part ain't in the legends about me." He sighed. "Don't know who it was that captured me, 'cause they didn't keep me very long, but they did things . . . mean, rotten things . . . and to this day I still can't figure out why. It makes it worse, somehow, not knowin'." He scratched his chest, and his fingers made a soft rustling sound on his cotton shirt. "I don't know why they let me go either. But when they did, I promised myself I'd die before giving up my freedom again. That's why I became an outlaw."

Archer touched his fingers to his forehead, his way of asking a question.

The captain chuckled in a hard, barbed-wire way. "No king but the wind, no law but the water."

Jaunty nodded.

When Archer frowned, Captain Reed took off his hat and ran his hand through his hair. "What I mean is, we're free. We choose what we want to do and who we want to be. Sometimes you gotta fight hard for it, but it's worth it, to choose for yourself."

Jaunty curled his lip in a lopsided smile, exposing a few stained teeth. "But you don't gotta be an outlaw to do that," he said.

Archer glanced at Captain Reed, who nodded and stuck his hat back on his head, ending their conversation. Both he and the helmsman returned to watching the water.

But Archer wasn't done. Ever since Sefia had broken him out of that crate, he'd been half-person, relearning simple tasks like feeding and clothing himself, and half-animal, killing without thought or remorse. He could feel that mad stinking creature from the crate starving for blood inside him, its sunken features lurking behind his own face, but maybe it didn't have to be like that. Maybe he could choose to be all-person: Archer, hunter, protector, artichoke-trimmer, gambler, ship's boy, quartz-holder, friend. This realization began to simmer inside him, slowly at first, but then faster and fiercer, until he was hot and brimming with it.

Maybe he could choose.

He found Sefia exactly where she'd been the last time he looked: bent over the book, her bare shoulders slender and dark with sun. Grinning, he bounded up to her in a few quick strides and sat down beside her.

As she looked up, the wind whipped a lock of hair into her face and she sputtered, pawing it down again. "Hi."

At her smile, his heart quickened. He leaned over, daring to brush her forehead with his fingertips, half-afraid that she'd pull away. But she didn't, and he slid her hair back until it curled around her ear.

She smiled, with the barest suggestion of teeth. "Thanks."

He could not remember wanting anything so badly as he wanted to kiss her now. To be *that* close to her, mouth to mouth, testing the shapes of her teeth and her lips. It was as if he'd never really wanted anything, and now this wanting blazed inside him like a lamp, the light reflecting out of him as bright as a beam from a lighthouse.

But he didn't dare.

He looped his arms over the rails, and made his sign for the book.

And Sefia began to read to him, her voice clear and strong in the wind, and that was enough. It didn't matter what the book or the legends said. What mattered was that he and Sefia were *there*, legs kicking idly off the edge of the quarterdeck, with the breeze and the bright afternoon sun pouring over them. What mattered was that they were together . . . and he was happy.

And they still had two more hours till their next watch.

CHAPTER 33

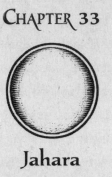

Jahara

Jahara was a mostly neutral island governed by a council of representatives from each of the Five Kingdoms, though due to its proximity to the southern coast of Deliene, the Delienean councilor's vote held twice the weight of the others. Separated from the Northern Kingdom by the narrow Callidian Strait, its location in the Central Sea made it an ideal port for commerce, and all manner of folk, from criminals to outlaws to court ambassadors, were welcomed to the city, under the promise that no person in Jahara could be charged or killed for crimes committed elsewhere. Out of respect for the city's neutrality, even Oxscinian and Everican civilians kept to this one cardinal rule. Though lately, the number of stabbings, shootings, and acts of arson had climbed so high that the Red and Blue Navies were no longer permitted in Jahara.

The *Current of Faith* reached the city at dusk, when the sun was a globe of molten glass sinking into the black water. The lamplighters were already at work, and the hills twinkled with hundreds of tiny quivering flames. Lined with lamps, the long piers jutted into the water, crossing one another in a twisted maze of ships and docks, so the whole city appeared out of the twilight like a glittering labyrinth, teeming with life.

As the gangway settled against the pier, some of the men cheered. They counted their coins and gathered their things, planning their night ashore.

Sefia looked down the dock, feeling very small. They were still a long way from land, separated from solid ground by an array of ships from every corner of Kelanna. Sloops and cutters, brigs and barques, flagged with silks of red and blue and green.

"I grew up in Deliene," Sefia murmured. "Shinjai Province." Deliene was separated into four provinces: Corabelli Land in the south; then Ken and Alissar divided by the long spine of Rider's Wall; then Shinjai, the mountainous region that supplied much of Deliene's lumber; and Gorman in the far north, a land of stony islands and icy waters.

Archer looked at her, startled.

She shrugged. "But it's not home anymore."

As they made ready to disembark, the crew of the *Current* gathered to say good-bye. Sefia and Archer got hugs and handshakes and earnest invitations to find the *Current* again when their quest was over. Some of the crew members even gave them presents.

Cooky and Aly loaded them with enough provisions to fill their packs to the point of overflowing: smoked meats, dried fruit with supple flesh, and enough hardtack to last for weeks.

"Special recipe, that," Cooky said. "Tastes better and lasts longer than any dinner roll you'll find on land."

Meeks gave them money.

Jaunty nodded curtly at them, which was as good a farewell as anyone ever got from him.

"Where's Archer?" Horse shouldered in between Jules and Theo, who moved aside good-naturedly. "Come here, kid."

Archer stepped forward uncertainly. Though he wasn't short by any standards, he was dwarfed by the big carpenter.

"This boy saved my life," Horse announced. As he spoke, he extended his hands, palms up, and uncurled his fingers—Archer's sign for helping. "I owe him a blood debt that someday I gotta repay." He clapped Archer on the back. "Till then, I got somethin' for you."

Theo, Meeks, and Marmalade were grinning and nudging each other with their elbows, whispering. Together they passed forward a sword in a worn wooden scabbard and a gun. Horse took them solemnly and bowed his head for a moment before he said, "These belonged to Harison. I don't think he woulda minded me givin' them to you."

Archer took the gun from its holster and cradled it in his hands. It was a revolver with a walnut grip, simple but true.

"His pa gave him that gun," Meeks added.

Archer nodded and carefully holstered it again before pulling the sword from its sheath. Like the gun, it was a plain weapon, but it was sharp and well cared for. He let it shine for a few moments in the dock light before he slid it back into its scabbard. With some ceremony, he took the weapons and made a short bow to Horse, who slapped him on the back again.

When they were through with most of the good-byes, the chief mate stepped forward and presented Sefia with a thin wooden wand, straight and smooth.

"We don't give these out lightly."

The crew murmured in agreement.

She took the stick from him and ran her fingers along it. It smelled faintly of mint and medicine. "What is it?"

"A wand made from the same stand of trees as the *Current* herself. For calling us, if you need our help. No matter when, we'll come running." He explained that the same magic that tied him to the ship also tied him to the wand, and if Sefia and Archer spoke to it, he would be able to hear them as clear as if they were standing beside him. "Don't use it if you're not in trouble, though. We're outlaws, not nannies."

Sefia nodded and tucked the wand into her belt like a sword. "Thank you, sir."

He patted her shoulder. "Good girl."

She blinked back tears. Aside from Archer, the crew of the *Current* were the first friends she'd ever had, and the thought of not seeing them every day made her heart hurt in a way she hadn't expected. She looked from one to another, trying to find the words, but all she managed was a half-choked smile.

Archer bowed—a formal gesture, but the others nodded approvingly.

Then Captain Reed came striding down the deck in a long walking coat with his hat pulled low over his face. In one hand he tossed a small leather packet up and down; in the other he carried the book.

As he drew near, Sefia felt the weight of his gaze on her. "Good luck on your treasure hunt, Cap," she said. "I expect to hear stories about you and the Trove of the King any day now."

His blue eyes glinted. "One day, kid, but there's like to be a spot of trouble 'fore this thing's done."

"That's what'll make it a good story."

He chuckled and returned her lock picks, which she stowed inside her vest, and then he handed her the book. She took it solemnly and clasped it to her chest.

"I'm sorry I couldn't find your place in the book again, sir," she said.

He winked and patted his pocket, where he kept the scrap of canvas Sefia had given him a week before. "Got my name out of it, didn't I? You've given us all a gift, Sef. We won't forget it."

The rest of the crew nodded. There was a fever in their eyes and in their hearts, and it burned so hot they could never rest for long. For them, life was only as good as their next adventure, and they chased after the wildest ones like whalers hunting giants across the mighty seas.

The wind coming off the sea ruffled their hair and tugged at their clothing. Captain Reed raised his head and sniffed the air. "Be careful. Whatever you think you'll find at this place Hatchet mentioned, if it's got anything to do with Serakeen, it ain't good."

"We still have to go."

"You're outlaws now, kid. You don't *have* to do anything."

Sefia smiled grimly. "We have to find him. We have to know."

Reed looked down at her, and beneath the brim of his hat his eyes were very blue and very sad. He started down the gangplank, his boots thudding against the boards. "Sometimes you find things and you wish you hadn't," he said softly. "Sometimes you wish they'd stayed lost."

Once Reed had disappeared down the dock with Jules and Marmalade, the ship's fastest sprinters, and the other crew members had dispersed on their various errands and nightly adventures, Sefia and Archer were left standing on the pier with Horse and Meeks, who had found them a guide: a small ferrety man in a ratty green coat.

"This here's Gerry," the second mate said proudly. "No better guide in Jahara."

Horse looked skeptical, but Gerry nodded sourly and tugged at one of his fraying sleeves.

"So, where we goin', Sef?" Meeks asked.

She glanced at Archer, thinking back to the night they'd met: Hatchet's men trekking through the jungle, the smell of the roast and the idle chatter of his crew. Half of them were dead now—Patar and Tambor in the clearing, Landin and One-Eye, whose name she had never learned, and Palo Kanta by the cabin, at least two more on the dock. But she and Archer were still here.

"The Cage," she said. "I heard them talking about a place called the Cage."

Gerry flicked a sideways glance at her. "Pay up front."

Meeks wagged a finger at him. "Half now, half later."

The guide grumped and started down the dock, leaving the others to follow after.

According to Meeks, all kinds of people set up shop in the Central Port, using a network of catwalks and rickety wooden planks to connect their barges and narrow boats. It was said you could walk a mile in any direction and still not set foot onshore. Wealthy merchants built wide walkways leading directly to their stores, while poor ones jostled for room wherever they could find it. The web of shops and ships and rotting bridges changed so often that after a month, the port would become an entirely new labyrinth.

"And that's why you always hire a guide!" Meeks declared as they passed the last of the tall ships at the end of the dock. "I ain't got to tell you the scrapes I been in 'cause I didn't get myself a guide."

Ahead of them, Gerry snorted.

"The captain didn't hire a guide," Sefia pointed out.

"Yeah, but he's Captain Reed, ain't he? He don't need one."

"Neither did the rest of the crew."

"All right, if you're bein' exact about it. But you get the point, don't you? It ain't safe here."

The guide led them past the outer piers into the floating market. During the day, it was filled with colored tents and vendors of all sorts, but at night the barges were flat deserted spaces strewn with bits of trash and rotting fruit rinds. Oversize wharf rats skittered through the shadows.

As they traveled farther into the maze, the glass lamps

became scarcer, until only a stray torch or a narrow boat's dim lantern lit the rotting boardwalks. Archer and Horse were quiet and alert, searching for movement in the shadows. Overhead, the sky was a bruised yellowish-purple.

They passed run-down shacks and docks that ended in abrupt pools of dirty water, and beneath the tattered canopies skulked tired old women with no teeth and tawdry dresses, fat men who smoked and followed you with their eyes, hounds so thin you could count their ribs as they snarled at the ends of their chains.

"In these parts, folks are as likely to kill you as trade with you," Meeks whispered. "So be careful."

Archer nodded and pointed to his eyes. He had been watching.

"You remember what I said about scrapes, Sef?"

"I remember."

Finally, they stopped on a catwalk lined with dilapidated taverns. Under a few baleful yellow lamps, a handful of patrons staggered down the street, laughing and listing sideways as they walked. Their guide gestured to a nearby building that appeared to be abandoned. The tavern had no windows, only greenish-gray walls encrusted with mold and salt. Over its door, a hanging birdcage made a plaintive squealing sound in the breeze.

"Ain't that funny." Horse touched the wall with a rough hand and examined the grime on his fingers. "I been down this street plenty, but I ain't never noticed this place before."

Meeks nodded sagely. "Such is the way of the Central Port."

"Shut up, Meeks. You ain't seen it before neither." He turned to Gerry, who flinched under his huge shadow. "You sure this is the waterin' hole we're lookin' for?"

Their guide nodded. "Ask around. The Cage is the only place Hatchet comes to drink." He glanced up and down the street nervously, his narrow eyes flicking from side to side.

Horse knocked on the wall. "It don't even look like it's open."

The little man shrugged and tugged at his threadbare collar. "You wanted the Cage. I showed you to the Cage." He cleared his throat and rubbed his fingers together, staring at Meeks.

"Right, right." The second mate palmed Gerry a silver loy, and the man slunk off down the alley, leaving them alone in front of the tavern.

"You don't hafta do this, Sef," Horse said. "You can come with us."

"It'll be a great story," added Meeks.

She studied their faces. Horse's wide-set eyes and his constant smile, the dimples like brackets around his mouth. Meeks's broad nose and his one chipped tooth. And for a second she hesitated.

But then she looked up, and in the floor of the birdcage, like a spider in the center of a web, was the symbol she had been seeking.

It was small enough that you wouldn't notice it if you weren't looking for it, but Sefia knew it so well she could see it even when she closed her eyes.

Two curves for her parents, a curve for Nin. The straight line for herself. The circle for what she had to do: Learn what the book was for. Rescue Nin from the people who killed her father. And get her revenge.

"Look," she said, pointing.

Archer nodded solemnly.

"Well I'll be . . ." Horse muttered. Then he hugged them both to his massive barrel chest. "You see Serakeen, you even hear a whisper that he's around, you run, hear?" His voice rumbled on Sefia's cheek. "You run as fast and as far as you can."

She hugged him tighter.

"Lemme hear you say it. You won't mess with Serakeen."

"Yes, Horse."

Once the big carpenter released them, thumping them both on the backs for good measure, Meeks peered at them anxiously. "You got the wand the mate gave you?"

Sefia patted her belt.

Meeks hugged them, first Archer, then Sefia. "I know you want answers, Sef," he whispered in her ear. "You want 'em like I want stories, and if you're like me, you'll do anything to get 'em."

She nodded.

"Use the wand if you have to. Even if you have to use it tonight."

As he and Horse started off down the alley, they kept looking back at the two young people, until finally they turned the corner and were gone.

Sefia fingered the wand the mate had given her. "I guess this is it."

Archer nodded and pushed on the door, but it didn't open.

"Locked?" Sefia dug into her vest for her lock picks and went to work. In a minute, the teeth clicked and the door swung open. There was little light inside, but they could make out a stained floor, round tables, and row upon row of dusty brown bottles lining the wall to their right. The bartender was nowhere to be seen.

They crept inside, wary of ambush, but the place was empty. Breathing in the stale air, Sefia grew light-headed. She knew this place.

"Palo Kanta was supposed to have come here too," she whispered.

Archer looked at her sharply.

"Here." She stood at the corner of the bar and looked out over the empty tavern. Then she stepped back again. "And here." All around the room, she could see glimpses of the tall man with the cut across his chin: Laughing, mouth open, molars showing. His fingers fondling a gold mai. Dirt under his nails.

She wove between the tables, feeling as if she were walking in his footsteps, and stopped at the far end of the room. She thought she heard a few distant shouts. "And here," she murmured.

Archer came to stand beside her.

"He should have been here . . . and below here." She knelt, searching the floor with her hands until they found a round metal handle in the shape of the ⬯.

"I thought this tavern was on a floating barge like the others," she whispered.

With Archer's help, she heaved open the trapdoor, revealing a narrow stone staircase illuminated from below. The sounds of shouting, which she thought she'd only imagined, were clear now—excited and agitated.

"Palo Kanta was supposed to go down there." From her pack, Sefia took out a brush and the small jar of paint Horse had given her as a parting gift. Carefully, she wrote Palo Kanta's name on the inside of the trapdoor, near the hinge. She blew on the words to dry them and whispered, "You miss a man so much."

Archer's eyes looked large and bright in the dim light. As she put the lid on the jar and stowed it back in her pack with the brush, Sefia was reminded again of what Hatchet's men had said: *One of them big cats, with the golden eyes.*

Together they descended the stairwell. The farther they went, the brighter and noisier it became, and with every step Sefia felt Archer growing more and more tense beside her, until he seemed hard and brittle as glass.

"What's wrong?" She reached out, but didn't touch him, afraid he would break under her fingers.

He shook his head.

When they reached the bottom, they found themselves in a low stone room with a loud, stinking crowd of people clustered in the center. They were shouting—numbers, bets, odds—and laughing uproariously. The stone walls were wet with condensation, and the hot moist air smelled like sweat and iron and liquor.

Archer's breathing quickened. He shook his head again, gripping the hilt of his sword so tight his knuckles turned white. From somewhere in the center of the room came a sharp sound: *bang!—bang!—bang!* Metal on wood. Archer flinched.

"Oh no . . ." Sefia's heart sank in her chest. "It's a fighting ring."

CHAPTER 34

The Cage

Panting, Archer stumbled back against the wall, his eyes wide with fear. Sefia tugged him toward the stairwell. "C'mon. We'll come back later."

But it was too late. An old balding man detached from the crowd and came toward them, leaning heavily on a broom for support. "What are you doing here?"

Sefia was struck by his thinness, as if he had wasted away down here, and all he had to hold himself up now was the broom he clung to like a walking stick. Curled around the handle, his hands were as smooth and hard as river stones.

"Who's that?" someone cried from the crowd. The others began to turn. They had greedy gleaming eyes. Cut knuckles. Guns and swords and hidden knives. People accustomed to violence, who sucked it down like ale.

Archer cringed but remained at her side.

"I'm Sefia and this is Archer."

"I'm the Arbitrator here," said the man with the broom. "What do you want?"

Arbitrator. She recognized the word. Arbitrators were the men who ran the fights, men who worked for Serakeen. She swallowed hard. "We saw the sign under the cage."

The Arbitrator looked Archer up and down, his gaze resting fleetingly on the boy's neck. Archer swallowed so hard Sefia felt his entire body shudder. "We've already got two candidates tonight," the man said.

"Boys?" She glanced at the crowd. Were they impressors? Cutthroats and kidnappers, like Hatchet? Archer wasn't safe here. She twined her arm in his.

"Candidates." The Arbitrator swung back to the crowd. "It's all right. He's got the mark." He waved Sefia and Archer over with a large hand. "Come on, then. This is what you're here for, isn't it?" Without waiting for them, he shuffled back into the crowd, which parted for him like water parting for a stone.

The stairwell rose in a black spiral behind them. They could still get away if they had to.

She looked to Archer. It had to be his choice to go on.

He nodded.

Sefia tightened her grip on his hand, and together they waded into the throng.

The crowd had closed behind the Arbitrator, and they jostled her as she approached the wide depression in the center of the room. Some of them sneered. She caught glimpses of leering

356

wag-tongued expressions and slitted eyes. Beyond them, she spied a tunnel at the opposite end of the room. Another escape, maybe. In case they had to fight their way out.

As she reached the hole, she could feel Archer still quivering beside her. Inside, about ten feet down, the floor was strewn with straw and sawdust. On opposite ends of the pit were two wooden doors notched and spattered with dried blood, and behind them, in narrow stone chutes, were two boys.

One of them was tall and slender as a whip, with a shock of dark hair tumbling over his eyes. He leaned on a spear, silent and still, watching the other boy through the slats in the door.

His opponent was shorter and thicker, built like an ox, with a low jutting brow and broad cheeks, and he hacked and battered at his door, making it shudder and jump under his sword. Every time he struck, Archer flinched, gripping his sword tighter and tighter and tighter.

Both were shirtless and barefoot, like Archer had been when Sefia found him, and their arms were marked by fifteen burns— one for each of the fights they'd already won.

Forty-five fights.

All told, the three of them had killed forty-five other boys. At least.

Sefia's hand slid to her knife. That people could *do* this. Over and over again. With such rabidity.

She'd find out where Serakeen was. She'd find out what happened to Nin. And then—

"He's been marked?" Someone shoved her way through the crowd—a gray-haired woman with a hooked nose and a scar across her cheek. A whale-tooth necklace, the kind common in the northern parts of Deliene, hung around her neck.

"Yes, Lavinia, he's got the mark." The Arbitrator grunted.

"He can't be here unless he's got the count too," said a man whose old blue military cap marked him as a former member of the Everican Navy.

Sefia scanned the crowd. Clustered around one end of the fighting pit were people who must have been impressors from the Stone Kingdom of Everica. From above, they goaded and prodded the short boy, who responded by hacking away at the door with his sword. Opposite them, the impressors from northern Deliene waited while their boy stood silently in the chute below.

The rest must have been spectators, bettors who came to gamble on the outcome of the fight. It made her sick.

The Arbitrator leaned on his broom and peered at Sefia and Archer. "Where are you from?"

"Oxscini," she said. Clasping his hand, she could still feel Archer shaking like a leaf clinging to its stem.

"Is he one of Garula's?"

Sefia shook her head.

"Berstrom's?"

"No."

"Fengway's?"

How many impressors were there? She shook her head again. "He's his own."

"Then you're a fool for coming here." The Arbitrator scratched his forehead. "Do you even know what you're getting into?"

Sefia took a deep breath. "Where's Serakeen?"

Bang!—bang!—bang! The sounds echoed from inside the chute.

"But has he got the count?" said the man in the blue cap.

Sefia glared at him. "What's so important about this 'count'?"

"You really are a fool, aren't you, kid? It's how Serakeen vets the candidates. He's got impressors working for him in every kingdom except Roku. Candidates fight fifteen times in their own territory, and when they're done, they come to the Cage. I arrange a fight, and if they win, they get sent to Serakeen." The Arbitrator shrugged. "No one knows what happens to them after that."

"'Cause all that matters is we get paid!" someone shouted. There was a round of hideous jeering laughter.

Sefia squeezed Archer's hand. "We don't want to fight."

More laughter in the crowd. "He's got to," the Arbitrator explained. "No one moves on without a fight."

Archer collapsed at the knees, stumbling. The others laughed.

"We've never had a three-way fight before," said Lavinia, eyeing the Arbitrator carefully.

"It doesn't matter if he doesn't have the count," the man in the blue cap repeated. "He can't fight if he doesn't have it."

"I *know*, Goj," snapped the Arbitrator. "Don't make a fool of yourself."

"Stop it!" Sefia shouted. "He's not going to fight!"

"Then you're not seeing Serakeen."

She reached for her coin purse. "I'll pay—"

Lavinia laughed. Her canines were sharp in her mouth. "The last person who tried to bribe an Arbitrator had his tongue removed."

"Then how about—"

"Show us the count or get out," said Goj.

"He has my aunt! I have to find out—"

"You'll find out nothing if he doesn't make the kill." The Arbitrator pointed at Archer, who shook his head again. "And it doesn't look like he's up to it. Fight or leave. Those are your choices."

Sefia glared at the Arbitrator, but his eyes were stony and his jaw was set and she didn't need the Vision to know he wasn't going to relent. And then she turned to Archer.

The crowd seemed to have parted around him, and he was standing all alone, the lamplight glinting off his hair and glimmering in the wells of his eyes, and he looked at her, and never in her life had anyone seen her so perfectly, seen all the best and worst parts of her, and she had never wanted so badly for things to be different.

Serakeen was the only clue she had to the symbol on her book. The only way she could find out who had taken Nin. And if she was still alive.

But it would cost her Archer. Because he'd have to do what she'd promised, over and over, he'd *never* have to do again.

She had been right all along.

No one she loved was safe.

She longed to wrap her arms around him and tell him he didn't have to. He didn't have to fight again. But she didn't move, and the words didn't come, and while she hesitated, he tilted his head to the side in a movement that was so familiar it looped around her heart and pulled tight.

The corners of his mouth twitched.

And his pack dropped to the floor.

All around her, the crowd roared its approval. The cruel, many-throated sound was like a hurricane. And she realized what he had done.

"No—!" She picked up the pack and tried to return it to him, but it was too late. He pulled his shirt over his head.

The crowd rushed forward to see the burns on his arm.

"He's got it! He's got the count!"

"But do we get paid for *each* kill?" Lavinia asked.

The Arbitrator sighed. "Yes."

"Looks like we'll see two kills tonight!" someone cried.

Eager chatter spread across the crowd. Counting and calculations. Weighing the odds. Coins clinked in their palms. Money for blood.

"Fifty peschles on the new kid!"

"Twenty!"

"Another ten on Haku!"

Sefia shook her head. What had she done? What had she let him do? Archer passed her his discarded clothing, which she uselessly tried to press back into his hands. He hadn't fully recovered from the fight on the *Current*—his cuts were still healing, his ribs were still bandaged. She had *promised* him. "No. No! You can't—"

The low-ceilinged room echoed with shouting and the

jangling of coins. Bets made, money exchanged, taunting and heckling and whooping with greed.

Archer unstrapped his holster and was undoing the buckle on his sword sheath when the Arbitrator stopped him. "For this fight, we let the boys have their weapon of choice," he said, glancing at Archer's gun, "with the exception of firearms."

Archer stared at the Arbitrator for a full second before he handed his sword to Sefia. He was going to fight, not wildly, but willingly. As himself and on his own terms.

He stood at the edge of the pit, the crowd surging around him, hissing, mocking, their words scathing and dry as coals.

She fumbled with the clothing in her arms. "Archer." Her lips almost brushed his ear.

He looked down at her, and in his eyes she saw how afraid he was. His fear was a desperate, ragged thing inside him: the boy in the crate, malnourished and laced with scars, a feral creature that couldn't feed or bathe or dress itself, that knew nothing but the fear and the pain and the kill. The thing he had been and was terrified of becoming again.

"Don't do this," she whispered. "We'll find another way."

They were so close she could count the freckles on his cheeks. He blinked, his long lashes dipping, and she thought for a second he was going to nod. He was going to agree, and he wasn't really going to do it. He had some other plan in mind.

Instead he pulled her to him and folded her into his arms, and his skin was warm under her cheek, and for the first time since she left the house on the hill overlooking the sea, she felt *settled* . . . like all the frantic fluttering bits inside her had finally come to rest, here, in his arms. In the sudden stillness she could hear his breath stirring, his heart rustling, and she understood without words or hand signals that he was going to fight—he was going to do it for her, no matter what it turned him into—and nothing she said or did now was going to change his mind.

Catcalls rose up around them like flames—the voices crackled and snapped—and Archer released her. She gasped at the shock of their bodies parting.

He turned away—

She tried to hold on to him, but her hands grabbed uselessly at the air.

"No, wait! Don't!"

He jumped into the pit, kicking up sudden blooms of sawdust and straw.

"Archer!"

Thunder. The crowd roared. The sound of it spun around her like a mad deafening wind.

Lavinia leaned over, her whale-tooth necklace dangling in front of Sefia's face. "He's injured, isn't he, kitten?" Her voice slithered under the noise of the crowd. Lavinia pointed at the black-haired boy with the spear, staring coldly through his door. "Gregor's going to skewer him."

A sour taste rose in Sefia's throat. The other boy, Haku, rattled his door and slashed at it with his sword. *Bang!*—*bang!*—*bang!* The crowd hollered for blood, their voices and the stamping of their feet filling the room with a horrible drumming. She tried to breathe. *Don't die. Don't die. Don't leave me. Don't die.*

Archer drew the piece of quartz from his pocket and stood, rubbing his thumb along its sparkling sides, waiting for the fight to begin.

CHAPTER 35

The Cost of Immortality

Captain Reed reexamined the scrap of canvas and tapped each of the letters with his fingers: REED. Then he scratched his chest, above his heart.

He'd seen words before.

They'd been his first tattoos, before any of the ones he'd given himself.

For a long time they meant nothing to him except abduction: being captured and forced onto his back, his inability to fight, helplessness, pain. As soon as he'd gotten the chance, he'd drawn over them with his own stories, buried them beneath layers of ink so he didn't have to see them every time he looked in the mirror. But now, even though he'd found someone to decipher the markings, he'd never find out what they meant. The words were lost deep in his skin, obscured by decades of ink.

Reed folded the coarse fabric and crammed it back in his pocket.

"You ready, Cap?" Marmalade asked. Her round face was like a moon in the dim light.

He nodded. "This the place?"

The barge in front of them had two crossed spars above the door, just as Dimarion had described when they'd struck up the alliance between the *Crux* and the *Current*.

Somewhere inside was an old bronze clapper belonging to the bell of the *Desert Gold*, the ship that had gone down with King Fieldspar on his return from the Trove. Their next clue.

"I just hope it'll be out in the open," Jules said. "Easy to find."

Marmalade nodded. "Just gimme an opportunity, Cap. I'll filch it for ya." She was always eager, quick to please—and fast. Fast legs, fast hands. She'd been a first-class pickpocket before she joined his crew.

Captain Reed felt the old excitement stirring in his belly— the jittery, gut-jumping anticipation of a good adventure.

He flung open the door.

The walls were covered with knickknacks and baubles, keepsakes and trinkets that mounted up the beams to the corners of the ceiling, all crammed together in a chaotic jumble of odds and ends. Black velvet ribbons, jeweled brooches shaped like dragons, dented tin cups, rusted swords, candelabras, portraits, boots, buttons, awls, alabaster carvings of bears and orcas, broken scissors, bone-handled knives, a faded sketch of a woman in a bear-skin cloak.

A waitress in a long dress with a patch over her right eye swayed up to them. "Welcome to the Crossbars, folks. Who do we have the pleasure of entertaining tonight?"

"I'm Reed. This is Jules and Marmalade. They're part of my crew."

"'Course they are." The woman winked her good eye at him. "I'm Adeline. Good to see you again, Cap. Take a seat anywhere."

Reed glanced back at Jules, who shrugged. Ordinarily, people shook his hand or asked for a story or laughed in disbelief when he introduced himself, but this was a stranger, despite sharing the name of an old friend, and she greeted him like they'd known each other for years.

At the largest table, six ragged men laughed and clinked glasses with old women in wrinkled dresses and faded lace.

"To wealth!" one man cried, raising his mug.

"To youth!" The old woman beside him tittered.

Reed, Jules, and Marmalade slid onto the bar stools and swiveled to survey the rest of the room. Wooden buckets and lanterns and knots of rope dangled from the ceiling.

Jules shrugged. "So much for easy findin'."

They searched the walls for signs of the clapper, but though they found silver bells and strings of glass beads, tambourines and bunches of dried flowers, there was so much junk in the tavern that finding any one thing might take weeks. That is, if the *Beauty* hadn't already gotten it. Reed cursed under his breath.

"Hey, uh . . . Cap? Ain't that your story?" Marmalade pointed to a nearby booth, where an ordinary man with wispy blond hair and a gap in his front teeth was regaling his table-mates with the story of Lady Delune.

"The woman was mad as a bat, screechin' and flappin' about,

her black petticoats all torn and flutterin' around her ankles as she dashed through that big lonely house of hers." Spittle came flying out from between his lips. "I barely caught her before she ran plumb off the balcony . . . not that the fall woulda killed her. She'd survived worse'n that in her long years . . ."

Marmalade leaned over, whispering, "That ain't how it happened, is it?"

"No." Reed drew two interconnected circles on the bar top. When he met the Lady, she'd been sitting in her ruined garden, still as a stone. In fact, among the overgrown shrubbery and fallen leaves, he had mistaken her for a statue, covered as she was by moss and vines. Her face was sad and her eyes were dull, and for all her perfect curves and symmetrical features the only thing that sparkled about her were the jewels in her necklace. They'd had a good long talk while the sun went down and the stars came out, all dusty white in the blue sky, and when dawn appeared pale and pink in the east, he took the diamonds off her, and with the faintest shudder she dissolved and collapsed into a pile of dust.

He started off his stool. The man was getting it wrong. The Cursed Diamonds of Lady Delune was a story about the cost of immortality, not the assault of a two-hundred-year-old woman.

Before he could say anything, Adeline sidled up to them with their mugs in hand. "Good story, huh? Sometimes we get three or four Captain Reeds in one night. I can't tell you how many times I heard that legend. It's never quite the same, is it?"

Reed stacked eight copper zens on the bar. "He's gettin' it wrong."

"Hush your mouth!" She leaned closer, so he could see clots in her makeup. The real Adeline, the Lady of Mercy, the original owner of his legendary gun, didn't wear makeup and wouldn't be caught dead in a dress. "Don't you know? Why'd you come here if you didn't know?"

Marmalade swigged her drink. "Know what?"

Jules sipped at her own mug; over the rim of her glass, her quick observant eyes scanned the room.

"None of these folks are *really* who they say they are," Adeline whispered.

"You don't say."

She laughed and pushed Reed playfully in the shoulder. "I mean, don't tell anyone I said this—especially Clarian, who owns the place"—she pointed to a doughy middle-aged man pouring drinks behind the bar—"but the Crossbars is a tavern of *liars*. Folks come here to tell someone else's story, pretend it's their own, and be believed. No one contradicts anyone else. Those are the rules."

Reed rubbed at a stain on the bar. If you didn't like your own life, you changed it. You ran away. You did something spectacular. You didn't steal someone else's story and pretend it was yours.

In a corner booth, an old woman claiming to be Eduoar, the Lonely King, rambled on and on about the succulent, mouthwatering meals they served at the castle in Corabel.

Pretending to be the Old Hermit of the Szythian Mountains, a man with missing teeth exclaimed over the exquisite footwear of his neighbors and fluttered his fingers along their buckles and aglets.

Adeline drew a pair of imaginary guns from imaginary thigh holsters and posed, fingers pulling imaginary triggers, making little *pew! pew! pew!* sounds with her red mouth.

Reed shuddered. It was like all the good and true things he'd ever done didn't matter, and he, who he was, the legacy he'd worked so hard for, was dissolving, frittering away with every lie they told.

"Lady," he said, "I hate to break it to you, but—"

"Cap." Jules turned the mug in her hands, slyly pointing to the wall behind the bar.

He swallowed his insults, grinned, and stuck out his hand to Adeline. "It's been so long, I didn't recognize you in this light. Good seein' you again. You give my regards to Isabella."

Giggling, she shook his hand and sauntered away, the fringe of her dress whispering against the floorboards.

"Left side," Jules murmured into her drink.

Behind the bar was a mirror and a set of glass shelves cluttered with bottles, but on either side the wall was overlaid with used instruments: drumheads and covered mallets, guitars with no strings, panpipes and flutes and fiddles. But most of all there were bells: big brass bells, old tarnished handbells, little jingling bells on silver chains, with a few gongs and chimes hanging amidst the rest. And there, on a hook, was an old brass clapper, dull and green, with an engraving of a sunrise over a desert half-hidden beneath the crust of verdigris.

The mark of the *Desert Gold.*

All someone had to do was inch behind the bar, snatch it off the hook, and after that it was only a few steps to the door. He glanced at Marmalade, who caught his eye and nodded. She drained the rest of her beer and signaled for another.

Clarian, the owner, began filling another mug with golden ale while he spoke to the pretty young woman seated across the bar from him. "What do they sound like?"

She tilted her pink face and closed her eyes. "Well," she said, "they sounded like trees, but also more than trees. I knew them so well I could hear one leaf rasping against another and know which of them was speaking to me. We'd spin long conversations out of nothing but the rustling leaves and clacking branches. These days, I even miss their creaking, the rough scuttle of squirrels racing over their bark."

The bartender watched her with fascination, his gaze fixed on her lips long after he'd finished pouring Marmalade's drink. "I like to go into the hills," he said finally. "The woods aren't magic, but they still speak: the branches rasping in winter, and the rustling wind. I like the creaking leaves and the birds scuttling their wings." There was something strange about the way he reused the woman's words, but as he spoke, he seemed to light up from the inside, as if his skin and skeleton were nothing more than a lampshade concealing his glowing heart. He slid Marmalade's drink across the worn wooden bar top, where she caught it without spilling a drop.

Reed left another four zens on the bar. "You ever hear the one about the bell of the *Desert Gold*?"

When Clarian ignored him, Reed cleared his throat. It wasn't until the young woman directed the bartender's attention his way that he turned, fixing his light blue eyes on Reed.

"What's that?" he said.

"The Bell of the *Desert Gold*."

"No, never heard that one." As he spoke, his gaze didn't waver from Reed's face.

Out of the corner of his eye, Reed saw Jules shake her head. The man hadn't looked toward the clapper. Either he didn't know which bell it belonged to, or he was a really good liar. In this place, both were possible.

Reed continued, watching for a flicker of recognition in Clarian's pale face, "They tell this story 'round Liccaro, when the sun goes down in the dusty sky. When King Fieldspar's ship sank in the middle of the Ephygian Bay, everything on board, includin' the sailors and the officers and the secret to where he hid all his pretty treasures, was lost with it. But as legend has it, some days if you're out on the bay, you can still hear the tollin' of the ship's bell from under the water. That mournful sound, like all the folks of Liccaro are cryin' out for what happened to their kingdom. Cryin' out for justice against the regents. Cryin' out for the things they lost, and the poverty, and the long hot days of nothin'."

Clarian gobbled up the description, his eyes feasting eagerly on the words, following every curve and closing of Reed's lips with the same fascination that Sefia had while reading the book, and that's when the captain understood: the man was deaf. His patrons pretended they were more famous or more important than they really were; Clarian pretended he could hear. And in this place, where no one pointed it out or treated him different, maybe that was another kind of spectacular.

His watery eyes drank in the description of the bell, as if he could really hear the deep tolling and the voices keening in the water.

"I'm sorry, bartender," Reed said, "for what's about to happen here."

"What do you mean?"

The man with the wispy hair finished his tale about the Lady Delune by wagging his tongue and thrusting his hips.

Reed spun on his stool and stood. "That ain't how it happened!"

The man's armpits were stained and his shirt was soaked with sweat where it curved over his belly. "That so?"

"You think assaultin' a woman's something to crow about? If you'd ever met the Lady Delune, you'd know she's ten times more beautiful'n you described, and she could easily wipe the floor with a pasty little runt like you." He caught Marmalade's eye and winked. She guzzled her drink and filched a glass of bourbon from a nearby table. Her cheeks were pink, and her eyes sparked. She was ready.

The other people at the man's table chuckled. They tried to hide it by putting their hands over their mouths, but their laughter escaped through their fingers and fell tinkling onto the table.

"I don't get it." Reed laughed. "Why're you lyin' to yourselves like this? You ain't special. You ain't gonna be remembered. Why in all the blue world would you sit here makin' up stories when you could be out there *makin'* stories?"

The others stared at him. They were tense, their faces

peaked, their eyes narrowed. Beside him, Jules sipped her drink and rolled her eyes at his speechifying.

"Who are you to talk to us like that?" the wispy-haired man demanded, starting forward. "You're in here with the rest of us."

Clarian came out from behind the bar, his arms crossed, his gaze stony.

Their anger roiled like a thundercloud. Reed could feel it rumbling inside them, threatening to burst from their clenched fists and teeth.

"I'm Captain Cannek Reed," he drawled. He drew back the folds of his coat, exposing the revolvers holstered at his thighs: one ivory grip, one black. There was a collective gasp.

"Listen," he continued. "We work hard for our stories. They're what *we* leave behind when we're gone. They ain't for some nobodies in a back-alley bar to twist however they so please. So go on. Get outta here. Go do something worth tellin' people about, instead of stealin' from folks like me."

He turned, and the impostor-Reed leapt forward and struck him square across the jaw.

The real Captain Reed came up grinning. "That's right. Come on!"

The little room erupted. Marmalade kicked the chair out from one of the beggars at the big table and he toppled over. Reed laughed. Someone hit him in the head with a mug. Glass and ale poured around his ears. Jules was trading blows with the impostor-hermit. Reed laughed again. A brawl! He just needed to keep them busy. Fighting him. Fighting each other.

The whole tavern was a mess of blood and curses, broken chairs and fists and faces. Clarian punched him in the gut. He doubled over, wheezing and chuckling at the same time. The old woman pretending to be the Lonely King slapped the bartender across the face when he turned around.

Out of the corner of his eye, Reed saw Marmalade wrench the clapper off the wall, tuck it into her coat, and dash for the door. She was so small and quick that no one noticed her in the melee.

Captain Reed let out a shrill whistle.

"Cap?" Jules's voice rang across the room.

"Let's skedaddle!"

She was at his side in an instant, grinning, a bruise coming up red and purple on her cheek. He tossed his coin purse behind the bar and they left, trading a few more blows on the way, bursting out of the door into the night.

Inside the tavern the brawl continued. Glass shattering. Tables breaking. People hollering and cheering. Their wild laughter wafted through the broken windows and steamed in the cool air.

A few docks down, Marmalade was waiting for them, perched on the rail of a houseboat and kicking her legs over the water. As they approached, she popped to her feet and brandished the clapper like a wand. "Ta-da!"

Jules clapped her warmly on the shoulder. "Fast fingers, Marmalade. I wasn't sure you could do it, after the drinks you had."

The ship's girl grinned impishly. "Cap was buyin'. I couldn't help myself." She passed the clapper to Reed, who traced the engraving of the rising sun with his fingernail. According to legend, if they were close enough, any sound the clapper made would be echoed by the bell, still lost in the Ephygian Bay with the *Desert Gold*. He swung it hard into a wooden piling. The post dented, but the clapper let out a dull resounding hum.

Jules touched it with the tip of her finger, absorbing the sound into her skin. "That the right clapper?"

"Oughta be." He tucked it inside his jacket.

They began trotting down the dock, back toward the *Current*, Marmalade chuckling every so often under her breath. "Did you see their faces when the Cap started whoopin' and hollerin' about stories?"

Reed grinned. He could smell the sea, hear it washing against the docks and the faraway shores, calling him to wilder waters, to bigger monsters, and to stories yet to be earned. He chuckled. "Guess they have somethin' to talk about now."

Chapter 36

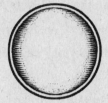

Kill or Die

Sefia stood at the edge of the stone pit, still reeling from the touch of Archer's arms on her arms, his chest on her chest. Her heart beat madly inside her like a trapped bird, feathers flying, wings breaking against the bars, but inside the ring Archer was as still as he had ever been. Waiting, ready.

The roar of the crowd swelled up to the ceiling—a terrible thunder of shouting and stomping and mad laughter—and then it broke across the room like a flood. Men and women swarmed around her, hot and sweaty and howling like animals. The bloodlust was ripe in their eyes and in their teeth. The chute doors swung open. The fighters were loose.

Archer and the boy with the spear reached each other first. Like jaguars battling in the undergrowth, all teeth and muscle and razor-sharp claws, they fought. Fists and the flashing tip of the blade, clouds of dust rising beneath their feet. They were so quick Sefia only caught glimpses of it: Archer grabbing the spear shaft; the other boy, Gregor, sprawled on the ground; craters of sawdust beneath him.

The third boy, Haku, attacked with a sword, but Archer had the spear now. The sounds of metal striking wood rebounded off the stone walls. Chunks of the spear shaft sheared away beneath the sword.

Archer landed blows again and again, cracking bones, causing bruises. Gregor staggered to his feet and joined Haku's attacks, but Archer's movements were effortless—beautiful and awful in their efficiency. It was like he could see every dodge and feint and parry as if they were individual threads in the violent tapestry of the fight, and he could warp and weave and cut them as he pleased.

Sefia was mesmerized and horrified at the same time, because he made it look *easy*.

Like he had been born doing it.

Like he was born *to* do it.

Archer swung the spear. It whirred through the air, a noise that cut off abruptly when its wooden shaft slammed into Haku's neck.

There was no blood. The blade had missed.

No, Archer had spared him.

Haku crumpled, groaning.

In the roar of the crowd, Lavinia muttered, "That was a perfect opportunity. Why didn't your boy kill him?"

Sefia pressed her hands over her ears.

Grabbing Haku's fallen sword, Gregor struck at Archer. The

spear split in two, showering the floor with splinters. Archer was cut. There was *cheering*. Blood matted his hair, dripped down the side of his face—bright red. Gregor swung the blade back and forth, testing its weight.

Then Archer was attacking, his hands a blur, the broken ends of the spear pummeling Gregor's long arms, his shoulders and legs and head in a broken rhythm of blows and bruises and split skin. *Crack!* Archer shattered the bones in the boy's hand.

The sword dropped.

The crowd cried out.

Another blow. Gregor's feet went out from under him and he hit the ground on his back.

The point of the spear hovered just above his throat.

It had taken less than two minutes for Archer to knock one boy unconscious and pin the other to the ground. He wasn't even breathing hard.

The crowd went berserk, hollering, bloodlust throbbing in their throats and eyes as they called eagerly for the kill.

Gregor cradled his ruined hand to his chest and stared up at Archer from beneath his bloodied mop of hair. On the ground, the boy didn't look afraid. He looked . . . ready.

All around her, men and women were shouting, veins bulging in their necks and foreheads, their eyes wide. Sefia tried to shut out the sound of them but their inarticulate cries engulfed her, rushing under her skin.

Archer hefted the spear. The noise of the crowd surged through him. Thunder in his blood. And suddenly he didn't look like Archer anymore. He looked like the boy in the crate.

An animal with bloodshot eyes. A murderer. The smell of dust and stone and sweat intensified.

The crowd swelled. They were hungry for it. There had to be a kill.

Sefia watched him, willing him to look at her. She blinked, and the room burst into a fine gold powder, spinning and sparkling, with Archer and the spear and the boy at the center—all the lines of their lives culminating in this moment: kill or die. A choice you couldn't unmake. Sefia was afraid to breathe, afraid of disrupting those glimmering currents, but she watched, and she hoped. *Not this. You don't want to do this. You don't want to be this. Look up. Please, look up.*

Then he did. His eyes lost that feral look. He became Archer again.

He let his arm drop.

He walked away.

The crowd roared. Dismay. Disgust. Blinking, Sefia was shoved and shouted at—hands groping for her, words lashing at her. Then the pitch of their voices changed. They were excited, eager again.

Gregor had lurched to his feet. He had reached the sword. It was clasped in his uninjured hand. He barreled toward Archer with a wild look in his black eyes, lips pulled back from his teeth.

"Archer!" The word ripped out of her.

At the sound of her voice, he twisted out of the way—too late. The sword scored him across the side. He didn't waver; it was as if he hadn't felt it at all. He beat Gregor with the broken spear: a downpour of blows striking his torso, his kneecaps, his bleeding knuckles. Archer was too fast. The boy couldn't block all of his strikes. They pummeled him. They broke him.

Finally, Archer struck him in the face. Gregor dropped and didn't get up again.

Beside him, Haku stirred and groaned, but couldn't rise.

Both of them were alive.

Archer flung the pieces of the broken spear across the ring and climbed the nearest chute door. As he appeared out of the pit, it seemed as if he were rising out of a well in which he had been lost for a long time, and now all the parts of himself he hated and feared most were flowing off him like water.

Sefia tried to run to him, but a cold hand grabbed her wrist, stopping her. "Not so fast, kitten." The whale-tooth necklace swung in front of her like a pendulum. "There must be a kill," Lavinia said.

The crowd roared again.

Sefia's hand went to her belt, but the wand had fallen out. It lay on the ground near Archer's pack.

"We don't win anything if there isn't a kill!"

"He has to do it! Otherwise he doesn't go to Serakeen!"

Archer balled his fists, but no one dared go near him.

"What does the Arbitrator say?" someone asked.

Sefia squirmed, trying to free her wrist, but Lavinia's nails dug into her skin.

The Arbitrator sighed. "There's always a kill."

Sefia wrenched herself out of Lavinia's grasp, dove for Archer's weapons, and flung them at him. He caught the hilt of his sword in midair, its sheath sliding away, its blade gleaming. The crowd went still. All eyes were drawn to him. Sefia snatched up the mate's wand.

"There must be a kill," the Arbitrator repeated, his face gray as he sagged against the broom for support. "That's how it works."

But Archer was no longer listening to him. He advanced through the crowd, which parted for him like grass withering before a fire. They made no move to stop him as he shouldered his things.

When he was done, he stared intently at the Arbitrator, waiting. Blood ran over his left eye and down his jaw, but in that moment his predisposition toward violence was only a part of what made him so formidable. Violence had made the others take notice, but now his very presence gave him control of the room. He seemed to blaze as if he had swallowed the sun and it was shining through his eyes and teeth. To Sefia, he had never seemed taller.

The Arbitrator wilted under Archer's gaze. The muscles twitched in his jaw.

Then he nodded, and Sefia was not surprised.

"I can't pay you if there isn't a kill," he said weakly.

"We don't want your money. Just tell us where to go next. How to find . . ." The next word tasted foul on her tongue. "Serakeen."

His eyes flicked nervously toward Archer. "Up the tunnel."

The room exploded with objections. Raised voices. Threats of violence. Lavinia slipped out her pistol, a wicked-looking thing with a scrimshaw grip.

Goj, the impressor from Everica, took off his blue cap and shook it angrily in front of the Arbitrator's face. "What gives you the right—"

But the Arbitrator's hard voice echoed off the stone walls. "Do as I say, or Serakeen will hear of it."

Invoking the Scourge of the East silenced them, and for a moment, they peered around uneasily, as if something evil and dark would come seeping out of the cracks in the stones. Then Lavinia spat sideways, and with a little discontented grumbling, the bettors began refunding their wagers, returning bags of coins, counting gold mai and silver angs in their palms.

"The porter will be waiting for you," the Arbitrator said.

A porter. He'd be able to tell them where Serakeen was. If he'd seen Nin.

Sefia and Archer crept around the edge of the pit to the tunnel, where she took a lantern from the wall. They began to walk, Archer pulling on his clothes, leaving behind the scent of blood and the whimpering of the injured.

When the noise and the smell of the fighting ring had faded, Sefia set the lantern on the floor and flung her arms around Archer. He staggered back slightly at the impact, but then he hugged her to him.

"Thank you," she said into his shirt.

His hand stroked her hair, just once, and settled against her shoulder.

"I was afraid you would . . ." Her voice trailed off. His heart pattered beneath her cheek, and she remembered the warmth of his skin, the raised ridges of his scars touching her chin and the corner of her mouth. "But you didn't." She squeezed him once more and released him.

He nodded, touching the edge of his scar. The boys had been like him.

"It's only going to get more dangerous from here." She touched the wand. "Should we call them? They said they'd help us." *And we might need it,* she thought grimly.

He shook his head. He crossed his fingers.

"You're right." Sefia tucked the wand away. "This is for us to do. We'll scout it out, and if we need help then, we'll ask for it."

The tunnel seemed to stretch for miles. As they walked, she imagined them passing under the shoemakers, the bakers, the blacksmiths in their forges with the walls stained black. She felt as if she and Archer had disappeared beneath the world—the people, their conflicts, homes, jobs, and streets—and for a moment, they were almost able to steal away from their own lives, from Serakeen, from dead fathers, from books and violence, and when they reappeared aboveground, they would seem to have materialized out of nothing, with no past and no direction.

But when they climbed a wide flight of steps and found a door etched with the ⊜ at the top, Sefia understood that they carried their past with them, growing heavier and heavier each day.

Archer reached for her hand.

When she swung open the door, they stepped out onto a little dock cluttered with broken barrels and empty crates. To the east, the dull rumble of nighttime activity rose from the Central Port, but out here on the edge of the city, the evening was soft and blue, and the lanterns of the night boats glowed like amber fireflies on the black water. Across the Callidian Strait, the smudges of Corabel's skyline were visible, glittering with lamps.

Sefia started as someone stirred on the dock. Wrapped in a long oilcloth coat, the man was perched on one of the pilings like some enormous vulture with old scars crisscrossing his cracked lips. He didn't say anything, but he climbed into the boat, beckoning them aboard.

"Are you the porter?" Sefia whispered.

The man nodded. The valleys of his face shifted in the evening light, and she had a sudden urge to put her hand on his arm, to reassure them both, maybe, that he was real and solid and wouldn't drift apart the moment she touched him.

"Is Serakeen here, in Jahara?" she asked.

The porter pointed across the water, toward the mainland. Toward Corabel.

The Scourge of the East had left his territory around Liccaro for this? It might be their only chance to find him before the next fight in the Cage.

"Where in Corabel? We can get to Serakeen on our own if you tell us where he is."

The porter said nothing. He gestured to the boat.

Archer tapped four fingers on his cheek. He wanted her to read the porter, like she'd done to the bartender in Epidram.

Taking a breath, Sefia searched for a mark that would allow her to focus her Vision—the scars around the porter's mouth.

She blinked. The currents of light washed over her, and she realized the porter *couldn't* speak. He had no choice—he had no tongue. It had been cut out of him years ago, a lifetime, it seemed. He'd even forgotten how to moan.

He'd been an impressor, once, from Liccaro. He'd gotten to the Cage, where he'd tried to bribe the Arbitrator. The Arbitrator had sent him through to Serakeen, who'd removed his tongue.

Now he was the nameless porter, who came when he was called and did only things he was asked to do: Ferry candidates from Jahara to Corabel. Ask no questions and give no answers.

Maybe he deserved it, for what he'd done as an impressor. Sefia didn't know.

She blinked again. "I'm sorry."

But she was the only one among them who could speak, and she got no reply. She wouldn't get answers this way.

Stepping nimbly into the boat, she sat in the center with the pack between her knees. "He'll take us to Corabel's harbor," she said. "There's a warehouse. He takes everyone there."

If the porter was surprised, he made no sign.

Archer took a seat opposite her, where he could watch the porter, though there was nothing threatening about the man who hung up the lantern—just a silhouette against the starred sky. The porter loosed the sails.

As they left Jahara, Sefia cleaned and bandaged Archer's wounds with supplies from their packs. She mopped his side with a wet cloth, gently wiping away the blood.

When she was finished, she let her hands linger on the sides of his face. She wanted to trace the curves of his brows with her thumbs, to brush her lips against the soft freckled corner of his eyelid. A flush of heat rose in her cheeks, and she sat back, busying herself with stowing the canteen and dirty rag.

"We're going to find the people who did this to you. To them. To all of us." She didn't say what they would do after that. Learn what the book was for. Rescue Nin . . . And then . . .

She didn't know. The only thing she knew was that whatever she had set out to do a year ago, things had changed. *She* had changed. She wouldn't take another life. She'd find another way.

They rode in silence across the narrow Callidian Strait, with only the sounds of the water rocking against the boat to accompany them. The bruised sky above Jahara began to fade, replaced by the sight of Corabel at night.

Three spiral lighthouses took shape along the rocky coast, warning sailors away from the treacherous cliffs and quick riptides of Deliene's coastline. Great towers topped with rooms of glass and mirrors, they sent beams of light across the dark water, guiding ships into the smooth harbor of the capital on the hill.

Seven years had passed since she'd left Deliene, watching the scalloped snowcapped mountains disappear into the distance from the back of a tipsy old merchant ship. She'd been crying, her tears frigid on her cheeks, her nose red with cold, and Nin had stood behind her, wrapping the folds of the bear-skin cloak around the two of them.

"Will we ever go home, Aunt Nin?" she had asked.

The old woman squeezed her shoulders. "There's no going back, girl. Not for us."

Sefia bit back a sob.

"Home's what you make it." Nin shrugged. "Could be a ship. Could be what you carry around on your back day after day. Could be family. Or maybe just one person you love more than any other. That's home."

The porter brought Sefia and Archer to a secluded pier in the western arc of the harbor, inside the long, tall arm of the cliff. Lanterns flickered near the center of the port, where the road led up the hill to the city, but here was all shadow and starlight.

Silently, he led them around the harbor to an enormous warehouse hewn into the stone cliffs.

"Thanks," Sefia said. "We'll take it from here."

But he just shook his head and opened the door. Sefia and Archer tensed, preparing to run, but nothing stirred inside. Except for the stacks of crates and giant spools of rope, it was empty, cavernous, echoing. Cautiously, they followed the porter inside.

At the far end, he ran his hands over the wall and a panel of stones slid aside. A hidden door with a pressure-sensitive key. Sefia was reminded of her old bedroom, from a long time ago.

She glanced up and down the warehouse. "Isn't there another way in?"

The porter reached into the opening, where he found a torch in the shadows and set fire to it, illuminating a tunnel of dry stone.

In the light, Sefia could see he had the kind of face you'd see on your local baker, on your tailor, on the man who swept the streets at dusk, on your father or your uncle.

He turned abruptly and pulled his black hood over his head. He stepped inside the tunnel, waiting for them.

Archer paced along the warehouse wall, searching for another entrance. Sefia ducked into the foreman's office, running her hands over the floor, feeling for seams.

Still the porter waited.

Finally Archer returned, palms up to show he'd found nothing.

"This can't be the only door," she said to the porter. "Have you seen another entrance?"

He shook his head. This was the only way he entered and the only way he left. But she'd known that from her Vision. She'd just dared to hope.

"I guess we'll return in the morning. We can keep watch on this place, at least."

Archer touched her elbow.

"It's too dangerous. We don't know what's down there."

He shook his head. They knew exactly what was down there. The person they'd been searching for all these long weeks. Just beyond the threshold.

Sefia swallowed hard. This was what she'd come for. They'd go in only so far as they had to, until they found another way out. Then they'd turn back. Regroup. Plan.

With Archer behind her, she entered the tunnel.

Closing the door behind them, the porter led them down the narrow hallway, and the only sounds were of their own breathing, and their footsteps along the corridor, and the snapping of the fire.

At last, they arrived at an intersection. The tunnel forked on either side of them, disappearing into darkness, but before them was a metal door. It gleamed dully in the torchlight, dominated by a large iron circle inscribed with four lines, three curved and one straight:

It was pointed the wrong direction, but it was unmistakable. Sefia put her fingertips to the metal. "Serakeen?" she asked.

The porter glanced furtively to the left, and from the shadows there came a soft, "Just beyond the door."

Sefia started. A guard stepped forward, his arms crossed, leaning casually against the wall as if he waited for Serakeen's victims every night. His gaze skimmed over her.

"Are you here to make sure we go in?" she asked.

"Just here to make sure you don't go nosing about." Lazily, he brushed a lock of red hair from his eyes. "You're free to leave, though we were told you wouldn't."

"We?" she echoed as Archer moved behind her.

A second guard.

She glared at the porter. "You could have warned us."

The guards laughed as he opened his mouth, showing her the scarred flesh where his tongue had been.

She'd pitied him earlier. She didn't pity him now. "You should have found a way," she snapped.

Bowing his head, he withdrew, the slick shine of his oilcloth coat disappearing down the tunnel until he was swallowed by the shadows.

Archer was watching her. His eyes seemed more gold than usual, almost burning.

"Well, they know we're here," she said. She glanced at the redheaded guard, who smirked. "Are you ready?"

Archer nodded.

They turned to the door, to the symbol they had been hunting, and to what lay behind it.

Red Waters

Before the Crossbars, before Sefia and Archer, before the quest for the Trove of the King, Captain Reed and the *Current of Faith* were on a journey to the western edge of the world. They had passed the tear in the sky that had doomed Cat and her crew, but the wind had died soon after. The ship floundered. The sails drooped from the yards like stained drapes. Only Captain Reed kept them moving forward, seeking out sluggish currents in the still water, maintaining their course despite the blinding light and the blistering heat of the west.

The sun had eclipsed nearly half the sky, blasting it of all color. Reed wiped his dry brow. The heat pressed down on him, wringing him out, though there was nothing left in him to sweat.

He'd spent the whole night pacing the holds, touching each of the casks and crates one after another. Up and down the hatchways. Around the dwindling stores. *One, two, three, four*... Counting them over and over, as if that would replenish the empty water kegs and meager slabs of salted meat.

But nothing had changed by morning. The crew received a scant meal of hardtack, a strip of dried meat, and a half-pint of water. Few of them even had the energy to complain. Their bodies were slowly consuming themselves, shriveling until they were gaunt and dry as raisins, skin stretched over sinew and bone.

Captain Reed leaned against the bowsprit, struggling to stand. He had been there for hours, tracing interconnected circles on the branches of the figurehead, but no matter what calculations he made, the result was the same: They had exactly enough provisions—*if* the rats didn't get them and the sailing was smooth—for a return journey. If they turned around today, they might survive.

The sun was sinking into the sea, lighting it up like a lamp. They were close. But how close? The light was a subtle, shifting thing. They might pass beyond the edge of the world today, or tomorrow, or the next week.

Or never.

Maybe the ocean went on and on forever, and there was nothing for him to find out there. Nothing but endless empty water.

Beside him, Meeks squinted into the distance, searching for signs of change in the seas. Shadows yawned in the pits of his eyes. They had all begun to look alike—walking skeletons in gruesome masks like Captain Cat and the last sailor of the *Seven Bells*.

Reed rubbed his sore eyes. "Why'd you follow me out here, Meeks?"

The second mate grimaced. "You remember what Cat said, before she died?"

He remembered. Those six words came to him over and over again, circling back on him in the night. "'Who's going to remember your crew,'" he echoed.

"She was right, wasn't she? All these things we're doin', all the adventures we been on, eventually, folks are gonna forget that we did 'em. Not you. You're the captain. But the crew? Sooner or later, they'll forget to mention our names. They'll forget we were even here."

"Then why—"

"Because *you* won't." Meeks grinned up at him, splitting his cracked lips. "I saw you go into that fire on the floating island. I seen you give up rations so the crew could have more. Some folks, knowin' when they're gonna kick it, might play it safe. But not you. Knowin' you ain't gonna die makes you fight harder to protect those who might."

Reed put his hand on the second mate's narrow shoulder and squeezed. Maybe he could finally do what Captain Cat had wanted: save the crew—all of them, not just their bodies but their minds too, so that when they left this place, it wouldn't be branded in their minds the way Captain Cat's experiences had been branded in hers. They could be free of this wretched unending brightness, and they'd never have to think of it again.

The words stirred deep in the trenches of his heart: *We're goin' home.* They rose, rolling up through him like smoke, into his throat, poised there behind the gate of his teeth. *We're goin' home.*

Words that meant defeat. And failure.

And survival.

"Cap . . ." Meeks put his fists to his eyes and bared his teeth.

Reed peered into the second mate's puckered face and cursed. "Doc warned us about this."

Distortions. Blind spots. Pain.

Meeks tried to blink, but he couldn't open his eyes anymore. "I'm sorry, Cap. I wanted to help."

"Let's get you to the doc." Captain Reed took the second mate by the hand and began leading him toward the main hatch.

What else would be taken from them, before the end? If there was an end? The bright spread of water stretched on and on around them, finally merging with the white radiance of the sun.

A muffled explosion, like powder, struck the bowsprit. Reed turned. Pieces of the sun were tearing off and floating toward them, trailing long ribbons of light. Wherever they struck, they hissed and burst like clouds of dust, sprinkling the hull with specks of light.

The *Current* was passing into the setting sun.

Shouts of alarm rose from the crew.

"It ain't right!" someone cried. "We ain't goin' no farther!"

Meeks jerked his head in the direction of the voice. His hands fumbled for his guns. "Camey, that son of a—"

A puff of light dusted Reed's neck and cheek. It felt like nothing—even lighter and less substantial than snowflakes. He brushed the collar of his shirt, but the light was already gone.

They'd made it. He would have crowed, if he weren't so hoarse.

He nudged Meeks behind the foremast. "Stay here till I give word. I ain't losin' you."

"But Cap—"

"Do it." Without waiting for a response, he staggered across the deck, drawing the Lady of Mercy. He was so weak the floorboards seemed to roll beneath him.

"Anyone seen Aly?" Cooky called for the steward as he poked his head out of the galley. Reed stumbled past him and halted at the corner of the main hatchway.

Beyond the mainmast, Jaunty clung to the helm, where Greta held him by the neck with one thick hand. The other pressed the muzzle of a revolver to his head. Camey stood beside them, hawk-nosed and bright-eyed, guns drawn on the chief mate, who stood in the doorway to the great cabin.

"That's far enough, Captain." Camey jerked his head at the Lady of Mercy. "Toss that aside."

For emphasis, Greta jabbed Jaunty with her revolver. The helmsman coughed and tried to spit sideways, but nothing came out.

Greta's hair had begun to fall out, revealing flaky patches of skin on her scalp. Neither she nor Camey had voiced a complaint, not even in the form of a joke, in weeks. Reed should have known. But he'd been so focused on getting to the edge of the world that he hadn't noticed. Or hadn't cared.

Now she had Jaunty, though she was a little unsteady on her feet, a little unsure of her own limbs. Reed could draw faster than Camey, might even be able to kill him before he got a shot off. But not if it cost him his crew.

Reed let the Lady of Mercy drop. The silver revolver fell to the deck as Horse and Doc climbed out of the main hatch.

The larboard watch stumbled from the shelter of the forecastle, blinking at the brightness.

Jules started forward. "Camey, what—"

He shot at her feet. Splinters flew from the deck. The chief mate winced.

"Now," Camey said, "undo your gun belt and get rid of that too."

The barrel of Camey's revolver stared Reed down. Remembering the boar from the floating island—shot clean between the eyes—he obeyed, unbuckling his holsters and letting them drop—Executioner and all— beside the Lady of Mercy.

"Turn the ship around," Greta barked.

The helmsman grunted, his hands flexing on the wheel, but he didn't turn.

Puffs of light struck the sails and drifted down to the deck. Hushed cries rose from the crew. The sun loomed larger and larger, closer and closer in front of the ship, as flurries of light broke over the masts and rigging.

"Camey, it ain't dangerous—" Reed began.

"You don't know that. You don't know what's out there. You put us in one bad situation after another on this cursed voyage, and it ain't right. We've had enough."

"And if you'd pulled this stunt a minute sooner I might've agreed with you," Reed said. "But not now. Can't you feel it?" The edge of the world, waiting just beyond the circle of the sun. His fingers tapped against each other. A story worth telling.

Camey shook his head. "I ain't goin' in there."

Greta drew back the hammer of her revolver. "Be easier with your help, Jaunty, but we'll do it without you if we got to," she said.

"No!" Horse lunged forward.

Camey shot him. The bullet burst through his meaty shoulder and out the other side. He hit the deck. Doc rushed to him.

There was a rustling among the rest of the crew. One by one, they held up their hands—arms raised, palms outward—and edged away from Reed. None of them, not even Jules or Doc or old Goro, looked at him.

A grin spread across Camey's hawk-nosed face. "Harison, get his guns."

The fore of the ship passed into the sun, enveloped in clouds of light. Bright smoke covered the bowsprit. Reed cursed. Meeks was up at the bow.

The ship's boy looked from Camey to Reed and back again. He shook his head.

"C'mon, Harison," Greta said, "you're one of us." The light was so harsh her eyes were nearly closed shut. Reed watched her carefully. She didn't know where Harison was, where to direct her voice. She was as blind as Meeks, though she was trying to hide it. "You're from *home*," she said.

"No," Harison said, stumbling across the deck. "I am home."

Her determination drained away as her sightless eyes roved aimlessly back and forth. She'd been so sure he'd help them. So sure. Reed almost felt sorry for her.

Light engulfed the flying jib, the forestaysail.

Camey's yellowed eyes bulged from his face as he bellowed, "Turn!"

Jaunty bared his teeth. "Keep squawkin'. It won't do you no good."

The fore of the ship was covered in light now,

wafting over the deck and spilling over the rails. They were almost a third of the way through.

"Help me!" Camey cried to the others. "We're all gonna die if you don't!"

Jules and Theo moved forward, hands extended, not entirely sure of themselves.

Reed could feel the light licking at his shoulders, the back of his head. It drifted around the periphery of his vision. "Not today," he murmured.

The light overtook him. It swirled and whispered around him, bursting into clouds of dust where it touched his skin. It was so bright he felt like he'd be blasted clean at its touch.

The others were shouting. Someone whimpered.

A gunshot shattered the air.

Someone hit the floor, groaning.

Reed ducked, peering into the light, but all he saw was that brightness.

Someone stumbled over him. Someone else was crying. There were the sounds of a fight: grunting, shuffling, cursing, the banging of elbows and knees on wood, the *smack* of flesh on flesh.

A gun fell to the deck.

He felt for his discarded revolvers. His belt. Something.

"Cap?" Harison's voice at his shoulder.

"Stay down," Reed muttered.

The light cleared so abruptly that he felt like he'd

been plunged into a well. He fumbled for his weapons, but his hands groped at nothing. Everything was black. And cold. After the blazing heat of the other side of the sun, this cold was bone-deep. It crunched.

He found his belt and buckled it on. As his vision returned, he saw black sky and the white disc of the sun, which gave off little light and no heat. His breath frosted in the air.

Greta lay on the ground, clutching her chest and gulping fast, painful breaths. Blood seeped into her shirt, around her hands. Above her, Jaunty clung to the helm, his shirt spattered with blood.

Harison was on his knees beside the empty pigpen. Reed grabbed him by the elbow and pulled him to his feet. "Meeks is behind the foremast." The cold snapped up his words.

The ship's boy nodded and scrambled away, nearly knocking into Cooky, who stumbled from the galley, calling for Aly.

The crew were on their hands and knees or clutching the rails, shivering in the sudden cold. Horse crouched protectively over Doc, who tried to stanch his wound.

The chief mate was wrestling with Camey, grunting, grappling, each trying to get a hold on the other. One of Camey's guns had been flung clear across the deck, but he gripped the other with white-knuckled determination. The mate had his wrist and banged his hand over and over on the rail, trying to make him release it, but they both held on.

Camey tripped. He couldn't see. His arms spiraled wide.

But the chief mate was never blind on the *Current of Faith*.

He wrested the gun from Camey's grasp, turned it on him, and pulled the trigger.

Blood fountained onto the deck. Camey dropped.

The ship was silent as the stunned crew regained their sight. The sky was black as pitch, without even the pinpricks of stars in the darkness, and the faint illumination from the back side of the sun was dim and cold, more like mist than light.

In the sudden stillness, Aly climbed down from the foremast, her rifle swinging at her back. She stopped beside Greta's corpse. Her breath smoked.

From behind the galley, Harison appeared, leading Meeks by the hand. "What happened?" the second mate asked, his voice falling loudly in the silence. "Help me out, Harison." The ship's boy leaned over to whisper in his ear.

Reed squinted at the crow's nest and walked to Aly's side. "I wondered where you'd got to."

She shivered. "Couldn't let them take the *Current*, Cap."

The cold was sinking into their bones. It hurt to breathe. Reed put his arm around Aly's shoulders and rubbed her arm. She was trembling. The others were clustered together at the rails, pointing into the black emptiness beyond the ship.

The water was as black as the sky. It wasn't natural. As soon as any light touched the water, it sank beneath the surface and disappeared, gobbled up by the darkness. Even the sound of the waves lapping at the hull was wrong—like the clacking of teeth.

The backs of Reed's eyes burned. His breath caught in his throat. That deep cold set something howling inside the core of him, wailing and screaming to get away.

The others must have sensed it too, because soon Aly began to cry.

Horse, too, was whimpering like a little kid.

Red lights appeared in the deep, but they sucked in more light than they gave, illuminating nothing. Thousands and thousands of them, multiplied over and over as far as the eye could see in the dim world behind the sun.

The chief mate swiveled, but he could not see the red lights. He could only feel the cold, the disturbing disquiet that carved into your gut and heart and lungs.

Then the sound advanced from the darkness.

It rolled over them like mist over mountaintops, filling the spaces between them, howling—or was it moaning. Whispering and chittering and mad laughter. Voices or the tolling of bells or glaciers cleaving in two or cliffs crumbling to dust. The last rattling gasp of the dying. It was the most terrible sound in a world of terrible sounds, the kind of sound that haunts you in the late hours of the night when the darkness shutters you in and the cold creeps into you through the cracks. When you are suddenly gripped by the unwavering certainty that you are already dead—and gone forever.

They had reached the red waters at the edge of the world—the place of the fleshless.

CHAPTER 37

Answers

Sefia put her hands on the emblem in the center of the door and glanced at Archer. The cold iron bit into her palms. Two curves for her parents, a curve for Nin. The straight line for herself. The circle for what she had to do.

Archer nodded. They had come here for answers. They had come here to finish it.

Ignoring the guards watching from the shadows, she took a breath, swallowed her doubts, and began to turn. Inside the door, great metal cogs wheeled and clanked as the symbol rotated until it was facing the right way, until it was correct.

The pins in the lock clicked, and the door swung heavily, silently, inward.

Sefia squinted. After the darkness of the corridors, the room beyond was blindingly bright. Candles filled the wall sconces and the cups of the hanging chandelier. Flames tipped the tops of slim white tapers, illuminating rough walls muffled by tapestries and old portraits in which the painted eyes of their subjects glinted like chips of glass.

Opposite them, near the center of the room, was a writing desk. The varnished surface was piled high with sheaves of paper, bottles of ink, and dip pens Sefia had never even dreamed of, and she was seized by the sudden desire to open all the silver-handled drawers and riffle through their contents, seeking smoother parchment, smaller books, and penknives that would fit in the curve of her palm.

But behind the desk, with her hands crossed neatly in front of her, was a woman with silver-black hair, eyes like slush, and skin the color and smoothness of a sun-bleached shell.

She was a little lighter in complexion, a little broader in the jaw and shoulders, but from a distance, Sefia might have mistaken her for her mother.

The woman rose expectantly, as if she'd been awaiting their arrival. "Welcome." Her voice was as intricate and exact as metalwork. "I'm glad you made it."

As Sefia and Archer entered, their footsteps making soft depressions in a thick carpet of red and gold, a man in a dirty aubergine overcoat closed the door behind them. He was tall and lean, with a stubbled jaw and a thick mustache that framed his mouth. A purplish-red scar coiled along the left side of his face, making the corner of his eye droop.

At the sight of him, Sefia's hand strayed to the hilt of her knife. Beside her, Archer curled and uncurled his fingers, lightly touching his worn wooden scabbard.

The man tried to smile, but there was a mournful twist to his mouth, the glistening of his clear-water eyes. "Don't be afraid," he said. "I don't want to hurt you." As if to prove his point, he held up his hands and retreated until he reached the sideboard on the right wall, where he leaned back, his eyes never leaving Sefia's. He didn't even seem to notice Archer was there.

"Please, sit down," said the woman behind the desk. She gestured to the two leather armchairs across from her.

Sefia and Archer remained standing.

"Which one of you is Serakeen?" Sefia asked, her gaze flicking from the woman to the man and back again, not recognizing either of them from her Vision.

"My name is Tanin, and this is my associate Rajar." As she spoke, the woman crossed to a gleaming silver tea set on the left wall, her passage between the desk and side table creating a curling wake of cold air that rippled the waves of her hair and the embroidered silk of her blouse. "The man you know as Serakeen—the bloodthirsty warlord, the Scourge of the East— is a fabrication, a useful myth we've concocted. But I'm afraid he doesn't exist."

"What do you mean 'he doesn't exist'? Who's been attacking ships in the Ephygian Bay?" Sefia demanded. "Who's been pillaging cities in Liccaro? Who's been looking for boys with scars around their necks?"

"I have," Rajar whispered. He pressed down the ends of his mustache with his thumb and forefinger, but he wouldn't meet her gaze.

"Don't tell me Serakeen isn't real. Going by a different name doesn't make you any less responsible for what you've done."

"I didn't want to." He seemed to be pleading with her. "You have to believe I didn't want to."

"But you did."

Rajar looked helplessly at Tanin, who said nothing as she tipped the teapot over the bone-white china. To Sefia it seemed as if everything the woman did altered the very air around her, and even that small movement, twisting the threads of steam that coiled from the fragrant cups of tea, might weeks later form hurricanes over some distant southern ocean.

"Rajar acts in the interest of the greater good. There are far more reprehensible reasons to take a life," she said at last. "Base survival, for instance. Surely you've learned this lesson, in all your many travels."

Sefia swayed, remembering the clearing, the orange light through the cabin windows, and Palo Kanta with the crooked lips, his life dribbling through her murderous hands.

"Now," Tanin continued, "sit down."

As the last two words struck her, Sefia's knees buckled. Her pack slipped from her shoulders, and she sank into the chair behind her. Archer sat too, down and up again in an instant, visibly shaken.

That voice was powerful. Not magical, but irresistible and dangerous.

"Do you take cream or sugar with your tea?" the woman continued as if nothing unusual had occurred.

Sefia twisted the straps of the pack at her feet. "Who *are* you?" she asked.

Tanin dropped lumps of sugar in two of the cups and turned

around. "I'm the Director of an organization known to a select few as the Guard."

The Guard. Sefia mouthed the words. They fit her the way a key fits a lock, sinking into place, opening all sorts of doors deep inside her.

"And Serakeen works for you?" Sefia eyed the man by the sideboard. He crossed and uncrossed his arms. His leather coat creaked.

"*Rajar* is one of us," Tanin said crisply. "He does what he must."

"For the greater good."

"Yes."

As Tanin handed her a cup and saucer, she felt the woman's cool, ink-stained fingers brush hers. Sefia shivered. The spoon rattled against the porcelain. "Which is?"

"Peace." Tanin offered the second cup to Archer, but he didn't take it.

Sefia laughed. It was absurd. Exterminators extolling the virtues of mercy. Butchers preaching restraint. Archer glanced down at her, surprised.

Unruffled, Tanin settled in behind the desk and blew across the surface of her tea. "War can lead to peace, if the right people are the victors," she said.

"And you're the right people?"

"We have to be."

"That's delusional."

"Only to the uninformed."

"So inform me." Sefia put her cup on the table beside her chair and crossed her arms.

"You may not know us, but you know the results of our work. We ended the blood feud in Deliene. We broke Oxscini's hold on Roku. We united Everica."

"In war against Oxscini."

"Yes, Oxscini's always been a problem for us. But not for much longer."

"How?"

"One cannot withstand the many." Tanin smiled.

Sefia's gaze darted to Archer, then back to Tanin. "The Red War," she whispered, finally, truly understanding. "You've seen it in the book, haven't you? That's how you know a boy like Archer is involved. That's why you want him to lead your army. That's why you need the book back. You want to make sure it all comes to pass."

"What is written *always* comes to pass," Tanin said. "We don't know everything, but we've seen enough to know the Red War *is* coming. A boy with a scar around his neck—a boy just like your friend here—*will* lead an army, and his foes will fall before him like wheat before a scythe. Lives will be lost, but at the end of the war, the kingdoms will finally cease their petty squabbling. With this war, we'll create *lasting* peace for all the citizens of Kelanna."

For a second the idea glittered before Sefia like one of her Visions: the Five Islands working together in concert, all the warring kingdoms united, their turbulent histories smoothed over in a single decisive victory. The cost would be high. But the peace would be worth it.

Archer touched the scar at his neck. He'd wear the cost of their peace the rest of his life.

"For all the citizens of Kelanna," Sefia repeated slowly. "What about Archer? You call what you did to him *peace*? What you did to *me*? My family? The woman you sent to take the book from us, you think she got any peace when she—"

"Don't speak of matters you don't understand," Tanin snapped, her voice lashing out at Sefia like a whip. "We all make sacrifices for the greater good. Your parents knew that, once."

Sefia's breath went out of her. It took her a moment to find her voice again, and when she did, her words were little more than a gasp. "You knew my parents?"

"Didn't they tell you?" A tiny wrinkle of surprise appeared between Tanin's brows as she set her cup aside. "They were members of the Guard."

Sefia said nothing, but she felt the doubts cracking open inside her.

Her parents? They were *heroes*. They opposed people like Serakeen. They kept the book from him. They would *never*—

But how had they learned to read in the first place?

"Your father was my best friend," Rajar added quietly, "a long time ago."

Sefia's mouth went dry. Was this the connection between the symbol and Serakeen, the assassin and the book?

"My father?" she whispered.

"He was the Apprentice Librarian," Tanin said, her voice hardening. "It was his *duty* to protect the Book. But he broke every vow he ever made. He and your mother murdered Director Edmon and stole the Book from us."

Sefia shook her head, but she couldn't stop herself from wondering: What if she was wrong? What if her memories of her parents—her mother full of grace, bronze and dark and smelling of earth; her father cradling her chin when he dropped her off at Nin's—were fabrications too? Some elaborate masquerade they had performed to keep their true identities a secret?

Had they been part of the Guard?

What had made them change their minds?

Why did they steal the book?

"So I became the Director," Tanin continued, "tasked with recovering the Book and making up for a betrayal that set us back decades."

"No, it can't be. They would have told me."

"Oh, Sefia, you really don't know." Tanin shook her head, turning each of the items on her desktop as if she were searching for the right words with her fingers. "Mar— Your mother was an Assassin. She had more secrets than anyone."

"My mother wouldn't—"

"She certainly did. Your mother was *extraordinary*. She could choke the life out of someone from fifty feet away. She was so powerful she could have consumed entire cities."

Sefia shook her head and stared at the floor. Beneath her feet, the designs in the carpet overlapped and intersected in an impossible lattice of connections and unfathomably complicated knots, but she couldn't follow them any more than she could follow what Tanin was telling her.

It wasn't true. It couldn't be true.

But she couldn't help but remember the scars on her mother's hands. Her facility with a knife.

Tanin was still speaking, but only a few phrases reached Sefia through the haze of her confusion until, "Your father was no hack either—"

At the words, those two innocuous words, Sefia's anger came into focus like a beam of light through a lens. *My father.* She narrowed her eyes. Something sparked inside of her.

"—with a snap of his fingers—"

Her skin burned. She was volcanic, blistering, riotous. An avalanche of blackrock ready to ignite. She'd been thrown off by Tanin's nice manners, by Rajar's morose contrition, by the truth about her parents. But she remembered what she was doing here now. She remembered why she had come.

"—bleed lakes dry in a matter of seconds—"

Slowly, Sefia raised her head. The rest of the room blurred, white and hot, until all she could see was Tanin, resting easily behind her desk, her lips meeting and parting, sending words into the air like sweet, toxic smoke. "They weren't supposed to fall in love, you know, but they always did like breaking the rules." For a moment, grief flicked across Tanin's face like a cloud passing over the moon. "And then they broke their vows. They stole the Book. They betrayed everything we'd worked so hard for. Your mother passed away before we could get to her, but your father—"

Sefia stood. Her hand curled around the hilt of her knife. "You killed him," she said.

"I would have given anything not to do what I did," Tanin murmured. "But we needed the Book back."

Like a bullet, like an explosion of gunpowder and grief and

guilt and rage, Sefia launched herself across the desk. Her knife flashed. Sheets of paper scattered around them like startled birds.

Sefia knocked both of them to the floor and brought her blade to Tanin's throat. "You tortured him. Just like you did Nin." She dug the edge of her knife into the woman's creamy skin. "Where is she? Is she even alive?"

Tanin smiled, but her voice shivered with regret. "You *are* your mother's daughter, aren't you?"

A noise behind her caused Sefia to look back. Her knife eased off Tanin's neck as she caught sight of Rajar, his dark coat splaying out as he raised his arms, hands twisting and pulling at the air.

Magically, Archer's weapons were wrenched from his grasp. The sword and revolver sailed across the room.

With a flick of his wrist, Rajar hurled Archer into a chair and scooped the weapons out of the air before they hit the ground.

Horrified, Sefia turned back to Tanin just in time to see her open her eyes. Her pupils contracted to points of black in two pools of silver.

The Vision.

"No!" Sefia cried.

But it was too late. With a wave of her hand, the woman flung Sefia aside. The knife flew from her fingers as her back struck the desk. Pain rippled along her spine and she fell to the floor, groaning.

Brushing herself off, Tanin stood. She raised her hand again, lifting Sefia from the carpet as if on invisible strings, and sent her crashing into the chair beside Archer.

Sefia struggled, but her arms and legs were pinned.

At her feet, her pack was unbuckling as if opened by invisible hands. Out tumbled her belongings—pans and candles and the biscuits Cooky had given them—and then the book rose from its depths, shedding its leather wrapping as it floated toward Tanin's outstretched arms.

The woman gathered it to her chest like a lost child and sighed with deep satisfaction. "What is written always comes to pass," she whispered.

...ure on Tanin's throat eased as the girl
...er shoulder. By the sideboard,
...and lifted his hands.
...they were so out-
matched.

At Rajar's command, the boy's swor...
scabbard. The revolver twisted out of hi...
weapons arced through the air, glinting,
ti... ...r sent the boy flying backward...
armchairs.

With... ...he caught the blade by...
and... ...air...
...moning her ...se of
the ... ...piled across her
vision, ...vide eyes.

"No!" th...

But against Manipulation ... ...were useless. Lifting her hand, Tanin dispos...
...nshing lint from her sleeve. The girl hit the desk
...eak moan...

the thre... of light, ... body le... the floor ... into the second c...

The girl fo... ... ...ould do her ... good. ... ...ld her fast.

This was it. The moment ... waiting for. The mom... ...'d been promised.

... ... used Manipulation to ope... ... ...nd the desk, she dug through the ...ins and crumbling bits of pastry, the nubs of ... ...es and threadbare sets of clothes, until at last she came to the Book. Lifting it from the detritus, she ripped aside its wra...ings, revealing leather covers, edges stained with age, clasps that locked all its secrets inside.

Reaching out, Tanin beckoned it to her.

It seemed an eternity before the Book reached her, but as its weight settled into her arms, she finally felt *complete*. As if Lo... ...d M... ...h ...etrayal was a broken link in a chain that extended through all the years of her life, and it wasn't ... ...il she'd secured the Book again that she could solde... ...t c...ed. A sigh escaped her, and she whispered the words she'd repeated to herself so many times before, in her greatest me... "What is written al...ys comes to pass."

Runners

Before they became parents, Lon and Mareah were runners. They were running when they stole the Book. When they escaped that complex of mirrors and marbled halls in an eruption of fire and rubble and charred scraps of paper. One was clutching the Book to his chest, under his crossed arms, as if trying to press it into his ribs, until his lungs filled with letters and his heart became a pulsing paragraph. The other was holding on to his elbow, so she could catch him if he stumbled, so she could keep him going, urging him forward, forward, forward.

When they crossed the threshold, breaking into the night and the fresh air, they were running.

Chased through the water and the woods by men and women and hounds, they were running.

They ran across kingdoms, mountains, shorelines. Even forced into hiding, they were quick. Restive. They breathed fast. They were wild and furtive with the chase. And when they slept—if they slept—they did so fitfully, in turns, with the Book between them, always ready to go. To run again.

And then one day, when they thought perhaps they had run far enough, for long enough, because they could no longer hear the sounds of the hunters or feel the chase at their heels, they built the house on the hill overlooking the sea.

CHAPTER 38

The Boy with the Scar

Archer strained against his invisible bonds, testing his feet and each of his fingers, but he couldn't move anything but his head and neck. He was trapped.

It had happened so fast.

"Are you okay?" Sefia asked. A few stray locks of hair had come loose from their ties, and her clothing was rumpled, but she seemed unhurt. The green feather glinted behind her ear.

He nodded. As he watched, Rajar set Harison's sword and revolver on the sideboard and hugged his arms miserably. Archer knew that look. Guilt. Self-loathing. He'd felt it too, time and time again.

Whatever he'd expected of Serakeen, it wasn't this. It wasn't kinship.

Pulling open a drawer, Tanin plucked out some blotting paper and dabbed it against her neck, but there was little blood. With a sniff, she crumpled the paper and tossed it aside. She laid the book on the desktop and stroked the worn cover, her elegant inky fingers tracing the discolored leather. To Archer, she seemed sad . . . and angry.

After a moment, she sat down and crossed her hands. "Let's get this over with, then. Examine him."

Archer's eyes widened as Rajar crossed the room. The man circled the armchair, pulling again at the corners of his mustache. He hunkered down, placing a hand on Archer's knee.

"I'm sorry," he said. His breath smelled faintly of smoke and cloves and liquor. Standing, he flicked open a pocketknife.

Archer struggled against his invisible restraints. His hunting knife was sheathed in the shoulder strap of his pack, so close but so impossibly far.

"Leave him alone!" Sefia cried.

Rajar shook his head. "We have to know." Then, taking hold of Archer's sleeve, he cut away the fabric, exposing the fifteen burns on his arm, and stared down at the scars with lopsided blue eyes. His pupils shrank to pinpoints.

Archer cringed, but no blows came.

After a moment, Rajar folded the knife away and slipped it back in his pocket. "He's a skilled enough killer, though he didn't complete the final test at the Cage."

"You've no right to do that," Sefia snapped.

Rajar ignored her. He circled Archer again. "Who are you, boy?" he whispered. "Are you the one we've been searching for?"

Archer felt as if the man were scooping him up and shaking him, so all the things he'd blocked out for so long, all the things he'd tried to forget, would come tumbling out.

"Well? What do you think?" Tanin toyed with a silver pen-knife, twirling it impatiently between her fingers. "Fit for the Academy?"

"He was going to be a lighthouse keeper." Rajar rubbed his cheek. "He was going to protect people."

Archer felt faint.

The memories rose out of him like floes of ice.

A lighthouse poised on a rocky promontory.

The notes of a mandolin drifting like soap bubbles from an illuminated window.

A girl with curls the color of sunlight through yellow leaves.

He was remembering. After all this time.

Archer's head spun. It felt like he was breaking open on the inside, all the mental blocks he'd put up to protect himself rupturing one after another, flooding him with blood and bile.

All of a sudden, the ceiling felt too low, the walls too close. He was back in the crate again. The sour stench of his own urine. Claw marks. He felt the prick of splinters under his fingernails. Darkness. There would be no light until the crate was opened, and then there would be fear and pain. Ugly laughter and killing and then food, once someone was dead.

Every time he was unleashed there was fear and pain.

The boy Hatchet executed in front of him just to get him to pick up a weapon.

Training with Hatchet's other boys—the splitting of skin over knuckles, the heft of a sword—until he was the only one left.

Then the fights.

He shut his eyes, but he saw them all, felt every blow, heard every last gasp, saw every dead boy empty-eyed on the ground. Every one.

He slumped against his invisible restraints, panting. The piece of quartz was resting solidly at the bottom of his pocket, but he couldn't reach it. His hands wouldn't move.

"Archer?" Sefia's voice was muffled, as if coming to him through water.

He didn't look at her. He couldn't.

"He's not cut out for killing, Tanin," Rajar said. "He doesn't deserve to be here."

Tanin smirked. "See yourself in him, do you?"

"Yes." The whiplike scar along the side of Rajar's face twisted as the word left his lips.

In that instant, Archer pitied him as much as he hated and feared him.

"Destiny has a cruel sense of humor," Tanin said, "but she will not be denied."

Archer swallowed, felt the scar tissue tighten around his neck.

"You can use the Vision too," Sefia said.

"We call it the Sight." With one last glance at Archer, Rajar sighed and returned to the sideboard, where he wrapped his coat around himself, though the room was not cold.

Sefia's voice was sharp with surprise. "That's why you burned him. You had to have a mark to use the Vision on."

"We have to make sure the candidates complete all our tests."

"But he didn't. He escaped from Hatchet, didn't he? He didn't kill those boys at the Cage. He's not the one you want."

423

Archer's memories churned over and over inside him. After the lives he'd lived, and the lives he'd taken, who was he, really?

A son?

A lighthouse keeper?

An animal? A killer?

The boy with the scar, the one the Guard had been searching for?

"But he's with *you*," Tanin pointed out. "A reader. The daughter of two of the most powerful people I've ever met. You, Sefia, are what makes him special. Of course we want him."

CHAPTER 39

Choices

Sefia's stomach turned. "I never meant—"

But it didn't matter what she'd meant. Every time she had touched the symbol or read from the book or recited her vow, she'd been leading him, slowly, inexorably—all the while promising that she was his friend, that she would protect him—to the very people he should have been running from all along.

He didn't look at her. His breath was ragged in his chest.

"We've been searching for the Book for decades, and you've not only brought it here to us, you've brought along a candidate as well." Tanin traced the ⊖ on the cover of the book with her fingertips, just as Sefia had done hundreds of times herself. "There are no coincidences."

Was everything—her parents, the Guard, her search for answers, and what the impressors had done to Archer—

destined to turn out this way from the beginning? Were they all just stories whose endings had already been written, the dates of their deaths pinned to the page with periods?

Tanin fingered the edge of her vest, above her heart. "I think you're extraordinary, Sefia, even more extraordinary than your parents, if you discovered your power all on your own."

A flash of pride and curiosity flared in Sefia's chest, quickly extinguished by hurt and confusion. "I did. They didn't tell me."

They didn't tell me anything.

"I'm sorry." Tanin's voice softened. "I wish things had been different."

Sefia's eyes blurred with tears. She shook her head, blinking.

"I know you don't want to believe it," Tanin continued, "but I loved them. Your mother was like an older sister to me . . . family. If things had been different, you and I could have—"

"You *loved* them? You killed my father," Sefia interrupted.

Tanin pressed her lips together, as if to seal in her sadness, her regret. "Yes."

"Have you killed Nin too?"

"The Locksmith?" Tanin asked. "No, Sefia, we took her into custody."

Sefia tried to lunge forward, but the magic held her back. "Nin's alive?"

"Would you like to see her?"

"Yes!" The word burst out of her before she could stop it.

Rajar smoothed down his mustache. "Are you sure?"

"If she won't believe her parents betrayed us, maybe she'll believe the Locksmith," Tanin replied.

Sighing, he folded his coat around himself and swept out of the room through a back door, almost hidden behind a tapestry. Archer's eyes were closed. His face was wet with tears.

"Archer?"

In the silence, Tanin flicked open the clasps of the book, then closed them. Opened and closed them again. The wrinkle had appeared between her brows again, and she stared hard at the symbol in the center of the cover, as if she could bore through it with the sheer intensity of her gaze.

After a moment, she leaned in and whispered, as if to the book itself: "Show me where the last piece of the Resurrection Amulet is hidden."

She opened the book. The pages fluttered. Her eyes were hungry, gobbling up the words, and then . . . She looked up, blinking. It was like she'd forgotten where she was.

Sefia's breath quickened. Tanin was searching the book. Was that all it took to find what you were looking for?

Tanin licked her fingertips and leafed through the book. Then she looked up again, and her gaze narrowed on Sefia. "What did you—? Did Lon do this?"

"Do what? What are you looking for?"

Tanin ignored her. She flipped halfheartedly through the pages before closing the book and slumping into the chair.

Sefia didn't take her eyes from the cracked spine. She could search the book. All the questions about her parents would be answered if she could just—

The back door swung open, and someone was prodded into the room. Someone in a bear-skin cloak. Someone like a mountain of dirt. Someone with hands like miracles.

"Aunt Nin!" Sefia wanted to fling her arms around the woman, but she was still pinned to the chair. "I'm sorry. I'm so sorry. It's my fault." The words poured out of her like water over the lip of a dam. "I should never have let them take you. I should have stopped them."

It took Nin a few agonizing seconds to look up, but when she did, her muddy eyes couldn't seem to focus. There was something vague and uncertain about the slouch of her shoulders, the uneasy plucking of her fingers. "That you?" she mumbled.

"Yes, it's me, Sefia!"

A smile broke through the hardened lines of Nin's face. "Girl," she murmured. She was thinner than Sefia remembered, her movements more tentative, but in that moment she almost seemed like her old self.

Except she still wouldn't meet Sefia's eyes.

Sefia glared at Tanin. "What did you do to her?"

"She had vital information."

She darted a glance at Nin. She *knew* there was only one way the assassin could have known she had the book. She just hadn't wanted to believe it. "Oh," she said.

Nin's mouth moved. Her jaws worked. But no sound came out. Rajar took up his post by the sideboard and crossed his arms.

"Go on," Tanin urged. "Tell her about her parents."

As if on command, Nin began to speak: "What do you want to know, girl? Did they steal it? Did I help them? Yes and yes."

Her speech was different too. The words seemed to slide off her tongue, like she couldn't control them.

"Who are these people?" Sefia asked.

"The Guard is good. The Guard protects us all."

"Did my parents betray them?"

"Yes. They weren't who you thought they were, girl."

No, they weren't. A sob lodged in Sefia's throat. She couldn't look at Nin anymore. Her parents hadn't been heroes. They'd been traitors. Liars. Even to their own daughter.

"We had to get the Book back," Tanin said gently. "We couldn't let something so powerful loose in the world."

"Loose?" Sefia echoed. As if the book were some caged beast.

"People are weak. They can't be trusted. Can you imagine what Kelanna would be like if everyone could do what you and I can do? Men would be turned into dogs and never turned back. Castles would disintegrate with the wave of a hand. Thieves and murderers, slave traders and warlords, the worst kinds of people would rule Kelanna because *they* would use the word for evil. It would be chaos."

In his chair, Archer raised his head, and his eyes were glassy with tears.

Tanin leaned across the desk, her voice hushed and urgent. "When we unite the kingdoms under one rule, we'll make sure that never happens. We'll make sure no one is ever again corrupted by the power of the Book."

"That's what you think happened? My parents were corrupted?" Sefia felt like her skin had been sewn on backward. "Aunt Nin?"

But Nin still wouldn't look at her.

Archer strained against his invisible bonds. The veins along his arms and neck swelled. But he couldn't move.

"You could join us, you know." Tanin flipped the penknife in her fingers once more and set it on the desktop. "We could teach you to control your gifts. You could *help* people. Protect them. The way your parents were supposed to."

Her parents. Sefia's images of them were already fading, their features cracking and flaking away like old paint, revealing nothing but darkness beneath. They'd betrayed Tanin. They'd betrayed her too, keeping this from her.

"Sefia . . ." The word was so small she wasn't even sure she'd heard it.

Archer was staring at her, sweat glistening on his forehead, his lips parted, though no other sound came out. But he'd spoken. His voice was hoarse and deep, and the sound of it sang in her blood.

"Join you?" Sefia spat. "Don't make me laugh."

Tanin shook her head. "Sefia, I don't think you understand what I'm offering you—"

"No," she said. "We'll never join you."

For the first time, a smile graced Rajar's mournful face.

Beside him, Nin blinked. Her eyes seemed to clear. She rocked back and forth on her heels, flexing her fingers.

"Not after what you've done to the people I love."

As Sefia spoke, Tanin's expression went from amusement to doubt, and then to confusion, hurt, and finally anger. She drew herself up to her full height. "The people you *love*? Your parents lied to you. Your *Aunt Nin* gave you up." Her voice was cold and crackled like ice, but there was an undercurrent of pain in it, running deep beneath the surface, causing her anger to rupture and break.

Sefia glanced at Nin. Her face was going red. She bit her lips. She ground her teeth. And then the words erupted out of her: "I told them, girl. I couldn't stop myself. Your name. That thing you carried. I told them everything. I'm sor—"

But Tanin's voice cut through Nin's, her words digging into Sefia again and again. "*I* would have welcomed you with open arms. *I* would have given you everything your parents never did."

"Sefia, listen to me," Nin continued. "The Guard is powerful. More powerful than you know. They control Everica, Liccaro. Got someone in Deliene too. They're going to—"

"Power. Knowledge. Purpose. Time and time again, *I* let you live, Sefia. You were supposed to choose me."

"Run, Sefia." Nin's voice rang out like a broken bell. "Run!"

Tanin raised her fingers, and Sefia flung herself against her restraints. She knew that look. The narrowing of her pupils. The hurt and vengeance in her eyes.

Without even touching her, Tanin gave Nin's neck a sudden, violent twist.

There was a *snap*.

A scream rose in Sefia's throat. Nin buckled, as if someone had taken a sledgehammer to all her supports and she were bursting apart, falling, fading, and then . . . gone, her hands as limp as leather gloves.

She was dead.

CHAPTER 40

All the Ways That Matter

N in!" The word exploded from her and burst into a brilliant cloud of light.

Sefia raised her arms. The golden ropes of Tanin's restraints sloughed off her and dissipated into nothingness.

She stood, her Vision swirling and sparking around her like gusts of snow.

Archer was free too. She could feel him reaching for his weapons as Rajar's hands swept back the folds of his coat, exposing his guns.

Sefia lifted her hand. The silver penknife rose from the desk.

Tanin opened her mouth to speak.

But Sefia was done listening. Her hand cut the air.

The blade slashed across Tanin's throat. The skin opened up, red and hot and wide. Her hands went to her neck. She looked surprised.

Rajar was at her side in an instant, murmuring something,

cradling her body as it slumped to the floor. Tanin's lips moved, but her extraordinary voice was gone. Blood leaked through her fingers.

The light went out of her eyes.

Archer tugged at Sefia's arm, and she looked up. He had their packs on his shoulder and the book in his hands. In the candlelight, the leather binding shone, polished with hundreds of years of handling.

The book of her parents.

The book of Palo Kanta.

Of Tanin.

Of everything.

Dimly, she heard Rajar calling for reinforcements. She stole one last look at the collapsed hillside of Nin's body.

Run.

Then the book was in her arms, and they were running— out the door and into the tunnel, where they barely slowed as Archer knocked the redheaded guard unconscious and shot the other in the leg.

Their footsteps echoed off the walls.

Their breaths were ragged in their chests.

The torchlight batted at the ceiling as Rajar's voice bellowed behind them.

They burst into the dark open space of the warehouse, where the starlight made dappled patterns on the floor.

And then they were out, in the arc of the harbor with the shadows of boats on the water. They dashed to the nearest skiff, where they dropped their things and tackled the ropes, untying lines, hoisting sails.

The sounds of pursuit reverberated in the warehouse. Shouts. Pounding feet.

Breathlessly, Sefia and Archer pushed their boat away from the dock. A breeze filled the sails.

Shots fired.

They ducked.

Bits of the hull splintered around them.

People flooded the docks, rifles in their hands. Some of them ran down the pier in search of another boat. Others knelt and raised their guns again.

There was a burst of orange flame.

And the report of rifles.

Sefia blinked. She could see the bullets heading for them, could see their trails like wakes of light. With a wave of her hand, she dropped them harmlessly into the water.

Archer stared at her.

On the docks, their pursuers had reached another boat, but they were out of range now. They were hurtling out to sea, the black water ripping them past the lighthouses and into the swift currents of the Callidian Strait.

Sefia clung to the rail, staring at but not seeing the cloud-swept sky, the moonlight skittering across the waves.

Nin.

Oh, Nin.

Sea spray splashed over the deck, drenching her left side. Sefia blinked salt water out of her eyelashes and looked around. They were alone, cold and wet as the wind nipped at their faces and the tips of their ears.

She collapsed against the gunwale, her head in her hands.

After a moment, Archer sat beside her. "Sefia?" he murmured.

She buried her face in her arms. Tanin was dead.

But so was Nin.

"I'm sorry."

She looked up at him then. Out here on the water, the planes of his face were rimmed with blue light, as if he were a thundercloud brimming with lightning. "That's the second person I've killed . . ." Her voice dwindled into silence.

For a moment Archer didn't speak. Then his hand flitted to his neck. "I've killed twenty-four."

She wanted to say something, but what words could express all they'd been through, all the terrible things they'd done, all the answers they'd found, and all the questions they had yet to ask?

Lifting her hand, she touched her brow once and held up two crossed fingers in the darkness.

She didn't need words for this.

Archer traced her hand with his own, trailing his fingertips along the soft blades of her fingers until they were laced with his.

"Yes," he said.

He was with her.

They were together.

In all the ways that mattered.

Then he leaned in and pressed his lips to the corner of her forehead, just above her temple.

Sefia tensed, remembering the sensation of his arms around her, his bare skin, his heart drumming frantically in his chest.

Then she lifted her chin and pulled him down to her, and their mouths met for the first time.

The kiss wasn't hard or passionate or even sweet the way she'd imagined it might be. But it was tender and strong, as if the pressure of his lips could communicate all the things he felt for her, all the things he still didn't have the words in him to say.

It opened her up. Her emotions welled inside her and she could feel them washing against her insides: sadness and regret and anger and pain and confusion and relief and more she couldn't name. Tears splashed onto their twined fingers.

Gently, Archer wiped her hands, her cheek, collecting her tears.

"Where to now?" he asked.

Sefia looked at the book where it lay, gold clasps gleaming faintly, on the deck. The book could tell her. She could open it and riffle through the pages and find the answers she needed. It was all in there.

Instead she tightened her grip on his hand and looked to the horizon. "Anywhere but here," she said.

Acknowledgments

In some ways, I've always believed books are magic—transformative, incendiary, transcendent. Time machines and puzzle boxes and keys to doors we didn't even know existed, deep in our hearts.

But during this past year I've come to realize that books are magic because *people are magic*—brilliant, generous, talented beyond measure. This book wouldn't be here without the summoners and channelers, the conjurers and magicians who pull figurative rabbits out of figurative top hats . . . the readers and believers. Their touch has given this book a voice, a body, a life—and for that I am endlessly grateful.

Mountains of gratitude to my dragon-riding agent-warrior, Barbara Poelle, who swooped in and sent me off on this extraordinary journey. Not in my wildest dreams did I imagine I could be matched with such an incredible advocate and partner, and I could not be luckier, or prouder, to be a Poellean. You are a force of nature. Thank you for everything.

I knew in my first conversation with my editor Stacey Barney that she was the person to helm this book, and not once has she steered us wrong. Thank you for believing, for your unerring sense of story and your unflinching approach to revision, and for never letting me scrape by with anything less than my best. Your influence has made *The Reader* a better book and me a better writer.

Legions of thanks to Jennifer Besser and all the amazing people at Putnam and Penguin who've shepherded this story into the world: David Briggs, Emily Rodriguez, Elizabeth Lunn, Wendy Pitts, and Cindy Howle. With extra special applause and appreciation for Marisa Russell, my exceedingly talented publicist, and Kate Meltzer, who answers all my questions with kindness and always lets me ask more.

So much awe and gratitude to Chandra Wohleber and Janet Rosenberg for their attention to diction and detail. Thank you for making each sentence the best version of itself.

To all the people who have turned these words into a real, physical book: you are actual wizards. Thanks to Cecilia Yung, Marikka Tamura, and David Kopka for listening to all my ideas for hidden messages and puzzles and turning them into reality. It has been a rare pleasure working with mapmaker extraordinaire Ian Schoenherr—thank you for being the best kind of collaborator. I am grateful for (and still a little flabbergasted by) the sorcery of Deborah Kaplan and Kristin Smith, who furnished *The Reader* in such striking form, and I owe fountains of thanks to Yohey Horishita, whose breathtaking illustrations capture so perfectly the spirit of *The Reader*. Thank you all. You've made this book more than a book.

To Heather Baror-Shapiro, thank you for hoisting the sails and setting Sefia, Archer, and Reed on countless new adventures around the world.

Never-ending love and gratitude to my family for making sure I was never alone on this journey. To Mom and Chris, who always believed in me, thank you for giving me the opportunity and encouragement to do what I love most, and for showing me that success means working at it hour-by-hour, minute-by-minute. This book never would have been written without you. To Auntie Kats, thank you for all the little things: for letting me read your comic books, for TV nights and hiking trips, for letting me paint dragons in your closet. I am so lucky to be your niece. To Dad, who turned every day into a story, every trip to the park into an epic adventure, thank you. I miss you.

To Cole, thank you for putting up with all my anxious and emotional writerly ways, for cooking dinner and running errands and giving the dogs baths when I'm buried in edits, for never making it a secret that you're proud of me. All the words in this novel wouldn't be enough to thank you for your encouragement and support. I love you.

I'm indebted to my friend Diane Glazman, the toughest critic and sharpest reader I've ever crossed, for ruthlessly demolishing my early drafts and whipping this plot into shape.

To Matthew Tucker, this all began because you wanted me to write a fantasy story. Here you go.

Huge thanks to the inimitable Brenda Drake for hosting the best writing contest on the internet, and big hugs and high-fives to my fellow Pitch Warriors of 2014, especially my friend and teammate Kirsten Squires. Your support has shown me the importance of community in a profession that's often so isolating. I feel so lucky to be on this road with you.

I've said it once and I'll say it again: I wouldn't be here without Renée Ahdieh. If this were a storybook, you'd be some wondrous combination of fairy godmother, knight in shining armor, and ass-kicking best friend. Your belief, your guidance, and your friendship are irreplaceable. Thank you, thank you, thank you.

Thanks to my fellow debuts in the Sweet Sixteens and the Class of 2k16, in particular the magical wonders Jessica Cluess and Tara Sim, whose friendship has been a more valuable resource than any blog post, spreadsheet, or how-to-survive-your-debut-year guide. You two are the actual best.

And finally, to any student or summer camper who's ever chatted with me about books, TV, movies, or video games, who's ever named a ship, a character, or a kingdom—your imagination is *inspiring*. I hope you go after your dreams with passion, with tenacity, and with kindheartedness. I believe in your stories. Write them well.

Sefia and Archer must disrupt the Guard's plans before they are ensnared in a war that will threaten the safety of the entire world.

Turn the page for a preview of
Book Two of Sea of Ink and Gold

CHAPTER 1

The Dreams

Archer was dreaming again, and in the dreams he had no name. He didn't remember when he'd lost it, but now the men called him *boy* or *bootlicker* or nothing at all.

He stood in a circle of stones, large and pale as skulls, while men and women jeered at him from the ring, their faces turned into hideous masks by torchlight. When he shifted, bits of gravel dug into the bottoms of his bare feet.

"This your new candidate, Hatchet?" a man sneered. He had black deep-set eyes and sallow skin.

"Got him in Jocoxa a couple months back," Hatchet answered. "Been training him up."

Hatchet—stout build, ruddy skin, always picking at half-healed scabs.

The nameless boy touched his neck, fingers grazing the scars at his throat.

Hatchet had burned him.

The sallow man smiled, his teeth sharp and small like a ferret's. "Argo's already put down four underfed whelps like this one."

Turning, the boy with no name found Argo standing on the other side of the ring, the light flickering over four raised burns on his right arm. Through the short coils of his beard, he wore a slack-jawed smile.

The crowd began clapping and whooping. A signal, maybe.

Argo strode toward the nameless boy.

The crowd cheered.

The boy with no name tried to step sideways, but he stumbled.

"Watch it!" Hatchet snapped.

Then Argo attacked.

His fists were everywhere, raining on the nameless boy's face and head and chest. It got hard to breathe, hard to see.

The blows came faster, heavier, like hail.

The boy with no name doubled over, caught a knee in the face. The ground rose up to meet him.

Dimly, he heard Hatchet shouting, "Get up! Get up, you little—"

But he did not get up.

Argo flipped him onto his back, straddled his chest, and raised a hand to strike.

In that moment, the nameless boy understood: This was the end. He was going to die.

He would cease to breathe. Cease to be. Cease to hurt. It would be easy.

But he didn't want to die.

And knowing that, knowing he wanted to live, however hard it was, however much it hurt, something opened up inside him, something hidden and ugly and powerful.

Argo slowed.

Everything slowed.

As if the seconds were stretching into minutes, the minutes into hours, the boy without a name could see where the fight had begun and every hit he'd taken since, all unfurling before him in perfect detail. He could see bruises and newly healed bones beneath Argo's skin, could sense pressure points in his joints like buds of pain waiting to blossom.

The fist came down, but the nameless boy deflected it into the dirt. He trapped Argo's leg with his own and rolled, pinning his opponent beneath him.

"That's right, boy! Fight back!" Hatchet shouted.

The boy could have struck. But he leapt to his feet and looked around instead.

He could see *everything*. He knew which torches would be easiest to wrench from the ground and how long it would take to reach them. He knew which of the stones lining the ring would make the best weapons. He counted revolvers and hidden knives in the crowd, found loose patches of dirt where the footing would be weakest. He saw it all.

As Argo stood, the nameless boy hit him in the face. The flesh crumpled. He hit Argo again and again, quick and hard, where it would hurt most. Where it would do the most damage.

It was easy.

Natural.

Like breathing.

Argo's kneecap popped. Ligaments snapped. The boy without a name struck him in the collarbone. He could almost see the splinters of bone spring away from each other under the skin.

Argo was crying. He tried to crawl toward the edge of the circle, but his arm and leg were no longer working. His limbs were covered in dirt.

The crowd called for blood.

Kneeling, the nameless boy picked up a rock studded with crags.

It was almost over now. He could see the end. It was very close.

Argo's eyes were wide with fright. His gums were bloody as he pleaded for his life.

But the boy with no name did not listen.

Living meant killing. He saw that now. He knew what he had to do.

He brought the rock down onto Argo's face. He felt the impact, the sudden warping of bone and flesh and beard. There was no more begging.

He raised the rock again.